"Sharon's novels take you on a healing j   ory and spiritual direction in a way that both draws you in and invites you to heal. And she never rushes her characters through the process of transformation—much like God never rushes us through ours. If you want to get lost in a great novel and at the same time find healing for your own soul, read *An Extra Mile*. You won't want to miss one of Sharon's books."

Susie Larson, talk radio host, national speaker, author of *Your Beautiful Purpose*

"Yet again, Sharon Garlough Brown offers the perfect blend of a riveting story and spiritual content—this time during the season of Lent. Redeeming and refreshing, I highly recommend it, even though it means saying goodbye to literary friends I have enjoyed for four novels."

Lucinda Secrest McDowell, author of *Ordinary Graces* and *Dwelling Places*

"Author Sharon G. Brown has done it again! Once more she powerfully weaves the stories of women who are struggling yet desiring to grow their faith in everyday life with its ups and downs. . . . Ultimately, these women show us a way to embrace God's joy and his personal call on our own lives."

Marilyn Hontz, speaker, author, ministry coach, pastor

"I have thoroughly enjoyed all of the Sensible Shoes books and hated to say goodbye to these wonderful characters. But *An Extra Mile* provided a fulfilling close to this great series. Thank you, Sharon, for enriching my life with these novels and teaching me so much about my own journey of spiritual transformation."

Lynn Austin, author of *Where We Belong*

"I came to the final novel of the Sensible Shoes series with a feeling of grief. How I didn't want the story to end! But once again, as with the first three novels, I found within the pages of *An Extra Mile* beautiful nuggets of truth to hold on to. . . . With her characteristic shimmering prose and deep spiritual insights, Brown tells another story for our times as we journey with the Sensible Shoes club one extra mile."

Elizabeth Musser, author of *The Long Highway Home*

"If you've been journeying with Brown's beloved characters through their densely packed year of spiritual insights and practices, don't miss this last mile. Reckoning with loss, with life not going as planned, and with relinquishing plans altogether, *An Extra Mile* is as harrowing as it is satisfying."

Sarah Arthur, author, speaker, preliminary fiction judge for the *Christianity Today* Book Awards

"Sharon Garlough Brown has once again given us an irresistible page-turner, bringing this series to a satisfying close while celebrating that life with God is always unfolding anew. Rarely in fiction are we invited so deeply and generously into the secret contours of the spiritual life. Through the realistic stories of these four women, readers experience what it feels like to enter the darkest places of loss, resistance, and frustration, and find there the abundant grace of God."

Debra Rienstra, author of *Great with Child* and *So Much More*

"*An Extra Mile* is a testimony to the joy that comes with spiritual growth and increasing trust, even amid setbacks and sorrow. In Mara, Charissa, Hannah, and Becca, we see God faithfully renewing real, messy lives with grace and tender patience, stretching his beloved ones to greater love and service. In this final installment of the Sensible Shoes series, Sharon Garlough Brown offers a beautiful invitation to share in the deepening sacred journeys of her characters and to make this pilgrimage our own."

Rebecca DeYoung, professor of philosophy, Calvin College, and author of *Glittering Vices*

"I finished reading *An Extra Mile* at exactly midnight with a tear and a sigh. Sharon Garlough Brown has done it again! I loved this final book in the series, and especially enjoyed seeing the transformation of the characters who now feel like friends. In this book we experience grief up close and too personal—I wept with the friends at their losses. But I cheered with them too when they found meaning and hope in the God who loves them. How I will miss these women and their spiritual journeys."

Amy Boucher Pye, author of *Finding Myself in Britain*

"One of the greatest gifts a Christian author can give us is a realistic picture of what it looks like to be human and a follower of Jesus. In *An Extra Mile*, Sharon Garlough Brown offers us this exceptional gift. In this final book of the Sensible Shoes series, readers will grieve, pray, and celebrate the victory of love that comes to those who dare to walk an extra mile."

Beth Booram, cofounder and director of Sustainable Faith Indy, author of *Starting Something New*

An Extra Mile

A STORY OF EMBRACING GOD'S CALL

Sharon Garlough Brown

IVP Books

An imprint of InterVarsity Press
Downers Grove, Illinois

InterVarsity Press
P.O. Box 1400, Downers Grove, IL 60515-1426
ivpress.com
email@ivpress.com

InterVarsity Press® is the book-publishing division of InterVarsity Christian Fellowship/USA®, a movement of students and faculty active on campus at hundreds of universities, colleges, and schools of nursing in the United States of America, and a member movement of the International Fellowship of Evangelical Students. For information about local and regional activities, visit intervarsity.org.

Quotations from Psalm 13, Psalm 42:1-5, Psalm 84:5-7, Isaiah 43:18-19, Mark 16:1-4, Luke 23:36-38, Luke 24:5, John 20:19-20, John 24-2, Ephesians 5:1-2, and Revelation 7:12 are from the New International Version. Quotations from Numbers 6:24-26, Psalm 57:1, Mark 14:1-11, and Luke 23:27-31 are from the English Standard Version. All other Scripture quotations are from the New Revised Standard Version of the Bible, copyright 1989 by the Division of Christian Education of the National Council of the Churches of Christ in the USA. Used by permission. All rights reserved.

This is a work of fiction. People, places, events and situations are either the product of the author's imagination or are used fictitiously. Any resemblance to events, locales or actual persons, living or dead, is entirely coincidental.

"Roads" from New and Selected Poems by Ruth Bidgood is used by permission of Seren Books.

"Someone to Watch Over Me," recorded by Ella Fitzgerald, The George and Ira Gershwin Songbook, 1959 (George Gershwin [composer] and Ira Gershwin [lyrics], Oh, Kay!, 1926).

Cover design: Cindy Kiple
Interior design: Cindy Kiple
Cover images: watercolor background: © donatas1205/iStockphoto
workout group: © Lynn Koenig / Getty Images
bowl: © Rita Maas/Getty Images

ISBN 978-0-8308-4332-9 (print)
ISBN 978-0-8308-8931-0 (digital)

Printed in the United States of America ∞

InterVarsity Press is committed to ecological stewardship and to the conservation of natural resources in all our operations. This book was printed using sustainably sourced paper.

Library of Congress Cataloging-in-Publication Data
Names: Brown, Sharon Garlough, author.
Title: An extra mile : a story of embracing God's call / Sharon Garlough
  Brown.
Description: Downers Grove : InterVarsity Press, 2018. | Series: Sensible
  shoes series
Identifiers: LCCN 2018005765 (print) | LCCN 2018007263 (ebook) | ISBN
  9780830889310 (eBook) | ISBN 9780830843329 (pbk. : alk. paper)
Subjects: LCSH: Christian women—Fiction. | Spiritual retreats—Fiction. |
  GSAFD: Christian fiction.
Classification: LCC PS3602.R722867 (ebook) | LCC PS3602.R722867 E97 2018
  (print) | DDC 813/.6—dc23
LC record available at https://lccn.loc.gov/2018005765

P 25 24 23 22 21 20 19 18 17 16 15 14 13 12 11 10 9 8 7 6 5 4

Y 39 38 37 36 35 34 33 32 31 30 29 28 27 26 25 24 23 22 21 20 19

ROADS

No need to wonder what heron-haunted lake
lay in the other valley,
or regret the songs in the forest
I chose not to traverse.
No need to ask where other roads might have led,
since they led elsewhere;
for nowhere but this here and now
is my true destination.
The river is gentle in the soft evening,
and all the steps of my life have brought me home.

RUTH BIDGOOD

For Mom, Dad, and Beth, who have
modeled the way of love for me over a lifetime.
And for Jack and David, who daily demonstrate it.
I love you and thank God for you.

*Follow God's example, therefore, as dearly loved children
and walk in the way of love, just as Christ loved us
and gave himself up for us as a fragrant
offering and sacrifice to God.*

EPHESIANS 5:1-2

Contents

Part One

In the Shadow

—෧

Be merciful to me, O God, be merciful to me, for in you my soul takes refuge; in the shadow of your wings I will take refuge, till the storms of destruction pass by.

PSALM 57:1

one

Becca

In the three weeks since her mother's death, Becca Crane had learned one thing about grief: there was no predicting what might trigger a deluge of emotion. The simplest things could set her off—an American accent on the London Underground, a box of Cheerios (her mother's staple) on a shelf at Tesco's, the melodic, mournful strains of a violin played by a street musician on the south side of the Thames. For some reason nighttime walks along the river with the view across to the Houses of Parliament evoked such deep pain in her chest that she could hardly breathe.

She pulled her knit beret down over her ears and leaned forward against the cold metal railing. All along the South Bank, the globes on the wrought-iron lampposts cast soft light on couples walking hand in hand, while the laughter of children riding an old-fashioned carousel wafted toward her.

She wasn't sure why she subjected herself to these evening outings. Maybe she preferred the searing pain of loss to the numbness that had consumed her immediately after her mother died. In Kingsbury, her hometown, she had stumbled along dazed and detached, as if she were watching herself in a movie, a short, dark-haired orphan girl trying to convince herself and everyone else that she would survive "just fine."

"Call me if you need anything," her aunt had said on the phone shortly after Becca returned to London for the remainder of her junior year abroad. The words rang hollow. Rachel hadn't even bothered to attend the funeral, using the feeble excuse of a business trip she couldn't change. She had even reneged on her offer of part-time freelance work over the summer, initially extended so that Becca could spend the summer with Simon in Paris, free of any need for her mother's financial support or approval. But now, as Rachel had caustically noted, Becca had been provided for through her mother's modest estate. "What on earth will you do with a house like that?"

Becca didn't know. She didn't know anything. Except that she missed her mother. Terribly.

An evening cruise boat glided by, lit from within. Becca imagined the conversations of the young women flirting over canapes and champagne, with nothing to think about except the men they might hook up with. Like her friend Pippa. Pippa had tried to be understanding and compassionate, but apart from her frequent bad break-ups, she had never lost anyone. Her advice, though well-meaning, was one-dimensional: distraction. Alcohol, fun, sex—it didn't matter what Becca used, Pippa said, as long as it took her mind off the pain.

Everyone had advice to dispense. Maybe it made them feel better, like they were helping before absolving themselves of any further responsibility of care and concern. Becca had already heard the best her friends on both sides of the Pond could offer:

Your mum would want you to be happy. She would want you to move on with your life.

You should travel, see the world. Life's short. Make the most of it.

Just concentrate on all the good times you and your mom had together. Try to be happy.

Look at everything you have to be thankful for.

None of their platitudes helped. And whenever someone said, "I know just how you feel. When my—insert family member or favorite pet here—died . . . ," Becca wanted to scream, "You don't know how I feel! You have no idea how I feel."

She reached into her purse for a tissue and blew her nose. How could anyone know how she felt when most days she didn't even know herself? The one person she wanted to talk to about it—the one person she had, for most of her life, confided in—was gone. Forever. *She lives on in your memories*, Simon said.

Not good enough. Nowhere close to good enough.

She stepped away from the railing and headed toward the London Eye, which was illuminated in bright blue. There—right there at the base of the Eye, near the place where happy crowds queued for their half-hour ride in the large, slow-motion capsules—that's where her mother had waited for her in December. Becca, spotting her from a distance, had pointed her out to Simon, who laughed and said how small and apprehensive she looked, her head tilted back to survey the size of the wheel. "A bit high-strung, is she?" he asked. Becca nodded. When their eyes met, her mother fixed a strained and determined smile on her face. "Ah, now," Simon said, "she's going to love me." Becca had laughed and leaned in closer to him.

She lives on in your memories, Simon's voice repeated.

Not good enough.

As she watched families board the Eye together, Becca knew one thing: she would give absolutely anything to have one more ride with her mother. Just the two of them.

Her phone buzzed with a text from Simon: Waiting for you.

She wiped her face with her coat sleeve and replied: On my way.

Hannah

One month after submitting a resignation letter to the church she had served for fifteen years, Hannah Shepley Allen was confident of one thing: dispensability was easier to embrace in theory than in practice.

"You're indispensable to me," Nathan, her husband of twelve days, said as he stooped to kiss her furrowed brow. "And to Jake. He adores you. And so do I."

Hannah pushed her chair back from the kitchen table, her eyes still fixed on her laptop screen. Perhaps if she hadn't been so readily replaced, her ego wouldn't be so bruised. But the latest email from her longtime senior pastor, Steve Hernandez, indicated that, with dizzying speed, Westminster was progressing with plans for her successor. *We're wondering if you might be willing to consider a rent-to-own option for Heather to remain in your house.*

She swept her hand toward her screen. "Go ahead and read the whole thing." Nathan pushed his glasses up on the bridge of his nose and leaned forward to read the words Hannah had read three times. She waited until he stood up straight again, then asked, "What do you think?"

"Well, it sure solves the stress of trying to sell it. Sounds like an answer to prayer to me."

"No—I mean, what do you think about them hiring Heather?"

"He doesn't say they're hiring Heather."

"It's obvious that's what they're doing." Hannah set her jaw and read the words again. *If you're open to the possibility, please get in touch with her to discuss details.* "And why is Steve the one emailing me about it? Why didn't Heather just call and say, 'Hey, I'm taking over your job and your office, and I want to take over your house too!'"

Nathan closed her laptop and gently turned her around to face him. "Maybe he wanted to be the one to float up the trial balloon, see how you'd react."

Well, it was odd. The whole thing was odd. And not even Nate could convince her otherwise. Now that they had returned from their honeymoon and had begun to settle into a home-life routine, she'd had lots of time to reflect on her transition to West Michigan. Though Steve had framed releasing her from ministry as a gift, saying that it was important she be free to focus on her marriage and not return to Chicago out of obligation, maybe it had been a calculated attempt for control. "You really don't think this is weird?" she asked.

"Do you want me to think it's weird?" His brown eyes smiled at her even as his lips remained neutral. "'Cause I can embrace 'weird' if you want me to. I can run conspiracy theories with the best of them. Like, maybe they planned this from the get-go and devised the whole sabbatical as a ruse to get you out of the way so they could hire this Heather, who is carrying on an illicit affair with—"

"Oh, stop." Hannah lightly punched his stomach. "That's not what I mean. I'm just saying, the whole thing is very . . ." He waited for her to find the right adjective. "Weird." That's the best she could come up. Something was off.

"Well, I won't argue with your intuition, Shep. But maybe Heather's done a decent enough job filling your shoes, and they're eager to offer her something permanent now that they know you're not coming back. Saves them the trouble of a long-drawn-out search, and if she likes the house well enough to stay in it, then why not? Seems to me they're doing you a favor, doing us a favor, by taking away the stress of selling it."

And the stress of a double mortgage, which would begin the first of April. Though Nate hadn't mentioned anxiety over managing two mortgage payments, Hannah had begun to feel the weight of it. With no current income and limited financial resources to bring into their marriage, she ought to be jumping for joy at the prospect of such an easy transition. Instead, she felt resentful.

"Don't let pride keep you from seeing the gift in this, Hannah."

"I know." What she didn't need right now was a lecture. What she needed was time to process this by herself.

He glanced at his watch. "I've got to go. Jake'll be done with band rehearsal soon." He reached for his car keys, which he kept on the kitchen counter, not on the hook beside the coat rack. She had made the mistake of hanging them there the day before, and he'd ransacked the house looking for them, frantic when she didn't hear his call on her cell phone while she was out shopping. He had been late to class.

"How about if I go pick him up?" Hannah said.

"No, it's okay. I'll get him."

"I'll get dinner started, then. Pasta primavera okay?" She reached for the correct cupboard on her first try and removed a stainless steel pot that had seen better days. Once she emptied her house, she could replace some of his cookware.

"Uh . . . it's Thursday," he said.

Her hand hovered near the faucet. She had evidently forgotten the significance of Thursdays.

"Pizza night," he said. "An Allen Boys tradition. But if you've already got something planned, I'm sure Jake won't mind."

"No, it's okay." If Nathan had already mentioned this particular weekly tradition, she had forgotten. There were quite a few Allen Boys activities to keep track of. She would need to make a list.

"Jake and I usually get a hand-tossed meat feast, but I can get half veggies if you'd like."

"No, get your usual. That's fine." She crammed the pot back into the cupboard. "I'll fix a salad to go with it, okay?"

"Thanks. I'll be back soon." With a kiss to her cheek, he was out the door.

Chaucer, Nate's golden retriever, trotted into the kitchen and sat down on the floor mat, thumping his tail. "Do you want to go out?" Hannah asked. He did not move. "Out?" He barked once. She motioned toward the back door. "Outside?" she asked, trying to mimic Nathan's inflection. Chaucer lifted a single paw for her to shake. She took his paw in one hand and stroked his silky fur with the other. He barked again. "Oh, sorry! Treat?" He rose and spun in a circle. "Okay. Treat. Your dad forgot to give you one, huh?" She reached into the jar on the counter and tossed two treats onto the floor. "Don't tell him I gave you extra."

She rinsed off her hands, then searched cupboards until she found a salad bowl. In their five days of living together under Nathan's roof, the only moving-in task she had completed was hanging up her clothes in half of his closet. He had promised to clear shelves for her in the cramped third bedroom that served as his home office, but she was reluctant to invade his space. So the boxes of books and journals she'd brought with her on sabbatical remained in a corner of the basement. The rest of her possessions awaited sorting in Chicago. Nate had insisted he didn't have any emotional attachment to his furniture, and if she wanted to integrate some of her pieces, he was fine with that. *Decorate however you want,* he said. *It's been a bachelor pad way too long.*

A dark bachelor pad. During the winter months she hadn't noticed how little natural light shone inside. But now that the March days were lengthening, the house felt like a burrow with its heavy brocade drapes and predominantly taupe walls. Hannah had never been a fan of bold, bright colors, but maybe they should exchange his drab furniture and her neutral pieces for something cheerful.

She should have taken some photos of the Johnson's cottage while she was living there. Nancy had discriminating taste, and though Hannah could never splurge on interior design, she might frugally duplicate the light cottons and pastel palette. If not for the rift between them, she might even have asked for Nancy's help.

Upon returning from their honeymoon, Hannah had cleared out her scant belongings from the cottage, leaving Nancy a potted plant and a thank-you note on the counter. Fifteen years of friendship, and they were left communicating only via email. All of Hannah's overtures toward face-to-face reconciliation had been rebuffed by cool reserve: Nancy and Doug were very pleased she had enjoyed her time at their cottage, and they wished Hannah and her new husband success in their life together. When Hannah mentioned meeting her at the cottage to hand over the key, Nancy replied that she would have a friend with her when she came to ready it for their family, and she really wasn't sure what their schedule might be. Hannah could leave the key under the mat.

Chaucer, having inhaled both biscuits, plopped down on the kitchen mat with a sigh. "Exactly," Hannah said. Maybe someday Nancy would forgive her for manipulating and deceiving her. She hoped so. She opened a Caesar salad kit and dumped it into the plastic bowl.

Out of sync. That's what her life felt like. Eventually, she would find her equilibrium in her new reality, with all of its joys and challenges. The adjustment would take time. She knew that. Any grief counselor would look at her inventory of major life changes over the past six months and recommend she be very intentional about processing the upheaval. Even good upheaval brought stress. She knew that. She had walked alongside enough grieving people in pastoral ministry to understand the complicated dynamics of loss and transition.

She rubbed Chaucer's back with her bare foot while she mixed the croutons with the lettuce.

Change in employment? Check. First, a mandated sabbatical and now, a resignation.

Major move? Check. Twice. From her settled life in Chicago to the Johnson's cottage on Lake Michigan to Nathan's house in Kingsbury.

Marriage? Check. A first marriage at age forty.

Becoming a parent? Check. She was now stepmother to a thirteen-year-old boy.

Change in social circles? Check. She had been removed from all of her ministry colleagues and peers in Chicago and had begun to forge new relationships in Kingsbury, particularly with the Sensible Shoes Club, her companions on the spiritual journey.

Death of a friend?

She set aside the salad bowl as, with tears, Hannah realized she had lived almost a whole day without once thinking about her beloved Meg.

Mara

Never underestimate the horror of a magnifying mirror, Mara Garrison thought, or the importance of a good set of tweezers. She tilted her chin higher and tried again to snag a stubborn, wiry whisker. Ever since she turned fifty, her nemeses seemed to sprout overnight.

"Gotcha!" she exclaimed as the root yielded with a satisfying pop. She swiped her chin to verify success, a gesture that brought to mind her grandmother, who had frequently sat with a pair of tweezers in hand, squinting at her reflection in the oxidized glass of an antique dressing table. After she finished her primping rituals, Nana would pat the embroidered seat cushion, and Mara would position herself in front of the mirror and grimace while Nana combed out the tangles of her dark auburn hair. As Nana combed with firm but loving strokes, Mara would confide in her about the girls at school who had nicknamed her The Whale. "Don't you pay them no mind, Sweet Pea," Nana would say. "Sticks and stones will break my bones . . ."

Mara would finish the sentence with a valiant, sniffled, "But names will never hurt me."

Whoever made that up was a whale of a liar.

If she ever got wind of anyone calling her granddaughter, Madeleine, names, they would have one angry grandmother to deal with. An angry daddy too. Her son Jeremy wouldn't put up with any bullying nonsense, that was for sure. And besides, with all the anti-bullying policies and procedures in place, kids didn't get away with as much as they used to. At least, they weren't supposed to be able to get away with it. She'd heard enough bullying accusations against Brian to know that teachers and students and administrators were pretty vigilant about that.

She wrapped herself in her red plus-sized kimono robe and shuffled down the hallway. "You up, Brian?" she called to a closed bedroom door. She hadn't heard his alarm go off. Bailey, Brian's dog, stood on his hind legs and pawed at the wood. "Down, Bailey." She nudged him with her slipper. "Get down. Brian?" Still no answer. She cracked the door open, the stench of sweat and day-old pizza engulfing her. How many times did she have to tell the boys not to leave food lying around? Bailey bolted inside. "You awake?" She stooped to pick up a pair of gym socks and glowered at his bed, where his Green Bay Packers comforter lay in a rumpled heap.

"Where's your brother?" she asked fifteen-year-old Kevin, who, red hair awry, was plodding toward the bathroom the two boys shared.

"Dunno."

Bailey wove in and out of her feet as she descended the stairs to the family room—no Brian—and to the kitchen—no Brian. "Brian?" she called down to the basement. No answer. She flipped on the light switch and walked down far enough to verify that he wasn't asleep on the couch or playing video games.

Her youngest had been in his room when she went to bed. She'd heard his music—his latest moody grunge or metal band that supplied the soundtrack for his obstinate defiance of her authority—and she had almost pounded on the door to tell him to turn it down. But weeks ago, at her counselor Dawn's suggestion, she had decided to choose her battles with him more carefully. So far that strategy hadn't paid off. At. All.

Kevin trudged into the kitchen and reached for a box of Lucky Charms, which he poured into his mouth straight from the plastic liner.

"Hey! How about a bowl?" Mara opened a cupboard and set one down on the counter. He filled it without commenting and ate the dry cereal with his fingers, picking out the marshmallow pieces first. She decided not to insist on a spoon. "Run down to the basement and check if he's down there somewhere, will you, Kevin?" Maybe Brian hadn't heard her calling for him. Or maybe he was ignoring her.

"I'm eating."

Pick your battles, Dawn's voice instructed.

Fine.

She was halfway down the basement stairs when Brian, wearing boxers and a rumpled T-shirt, emerged from the laundry room. "What are you doing? Didn't you hear me calling you?"

The split second of panic on his face morphed into his usual expression of scorn. Without replying, he tried to brush past her on the stairs.

"Whoa!" She thrust out her arm and, before he could resist her, sniffed his hair, a swift maneuver she had learned years ago during Jeremy's adolescent experimentation with marijuana.

His nostrils flared. "What are you doing, you freak?"

"Nothing. Just wondering where you were, that's all."

"Yeah. Whatever." He snarled something else under his breath.

"Excuse me?"

"I said, Whatever." Bounding up the stairs, he shouted in anger when Bailey tripped him at the top.

"You're the one who wanted a dog," Mara muttered. She snapped her fingers and summoned Bailey. In the months since her soon-to-be-ex-husband, Tom, had bought Brian the dog in order to spite her, Mara had become quite attached to the little guy. She rubbed his face in her hands and patted him on the rear end before he raced off.

Hearing a door slam upstairs, she headed to the laundry room to see if anything was amiss. Years ago, when Jeremy was a little older than Kevin, she had found all sorts of contraband in the laundry room. She had survived Jeremy's rebellion, she reminded herself as she rummaged through a trash can. He had grown up to be a loyal, loving, and affectionate son, husband, and father. Maybe there was hope for Brian. If he didn't become even more like his dad.

The trash can was filled with nothing but lint and wadded up tissues. No cigarette butts and no baggies with suspicious substances. Brian had never done a load of laundry, had never even put away his own clean clothes. So what was he doing down here? She kicked at a pile of dirty clothes on the concrete floor, not sure what she was looking for until, Bingo. She found it. Buried beneath multiple pairs of jeans, boxers, and sweatshirts was a fitted twin sheet crumpled into a ball. He had been trying to conceal his embarrassment.

And she had been quick to assume he was up to no good.

No way she could talk with him about it. Tom was the one who had handled the puberty conversations with the boys, and she sure wasn't going to text Tom and ask him to reassure Brian that there wasn't some-thing wrong with him. She tossed the sheet and some towels into the washer and started a load. She would put clean sheets on his bed while he was at school, and he would know that she knew. Rather than him being grateful that she didn't mention it, he would probably be even more resentful toward her for finding out and fixing it. Because he didn't want to need her, Dawn had once explained. What he wanted was to go live with his dad in Cleveland.

Tom wouldn't have it. He had made it clear through their attorney negotiations that what he wanted were visiting privileges without day-to-day responsibilities. At least, that's the way Mara saw it. He insisted that primary physical custody be granted to her for both boys, no matter what Brian begged for. Tom would drive in and see the boys every other weekend, get every other spring break and alternate major holidays, take them on expensive vacations during his allotted summer weeks, and preserve his role as their fun, spoiling hero. The drudgery, the conflict, the day-to-day stress of single parenting two teenage boys—that would continue to be hers.

A week ago Tom had submitted a proposed financial settlement that to Mara's astonishment enabled her and the boys to stay in the house until Brian graduated from high school, at which point the house would be sold and the profit split. After crunching the numbers, her attorney advised her to take it. It was a good offer, he said, with equitable monthly child support for the boys. They would be well provided for. By ac-cepting the deal, she could stay out of court and be free to move on once their mandatory six-month waiting period expired in June.

She ought to be elated. Grateful. She ought to feel relieved. And she did. But she couldn't help feeling like Tom had played her. He would make sure both boys knew that his "generosity" had enabled their lives to continue with the least possible amount of disruption. Hero dad. That was the script. And if Mara didn't follow it, the boys would resent her.

She didn't want to feel indebted to Tom. Maybe what she wanted was a fresh start, a clean break. Maybe subconsciously she'd hoped that his settlement proposal would reveal him to be the bullying oppressor she had endured for the past fifteen years. Instead, he was coming off as magnanimous. Even with a gift that ought to have set her free from some financial stress, he had managed to retain control. She wasn't naïve. Anything that appeared to benefit her and the boys would actually be benefiting him first. He probably wanted to protect his investment, hold on to the house long enough for the market to fully recover so that in four years he would get more money for it.

In all likelihood, the proposal was also a manipulative attempt to keep her from prying into his personal affairs, including whatever agreement and relationship he had with the pregnant girlfriend Kevin had told her about. Maybe his attorney had recommended generosity as a way to cover an "indiscretion." His company might not look favorably upon him getting a woman pregnant and then divorcing his wife. If, in fact, it was his kid. She didn't know that for sure, and she wasn't going to ask Kevin to find out.

Let it go, she commanded herself. Let it all go. The bitterness. The desire for revenge. She had turned it all over to God the night the Sensible Shoes Club met at Meg's house to pray with the story of Jesus washing the disciples' feet. But Mara was daily reminded that she needed to keep letting go, especially when her buttons got pushed.

She picked through the rest of the dirty laundry pile, separating out all the dark colors. The agreement, at least, bought her some time to get on her feet. Maybe someday her part-time job at Crossroads House shelter would become a full-time job with benefits. Miss Jada had told her the board was open to that possibility. What an answer to prayer that would be! She loved coordinating meals and overseeing hospitality for the homeless and displaced guests who came in search of a safe place to land, just like she had done almost thirty years ago with the then-toddler Jeremy.

Brian was slouched at the kitchen counter, eyes riveted on his cereal bowl, when Mara lumbered up the stairs. Rather than calling attention to their silent transaction, she picked up her cell phone and checked for messages: one from Abby, saying she wouldn't need her to take care of Madeleine that morning; one from Hannah, confirming their Sensible

Shoes Club meeting that evening at Charissa's house; and one from Tom (who had been instructed that he needed to communicate any change of plans directly to her, not to the boys), informing her that he would pick them up an hour later than usual. "Dad will pick you up at seven," she said, "and I'll be gone. I've got my group tonight."

Neither one of them acknowledged the news. She replied with "Happy to come another time" to Abby, "Looking forward to it" to Hannah, and "Okay" to Tom. Then she packed the boys' lunches in silence. Where was the line between picking the important battles and enabling them to take advantage of her? She would have to have another conversation with Dawn about that.

I am the one Jesus loves, she mentally declared to her reflection in the microwave as she spread mustard onto white bread. Come to think of it, she had totally neglected that spiritual practice the past couple of weeks. All the time she spent plucking whiskers in front of the magnifying mirror, and it still hadn't become a regular habit to declare God's love for her to herself. She was so focused on removing the offending hairs that she lost sight of the larger opportunity to see herself as God saw her. Beloved. Favored. Chosen.

As Hannah would say, *That'll preach.*

She would have to remember to share that image of the mirror with the group. They hadn't been together since Hannah's wedding, and they had a lot to catch up on.

Mara wiped her nose against her sleeve and slid Kevin's ham and cheese sandwich into a plastic bag. She could still see Meg sitting at the back corner table near an exit door at their first retreat session at New Hope, the hives of anxiety rising to her chin as she tried to decide whether to stay for the sacred journey or bolt. The growth and transformation Meg had experienced was remarkable, and in many ways, she was the kind and compassionate bond that had knit them all together. Though Hannah and Charissa hadn't said it aloud, Mara wondered if the thought had crossed their minds too: she wasn't sure how the Sensible Shoes Club would survive without Meg Crane.

"Did you make me ham and cheese?" Kevin asked.

That was the drill. Every day she made him ham and cheese on white bread with mustard on only one side. "Yep."

"I'm kinda tired of ham and cheese."

She inflated her cheeks and blew the air out slowly. "Then tell you what," she said, fighting the temptation to toss the sandwich into the trash, "how about if you make your own lunch? Both of you. I think I'll take the day off. And Brian?" He was actually making eye contact with her. "You'll need to take your dog for a walk."

Charissa

What was it about pregnant women, Charissa Sinclair wondered as she stood in line at the Kingsbury Public Library, that caused even strangers to lose all sense of propriety and violate personal boundaries? The next person who reached out to touch her belly would be slapped. Or maybe she would reach out and rub theirs like a genie lamp.

"When are you due?" the latest offender asked.

To prevent any further infringement, Charissa positioned her gardening books against her burgeoning abdomen. "July."

"You look really good. You've got an advantage, being tall. I was ginormous. And then my doctor told me that I had—"

Here we go. Charissa fought the temptation to interrupt and tell her she wasn't interested in her pregnancy complications or labor horror stories. If she was subjected to one more personal narrative or narrative about a friend of a friend or a second cousin once removed who ended up in some kind of childbirth emergency, she was going to scream. Or throw something.

"Next?" The library assistant summoned the woman to the counter, cutting her off just as she was getting to the good part. Charissa watched her deflate.

"Well, good luck to you," she said over her shoulder, with a final appraising stare.

Charissa gave her a close-lipped smile.

Pregnancy was hard enough without strangers compounding the stress. There were women who exulted in being pregnant—Charissa was assaulted ad nauseam by their posts and photos on Facebook chronicling their "journeys"—but she wasn't one of them. She had finally begun to accept that reality without heaping guilt on herself. "You know I love our Bethany," she said to John when she got home, "but part of me wants to say, 'Wake me up when it's over.'"

"I know," he said. "How many babies would be born if men had to be pregnant?"

"None. You guys are wimps." She set her books down on the console table and hung up the key to Meg's car, which Becca had loaned to her. *No point in it just sitting in the driveway while I'm in London,* Becca had said while they were changing into their bridesmaids' gowns for Hannah's wedding. Charissa needed to send her an email, see how she was coping with everything.

"Jeremy and I are going to get something to eat and then head to Home Depot while you have your group," John said. "He wants to show me what he's thinking for the bathroom remodel."

"Just keep in mind your wife is pregnant, okay? And we've only got one toilet."

"I know. It's just some cosmetic updates. Nothing major."

"And budget, remember?" She glanced out the front window at the sound of Jeremy's loud muffler. "We're on a budget, John."

"I know. He knows that, he's good about that. Look what he's already saved us! We're running way under."

John was right about that. Mara's son had been a godsend. In the five weeks since they closed on the house, Jeremy had restored hardwood floors, reinvigorated kitchen cabinets, and helped them paint the interior, including the soft seashell pink walls of the room that would be their daughter's. Jeremy often voiced how grateful he was for the work. With his own new baby and reduced hours at the construction company, he and Abby were strapped for cash. He was hoping work would pick up again in the spring, counting on it. In the meantime, he was making himself available for all kinds of handyman projects.

John opened the front door to greet his new friend. "C'mon in!"

Jeremy wiped his work boots on the welcome mat and grasped John's extended hand, his shy smile revealing the gap between his front teeth. Mara had once confided to Charissa that she regretted never having the money to pay for braces for him. *He used to get teased because of his teeth,* Mara said. *Kids can be so cruel, can't they?*

Yes. They could. Though she hated to admit it, Charissa had once been one of them. Lately she had become quicker to recognize her critical and judgmental impulses, hard as it was to be honest about them.

Progress, not perfection. That was her new motto, far easier most days to declare than to live.

She greeted Jeremy and then said, "Is Abby off tonight?"

"Yeah."

"How's she doing, being back at work? How's Madeleine?"

"Good. Both good, thanks." He cracked his knuckles and turned toward John. "You ready to go?"

"Gimme just a sec." John jogged down the hallway to their bedroom.

Charissa pressed on the small of her back. She didn't yet know Jeremy and Abby well enough to initiate any prying conversations about money or stress. "Your mom's coming over tonight. We've got our Sensible Shoes group."

"Yeah, she told me. She always looks forward to that."

"Yes, it's always a good time together. For prayer and reflection, that is. I mean, it's not a 'good time' like most people think of when they hear the words 'good time.'"

He chuckled. "No, I guess you're right about that. These days, 'good time' for us means getting a few hours of uninterrupted sleep."

"I'm sure that will be the same for us in a few months." Charissa wasn't looking forward to that part. When she didn't get her six to eight hours, she became a thunderhead of irritability. There was a reason why sleep deprivation was a common method of torture.

Jeremy pointed with his chin toward the gardening books. "Gonna do some landscaping?"

"No, not so much landscaping; it's all pretty well laid out already. But I'm noticing lots of green things starting to poke up in the flower beds, and I don't have a clue what any of them are." She wondered how many of the plants Meg and Jim had tended when they lived in the house twenty years ago. She had planned on asking Meg about the flowers come spring and summer, but—

"Abby's always dreamed of having a flower garden," Jeremy said. "She does these pots of flowers for the patio at the apartment—real pretty—but I don't know what any of it is. Red and pink and white. That's all I know about flowers."

"I'm not much better than that. John's mom is a master gardener, and I'm hoping she'll be able to identify what's in the beds and give me some tips when they come down to visit."

"What about Mom?" John asked as he returned with his wallet and phone.

"I was saying she's got a green thumb."

"For sure. Mom can make anything grow. As for me, I look at plants, and they die."

"Well, don't you start killing things off before they even have a chance," Charissa said. "We'll have the prettiest garden on the block, just you wait."

"Says the woman who for our whole married life has insisted she couldn't bear the responsibility of a house plant."

"Go," she said, bopping him on the shoulder as he flashed his boyish grin. "You can go now. And keep an eye on him, Jeremy. Don't let him convince you that I've given him permission to buy anything other than what you recommend for the bathroom. Budget, John. Keep to the budget." This she said for the benefit of both of them.

John gave a mock salute, Jeremy a slight nod, and they were out the door.

Charissa kicked off her shoes, sank into an overstuffed armchair facing the fireplace, and put her feet up on an ottoman. She had hoped to vacuum the rugs again before Hannah and Mara arrived, but she didn't have the energy. The bathroom, at least, was clean. Good enough for today.

Though she had never been one to count down the days to the end of the semester, she was ticking them off her calendar with zeal: seven more weeks. Managing her own doctoral course load on top of teaching a section of freshman writing would have been challenging enough without sharing the inside of her body. But Charissa wasn't complaining. Or trying not to, anyway. Recently she had been pondering the idea of her body as "sacred space," a place where new life grew and took shape. She didn't yet fathom what that life would become, but she was trusting the process. Or rather, she was trusting God with the process. Or trying to.

Maybe that's why she felt compelled to garden. Given all of the deaths she had observed the past few months, spiritual and emotional ones as well as the death of a new friend, the miracle of green shoots emerging from the earth after the harshness of winter spoke to her.

At twenty-six she'd had very little exposure to death: her paternal grandmother when she was in first grade, a friend's father when she was in middle school, and a college classmate—a girl she knew only by name and sight—when they were juniors. As someone whose life had not been shaped by trauma or tragedy, Charissa hadn't given much thought to resurrection. Resurrection was merely a doctrine of faith she had always affirmed without hesitating, ever since she memorized the Apostle's Creed as a third-grader: The third day he rose again from the dead. Period. Or rather, exclamation point.

Words from Meg's funeral still pursued her. Hymns, Scripture, the pastor's homily—all of it quickened her to a promise she'd never had to cling to before. *We are Easter people,* Meg's pastor had declared, *practicing our hope.* In the midst of death. In the midst of change. In the midst of sorrow. In the midst of uncertainty.

The third day he rose again from the dead.

In a few weeks they would sing their alleluias again on Easter morning. Easter, which had never meant much more to Charissa than trumpet fanfares, lilies, and ribboned baskets filled with chocolate, had taken on new significance, not as a historical event to be commemorated once a year but as an ongoing reality to be lived daily.

The third day he rose again from the dead.

Meg's death had awakened in her a profound sense of vulnerability. Meg had been younger than Charissa when she buried her husband, younger than Charissa when she gave birth to their only child, the child who should have had two parents bring her home to the front room they had lovingly prepared for her.

Charissa glanced toward the room that now awaited Bethany.

She wasn't superstitious. But no matter how hard she tried to shake it, the cloud of morbidity that had descended on the house after Meg's cancer diagnosis would not dissipate. Even with all of Jeremy's remodeling of the space, Charissa couldn't stop thinking about the dreams that had been birthed, cherished, and shattered here.

She had suggested that the group gather and pray for one another instead of using one of the prayer exercises from their notebook. But maybe what each of them needed was a focal point for faith. For hope.

I am the resurrection and the life. That was one of the verses from Meg's funeral that pursued her, and it seemed a good text to ponder. Charissa checked her watch: forty-five minutes before Hannah and Mara arrived. Time enough to compose a short lesson plan. Or rather, an invitation for prayer and conversation.

MEDITATION ON JOHN 11:17-44
Resurrection and Life

When Jesus arrived, he found that Lazarus had already been in the tomb four days. Now Bethany was near Jerusalem, some two miles away, and many of the Jews had come to Martha and Mary to console them about their brother. When Martha heard that Jesus was coming, she went and met him, while Mary stayed at home. Martha said to Jesus, "Lord, if you had been here, my brother would not have died. But even now I know that God will give you whatever you ask of him." Jesus said to her, "Your brother will rise again." Martha said to him, "I know that he will rise again in the resurrection on the last day." Jesus said to her, "I am the resurrection and the life. Those who believe in me, even though they die, will live, and everyone who lives and believes in me will never die. Do you believe this?" She said to him, "Yes, Lord, I believe that you are the Messiah, the Son of God, the one coming into the world."

When she had said this, she went back and called her sister Mary, and told her privately, "The Teacher is here and is calling for you." And when she heard it, she got up quickly and went to him. Now Jesus had not yet come to the village, but was still at the place where Martha had met him. The Jews who were with her in the house, consoling her, saw Mary get up quickly and go out. They followed her because they thought that she was going to the tomb to weep there. When Mary came where Jesus was and saw him, she knelt at his feet and said to him, "Lord, if you had been here, my brother would not have died." When Jesus saw her weeping, and the Jews who came with her also weeping, he was greatly disturbed in spirit and deeply moved. He said, "Where have you laid him?" They said to him, "Lord, come and see." Jesus began to weep. So the Jews said, "See how he loved him!" But some of them said, "Could not he who opened the eyes of the blind man have kept this man from dying?"

Then Jesus, again greatly disturbed, came to the tomb. It was a cave, and a stone was lying against it. Jesus said, "Take away the stone." Martha, the sister of the dead man, said to him, "Lord, already there is a stench because he has been dead four days." Jesus said to her, "Did I not tell you that if you believed, you would see the glory of God?" So they took away the stone. And Jesus looked upward and said, "Father, I thank you for having heard me. I knew that you always hear me, but I have said this for the sake of the crowd standing here, so that they may believe that you sent me." When he had said this, he cried with a loud voice, "Lazarus, come out!" The dead man came out, his hands and feet bound with strips of cloth, and his face wrapped in a cloth. Jesus said to them, "Unbind him, and let him go."

For prayer and conversation:

1. Which sister do you identify with? Why?

2. Try to pretend you don't know the end of the story as you imagine yourself as that sister. How do you feel when you hear the news that Jesus has finally arrived?

3. What surprises you about Jesus?

4. What does it mean for you to know Jesus as the resurrection and the life right now?

two

Hannah

The candid wedding photos captured and chronicled a far more intimate and tender tale than the posed ones. Hannah peered over Mara's shoulder at a photo of Nathan and her talking with Katherine Rhodes, who had officiated their ceremony at New Hope. "Oh! I like this one," Mara said. "Look how Nathan's looking at you. Total adoration." Yes. His expression was soft and wistful. Hopeful. Proud, even.

Charissa agreed. "That one too," she said, pointing to the last one in the stack.

Yes. That was one of Hannah's favorites, the moment when her father placed her hand in Nathan's, all of their faces glistening with tears.

"Such a beautiful wedding." Mara gathered the photos together and returned them to Hannah, who tucked them into a manila envelope. Eventually, she would organize them into an album. It was the sort of project Meg would have been delighted to help with.

Charissa moved off the sofa where the three of them had huddled together and pulled her long dark hair into a tight ponytail. "I know I'm the one who suggested just catching up with each other tonight," she said, "but the more I thought about it, the more I realized I need something to help me fix my eyes in the right direction in the midst of everything that's changed. That's changing. So I hope you don't mind, but I put together a mini-reflection exercise—not as extensive as the ones Katherine wrote, but something to get us thinking about Easter. About resurrection. Then we can pray for one another. Does that sound okay?"

Mara nodded. "Works for me."

"Me too," Hannah said. She hadn't relished the thought of spending their entire time together talking about Meg and her absence. Much as she valued Mara and Charissa's companionship, she still preferred to process her grief privately.

Charissa passed them each a sheet of paper. John 11 was a text Hannah had already spent quite a bit of time meditating on, but she wasn't going to disregard Charissa's offering. As Charissa settled herself into her chair, Hannah stared at the lively flames crackling in the fireplace. Three Fridays ago they had gathered in Meg's parlor in front of a dancing fire to ponder the depths of Jesus' love and to wash one another's feet. When Meg had knelt before Hannah and reverently washed and dried her feet, both of them were overcome with quiet tears. And then, to Hannah's surprise, Meg placed a kiss on the top of each foot, her face illumined by the firelight and by something else. By Someone else. It was as if Jesus himself had stooped to wash her feet.

She had forgotten to tell Meg that.

She clenched her eyes shut, trying to fend off the sudden onslaught of grief.

"Oh, honey," Mara murmured as Hannah's chest began to heave. It was no use. Hannah leaned her head against her friend's broad shoulder and cried.

Friday, March 13
7:30 p.m.
Mara and Charissa both said we could skip journaling about the text and just talk and pray together. I think they were both caught off guard by my flood of tears. But I need some time for quiet reflection. I need space to listen and breathe before I talk about it.

I've pictured myself as Martha before, charging out to confront Jesus and accuse him of doing nothing to intervene. So tonight I'm picturing myself as Mary, refusing to leave the house to meet Jesus because she's so utterly disappointed that he didn't come when they desperately called for him. I'm imagining myself sitting there when they get the news that he's finally arrived—four days too late. He couldn't even be bothered to come to the funeral, and now he shows up?

No. Not okay.

"You coming?" Martha asks as she grabs her cloak. No. I'm not coming. What kind of Love does nothing when it's in Love's power to intervene?

I feel the gravitational pull toward giving the right answer. The theological answer. The answer I have come to know and trust. But I think I need to stay longer with Mary and feel the weight of her sorrow and disappointment. Because maybe, if I'm really honest and take the time to listen to my own grieving soul, maybe I'll discover that I'm still harboring resentment that he didn't answer my prayers—our prayers—the way I wanted him to.

I've spent all day running through the "if onlys" again. If only I had noticed something was really wrong with Meg sooner. If only I had seen that it wasn't bronchitis. If only I had pushed her to get to a doctor faster. If we had caught it even a month earlier, would the prognosis have been different?

And what if I'd encouraged her to explore chemo, even though the doctor said the cancer was too far progressed for it to be effective? What if I'd urged her to do everything she could to fight it? To live?

I write the words "to live," and I see the irony. What's my definition of "to live"?

Jesus said to Martha, "I am the resurrection and the life. Those who believe in me, even though they die, will live, and everyone who lives and believes in me will never die. Do you believe this?"

Yes, I believe, Lord. Help my unbelief.

Do I think for a moment that Meg would return here after glimpsing your glory? Do I forget that she lives? That she lives more fully now than she ever lived here? Do I forget?

I'm sorry, Lord. But it hurts.

I know she died with sorrow over Becca. I know she was worried over all that was left unsaid and undone. By putting me in charge of her estate, Meg was also entrusting me with her daughter. She hoped I'd watch over her in prayer, not just oversee the disbursement of assets. She hoped Becca would reach out to me if she needed anything, that Becca would be open to forming a connection with me. I don't know if that will happen. How do I honor Meg's desires while giving Becca freedom to choose her own way?

I pray. I offer help and encouragement. A listening ear if she needs it. So far, she hasn't replied to any of my recent emails. I don't know how hard to push.

If you can just be available, Meg said, if she ever needs anything. She didn't ask me to try to become a mother figure for Becca. She didn't ask me to try to lead her to Jesus or try to persuade her to get out of her relationship with Simon. Just be available.

I can see her face and hear her voice say, "I'm so thankful for you, Hannah." Not for my help. Not for my prayers. Not even for my time. But for me. I wanted to do so much more for her. When we prayed in this house in February and anointed her with oil, I wanted to anoint her for healing, not for death.

And I hear your voice remind me—again—that I did anoint her for life.

Why do I still get confused about who is alive and who is dead? Bring Becca from death to life, Lord. And thank you for bringing Meg from life to life. Thank you for giving me the privilege of being there when she crossed into your near presence. Please let the memory of that moment become a source of comfort rather than distress for Becca. Bring her to life. Please.

I look at the text again, and I'm reminded of how differently the two sisters grieved. Martha, the confronter. Mary, the avoider. I've been both sisters. I've had my moments of angrily accusing you of not caring, and I've had my moments of keeping my pain to myself and privately nursing my disappointment.

I watch Mary sitting there in the house, surrounded by people who are probably wondering aloud about Jesus' power—couldn't the One who healed the blind man, they ask later, have kept this from happening?—and none of their words comfort or soothe. They just compound the pain. Then Martha reappears in the doorway, and her countenance is softened, and she speaks gently and says, "The Teacher is here, and he's calling for you."

That's what breaks the stewing. The ruminating. The rehearsing of the confusion and the wound. "Jesus is here, and he wants to see you. He's calling for you." Those summoning words shift everything and gently move Mary forward in her grieving. Those are the words I need to keep hearing, Lord, as I move forward with all of the losses and all of the gains. So many joyful gains to celebrate even as there are so many deaths to mourn. You summon me. I summon you. Come and see the things I have buried. Come and see the places where I'm disappointed and the places where I hope. Meet me here with resurrection life. Not just me. All of us. Please.

Mara

As the others recorded their insights, Mara stared at the handout and tried to focus. It would have been easier just to talk about the questions out loud and then pray. She really wasn't good at writing down her reflections. She had tried a few times over the past several months, but it didn't stick. She would never be a journaler like Hannah. She needed to be okay with that.

She read the text again. Which sister did she identify with? The loud-mouthed one. The one who had no problem telling Jesus how she felt. They'd sent a message to him to ask for his help, and he hadn't even bothered to come. She would have gunned for him, just like Martha. And she might not have been as polite.

She also wasn't sure she could have been as full of faith. Martha trusted that Jesus could do anything, even when he hadn't done what she wanted him to do. That was big faith.

But Martha also doubted. There she was, saying she believed that Jesus could do anything, that he was the resurrection and the life, that he was the Messiah, the Son of God. And then when Jesus told them to roll away the stone, she argued with him because it would stink too bad to open the tomb.

Mara liked Martha. She liked her a lot. Because she'd had the same kind of arguments with Jesus about opening the tombs of old dead things she had buried long ago: traumas and hurts and sorrows, regrets and guilt and shame. She'd also been afraid of being overwhelmed by the stench of it. And if the stuff was dead and buried, why visit it again? Why open the seal?

Because sometimes, she had learned over the past few months, Jesus asked questions like, "Where have you laid him?" and you could either say, "Never mind. I don't want to go there again," or you could say, "Come and see."

That's one of the things Mara had come to love about Jesus: he never forced his way anywhere. He just asked the probing questions and promised not to leave her when she drummed up the courage to go to the tomb. Tombs, plural. Many of them.

Mara had spent enough years in counseling to know that it was by opening up those stinking tombs of rotting sorrows that you could experience healing. Resurrection life, even. Just like Jesus promised. She had experienced a fair bit of that over the past few months—rolling away the stones and letting Jesus speak new life and power to old hurts. She had also experienced the gift of doing it in community. She wasn't alone at the tombs.

Talk about new life. She wasn't, thank God, alone.

—☙—

At least they had the first meeting without Meg under their belt, Mara thought as she watched Hannah drive away shortly after nine-thirty. She wriggled into her coat. "You think she's okay?" she asked Charissa.

"Not sure."

"Me neither." After her brief cry on Mara's shoulder, Hannah had insisted she was doing all right. She said she was navigating lots of transitions, trying to find a new equilibrium, working things out with the church in Chicago, wondering how best to support Becca, missing Meg. *Enjoying being a newlywed?* Mara had asked. At this, Hannah had blushed and replied, *Absolutely.* Not that Mara would have expected Hannah to confide about intimate details, but she thought maybe Hannah would at least gush about how wonderful a husband Nathan was or how blissfully happy they were together.

"She and Meg had grown so close," Charissa said. "Not that I wasn't close to Meg, or that I'm not sad, but . . ."

"No, I know what you mean. The two of them had something special." Mara was ashamed to think of it now, how she had responded with jealousy when Hannah chose Meg to be her maid of honor. If she had known then that Meg wouldn't even make it to the wedding, she wouldn't for a moment have begrudged her any of that joy.

Charissa was typing into her phone. "Sorry. Message from Becca."

"How's she doing?"

Charissa looked at her watch and counted off on her fingers. "She's five hours ahead of us, so middle of the night there, and she's replying to an email from one of her mother's friends? I say, not so good."

Poor girl. "I'm glad she's reaching out to you. Meg would be so happy about that." No huge surprise that the two of them had connected. With only a few years between them, Charissa and Becca had discovered quite a lot in common at Hannah's wedding. Both were English literature majors, both had studied in England (Becca in London and Charissa in Oxford), and now, in God's very small world way of weaving stories together, Charissa was living in Meg's old house.

"I used the excuse of having a question about the car," Charissa said. "Anything to keep communication lines open, right?"

"Right."

It had been a God thing when, while Mara was zipping up the back of Becca's bridesmaid dress, Charissa mentioned the hassle of only having one vehicle. Mara, admiring an intricate butterfly tattoo on Becca's left shoulder, wasn't looking at Becca's reflection in the mirror when she offered the car, but Becca must have caught Mara's lingering gaze because she reached over her shoulder, touched the butterfly, and said with the slightest pinch in her voice, "Mom didn't know about that. She had a tough enough time with the nose ring."

Becca was spirited—no question about that—and determined to defend her relationship with a fortysomething former philosophy prof to anyone who might question it. Though Mara did not pass any sort of judgment (who was she to throw stones?), Becca seemed to assume that she and Charissa would share her mother's opinion about the perils of being involved with an older man. "At least he's not married," Mara had commented while she stuffed herself into her own bridesmaid dress. When Becca eyed her quizzically, Mara said, "Been there, done that, got the T-shirt."

A loud engine rumbled in the driveway, and Mara squinted out the Sinclairs' front window. "Is that Jeremy's truck?"

Charissa put her phone away. "Yeah, boys' night out. He and John went shopping for the bathroom remodel."

On a Friday? Abby didn't usually work on Friday nights. Maybe she was home alone with the baby. Or maybe she was out with friends and they'd hired a babysitter when they didn't have money to pay for one. How many times did Mara have to remind them that she would be happy to babysit and give them a date night, even if it meant missing her group?

She waited for the headlights to turn off, ready to chide her son for not accommodating an eager grandmother, but only one car door opened and slammed again, and soon John was at the front door, and Jeremy was pulling out of the driveway. Maybe he hadn't noticed her car on the street.

"Hey, Mara," John said as he yanked off his shoes near the door. "Sorry! Interrupting?"

"No, we're finished," Charissa said. "Any luck?"

"Say goodbye to those peach tiles and funky wall sconces. Your son's a magician, Mara. An absolute magician. He's got it all figured out and yes"—he held out a single finger to keep Charissa from interrupting—"it's all in the budget. Under budget, actually. So we'll have even more money to play with. What shall we do next? Maybe a deck?"

"Uh, no." Charissa planted her hands on her hips. "You've got a funky math system going in your head."

"Yeah, well. Anything for my baby girl."

"Your baby girl needs a deck?"

"She needs her daddy to rock her outside and look at stars. So, yes."

Charissa exhaled loudly.

"Jeremy okay?" Mara asked.

"Yeah, good. He said to say hi."

Oh.

"Abby was waiting for him, so he had to get going."

Oh. Okay. "Well, I need to get going too." Mara leaned against the back of their sofa to balance herself as she put on her shoes. "Thanks for hosting, Charissa. Let me know when you want to go shopping for some more maternity clothes. I'm happy to go with you."

"I think I've got what I need, but thanks." Charissa tugged at her elastic waistband. "I'm hoping to get over to Crossroads next Friday to help serve lunch, so put me on your volunteer list, okay? I want to make a regular habit of it."

"You got it. Thank you."

As soon as she got into her car, Mara dialed Jeremy's cell phone number. "Hey! Sorry I missed you," she said.

"Yeah, sorry about that. Maddie's having a rough time, and I didn't want Abby to have to wait any longer for me to get home."

"So Abby was off tonight?"

"She doesn't work Friday nights."

"I know, that's what I thought. So I was surprised when Charissa said you were out with John."

"It's work, Mom. A potential job."

"No, I know. That's great. I'm so glad they've got some work for you to do."

"At least somebody does."

The resignation in his voice panged her. "Oh, honey. I wish there was something I could do to help. You know I'd do anything for you. For all of you." He didn't reply. "Is there anything I can do?"

"Abby called her folks. They're going to give us a loan."

Oh. That was exactly the type of help she couldn't offer.

"Do you have any idea how much I hate that?" he went on. "How much it kills me to ask them for help? I hate being a charity case."

"It's not charity. It's help. There's nothing wrong with asking for help. Nothing shameful about it. If I'd had an option like that when you were little, someone who could have stepped in and given us a little bit to keep us going, I would have jumped at it." She *had* jumped at it, come to think of it. She'd jumped toward Tom and his fancy suits and platinum credit cards when Jeremy was a teenager because she didn't have family to help, and she was tired of struggling to make ends meet.

"Well, you're you," Jeremy said. "I'm me. And I'm telling you, it sucks."

"No, I know, honey. I know. I'm sorry."

Mara had only met Xiang Liu, Abby's father, once. Though Abby had translated cordial greetings from him and from her mother, Ellen, at the wedding rehearsal dinner, Mr. Liu (Mara could never call him Xiang) had not seemed at all pleased by the merging of the families. After the brief translation Abby offered during family introductions, he spoke in whispered words that Abby listened to without interpreting, her mouth fixed in a smile that wanted to be serene.

"I gotta go, Mom. I'm pulling into the apartment now."

Mara offered the only help she could. "I'll be praying for you, Jeremy. For something to open up for you. You pray too, okay?"

If he answered, she didn't hear him.

When she reached her own driveway a few minutes later, she flicked off the headlights and sat in the dark, the moonlight reflecting off patches of lingering snow. The boys had left the house without turning on the exterior lights. They probably had also neglected to walk Bailey. As soon as she opened the garage door, he would bark, and she wanted a few minutes of quiet.

She exhaled slowly. If construction work didn't pick up in the spring like Jeremy hoped, he and Abby might find themselves struggling to pay rent. And if they found themselves struggling to pay rent, they would have to rely more and more on Abby's parents for support. Jeremy wouldn't go for that. Not long term.

So what if she offered their basement as a small apartment for them? It wasn't ideal for a couple with a baby, but it had a bathroom and an open living space, with a bedroom Tom had used as an office. If she moved the washer and dryer into the mudroom area next to the kitchen, they might even be able to put in a kitchenette. Jeremy could do that work, no problem.

She would have to appease the boys somehow. They would resent giving up their video game lair. But maybe she could clear out the guest bedroom upstairs and give it to them as a game room.

By the time Mara entered the house, she was already picturing a happy life together under the same roof, the shared meals at the table, the evenings spent in conversation, the unhurried hours she would enjoy with Madeleine. Maybe they could transform the backyard into a little girl's paradise too, with a swing set and playhouse more magnificent than any of the ones she had envied or imagined when she was a child. "Down, Bailey," she commanded as she flipped on the kitchen light switch. As expected, there was a puddle on the tile floor. Without removing her coat, she cleaned up the mess and grabbed his leash off the hook. "C'mon, dog. Walkies."

With a spring in her step, she walked back and forth along the cul de sac until Bailey did the rest of his business on a neighbor's lawn. Humming, she cleaned it up and carried the plastic bag home, swinging it in rhythm with her stride.

Becca

Becca stepped out of Simon's bathtub onto the grimy linoleum and wrapped herself in a stiff, stale-smelling towel. What she wouldn't give for a long shower with consistent temperature and powerful pressure! Even after almost eight months in England, she still hadn't mastered the knack of combining scalding and icy water from two different taps.

She was fastening her bra when Simon rapped on the bathroom door. "Just a sec!"

Without hesitating, he flung open the door. She shoved her arms into her shirt. "What! Gone all prudish?" he said. She snatched her jeans from the yellowed floor.

He seated himself on the edge of the tub and motioned for her to sit on his lap. "I don't have to leave for another two hours," he said.

She averted her eyes and slipped into her jeans. "I can't."

"Can't?"

"I promised Harriet I'd help her with an essay."

"So reschedule." He grabbed her hand and pulled her toward himself, more forcefully than usual.

It was the daylight. That's what it was. There was something romantic about the darkness of evening, the cloak of nighttime that enlivened passion and longing. She caught a glimpse of herself in the chipped mirror above the sink, and she didn't look anything like Simon's "seductive schoolgirl" from the night before.

"Simon, please."

He released her wrist with a gesture of disgust. "Suit yourself."

Something in his tone terrified her. "Wait, how about this? I'll go help her for a little while, tell her I can't stay long. I can be back here by lunchtime."

"I've got other plans for lunch." He turned his back toward her.

No! He couldn't walk away. "Simon!" But that voice sounded childish and desperate. "*Professor . . .*" A little better. He glanced over his shoulder. "I made a mistake." There. She'd found the alluring voice again. "I was wrong. I have time after all."

Hannah

Saturday mornings at the Pancake House were an Allen Boys' tradition, a tradition Hannah had participated in months before when, having fled New Hope because the retreat content was hitting too close to home, she had ended up lost and locked out of her car in the restaurant parking lot, pounding her vehicle in frustration when Nathan and Jake happened to arrive. Nate still teased her about the memorable first impression she'd made upon her future stepson.

"You sure you won't join us for blueberry pancakes?" Nathan asked as he rinsed his coffee mug in the sink.

"I'm sure." She brushed lint off her cardigan. Some morning she might feel comfortable enough to come downstairs in her pajamas or bathrobe, but for the past week, she had made a point of being dressed before Jake awoke. Exiting his father's room in a robe still felt awkward. "I think it would be good for the two of you to have some father-son time, so Jake doesn't feel like I've been inserted into everything."

"He doesn't mind."

"Not yet, he doesn't."

Nathan looked over his shoulder at her, eyes narrowed. "What's that supposed to mean?"

"Nothing. I'm just saying, I don't want Jake to resent having me around." She opened the dishwasher and reached out her hand for his mug. Nathan had a habit of rinsing mugs and glasses only to abandon them on the kitchen counter. On any given day he'd go through half a dozen.

He clasped the mug with both hands. "Has he said something to indicate he resents having you here?"

"No, of course not. Jake's the most easygoing teenage boy on the planet."

"Okay, then." He handed over the mug.

"Okay." She set it on the top rack.

"So are you coming with us?"

"I think I'll—morning, Jake!" Jake entered the kitchen in his pajamas, his eyes darting from his father's face to hers. She hadn't heard him come down the stairs.

"Hey, bud," Nathan said. "Ready for some pancakes?"

"Are we going?"

"Absolutely! Hannah and I were just talking about it."

"And I was saying I thought maybe it would be nice if you and your dad had a chance to go together, just the two of you." She hoped Jake didn't think they regularly spoke about him behind his back.

"Oh," Jake said. "Okay."

There. See? She gave Nathan a pointed glance when Jake turned toward the cupboard to get a glass. "I've got some work to do over at Meg's house," she said. "I'll get it done this morning, and then the rest of the day's open."

"I was going to go with you and help, Hannah."

"I know. But I think I need some time over there by myself, just to work some things through." She hadn't set foot in Meg's house since returning from the honeymoon, and there were tasks she could no longer avoid, like mail to collect and sort. And Becca probably hadn't disposed of all the flowers before she flew back to London.

Nathan tightened the sash on his terry cloth robe and said, "Well, I'll go shower, then. Leave in half an hour, Jake?"

"Yeah."

Nate was annoyed with her. She could tell. But if she followed him upstairs to continue the conversation, Jake would know there was something wrong, and she didn't want to call attention to a disagreement. She waited until she heard footsteps on the floor above and then said, "So tell me about this science fair project your dad said you're working on. What are you trying to do?"

Jake sat down at the table and took a sip of orange juice. "It's called the McCollough effect, and it's really cool. Have you heard of it?" She hadn't. "It's this visual perception thing where black and white horizontal line patterns look like they're different colors because you've used induction to produce . . ."

She was already lost, but she sat down across the table from him with a bowl of cereal and listened like she understood. When he asked if she would be willing to be a test subject, she accepted. Gratefully.

The first time Hannah had entered Meg's Victorian house, she had been struck by its resemblance to a funeral parlor. Now as she entered, the mustiness of the space and the pungent odor of decayed flowers overwhelmed her. She removed her shoes and stood in the foyer, feeling the weight of the silence. Even the grandfather clock, which once echoed through the house with its melancholy chimes, had ceased its ticking.

Setting a stack of mail on the entry table, Hannah stared into the front parlor with its stuffy and lifeless antique furniture, the faded burgundy velvet drapes closed at the window and pooled on the floor, with gray dust clinging in creases along the deep folds. On the mantel sat a snow globe with a multi-spired castle, a gift Meg had purchased for herself in London because it was like one Becca had broken when she was a little girl. Hannah had watched Meg place it there in a small act of defiance—or perhaps as a declaration that she would no longer be governed by her mother's house rules. Though she had enlisted Hannah's help in rearranging some of the furniture and hanging family photos, there was so much they had left undone.

Hannah stroked the back of the sofa where the two of them were sitting the night Meg received the doctor's phone call that the x-ray had revealed "something suspicious," the same sofa where they'd sat the night of the foot washing. On the marble coffee table a magazine lay open to a page with photos of bridal bouquets. She couldn't bring herself to touch it, not when Meg, who had planned to arrange her bouquet, had left it there. If she could have closed a door to the room, she would have done so. But there was no door.

Her lips firmly pressed together, she stepped across the foyer into the music room, where the piano was still covered with get-well cards Meg had placed there, along with handwritten notes of encouragement from friends and drawings and thank-you letters from her young students.

Mingled among them were cards Becca had evidently received after her mother's death: "Praying for God's comfort" and "Thinking of you in your grief" and "In your time of sorrow, remember" cards she'd chosen not to take with her to London. Becca had also left the funeral bouquets here, along with the collage of pictures she had assembled for the memorial service. A shrine, Hannah thought as she touched the cheek of a smiling Meg. Becca had left a shrine.

She had told Becca she would take care of the house until she returned from London; she would see to it that bills were paid so that Becca didn't need to worry about those details. At least, not for now. At some point Becca would need to decide whether to keep or sell it, a decision Hannah wished a twenty-one-year-old didn't have to make. For so many reasons.

She stooped to stroke the drooping leaves of an amaryllis, the tall stalks now collapsed, the white flowers wilted and browned. She would keep this pot and its bulb. Meg would want that. As for the rest, Becca could decide what to do with the cards and photos when she returned at the end of April to organize her mother's things. Hannah would help her, if she wanted help. But for now her only tasks were to dispose of the flowers and sort the mail.

The grass withers and the flowers fall, she thought as she emptied murky water into the sink and tried to keep orange pollen from the lily stamens from dusting the kitchen rug. Maybe the wilted petals of the roses could be dried and saved. She didn't know anything about making potpourri, but Mara probably did. She removed as many petals as she could, then placed them in a plastic bag. She would ask Mara to make something lasting out of them. Sachets, maybe. Becca might want one. Or maybe she would think that was morbid. If she had left the flowers to fade, then maybe she didn't want any reminders from her mother's service.

Hannah unlocked the back door, startling the sparrows and finches investigating empty birdfeeders. She would fill them with seed. Meg would want them filled. She would even want the squirrels fed, especially the one with the bare patch on its back, an impudent squirrel Meg said had won her over with its persistence and ingenuity in finagling seed from the squirrel-proof feeders.

She was just about to walk down the stairs to the yard waste container when she spied multiple cigarette butts crushed on the concrete. Hannah flushed with anger. She had watched Simon from the kitchen window that night, his face partially lit by the porch lamp as he puffed smoke into the frosty air. With stunning disregard for the woman who had welcomed him into her home—the woman who, having never smoked a day in her life, had been struck down by lung cancer, of all things—he'd had the gall not only to contaminate her property but to leave the foul debris behind. By the time she filled the birdfeeders and began sorting the mail, Hannah had imagined several gratifying scenarios, the mildest of which ended with Simon saying or doing something so callous and conceited that Becca decided she was done with him.

If only.

She set aside a few handwritten envelopes to forward to Becca, along with paperwork concerning the estate. At some point she would need to try to pin Becca down about her summer plans, whether she would still accompany Simon to Paris or whether she might choose instead to spend the summer in Kingsbury. Not that Hannah would blame her for not wanting to spend the summer at home. What did Kingsbury hold for her now? Sorrow. And a big empty house that amplified it.

At the bottom of the stack of mail was one final handwritten envelope addressed in unsteady cursive not to Becca but to Meg. Hannah pulled it closer to decipher the return address: Loretta Anderson, Winden Plain, Indiana.

Meg's beloved Mrs. Anderson. Maybe her card had been lost or delayed in the mail. Hannah checked the postmark. No. It was stamped five days ago.

"What should I do with it?" she asked Nathan when she returned to their house shortly before noon.

"Open it."

"I don't know . . . it feels a little intrusive."

"Meg made you the executor, Hannah. Her business is your business." His tone was uncharacteristically clipped.

"Maybe I should just write a letter to Mrs. Anderson and let her know. Or call her." She could probably track down a phone number online.

"Whatever you think is best." Nathan glanced at his watch and took a last gulp from his coffee mug. "I've got to go." He pushed back his chair. Chaucer, who had been sleeping at his feet, jumped to attention.

"I thought the rest of the day was clear, for all of us."

"I know, I'm sorry. Something came up while I was out with Jake. I won't be long, I hope."

"Something with a student?"

"No. With Jake."

She waited for him to elaborate. Instead, the silence between them billowed. She rotated her gold floral earrings, then tucked her hair behind her ears. "Are you mad at me?"

"Mad at you? Why would I be mad at you?"

"I don't know . . . the pancakes . . . not going with you and Jake."

He rinsed out his mug and set it down on the kitchen counter. "I've got lots of faults, Shep, but passive aggressiveness isn't my style. You know that. When I'm mad at you, I'll tell you." He put on his coat. "I'll be back soon." Before she could ask him any more questions, he was gone.

Chaucer sat in the middle of the kitchen floor, thumping his tail. "Neglected again, huh?" She tossed him a treat from the jar, then opened the envelope from Loretta Anderson.

My darling Meg,

What a joy to receive your beautiful drawing of the cherry tree, and what a deeply moving reflection you wrote about its resilience. I look forward to receiving your photos when it blooms in the spring.

In the rest of the note she offered updates about her health (her eyesight was failing, but she was otherwise well and well-cared for), and she expressed her thanks for Meg's kind words of love and encouragement. *You have always been one of my deepest joys. I thank God for the gift of you.*

No mention of Meg's cancer diagnosis. Meg must have chosen not to tell her, for whatever reason. But there was no reason now for keeping it secret, especially if Loretta was expecting further contact. Taking the card with her, Hannah retreated to Nathan's office and found some non-monogrammed stationery in a desk drawer. Painful as the truth would be, silence would be unkind.

three

Seeds, Charissa was reading online, could lie dormant for centuries—millenia, even—and then, when planted in good soil and given the right amount of moisture and sunlight, they would sprout and bear fruit. "They actually planted seed they found in one of the Egyptian pyramids, and it grew," she said to John, who was reclining on the couch with a remote control, waiting for the March Madness brackets to be announced.

"Grew into what?"

"Grain, I guess. Wheat. Isn't that amazing?"

"More amazing if it had grown into mummies."

"Oh, no. Wait." She clicked on another link. "I take that back. Nope. Sorry. Not true."

"No mummies?"

"No sprouting. Not from the tombs, anyway. But that would have been a great story." In principle, however, seed viability was real. Scientists, she read, had extracted embryos from some ancient seeds buried by Arctic squirrels, and the seeds had germinated in the laboratory.

"Sounds like *Jurassic Park* stuff," John said when she relayed this information. "Cool." He sat up on the couch and turned up the volume. "Ahh, here we go. C'mon, State."

This was her cue to leave. She rose with her laptop.

"You're not going to watch with me?"

"I want to keep reading." Though she was reluctant to admit it, Pastor Neil Brooks's sermon on the parable of the sower that morning had spurred her curiosity in ways that years of listening to the Reverend Hildenberg's sermons had not. She had spent all afternoon studying Scripture references to seeds and sowing.

"You've got your seeds," John said, rubbing his hands together in anticipation, "and I've got mine."

Every year with the basketball thing. Charissa didn't understand it, the game or the madness. She only knew that for the next however many weeks, John would be obsessed with his brackets, engaged in friendly and sometimes not-so-friendly competition with friends and work colleagues. From the bedroom she could hear him on the phone, running loud commentary as the drama unfolded.

The son of Michigan State alums, John cheered for the Spartans as if he'd attended there himself. If he'd been a foot and a half taller, he often lamented, he might have gotten an athletic scholarship. But where height failed him, heart compensated, and he'd played on the Kingsbury University team with the same intensity and gusto that characterized all of John's endeavors. Though Charissa couldn't care less about the difference between a jump shot and a lay-up, she understood the meaning of Most Valuable Player and had celebrated with John when he was given the honor their senior year.

"Yeah, baby!" he yelled before appearing in the doorway, phone still pressed to his ear. "Number two seed!" He gestured at her with his fingers in victory formation. She gave him a thumbs up, and then he disappeared. He had already purchased several green Spartan shirts in all different sizes for Bethany. His parents had bought her Spartan onesies, bibs, cutlery, and pajamas. Charissa had drawn the line at the baby football jersey. *How about a cheerleader's outfit, then?* John had teased.

He was incorrigible. Loveable, but incorrigible.

Opening to Mark 4, she read the text again: "Listen! A sower went out to sow. And as he sowed, some seed fell on the path, and the birds came and ate it up. Other seed fell on rocky ground, where it did not have much soil, and it sprang up quickly, since it had no depth of soil. And when the sun rose, it was scorched; and since it had no root, it withered away. Other seed fell among thorns, and the thorns grew up and choked it, and it yielded no grain. Other seed fell into good soil and brought forth grain, growing up and increasing and yielding thirty and sixty and a hundredfold." And he said, "Let anyone with ears to hear listen!"

Before attending the sacred journey retreat at New Hope, Charissa would have never paid attention to the parable for herself. If asked what category of soil her own soul was—if asked to assess her own capacity to receive the Word of God and be fruitful with it—she would have replied without hesitating: she was the good soil. Didn't her good and upright life attest to that?

But for the past six months she had been weeded and plowed, vigorously and relentlessly. Achievements she had for years named as wheat had instead been revealed as tares rooted in her desire for honor and recognition, her pursuit of excellence, her idolatry of reputation, and her addiction to esteem. All of it had been exposed and gathered up and burned, leaving her with scorched ground. Thorns and thistles, that's what had characterized her life. She had been choked by thorns without even realizing it.

Yet there was good news too. Thank God her eyes had been opened to the truth of the depth of her sin and her desperate need for grace. Over and over and over again. She had been led firmly and persistently toward repentance. Daily. And now could she be patient with the process of transformation? Could she trust the viability of the good seed planted in soil tilled by the Spirit?

Be mindful of the condition of the soil, Neil had said, *and submit to the process of being composted and amended. The Lord knows what to remove from us and what to work into us to make us fruitful. Trust the wisdom and the slowness of his work. And trust the power of the seed. Give a seed good soil, and it does what seeds do. It grows.*

Let anyone with ears to hear listen.

Her temptation, she knew, was to want immediate results, to plant the seed in the ground, monitor it daily for progress, and then become obsessive about comparing it to seeds planted in other gardens, in other souls. Her temptation, she knew, was to be too quick to weed her own garden. Sometimes, however, it was hard to tell the difference between the wheat and the weeds. Sometimes, Neil reminded them, you needed to let the wheat and the weeds grow up together for a while before you could discern which was which.

But waiting was not her strong suit. Charissa was a fan of efficient planning, measurable goals, and straight lines to the destination. The long, slow, circuitous nature of growth and transformation was dizzying and disorienting, even infuriating at times.

She recorded some notes in her journal, then turned her attention toward literal rather than figurative gardening. Even though she ought to be working on her lecture for Tuesday or her metaphysical poets paper due on Wednesday, she would give herself the luxury of one more hour.

She typed "planting seed in Michigan" into her search engine and perused the results: beans, beets, broccoli, Brussels sprouts. She hadn't considered planting vegetables. Could she actually grow broccoli in her garden? The thought of planting something they could serve for dinner seemed beyond her horticultural reach. Most of the planting was still indoors—no way she could manage the time and attention that re-quired—but come April, she could start planting seeds that could sprout into green things. "As long as I don't have to eat those green things," John said when she mentioned this to him later.

"They're good for you. Good for Bethany. I could make spinach smoothies."

He grimaced. "Good thing you're the pregnant one." He reached into the fridge for a soda. "Just don't be hiding any of that nasty stuff in my food."

"I don't cook."

"Exactly. Guess I'm safe." He popped the can open and strolled back to the living room, sipping as he walked.

"I could learn!" she called after him.

He laughed.

"Okay, mister." She pursued him and spun him around, extending her hand for him to shake. "Right here. Put it right here."

"What are we shaking on?"

"A bet. You've got your madness bracket thingy, so I'm doing my own competition. One meal from scratch, using all fresh ingredients, once a week until the baby's born. You choose a night, I'll choose a night."

He laughed again.

"I'm serious, John. Why can't I?"

"'Cause you're the one who's always joked about what you could make if you knew how to boil water."

"Well, maybe I'd be good at it. Enjoy it, even."

He stared at her a hard second. "Nothing from a can?"

"No."

"No frozen anything?"

"No."

"Ooooh. You're on, Riss. And how do we determine a winner?"

"I say, given my disadvantage going into this, if it's edible and we don't get sick after eating it, I win for the week."

"What's the prize?"

"You'll have a wife who knows how to cook. What more do you want?"

He flexed his eyebrows playfully at her. "How about a deck?"

—⟟⟨

"You'll help me, won't you?" Charissa said to Mara on the phone a little while later. John, who had wheeled the garbage can to the curb, was now talking with the next-door neighbor. He could easily be occupied for the next twenty minutes, even in the cold.

"I'm no gourmet cook, girlfriend. I use lots of cheats and shortcuts because Tom and the boys never wanted froufrou meals. Why'd you set the bar so high?"

What a great question for her life in general. "I figured I might as well go for it if I've got the motivation." How hard could it be?

"Well, I'm more of a baker than a chef, but I'll give it a whirl. When do you want to start?"

"I told him I'd cook on Friday. So maybe we could go grocery shopping after we finish serving at Crossroads? Or will you be too tired?"

"No, that's fine with me. Let me do some research this week, figure out a good recipe for you to start with. And then we'll go from there."

"Thanks, Mara. I told him you'll be my coach, at least for the first couple of weeks. And then I'm on my own."

"You'll be fine. Quick learner, I bet."

Charissa switched her phone to the other ear. "I didn't think I'd succumb to the whole nesting thing, but maybe there really is something biological to it. Or maybe it's moving into our own house that's made a difference, having a yard for the first time. Whatever it is, I'm feeling a longing to become domestic. Don't tell anyone."

Mara laughed. "No, I remember the same thing when I was pregnant with Jeremy. But there wasn't really a place for me to nest. Just a crummy apartment Bruce kept on the side, without Tess knowing about it. So it pretty much sucked. My own fault, I know. But I wouldn't give Jeremy up for anything, that's for sure." She paused. "Did you guys happen to see him at church this morning?"

No, they hadn't. After a few weeks of sitting with John and Charissa for worship at Wayfarer, Jeremy and Abby hadn't shown up that morning, and Jeremy hadn't replied to John's text. "We looked for them, but I don't think they were there."

Mara sighed. "That's what I was afraid of."

"What do you mean?"

"I think I really screwed things up." Mara related her worries over Jeremy's financial situation, her desire to help them, and her offer to give them the basement as an apartment. "You know, just in case they need it. But Jeremy got really upset, said something about living in his mother's basement. I hadn't even thought about the way it would sound, offering him a place, you know? I just wanted to help, to try to take some of the pressure off. God knows I didn't mean to offend him or make him feel even worse about himself. And when I called back later to apologize, he wouldn't pick up his phone, and Abby said she wasn't sure where he was."

"I'll ask John to call him."

"Would you?"

"Of course." If he ever stopped chatting to the neighbor. He was probably inviting him over for dinner or to watch basketball. John could befriend anyone, anywhere.

"Thanks, Charissa. Keep them in your prayers, okay?"

Charissa had never been one to pray regularly for others, and she always felt a bit guilty when people asked her to pray because she knew she would probably neglect the task. Some of her friends kept a list of people and requests, committing to daily intercession and chronicling updates and answers. Maybe she should begin a new daily discipline. But start small. Pray regularly for only a few people. "I will," she said, and tried to mean it.

—☙

After a year of trying to forge relationships at the apartment with neighbors who did not want to socialize, John was in heaven. When he finished recounting everything he had learned about Chuck, the neighbor, Charissa asked if he could call Jeremy and check in. "Mara's worried about him."

"What should I say to him?"

"That we missed them at church, that we're wondering how they are. I don't know—use the excuse of finding out when he wants to start work on the bathroom."

While John dialed Jeremy's number, Charissa skimmed the lecture notes that had been provided for her about research strategies and citation styles. Maybe they were adequate. She had begun the semester thinking she would revise and improve everything that had been given to her, but when she agreed to take over the writing section at the last minute, she hadn't factored in the time it would take to read and grade papers or to meet with students who needed input on assignments—or more rarely, to encourage students who had life issues they were struggling with. Those were the conversations that had most surprised her, that a student would seek her wisdom not about writing technique but about life.

The memento mori exercise she had adapted and assigned them in February had prompted a few of them to ponder the trajectory of their lives, to consider what they were devoting their energy to and why. Prayerfully engaging the exercise herself had stirred up her own questions about why she was pursuing a PhD and why she wanted to teach, questions she had avoided giving serious time to contemplate because she wasn't sure she was ready to listen for her soul's deepest answers.

"Hey, Jeremy," John said. "Missed you guys this morning . . . Yeah, yeah . . . No, I get it. Totally. You need your rest."

She shifted position on the couch as Bethany punted.

"No, I know," he said. "Glad you guys are okay. And whenever you're ready to start on the bathroom, let us know."

Much as Charissa wanted the tile and fixtures revamped as quickly as possible, she wasn't looking forward to sharing the space. Maybe Jeremy could work during the day, and she'd plan to stay on campus, with close proximity to restrooms.

"Yeah, I'll check. Riss?"

She looked up from her notes.

"Okay if he starts tomorrow?"

Tomorrow? She mentally scanned her schedule. Yes, she could spend the day on campus. "Sure." Maybe he would be done by the end of the week. She was amazed by how efficiently Jeremy worked. But since he charged by the project, not by the hour, he probably was eager to move on to other jobs. She hoped he had some scheduled.

"Did he say if he has some other projects?" Charissa asked when John hung up the phone a few minutes later.

"Nope. Didn't mention anything."

"Did he mention Mara offering to convert her basement into an apartment?"

"An apartment? No. Like, for them to live in?"

"Yes."

"That's what every husband and father aspires to," he scoffed, "living in his mother's basement with his family."

"It was a kind offer from her, John. She's worried."

"And they'll find their way. Economy's bound to pick up soon, right?"

Charissa closed her lecture notes and opened her journal. Maybe it would be easier to intercede if she wrote out her prayers. For Becca. For Mara. And for Jeremy and his family.

Hannah

Hannah rolled over on her side of the bed, where she had spent the past hour trying in vain to nap while Nathan and Jake watched an Indiana Jones movie downstairs. Whatever it was that had required an hour of Nathan's time yesterday, he wasn't sharing details. "Just some teenage boy stuff," he'd said when he arrived home. "Nothing to worry about."

With fifteen years of pastoral experience behind her, Hannah understood the complicated dynamics of confidentiality. Boundaries, however, had been far more well-defined when she was single and working out of a church office or when she was ministering in a hospital room or restaurant booth or nursing home. As for developing intimacy as a married couple while honoring the intimacy of a father-son relationship, she was at a loss. If some issue had arisen with Jake that needed resolving, what role did she play? She was "Hannah" to Jake, not "Mom." If Jake were "their son," then she and Nate would work together to help him. But so far, Jake wasn't asking for her help with anything. She would be a test subject for his science project. That was all. Jake cleaned his own room, made his own lunch, asked Nathan for help with homework, and politely welcomed her into their space, like a long-term houseguest.

"It's still early days," her mother had said on the phone when Hannah casually mentioned she wasn't sure how to function as a stepmother. "You'll find your way. Tell me about your honeymoon. How was Ludington?"

The details she felt comfortable sharing with her mother were ones about the bed and breakfast, a Victorian house with four-poster canopy beds, a fireplace and Jacuzzi in their room, a cozy nook for reading, and delicious food elegantly served. She spoke about their proximity to the lakeshore, where they had enjoyed leisurely walks along the beach and savored sunrises and sunsets. She also described their outings into the Manistee National Forest, where Nathan had taught her how to cross-country ski and persuaded her to join him on a two-person snowmobile for an exhilarating ride she would never forget and hoped someday to duplicate. With her helmet pressed against Nathan's back and her arms wrapped around his waist, she began the ride with eyes closed. But eventually she lifted her head, loosened her grip, and cried with the sheer beauty of it, shouting her enthusiasm as he increased velocity to soar through the deep snow-covered woods. *A speed addict,* Nate reported to Jake after he returned from his spring break trip with friends. *You should have heard her.* Jake had smiled his shy smile. He was the one who had first suggested snowmobiling as a way for Hannah to learn how to play.

What she didn't tell her mother (did any new brides confide such details to their mothers?) was that she had also cried, not with wonder, joy, and pleasure, but with shame as she struggled to offer her body to her husband. She had been ill-prepared—emotionally, mentally, and spiritually—for the uneasiness she would feel in those early days of exploring oneness. Nathan was tender and patient, gently reassuring and demanding nothing more than she was prepared to offer. For this she was grateful. But even so, she couldn't shake a gnawing sense of inadequacy. And to whom could she confide? For years she had offered pastoral counseling to married couples struggling with everything from financial stress to parental challenges to sexual difficulties and dysfunctions, couples who forgot—or didn't mind—that the pastor they consulted offered remedies derived from theological and therapeutic wisdom rather than from personal experience.

She could have told Meg, and Meg would have understood. Meg might even have commiserated with her, offering wisdom from her own experience as a newlywed.

Hannah reached for a photo she had removed from Becca's memorial collage to scan and keep for herself: a picture of Meg at the Kingsbury Gardens with an impossibly blue butterfly poised on her shoulder, her face lit with the same light that had radiated from her when she knelt to wash Hannah's feet. Luminous. That was the word. Even with her protruding collarbone and weary eyes, Meg's unveiled face reflected God's glory and revealed his image.

Even though our outer nature is wasting away, our inner nature is being renewed day by day. That was Meg's testimony. She had crossed the finish line with radiance, with love. Like the butterfly at rest on her shoulder, she had endured the rigors of transformation to discover wings.

Hannah kissed the photo and fell asleep clutching the image of her friend—her sister—to her breast.

———Ꙅ———

"Thought you might sleep straight through," Nathan said, glancing up from his book when Hannah shuffled into the kitchen. She rubbed her eyes, still mildly disoriented. It was pitch black outside.

"Where's Jake?"

"At a friend's, working on a history project."

"Is everything okay with him?"

Nathan hesitated. "Yeah, he'll be okay. Some older boys were teasing him in the locker room, and I know one of the dads. We got it taken care of."

The Allen Boys, doing their thing.

He rose to his feet and went to the fridge. "Sorry—we went ahead and ate without you. I wasn't sure if I should wake you up or not. How about some pasta?"

She shook her head. Cereal, maybe. And some toast. "I'm okay. Not very hungry."

"You feeling all right?"

"Just tired."

"You sure?"

"Yeah."

But when he reached for her hand, her eyes burned. "Hannah?" She pressed her lips together, trying not to cry. He enfolded her in an embrace. "I'm sorry," he murmured, "I know all of the upheaval has been hard on you."

She wanted to refute that. She wasn't unhappy. Was not. She had every reason to be happy, to be grateful. And she was. So grateful. And so sad.

"I was thinking earlier about regular rituals you and I can practice," he said as he stroked her hair, "like a date night. Something fun to keep that play discipline going. I don't want to lose that."

She straightened herself to look him in the eye. "That sounds good. Thank you."

"And I was also thinking about Sunday nights, how maybe we could light our unity candle and practice the examen. Just as a way of reviewing our life together with God, to see what we're noticing and talk about it. What do you think?"

"I'll get the candle," she said, and kissed him.

———⌒———

While Nathan wrote fluidly in his notebook, stopping periodically to gaze at the flame or close his eyes in a listening posture, Hannah found that her words wouldn't come. What was she noticing about her life with God? She had already journaled about her grief and disappointment and didn't feel like writing it out again. She was weary of grief. She flipped back a few pages to see her journal dates. Apart from writing out her reflections at Charissa's house about Mary and Martha, she had written nothing the past few weeks. Not since Meg's funeral. Nothing about their wedding. Nothing about their honeymoon. Nothing.

She stared up at the kitchen ceiling, eyes fixed on a red smudge. Like insect blood. A swatted mosquito, maybe. She couldn't paint over it without painting the whole ceiling. Then if she started painting the kitchen ceiling, she would have to paint the ceilings in the hallway and the family room and the stairwell. And then if the ceilings were freshly painted, the walls would look dingy.

She didn't like the mint green walls in the kitchen. It looked antiseptic. Her kitchen in Chicago was a soft buttercream yellow. Natural, not artificial. And when the morning sunlight streamed through her eastern-facing windows, the whole room glowed with warmth and welcome.

Nathan wouldn't object to her painting the walls, and it would give her a project with tangible results. She would pick up some paint color cards while she was out running errands on Monday and experiment with coordinating palettes so that the rooms had more cohesion.

Painting was one of the first things her parents had done together whenever they moved. They would show Hannah colors she could select from for her bedroom—she usually chose pale yellow—and then she would help by covering the baseboards with painters' tape. Dad would let her work on the first coat, but then he and Mom would finish the second coat together. Hannah would lie on her bed, positioned temporarily in the middle of the room away from the walls, and read her Laura Ingalls Wilder books and pretend she wasn't listening to their conversations about new neighbors and sales clients and Dad's travel schedule. She couldn't remember them arguing while they painted. Wasn't painting one of those potentially stressful married couple's activities? Or maybe that was wallpapering. Maybe that's why they never had wallpaper in any of their houses. Or maybe her parents stripped the wallpaper or painted over it while she was at school. She couldn't remember.

She remembered getting library cards. That was one of the first places she would go with her mother whenever they moved into a new town. Getting a library card with her name and new address on it helped her feel like she belonged somewhere. Books were her first friends in any new community, sometimes her closest ones. Reading Laura's stories about moves and adventures gave Hannah courage for her own, and she had read Laura's stories over and over. Those dog-eared books were still on a shelf at her house in Chicago. There was no room for them here.

"How's my favorite girl doing?" Daddy would ask, usually a few weeks after a move. He would come into her freshly painted room and sit on the edge of her bed and ask her about school and teachers and friends and the kids who played every day together in the neighborhood. Hannah would grip Brown Bear to her chest and smile and nod and say that school was fine and that she liked her teacher and that she was making new friends. And Daddy would say, "I knew you'd like Colorado." Or Arizona. Or California. Or wherever else she had landed, with shoes and jeans that weren't what the other girls were wearing.

Nathan looked up from writing. "Done?" he asked quietly.

She supposed she was. She closed her journal before he noticed the blank pages in front of her.

She would invite him to speak first. And then she would speak about what she was noticing. Some of it. The deepest truth she would keep to herself: that even with all the blessings and gifts of her new life, she missed the familiar comfort of the old.

Mara

Mara flipped through her five ingredients or less cookbook, searching for something easy that Charissa could try to make for dinner. She had suggested a pasta dish, but Charissa said she would have to make her own tomato sauce from scratch. Way too much trouble. So Mara had suggested tacos. But John liked spicy salsa, and she would have to make that from scratch too. "I've got it!" Mara said to her on the phone Thursday afternoon. "Stir-fry. And don't tell me you're not allowed to use soy sauce."

"But I—"

"You made the rules for this thing, you can bend them. We can go shopping tomorrow afternoon, get all the veggies, and make it with rice. You know how to cook rice, don't you?"

Charissa took too long to reply.

"Ohhhh, girlfriend." Mara made sure there was no hint of condemnation in her voice. But seriously. How did someone live to be twenty-six without knowing how to make rice? They had come from two different worlds, the two of them. "Okay. I'll teach you how to make nice, fluffy rice." They would have to make it without a chicken bouillon cube. She wondered how the boys would react if she told them they were having a vegetable stir-fry for dinner. Cooking a double portion at Charissa's house made more sense than coming home to fix something else. If they didn't like it, they could eat cereal.

"You see Jeremy this week?" Mara asked, changing the subject as smoothly as possible. She had only talked with Jeremy once since the whole basement apartment debacle, and it hadn't been a long enough conversation to determine how he was doing. Abby was fine, he said. Madeleine was fine. They didn't need her to babysit that week because Abby had a few days off, and they were managing okay. She tried not to take it personally.

"He's been working on the bathroom," Charissa said, "and I think he's almost done. It looks great in there. Amazing what a few small changes can do."

Mara hesitated. "Does he seem"—what word did she want to use? Depressed? Angry?—"okay?"

"A little on the quiet side, maybe, but I don't really know him well enough to say for sure."

If there weren't such a language barrier with Abby's mom, Mara would have tried fishing for information. She had sent Ellen an email under the pretense of sharing some "grandmother photos" of Madeleine. She had also thanked her and her husband for their financial help, hoping that Ellen would divulge more details about their support. But the only reply she received was a brief email thanking her for the pictures and saying she was continuing to pray for their children and granddaughter "in all times." Mara wondered what Abby had confided to her.

"Is there anything John and I can do to help?"

Mara couldn't think of anything. "You've already done so much. Thanks for giving him projects."

"Wish we had some more. John is scheming for a deck, but so far, I'm holding my ground. For budget reasons," she added quickly, "not because of anything to do with Jeremy."

"No, I know. I keep praying for his company to land some big contracts. Maybe once spring hits." She eyed the clock on the microwave. "I gotta go. The boys will be done with basketball practice soon. But I'll see you tomorrow at Crossroads, right?"

"I'll be there about ten-thirty. Not that I'll be much help in the kitchen."

"I'll put you to work," Mara said. "We'll have you chopping veggies like a pro in no time. Just you wait and see."

Bailey, his shaggy little face pressed against the passenger side window, wagged his whole body with excitement as Mara backed her SUV out of the garage. She had only planned to take him for a car ride once, but a single trip to the school to pick up the boys had attracted so much enthusiastic attention from some teenage girls that Kevin had asked if she could make a regular habit of it. "You little chick magnet, you," she said as Bailey spun in the seat.

All along the cul de sac, spring was emerging. With the temperature above fifty degrees for the first time in months, the neighborhood had burst into life. Soon the über-mowers would begin their twice-weekly obsession with maintaining their lush carpets of weedless checkerboard lawns, and her flaws would be even more noticeable, with the brown patches of dog pee and unruly crabgrass. So be it. Since she was staying in the house for the next few years, she might as well stop worrying what people were whispering about her and manage as best she could.

She waved at a short-sleeved neighbor who, golf club in hand, was swinging stiffly at imaginary balls in his yard and sending chunks of snow flying. In front of Alexis Harding's melting driveway glacier, a little girl dressed in a pink crinoline tutu and snow boots rode her training wheeled bicycle back and forth through puddles while her brother maneuvered around her on his skateboard.

Mara looked forward to buying Madeleine her first tricycle. She would get her a pink one with a bell and streamers on the handlebars. Or maybe Madeleine would prefer purple. Or blue. Maddie could have whatever color she liked. Maybe she would buy herself a bicycle someday, and the two of them could ride together. Mara hadn't ridden a bike in years, not since she had pedaled her rusty one back and forth to junior high. But someone had stolen her bike from the rack in front of the school one day, and Mother didn't have money to replace it, not even with a used one from the Salvation Army. Mara figured it was a prank: her bicycle wasn't good enough for someone to want to ride. Someone had probably taken it and ditched it somewhere, just to be cruel. She had searched the woods near the school for it, but she never found it, and she never saw anyone riding it.

"Pretty optimistic there," Mara said as she passed a landscape company's truck, the driver pausing to remove the orange snowplow sticks lining driveways.

Maybe Jeremy could find work with a landscape company if construction didn't pick up. Only a few of the neighbors did their own gardening. No shame in putting around flyers to advertise his services if he would agree to it. Since he was obviously still smarting from her basement offer, it probably wasn't a good time to suggest he could make some money mowing lawns. That's what he'd done as a teenager, and he'd made good money. *Under the table money,* Tom called it. Maybe she would suggest that kind of work to Abby. Every little bit helped. She wouldn't mention the "under the table" part, though. Let them decide how to do it. She hadn't asked Jeremy how he was handling the money he'd been getting for odd jobs. She didn't want to know.

"What's the matter?" she asked Kevin as he pushed Bailey aside and slumped into the front seat.

"Nothing."

"Good day?"

Kevin shrugged.

"Where's your brother?"

"Dunno."

"He wasn't at practice?"

"Nope."

"You didn't see him after school?"

"Nope." He clicked his seatbelt into place and patted his lap for Bailey to return.

"Kevin!"

"What?"

She puffed out a chest full of air and craned her neck behind his seat, scanning the school entrance. "Go back in, please, would you? Go look for him."

Kevin replied with his own irritated sigh. "He probably left with Seth."

"Go check. Please."

"Just text him. Or call Seth's mom."

"Kevin Mitchell . . ." When he was a little boy, the double-name tactic had worked wonders. She hadn't tried it in years.

He drummed on the window, face turned away from her, and then growled, "Fine. But I told you, he's probably with Seth." As soon as Kevin slammed the door behind him, Mara texted Brian. No reply. She waited a few minutes—no sign of Kevin or Brian—and then scrolled through her phone contacts.

Jackie, Seth's mother, picked up on the third ring. She was glad Mara had called. She was just going to call her. Seth wasn't with her, was he? She had been sending him text messages for the past hour, but he hadn't replied.

"I was hoping Brian was with you," Mara said.

For the next few minutes Mara listened to Jackie rant about all the bad influences on her son, about how he had been a poster child for obedience and virtue—"a good Christian kid!"—until he started hanging around the "wrong crowd," of which Brian, though she didn't name him, was doubtless the ringleader.

"At least they're probably together," Mara said. "Safety in numbers, right?"

Jackie clearly was not comforted by this thought. She hadn't been able to reach her husband yet—he was giving some deposition as an expert witness, yada yada—but he would have a way of tracking the phone. She would let Mara know as soon as she heard something. "And we'll be grounding Seth," she said in a tone that communicated that Mara needed instruction on what to do with her own son. "Severely grounding him."

As soon as Jackie hung up the phone, Mara texted Brian again—still no answer—and waited for Kevin to appear. Ten minutes later he emerged from the administration building, Brian and Seth shuffling behind him, their hands shoved in their pockets. "Where were you?" Mara demanded as soon as they opened the back doors.

"Detention," Kevin replied for both of them.

"Detention? For what?" In her rearview mirror she watched Brian glance at Seth.

"They took our phones," Seth said.

"And didn't let you call your mothers to say what was going on?" Not likely. "Text your mother right now, Seth. Let her know I'm bringing you home." While Seth typed a message, Mara turned around in her seat and narrowed her eyes at Brian. "Detention for what?"

Brian also began typing on his phone. Mara snatched it away from him and held it out of his arm's reach. "I said, detention for what?"

"Hall passes."

"Hall passes?"

He stared at her without blinking. She turned to Seth, who had finished typing and was fidgeting in his seat. "Seth?"

He stared at his hands. "Brian stole a stack of hall passes from Miss Cooke's desk, and we sold them at lunch."

"You what?" She was so relieved it wasn't drugs or bullying or sex or vandalism that she nearly laughed out loud. Digging her nails into her palms, she manufactured a suitably stern expression.

Seth leaned his head back and sighed. "Mom says I'm grounded for a month."

Mara kept her opinion about that to herself. "We'll talk about your punishment later, Brian."

Muttering something under his breath, Brian shooed Bailey away and turned his face to the window, arms crossed against his chest.

One week, no cell phone, no video games, no arguing. After Brian unleashed a foulmouthed litany of names at her, some of which she'd been called many times before, Mara upped it to two weeks. He was more frightening—did he know this?—when he wasn't yelling at her. Far more frightening when, with cold hatred in his eyes and a slight sneer on his lips, he stood silent, jaw raised, staring at her. She tried not to blink. When he finally turned away and vaulted up the stairs, she breathed slowly. Like the breath prayers Meg had learned from Katherine. *Inhale:* God. *Exhale:* Help me.

"I'm at my wits' end with him," she said to Charissa the next day as they worked side by side in the Crossroads House kitchen. "No clue how to deal with him."

"Does Tom know what happened?"

"Attorney says I have to keep him in the loop with anything big that happens with the boys, so yeah, I texted him. His comment? 'Boys will be boys.'"

Charissa snorted her disgust.

"I'm not minimizing what Brian did. He stole. He probably got off easy with detention instead of being suspended. But I'll tell you, I was so relieved it wasn't something bigger, something that hurt someone else. All the kids got their money back. No harm done, I guess. But still."

Charissa was peeling the life out of a carrot, slowly turning it to inspect whether she had removed all the tiny little hairs.

"Here, just wash and scrub them. You don't have to peel them."

"But all the—"

Mara pried it away from her. "I know. It's just going into the soup, so don't worry about it." She rapidly chopped it and added it to the pot simmering on the stove. "Want to try the celery?"

Charissa eyed the stalk critically.

"Watch." Mara reached for the large knife. "Cut off the leaves"—thwack—"and then"—chop chop chop chop—"see? Nice and thin."

Charissa shuddered.

"What?" Mara asked, scraping the celery off the cutting board into the pot.

"I think it's the knives." Charissa gingerly made her way to the corner of the kitchen and sat down in a metal folding chair, head in her hands. "Makes me feel a little woozy."

Mara laughed and rearranged her hairnet. "You've seriously never chopped anything? Sliced apples? Cut broccoli? Nothing?"

"Not fast like that. I'd be afraid of slicing off a finger or something."

"How's it going in here?" Miss Jada asked, entering the kitchen from the main hall.

"Right on schedule," Mara said. She emptied a bag of rolls into a bowl.

"You all right, Charissa?" Miss Jada asked.

Charissa looked up and gave her a wan smile. "Feeling a little dizzy. I'll be okay."

"You're not sick, are you?" Miss Jada was a stickler when it came to volunteers and staff being healthy. The guests had enough problems to deal with. They didn't need to be exposed to germs from someone serving them.

Charissa rose unsteadily to her feet. "No. Not sick."

But before Mara could rush to her side, Charissa swooned and collapsed onto the floor.

—☙

"I fainted, that's all," Charissa said when John skidded into Miss Jada's office half an hour later. "I'm fine. Just a bit embarrassed." As soon as Charissa had regained consciousness and recovered enough to walk, Mara had gently escorted her out of the view of concerned onlookers.

"I think she's okay," Mara said. "It happened to me when I was pregnant with Brian. Pretty common, I think. Nothing to worry about." At least Charissa hadn't hit her head. Somehow, she had managed even to faint gracefully. Mara had crumpled like a big old sack of potatoes when she fainted, Tom crowed afterward. He hadn't even offered to get her a cold cloth. He just laughed, thought it was all very amusing, and told his friends about it later. Right in front of her. The story got bigger and bigger, and she got fatter and fatter every time he narrated it. *Bam! Like one of those humpbacks crashing into the water, you seen those?*

"I got up too fast, I think. I'm feeling better now." Charissa handed Mara the wet towel and shifted position.

"Ooh-ooh," John said when she swung her legs around and tried to sit up. "Take it easy."

"I'm fine." She sat with her head in her hands, then glanced up at John. "Really."

He sat down beside her on the couch, arm draped around her shoulders. "I don't think she should drive," he said to Mara. "Okay to leave the car here for a few hours? We'll come get it later."

"No problem."

He kissed Charissa on the cheek. "Quite a dramatic way to get out of cooking me dinner."

Charissa smiled. "Raincheck."

A few minutes later Mara watched the two of them leave together, hand in hand, John opening the door for her and helping her into his car. Did that girl have any idea how lucky she was? "Blessed" was a better word. Did she have any idea how blessed she was?

"She okay?" Miss Jada asked, sidling up beside Mara and tracking her gaze to the parking lot.

"Yep," Mara said, "she's gonna be fine."

Becca

Becca leaned back against the red leather booth at the Cat and Mouse Pub and yawned. "I've got to get going," she said to Pippa and Harriet as she took a last sip of her Strongbow cider.

"But it's so earrrrly!" Pippa chided. "We thought we'd head to the club for a while. Karaoke night."

Pippa was already halfway to being plastered, and Becca wasn't interested in watching her friend belt out a boozy anthem in a skin-tight top that showed off her breast implants. Harriet could be her chaperone. "I can't, Pippa. Not tonight."

"Oh, come ohhhhn. Simon can wait."

"Simon's at a quiz night." Becca had planned to go to The Lamplighter to cheer on his team as they vaunted their trivia expertise, but he said he wanted a night out with "the lads." He had obviously forgotten it was the four-month anniversary of their official first date. She had decided not to remind him.

"So, what's the rush?" Pippa winked at one of the young bartenders delivering trays of food to a nearby booth before focusing bleary eyes on Becca. "You're not going on one of your morbid walks again, are you?" Harriet tried to shush her with a nudge of her elbow.

Becca reached for her purse. No, she wasn't going on "one of her morbid walks." She was going to the British Museum, which was open late. But she didn't tell them that. They wouldn't understand.

Pippa grabbed her wrist. "Sorry! Staaaaay. Come on. Harriet and I are worried about you, aren't we, Harry?"

"Bit more worried about you at the mo," Harriet said as she checked her lipstick.

"See?" Becca said. "I'm fine." She rose from the booth. "See you guys tomorrow." No need to worry about her. She'd been an orphan for what? Almost a month now? Ought to be over it by now, right? Back to normal, whatever "normal" was? She threw on her coat and wove her way through the crowd before either one of them tried to stop her.

The larger than life marble Lion of Knidos, its eyes gouged and lips parted in the prelude to a roar, confronted Becca the moment she entered the museum's Great Court. That's where she ought to have met her mother in December, near the lion at lunchtime. She should not have met her there just before the museum closed. And not with two friends in tow. She could still see her mother rearrange her disappointed face when she realized she and Becca wouldn't be having a mother-daughter dinner.

"Look, Daddy!" a little boy exclaimed, barreling around Becca to reach the reclining lion. "Aslan!"

Becca couldn't remember much of the Narnia mythology—she had been little, maybe six or seven when her mother read her the books—but she didn't think Aslan was a stone lion. Killed on a stone table or something. That part had made her cry, how the lion didn't fight back but submitted himself to cruelty and died.

But wait! her mother would say, rocking her in her arms and wiping away her tears. *Wait and see what happens!* Too bad she had outgrown fairy tales. What she wouldn't give for an embrace from her mom now, for words of reassurance that all would be well.

How long, she wondered as she watched the little boy skip around the statue, how long would she be able to play her mother's voice in her head? How long before the memories of her scent, her laugh, her nervous tics became memories of memories rather than memories of the real substance of her? How long?

Maybe that's why she felt compelled to visit all the places her mother had been, so she could imprint the memories of her posture, her gait, her facial expressions, her words, even her sighs while it was all still fresh in her mind. She wanted to remember everything vividly because there was so much she had not savored when she had the opportunity. Why had she not taken more photos? Why had she not thought to record her voice in ordinary conversations? Why had she not seized every possible chance to be with her in London and tour these places together?

"What good does it do to punish yourself?" Simon had frequently asked over the past few weeks. "Regret gets you nowhere."

No, and neither did anger. But she battled both. The stratum of strong emotions lay directly beneath a shallow surface of self-control, and these days it didn't take much to drill straight through.

She left the little boy and his dad, who was commanding him not to jump up and touch the lion, and strode past the gift shop. If only she had met Simon after her mother's visit. She didn't regret meeting Simon—not at all!—but if they had met at the pub a few weeks later, maybe things would have been different. Then she would have at least been able to enjoy her mother's visit without feeling the need to conceal such a huge part of her life. If Simon had been a peer from school, someone she had met at a lecture or in a tutorial, she would have introduced them immediately. But she had known her mother would have a meltdown over her dating an older man.

Becca shadowed a tour group into the Department of Ancient Egypt and Sudan, where crowds of eager visitors pressed around a glass display case. In the glare of the artificial light it was difficult to see the inscriptions on the black granite. She wasn't sure if her mother had stopped to look at the Rosetta Stone. She had never asked her.

She stepped aside so a towheaded little girl could get a closer view. "What is it, Daddy? A very old rock?" The earnest lilt of her voice made Becca smile.

"It's a very, very old rock with pictures that are actually words," he said. She stood on her tiptoes, straining to see. "And no one knew what those pictures meant until they found this stone. This stone was the mystery decoder."

"It's magic?"

"No, not magic. It just gave clues for how to solve an ancient mystery. It told us what the lost language was saying by using words we could understand."

The tenderness in the father's voice pierced Becca. Losing her mother had reopened all the old aches over not having a father too. It was like she had lost him again, just when she was finding him. She had lost every opportunity to know him through her mother's eyes, through her stories.

Lyrics from an Ella Fitzgerald recording she had loved when she was a little girl floated through her memory, a song she had often insisted her mother play on her grandmother's old record player: *I'm a little lamb who's lost in the wood. I know I could always be good, to one who'll watch over me.*

If she hadn't met Simon, she thought as she exited the museum an hour later, where would she be?

Lost. And entirely alone.

Notting Hill was not the sort of neighborhood her mother would have chosen to visit on her own ("Way too alternative," Becca had explained to Simon), and Becca, not eager for her mother to see the flat where she spent most nights, had steered clear of mother-daughter outings near Portobello Road.

Though Simon complained about gentrification and multinational chains supplanting independent cafés and quirky shops, Becca loved Notting Hill for nevertheless retaining its sizzling energy and bohemian spirit. Not far from the posh Kensington sidewalks where nannies pushed babies in prams, Notting Hill—a place of communal gardens and terraced houses painted in vibrant Mediterranean colors—had long been home to artists and writers, as evidenced by the blue plaques marking houses of the notably famous. George Orwell's former residence wasn't far from the basement flat Simon had rented ever since his divorce, and Simon, an aspiring novelist, often said that someday there would be a plaque outside his flat as well. Becca had no doubt that he would one day publish international bestsellers. It was only a matter of time. Simon said she would be in his acknowledgments page as his muse.

Exiting the Tube station, she strolled past bookshops, tourist traps selling Queen Elizabeth bobble heads, and the tandoori restaurant where she and Simon often ordered takeaway curries and kebabs. If he were home, she'd pick up two orders of chicken korma. That's what they had eaten the night she first accompanied him to his flat.

Her fingers lingered on the wrought-iron gate, remembering the brush of his hand against hers as he opened the latch and invited her to follow him down the stairs. Simon had awakened her that night, awakened her to passion and longings she'd never felt before. Physical intimacy, Becca had discovered, was far more than carnal drive and desire. It was a gateway toward a union of souls, a oneness of being. To use a word she didn't usually apply to herself, their love was something "spiritual." There was no other spirituality she needed. She was fulfilled.

Much as it had pained her mother, Becca could never embrace her brand of spirituality. After all, what kind of God allowed daddies to die before they held their baby girls and moms to die before their daughters grew up? Not any sort of God she wanted to know, that was for sure.

"Waiting for you," she texted to Simon as she undressed in the dark. But there was no reply. At midnight, unable to stay awake any longer, Becca crawled into bed, the strains of Ella Fitzgerald's song soothing her to sleep.

Hannah

After discussing it in low voices behind a closed bedroom door for half an hour Saturday morning, Nathan finally agreed to Hannah's proposal: the Allen Boys would keep their Pancake House tradition as father-son connection time, and the three of them would decide on something weekly to enjoy together on Sunday afternoons as part of a family Sabbath practice. "But I want you to suggest something you'll enjoy, Hannah. Please."

"Okay."

"There's still plenty of snow up north if you want to go snowmobiling."

Driving a couple of hours each way for an afternoon outing seemed excessive, especially on a day set apart for rest. "Maybe a movie," she said. "Or a game."

But when Sunday morning came around, she didn't even feel like going to church. "A headache," she said when Nathan eyed her with concern. "Nothing to worry about. But I think I'll stay home this morning."

He removed his bathrobe from his closet. "I'll bring you some Tylenol."

"No, it's okay. I'll sleep it off."

"You sure?"

"Positive."

But as soon as she heard the front door close an hour later, she shuffled downstairs to make herself a cup of tea. Truth was, ever since submitting her resignation letter to the church, she had found it difficult to be in worship. Now that she knew she wouldn't be returning to Westminster—now that she knew her time away was not temporary rest but permanent removal—she felt agitated on Sundays. Wayfarer Church was a good church. Neil Brooks was a gifted preacher, an attentive shepherd. But it was Nathan's church. Nathan's house. Nathan's world. And though he continued to try to make room for her, she still felt like a long-term guest.

The thought had occurred to her that they should explore buying a house together now that she was negotiating a contract with Heather that would take care of the Chicago property. But Nate and Jake were both happy in their house, and she didn't want them to go through the upheaval of a move. Then again, compared to all the upheaval she had been through lately, maybe the two of them could manage a change of houses quite easily. But if Nate were open to a move, he would have mentioned it. Instead, he had eagerly agreed to a cosmetic makeover of paint, furniture, and curtains. *Whatever you want*, he had reiterated.

She didn't know what she wanted. That was part of her problem.

Did she want her old life back? No. She missed her old life, but that didn't mean she would choose to return to it. She chewed on that thought a moment longer, just to make sure it was true.

Yes, it was true.

Nathan's old tea kettle whistled, and she removed it from the burner to fix herself a cup of Earl Grey. Maybe if she found pastoral work in Kingsbury, that would ease her grief. But there weren't any openings for paid staff at Wayfarer. And how would Nathan feel about her searching elsewhere? They hadn't discussed her plans for ministry. In his mind, she still had sabbatical time left, time she should make the most of.

She glanced at the clock on the wall. The first service would be starting soon at Westminster. She wondered how long it would be before they made an official announcement about Heather taking over as associate pastor. She had listened to the past couple of weeks of Steve's sermons online—no mention of any changes verbally or in the bulletins—and as of Thursday when she last checked, nothing had been posted on the website. She opened her computer, clicked on the book-marked page, and selected the "Staff" tab. Senior pastor, Steve Hernandez. Youth pastor, Cory Sheldon. Children's ministry coordinator, Megan Fields. Seminary intern, Heather Kirk. No associate pastor.

As in, no mention of Hannah at all. Her fingers hovered above the keyboard. On Thursday, her photo had been beside her name, her old name. *Hannah Shepley, Associate Pastor for Congregational Life.* Now the position had been removed. She had been erased. Expunged. Permanently.

The reasonable voice inside her head reminded her that she had resigned a month ago and that it was appropriate for her not to be listed on the website. The reasonable voice inside her head reminded her that the church had shown patience by allowing her to delay clearing out her office until the end of March, when she planned to pack up her house so that Heather could fully move in. But the louder voice protested, *I gave you fifteen years, and there's not even a thank you?*

"They offered to throw you a party," Nathan said when he returned at lunchtime, "and you told them no."

"Because they were spreading all those crazy rumors about me, about us!" She didn't care that Jake was hovering in the family room within earshot. She had tried to pretend she was over it. She had tried to convince herself that because she had prayed about surrendering her reputation to Jesus, she had moved on. She had not. If, as Nancy had reported, some people thought she had taken advantage of the church by not returning to serve—or worse, that she had contrived the sabbatical as a ruse to reconnect with an old boyfriend and then had shacked up with him—

"Hey," Nathan said gently, kneeling beside her, his hand on her knees. "How about if you email Steve and tell him you'd love to have a small reception? They can have it while we're down there to clean out your house."

"No."

"C'mon, I think it would be good for you. For some closure. Let them thank you publicly, pray for you, send you out with their blessing."

"No."

"You can't just slink out the side door, Hannah. There are people there who love you, who are grieving that you're gone. They need a chance to say goodbye. So do you."

Her shoulders heaved forward, and Nathan held her as she cried.

She did not have the capacity to pray the examen right now, Hannah confessed as Nathan prepared to light their unity candle that night. He understood. She did not have the energy to journal her reflections about how she was glimpsing God or how she was responding to or resisting his invitations. He understood. She was too tired to plumb the depths of her soul and share what she discovered with him. He understood.

There were seasons, Hannah knew, when words did not come, and it was all right that words did not come. There were seasons when faith meant trusting the groans of the Spirit to interpret the depths of longings and sorrows that could not be articulated but only offered. There had been seasons in her life—many of them—when she had been tempted to put too much confidence in her words, when she had been tempted to use her words in a frantic, futile effort to control or manipulate God into acting quickly to fix or solve or rescue. Silence invited deep trust, a different way of knowing and being known. She knew this. And besides. She was tired, too tired for words.

four

Charissa

No matter how hard Charissa tried to flatten and smooth the bulges, her light blue cardigan retained the shape of the hanger. She should have double-checked in the mirror before she left the house. Now she would have to stand in front of her freshmen with protruding horns on her shoulders.

Great.

She wasn't going to lecture in her shell top. Justin Caldwell and his back row posse would be distracted by her enlarged breasts. Since undertaking the freshman writing section, Charissa had perused the professor ratings site multiple times, and she could guess which students had given her chili peppers for hotness. She was not flattered. She *was* flattered, however, by the students who ranked her as hard. "Professor Sinclair" was no easy A, several complained. This gratified her. One student had written that the course had "confirmed his desire to write." But then he'd proceeded to say that Charissa had helped him "hone his grammer skills." Obviously, he hadn't put his review through a spellchecker.

She really shouldn't put much stock in the reviews, she thought as the students straggled into the classroom. She also shouldn't be Googling her name. But it was a regular habit now, one she had tried unsuccessfully to fast from. Maybe next Lent she would apply more diligence to conquering her vanity.

"I'm returning your first drafts," she said once she had taken attendance and closed the door. "Phone away, Justin." She handed him his paper. He kept typing. She stood beside him, waiting, wishing she could snatch the phone out of his hand and bop him on the head with it. "Now." He shoved it into his backpack.

"For the most part, these were strong first efforts," she said, returning to the lectern. "However, I noticed that some of you only concentrated on the first paragraph of the article in your analysis. In your revisions, you'll need to incorporate the entire breadth of Berry's essay. In other words, make sure you read all of his argument before you attempt to write your interpretation and critique." Honestly. Did they think she was stupid? That she wouldn't notice they had only read the first page of the essay? "The other thing that was lacking in most of your reflections is the acknowledgment that he wrote this essay in 1971. So in what ways are his observations about American politics and culture prophetic and timely for our postmodern context? Don't merely quote from his essay. I don't want summaries of his salient points. Interpret it. Wrestle with it. Demonstrate you're thinking critically, and then use the rhetorical skills you've been learning to respond with high-quality prose."

Most of the students were too busy skimming through her margin notes on their papers to be listening. She took a sip from her water bottle and waited for their attention. "Before I divide you into pairs for peer review, I want to offer some thoughts about the revision process in general. Many students, when they undertake editing, consider only the lexical level of the text. They look only at word substitutions, believing their primary task is to choose better words. And while word choice is important to our prose—while strong, precise language enhances our arguments—revising is not simply a matter of using a thesaurus as you rewrite. Think big picture. Think about theme. Think about—"

Not passing out. She was suddenly lightheaded again. She took a longer sip of water. The websites said it was important to stay hydrated, to—

"Think about big picture. Big picture themes and—" She wiped her brow with a hand that was becoming blurry. "Don't be afraid to cut sections that don't serve the larger purpose of—" *Even if you're attached to—*

Faces spun and swirled. She was grabbing, grasping, staggering, plunging. Down.

If this incident ended up on social media, heads would roll. Charissa wasn't sure which student had first raced to her aid, but Justin was way too close when she came to, and she didn't like the smirk on his face when he glanced at his phone before pocketing it. "Are you okay, Ms. Sinclair?" Sidney, one of her favorite students, was kneeling beside her.

Charissa rolled gingerly to her side. She still felt too woozy to stand.

"What can I get you?" Sidney asked.

All around Charissa students were stooped and staring. Thank God she had worn slacks and not a skirt. "I'll . . . nothing. Nothing." She pushed herself up to a sitting position and rested her head on her knees. If this fainting drama was going to become a regular game in Bethany's repertoire, she didn't want to play. "I'm okay, everyone. Back to your seats." But she hesitated to rise.

"Can somebody go get someone?" Sidney called out.

"No. No, I'm fine." Charissa willed herself to stand but then gratefully sat down in the chair Ben dragged forward. She should carry snacks in her bag, almonds or cheese, something with protein. She would be fine once she ate something.

"Ten minute break," a voice commanded. She looked up to see Nathan Allen enter the classroom, motioning for students to head out. "Back in ten," he repeated as they exited, chattering. He closed the door behind the last one. "Let me call John for you."

"No, I'm okay."

"Charissa."

"He'll just worry." She hadn't landed on her belly, thank God, but her elbow was sore. She must have absorbed the force of the fall on her right elbow. She clutched it against her body.

Nathan eyed her with concern. "I think it's unwise not to get checked. Make sure you didn't injure yourself."

"I'll be okay. Just another bruise to the ego." She attempted a wry smile. "No permanent damage done." Which was more embarrassing: missing her final presentation last semester because she overslept or fainting in front of a room full of students? Though no blame could be assigned to this mishap, it might prompt Dr. Gardiner and the other faculty to question whether she was fit to fulfill her responsibilities. She would need to talk with Dr. Gardiner as soon as possible to preempt decisions being made on her behalf.

"Let me take the rest of your class today," Nathan said. "I've got nothing scheduled for the next hour."

"I'll be fine. Thank you, though." She stood up—too fast, apparently—and caught herself before she lost her balance. At a minimum she wasn't fit to finish her lecture, and it wasn't fair to the students to place them in peer groups without proper instructions. She gave a defeated sigh. "On second thought, maybe I should head home."

He reached into his blazer pocket for his cell phone. "I'll call Hannah. I'm sure she wouldn't mind coming to pick you up. I don't think you should drive right now."

The way she felt at the moment, she wasn't going to argue.

True to Nathan's word, Hannah arrived at the university library parking lot half an hour later. "Where to?" she asked as soon as Charissa clicked her seatbelt into place. Belts were increasingly uncomfortable.

"Home, please."

"You sure you don't want me to take you to the doctor?"

"I'm sure. I think I just need to eat something and lie down." The two-pack of oatmeal cookies from the vending machine hadn't alleviated her lightheadedness. "Thanks, Hannah."

"No problem."

If Mara had been the one to chauffeur her home, Charissa might have been peppered with questions or subjected to well-intentioned pregnancy tips and personal anecdotes. But Hannah was quiet on the drive, and Charissa, who was not adept at small talk, wasn't sure how to engage her in conversation. Usually, Hannah was the one who guided meaningful interactions. Maybe she was tired. "You feeling okay?" Charissa asked after traveling several blocks in awkward silence. "We missed you in worship on Sunday."

"Yeah. Thanks. Just a bit of a headache."

"Nathan was telling us at church about your house. That's great you don't have to worry about putting it on the market."

"Right. Big answer to prayer."

"When do you have to go down there to pack everything up?"

"Saturday, I think."

"Well, if you need any help when you get back here unloading boxes or anything, I'll volunteer John."

Hannah did not take her eyes off the road. "Thanks. I appreciate that."

When they arrived at the house a few minutes later, Hannah did not turn off the car. "Do you need some help getting inside?" she asked.

"No, I'm fine, thanks. You're welcome to come in for a minute, Hannah, if you'd like."

"No, that's okay. I'll let you get your rest. Let me know if you need anything else, though, all right?"

"I will," Charissa said. "See you Friday, then?"

"Friday?"

"For our Sensible Shoes—"

"Oh, right," Hannah said. "Friday."

As Charissa carefully ascended the front steps, she added another name to her growing list for prayer: Becca, Mara, Jeremy, Abby. And Hannah Allen.

Becca

In the land of knights and castles, chivalry was dead. With a disdaining glance Becca passed by half a dozen guys who kept their seats on the Tube, not even rising for a mom with two little kids. "Hold on here, sweetheart," the mother said, placing one child's chubby hands onto a pole while clutching the younger one. The only people speaking in the carriage were tourists, distinguished by their accents and lack of balance as the train sped out of the station and pitched to the right. Becca had once stood with the same two-fisted grip on the overhead bar. Now she made a point of trying to stand nonchalantly so as not to call attention to herself. Not that Londoners were bothered to pay much attention. She focused on the colorful grid of crisscrossing lines on the maps above the windows and exited when the train screeched into Russell Square station.

"Could I have a coffee, please?" she asked the elderly cashier at the café in the square. On this unseasonably mild early spring morning, the park was filled with dog-walkers, joggers, and readers. As the cashier poured her drink, she watched a few patrons disregard the instructions not to feed the birds. The brazen pigeons weren't fooled by the hawk and owl statues.

"There you are, love," the cashier said, setting her drink in front of her. His kind smile nearly undid her. Becca quickly counted out her change and found a table where she could study without distraction. She was way behind on a few assignments, and though her professors had been patient, her grace period was drawing to a close. Mourning, she had discovered, had an expiration date beyond which there remained little sympathy and understanding, except perhaps by those who had also suffered loss.

"But we just want the old Becks back!" Pippa had said when Becca bowed out of another invitation to a karaoke night. "Come on. It would do you good to have a laugh."

She wasn't interested. She looked up as a man in a tracksuit jogged by and began doing lunges, stretches, and push-ups against a nearby park bench.

Not interested.

Even her high school and college friends, some of whom had sent a flurry of concerned and consoling emails when they first heard the news, had returned to the preoccupations of their own lives. She didn't blame them. Not much, anyway. No doubt some of them had suffered losses she had never acknowledged or understood, either.

At the table adjacent to hers, a young woman about her age was tossing crumbs toward a white pigeon. "Shhh," she said, when she saw that she'd been spotted. "Don't tell anyone." She brushed off her hands and poured from a small ceramic teapot on her tray.

Becca studied her face. The gesture of pouring tea had triggered a memory. "You look familiar," she said, scanning for possibilities until she landed on the most likely one. "You don't work at the hotel near here, do you?"

"Yes, at the Tavistock. But I've got the day off today." She pivoted toward Becca, her expression brightening with recognition. "I know you; you came for tea with your mum a few times, right? Americans. She was over here to visit before Christmas."

Becca tried to push down the lump in her throat. Why had she started the conversation? Now the inevitable question was on its way. Of all the places to land for coffee . . . of all the people to land next to . . .

"Such a nice lady, your mum. She wrote a commendation letter for me and gave it to my manager when she left. I've never gotten a letter like that before, and I didn't have a chance to thank her. So kind of her."

Yes, Becca thought, that was the sort of thing her mother would have done. Before any polite inquiries could be made, she blurted out, "My mom died."

The girl looked stricken. Maybe that's what Becca was hoping for when she stated it so bluntly: shock. Maybe she wanted sympathy from a stranger since sympathy from friends was waning. "Your mum—"

"Yeah. Cancer."

"She never said—"

"She didn't know." Becca wrapped both hands around her coffee cup and stared at a trio of pigeons vying for more crumbs. "I'm Becca, by the way." If she was going to confide such news to someone in a park and potentially depress them, it seemed only fair to introduce herself.

"I'm Claire. And I'm sorry, I don't remember your mum's name."

"Meg. Meg Crane."

"Mrs. Crane. Yes." She looked at Becca with deep compassion and said, "You have her eyes."

Those eyes now welled up with tears. Pippa had met her mother. Harriet had met her mother. Simon had met her mother. But none of them had ever thought to make that simple observation. *I hope our baby has your eyes,* her father had written to her mother the day they saw the ultrasound picture. Becca had found the card on her mother's desk and had tucked it into her purse after the funeral, one of the few cards she had decided to take with her to London. It was a well-traveled card.

"I'm sorry, Becca, I didn't mean to . . ."

"No. It's okay. It's just . . ."

Claire nodded. "I know." Something in her voice told Becca that she did, in fact, "know." Maybe part of experiencing grief meant developing a fine-tuned radar for identifying kindred spirits. "I knew she was feeling poorly when she was here," Claire went on, "that she had to go home early, but I had no idea she was so unwell. I'm so sorry."

That wasn't the cancer, Becca silently replied. *That was her grief. Over me.* She reached into her bag for a tissue and blew her nose. "Thank you. I remember she said you were kind to her." *Kind when I wasn't,* she thought, and the truth of that admission pained her to the core.

"Do you want to talk about it?" Claire asked. "About your mum?"

Becca considered this a moment, then repositioned her chair slightly. Yes. As a matter of fact, she did.

It was the airplane effect, Becca told herself as she poured out her heart to Claire over the next hour: sit down next to a stranger on a plane in Chicago, and by the time you've reached, say, Philadelphia, you know their entire life story. Or they know yours.

While Claire listened without interrupting, Becca recounted some of her favorite childhood memories: watching old Cary Grant films together, dancing with hairbrush microphones to Frank Sinatra standards and ABBA songs while Gran was away, listening to her mother play Debussy or Chopin or Liszt. "She tried to teach me to play piano, but I was more interested in ballet. So Mom saved for lessons for me and came to all of my dance recitals."

"She sounds like a wonderful mum."

"She is. Was." Becca bit her lip. "Here"—she reached for her phone— "I'll show you a picture of her. I mean, you've seen her. But this was just a few days before . . ." She scrolled through photos until she found the one she was looking for, the one with the blue butterfly resting on her mother's shoulder. It was one of her favorites, not just because of the expression on her mother's face—the surprise, the wonder, the joy— but because something in the way the light was shining into the atrium made it look like her mother's face was shining too.

"Ohhh. She's beautiful." Claire's eyes brimmed with tears.

How could it be that a relative stranger could be so deeply moved by her pain when her friends hadn't expressed any interest in photos or stories? "The color of the butterfly, that's the same color as the dress she was going to wear for her best friend's wedding. But she died the week before. So I offered to wear the dress and stand in her place."

"I'm sure your mum would have been happy about that." Claire handed the phone back to her.

Becca couldn't help it; she kept talking. "She told me this story about my dad—he died before I was born—how he had invited her to a Valentine's Day dance when they were in, like, ninth grade. And she saved and saved her money because there was this blue chiffon dress she wanted to buy. But when she took my grandmother to the store to see it, Gran didn't like it. So Mom didn't buy it. But then when she saw this bridesmaid dress, it looked just like the Valentine's gown." Becca pressed her palms against her eyes. "I wish she'd had a chance to . . ."

It was all the chances, wasn't it? All the missed opportunities that fed Becca's regret, all the future opportunities that fed her sorrow. "You know what I've been thinking about the past few days?" Becca said, rubbing her face. Claire waited. "My own wedding."

"You're getting married?"

"No. I mean, not yet. I mean, I'm in a serious relationship with someone, but . . . no." She wiped her nose with her sleeve. "I've been thinking about the future, about how I won't have a dad to walk me down the aisle, how my mom won't be there to share the moment with me. To share any of the moments with me." That's the part she couldn't fathom, couldn't accept: the finality of it all, the never, ever again-ness of it. Never, ever again would she receive her mother's comfort. Never, ever again would she share her mother's joy. And though they had said goodbye with love and tenderness, never, ever again would she have the opportunity to regain her mother's trust. Or her approval.

"That's really hard," Claire said. "I'll be praying for you."

Even though Claire didn't say the words in the carefree, flippant way Becca had heard others say them, she stiffened. Prayer was the easy offer people often made to those who were grieving. Whether they ever followed through with it, she couldn't say. It didn't really matter, either. What good was prayer? Prayer was just words spoken into an empty void that might make the person praying feel better but didn't accomplish anything of any significance whatsoever. "Well, thanks for listening." Becca gathered her trash and shoved it into her empty cup. "Sorry to dump on you like that."

"It's no problem. Any time. I mean that. You can drop by the hotel any time." Claire removed a scrap of paper from her purse, scrawled a phone number on it, and handed it to Becca. "Do you go to church at all?" she asked.

"No." Becca wasn't going to have this conversation. A shame too, a potential new friendship being aborted as soon as it began. She shoved the scrap into her purse, just to be polite. "Sorry, I've got to run."

Claire looked like she wanted to say something more, but Becca slung her bag over her shoulder. "Please drop by any time," Claire said, "if there's anything you need."

Yeah, no. Becca thanked her and with a casual wave, strode across the park. Obviously, Claire was a "Jesus person." And what Becca didn't need was Jesus.

Mara

"She'll be rolling over in no time," Mara said to Abby as Madeleine lifted her head and did a mini-pushup on the apartment living room carpet. "That's how Jeremy used to get around. He'd roll from one side of the room to the other." She couldn't believe how much her granddaughter had changed in only two weeks, and this cemented her resolve: even if Abby and Jeremy privately accused her of being overbearing, she was determined to see Maddie weekly, if not several times a week. She wouldn't let them renege on their babysitting offer.

If Abby had been surprised to see her mother-in-law at eight-thirty in the morning, she hadn't voiced any objection. After dropping the boys off at school, Mara, on a whim, had decided to pop in unannounced. "Why don't you go lie down?" she said. "I'll watch her. I don't have to be at Crossroads for another hour."

"Jeremy didn't tell you?"

"Tell me what?"

"My shift at the hospital changed. I work second now. I'm so glad to be off nights."

"Oh. Guess he forgot to mention it."

"It's a new change. Just started this week."

So they probably wouldn't need her to help out with babysitting a few mornings a week. Maybe she could help with evenings when they both had to work. If Jeremy had work.

Abby rolled Madeleine onto her back and set the activity gym above her, rattling a plastic monkey to get her attention. Maddie beamed. "Who's a smiley girl?" Abby said, moving her face toward Maddie's to touch noses. Maddie giggled. "Who's a smiley girl?" Maddie laughed, a gurgling little baby laugh that made Mara laugh too.

"Oh, that baby!" Mara said, sliding to the floor to be near her. "I just want to gobble her up, she's so cute." Mara squeezed the blue elephant's belly. The squeak made Maddie laugh again. "Is she sleeping any better?"

"I think we're getting there."

"Amazing, the difference a good night's rest makes."

Abby nodded. "Can I get you something to drink?"

"No, I'm fine. Thanks. But get yourself something. I'll watch her."

While Abby made herself a cup of tea, Mara lay on the floor beside her granddaughter, tickling her tummy and rattling her toys. Baby therapy made the whole world better. "I think maybe I upset Jeremy last week," Mara said when Abby returned with her steaming mug. "I assume he told you about my basement idea."

"Yes. It was a really generous offer. We were grateful for it."

"I'm not sure he was." Mara sat up on the carpet, her fingers resting on Madeleine's tummy.

"He knows you want what's best for him. For us. I think it's the whole needing-to-provide-for-his-family thing."

"Yeah, I get that. I wish I had thought it through before I offered. You know me, I get in trouble for speaking without thinking."

"No harm done, Mom."

Mara kissed Madeleine on both cheeks. She would do anything for any of them. Anything in her power.

"I'm glad you stopped by this morning," Abby said, her face partially concealed behind her mug. "I was about ready to call you." Mara raised her eyebrows inquisitively. "I'm worried about Jeremy. I think he might be drinking again."

Mara felt a fist strike her gut. "What makes you think that?"

"Last week before my shift got changed, he came home late a few nights. I thought maybe I smelled it on his breath. He acted okay, but . . ."

"No. No, I get it. Even a little bit could . . ."

"Right."

Alcohol was not something Jeremy could manage in moderation. He'd been sober for five, maybe six years now, and he had worked terribly hard to get there. Though Abby no doubt knew about his past struggles with addictions, she had only ever known him as clean.

"He's under a lot of stress right now," Abby said, "and I know he's feeling discouraged. Depressed, even. I told him I'm willing to move. If the economy doesn't pick up here, we should go some place where he can find a job."

Mara pretended this news was not also a fist to her gut.

"My parents said it's a bit better down in Ohio. But I'm thinking maybe even farther south. Like Texas, where he could work construction year-round."

Texas?

Abby set her mug down on the coffee table and swept Madeleine up into her arms, nuzzling noses. "If he could find something full time with benefits, I could quit my job and stay home with Maddie. He knows that's what I want, what we both want."

Mara would do anything for them. Anything in her power. But letting them go?

Oh, God.

No.

Later that afternoon, while supervising meal preparation at Charissa's house, Mara asked her if she knew anything. "No, nothing. John hasn't said anything to me about it." Charissa repositioned her knife and continued her slow chopping of vegetables for the stir-fry. She was determined to win her cooking bet for the week. "And I hope it's not John that led him into temptation. I overheard him invite Jeremy out for drinks one night. I never asked where they went. I'm sorry! If we had known about this, we never would have—"

"No, I know."

"He hasn't been at church the past couple of weeks." Charissa scraped the green peppers into the oil and jumped back, startled, when the pan sizzled and spit. "Abby came alone with Madeleine last week—she's asking great questions about life and faith—but I don't think John got very far when he tried to ask Jeremy how he was doing. I'm sorry, Mara. I'll be praying. Is there anything else we can do?"

No. Nothing. There was nothing else anyone could do.

Hannah

Hannah poured herself a first cup of tea and stared into the predawn darkness. She ought to have returned Mara's frantic phone call about Jeremy. Instead, she'd waited a few hours and then emailed a perfunctory message to say she would pray. So far she hadn't. Not wholeheartedly, anyway.

She wished she could skip the Sensible Shoes Club meeting. She supposed she could tell them that she was leaving for Chicago early tomorrow morning and didn't have the energy to undertake both. That wasn't technically a lie. She didn't have the energy. More than that, she lacked desire.

At Nathan's urging, she had emailed Steve early in the week to let him know she would be coming to town to pack things up. He had immediately replied, inviting her to participate in the worship service. She declined. "Then how about a farewell reception after the second service?" he wrote. "A chance for us to wish you well." Reluctantly, she agreed. She wondered if Nancy and Doug would be there.

Nathan shuffled into the kitchen in his robe and slippers. "You're up early." Usually Nathan was in his chair with his Bible and journal by the time Hannah came downstairs. "Did you sleep okay?"

"Not great."

"Was I snoring again?"

"No."

He measured out the coffee grounds and switched on the pot. "A lot on your mind, huh?"

She nodded. Tomorrow she would cross the threshold of her house for the first time in almost eight months. She and Nathan would pack up her possessions at her home and her office—with both of them working at it, they might finish in a single day—and spend the night at a hotel. Then, after enduring the hastily organized reception, the speed and timing of which would only heighten the rumors swirling about the "real reasons" for her departure, they would load up the U-Haul and leave her life behind. "I really hope Heather's not planning on hovering around while I pack up," she said, still staring out the kitchen window into the darkness. "I want time alone in my house."

"So tell her that."

"I'm not going to tell her that."

"Why not?"

"Because I don't tell people what I want."

"Or what you need," he added quietly. He probably didn't mean for the words to sound like an accusation.

Hannah set her mug down on the counter. He turned her gently toward him and took her hands in his. "So practice," he said. "Practice with me. Say one thing you want."

She hesitated. If she said the words, "I want," then there ought to be something significant that followed. The coming of the kingdom, for instance. Or being a faithful steward of everything God had entrusted to her. Using the words for lesser things seemed selfish.

"C'mon, Shep. Anything."

She stared at him a moment. "I'd like . . ."

"Try fast. Unfiltered. I want . . ."

Okay, fine. He wanted direct? She would be direct. "I want to sleep on your side of the bed."

Nathan laughed. "Okay. Now we're getting somewhere. It's yours. We'll switch tonight. What else?"

When she didn't reply for several long minutes, he asked, "Are you self-editing right now, or do you really not know what you want?"

"Both."

"Okay. Say something you're editing, then."

Hannah closed her eyes and blurted, "I want a house that's ours." She opened her eyes to check his. Inscrutable.

"Say more."

Since there was no turning back, and since he would continue to ask follow-up questions until he was satisfied she was telling the whole truth, she took a deep breath and said, "I want a house where I feel like I'm not a long-term guest, where I feel like I'm not invading space."

"You're not invading—"

"No, listen"—she held up her hand and touched her finger to his lips to keep him from interrupting—"you asked, and I'm telling you the truth, Nate. This is your space. Yours and Jake's. It'll always be that. No matter how we redecorate or rearrange, it's your house. And I don't know how to fit into it, how to make it mine. Ours."

The coffee pot stopped gurgling. Upstairs an alarm clock buzzed. Jake would be rising for school soon. She should not have started this conversation. "See? I should've kept it to myself."

He poured himself a cup of coffee. "That's not what I was thinking."

"Then say something. What are you thinking?"

"That I wish you felt comfortable talking to me about your heart. I thought we had worked through some of this, that you were being honest with me, that you weren't hiding behind the 'everything's fine' mask."

"You knew everything wasn't fine. I told you I was struggling."

"I know," he said. "I know you've been struggling over everything with Westminster, with Heather, with Meg. But I didn't know you were unhappy here."

She wasn't unhappy. Did she say she was unhappy? He had asked her to name desires, and she had named one. Now she wished she hadn't. This was why she didn't speak her heart, because speaking the truth created too much possibility for conflict. Easier to keep quiet, offer her longings privately to God, and pray for the grace to accept whatever gifts were given rather than trying to orchestrate them for herself. "Forget I said anything. I wasn't going to say anything."

"So what were you going to do, continue to feel miserable and displaced and keep it to yourself? That's no way to do marriage, Hannah." Footsteps padded upstairs; Jake was on his way down. "We'll talk about this later," Nathan said, in a tone that probably was not intended to make her feel like an eight-year-old. Then he greeted Jake with a cheerful, "Hey, bud! How about some eggs?" Without finishing her tea, Hannah tightened the sash on her robe and went upstairs.

───⟡

He had a point, she thought as she filled the birdfeeders and sorted mail at Meg's house. But he wasn't sharing his heart, either. There were obviously things going on with Jake that Nathan had decided not to confide to her. She wasn't asking him to betray Jake's trust. But surely there was a way to talk about how he was negotiating his stress as a dad without disclosing private details about his son. How did a husband and wife share their inner lives if that husband wouldn't talk about his role as a father?

From the kitchen window she watched grateful chickadees swoop toward the feeder. How she wished she and Meg could sit at the table together over a pot of tea. Meg wouldn't judge her for feeling desolate, for feeling like a stranger to her new life. Meg would listen with compassion and pray for her. Not that Mara and Charissa would be unsympathetic. But Hannah didn't feel the same sort of connection and intimacy with them as she had felt with Meg. It was that simple. She missed her friend. Desperately.

Funny how Meg's house, which had felt so oppressive and lonely the first time Hannah entered months ago, had now become one of the few places where she felt like she could listen to her own soul and breathe.

She sat down at Meg's table, head in her hands. Two weeks. Only two weeks until Good Friday, and she had never felt so unprepared. Usually she was diligent about praying through Lent, reflecting on the ways she was being invited to die to self and live to Christ. Maybe she hadn't thought much about Good Friday and Easter because she had spent so much time thinking about it when Meg was dying. She had spent hours meditating on the crucifixion and resurrection texts. So why did she avoid them now?

Charissa had asked her to choose the text for reflection tonight. But when she had thumbed through the prayer exercise notebook, nothing grabbed her. It sounded terrible to say, didn't it, that nothing from Scripture grabbed her attention and invited her in? But it was the truth. She didn't feel like reading the Word. She didn't feel like praying. At least she wouldn't have to participate in the worship services at Westminster. Attend, yes. Under compulsion. But lead? No.

She rubbed her eyes. She was yielding to spiritual dryness without searching for springs. She knew that. But she was too tired to search. That was the truth. Maybe she needed God to pursue her in the barren, weary landscape of her soul.

Part Two

Broken and Poured Out

As the deer pants for streams of water,
so my soul pants for you, my God.
My soul thirsts for God, for the living God.
When can I go and meet with God?
My tears have been my food
day and night,
while people say to me all day long,
"Where is your God?"

PSALM 42:1-3

five

With all the deadlines pressing in on her—books to read, papers to write and grade, lectures to revise—Charissa had discovered that offering a few hours of volunteer time at Crossroads on Fridays helped keep her life in perspective. Being surrounded by people who had nothing helped her remain grateful for what she had been given. The intentional practice of serving others had shaped her in ways she couldn't have anticipated.

"The stir-fry was a big hit," she told Mara as they set out bowls of salad and pots of soup for the Crossroads guests. "John says I won for the week since neither one of us got sick afterward." Mara did not reply. "Thanks again for helping me."

Mara smoothed the edge of the tablecloth. "I told you, you'll conquer it in no time."

"I don't know about that, but if I have a couple of healthy meals in my repertoire, that will be a big improvement." Charissa looked forward to planting and cooking from her garden. She had been studying seed catalogs the past week and was becoming quite the expert on heirloom tomatoes. *Want to become an expert on basketball seeds?* John had teased. She did not.

"You feeling better today, Miss Charissa?" Billy asked when he made his way through the line. A regular at the shelter, he had spoken to her a few times about his military service in Vietnam. "I seen you last week. You were out cold."

"I was," she said. "But yes, I'm feeling better. Thank you." Her students, even Justin, who had not posted on social media—she had checked— had made similar inquiries about her yesterday. She ought to let go of the embarrassment and let people express concern and offer opinions, hard as it was. Bethany wasn't even born yet, and already she was offering lessons about giving up control.

"You need to make sure you're getting enough iron," Ronni, a single mom of three, commented as she held out her plate for salad. "Doctors said I was anemic. Tell you what, I felt crappy. You tired?"

"Not too bad."

"Well, that's good."

Yes, it was. Now that Charissa had hit the six-month mark, she felt like she was heading into the homestretch. In a few more weeks she would finish the semester, and then she could turn her attention toward preparing for Bethany's arrival: decorate the room, stock up on diapers, buy newborn clothes and other paraphernalia. John had been researching strollers and cribs and car seats for months now, but she hadn't yet given him the green light to purchase the larger ticket items. They'd had too many other expenses with remodeling the house.

Not that she was going to complain, she reminded herself as she served the salad. Most of these people didn't have houses. And she bet most of the moms hadn't been able to buy anything new for their babies.

"Are you okay?" she asked Mara after the last of the patrons had passed through the line.

Mara shook her head. Normally gregarious with each guest, she had served today without much interaction, even with the regulars. She picked up the empty soup pots and motioned for Charissa to follow her to the kitchen. "Usually it doesn't bother me," she said in a low voice. "But today the smell of booze got to me. Every time I smelled it on their breath or saw it in their eyes, it pushed all kinds of fear buttons about Jeremy. I just feel so helpless about everything." Her eyes brimmed with tears.

"Can I pray for you?" Charissa asked. Mara nodded.

___᠅

Later that afternoon Charissa received an email from Hannah, apologizing that she hadn't had a chance to select a text to pray with. She wasn't even sure she would be able to come to the group, since she was leaving early the next morning for Chicago.

Charissa wished she could call Meg. Meg would have known how to reach out to Hannah and encourage her. *Don't worry about choosing a prayer handout,* Charissa wrote back. *I'll find one. Just come. Even if you can only stay a little while, we can still pray for you.*

"Did you get ahold of Jeremy?" she asked John when he entered with shopping bags shortly after five o'clock.

"Yeah. He's home with Madeleine tonight."

"And?"

"He sounded okay."

She followed John to the kitchen and started unpacking groceries. Chips. Cookies. Soda. No wonder he'd offered to stop at the store after work. Charissa didn't buy junk food. "What about going over there?" she asked.

"Just showing up? That'd be weird."

"How about watching basketball together? It's Friday. Somebody's got to be playing, right?"

"Um, you're cute." He opened a Pringles canister and poured out a stack. "Michigan State against Kansas, remember?" She stared at him. "Regional semifinal."

"Okay, then. Offer to take a pizza over there and watch the game with him."

"Chuck and I are going to Buffalo Wild Wings to watch the game with some of his friends."

Charissa closed the pantry cupboard. She would organize it later. "Take a raincheck with the neighbor, okay? And call Jeremy back. Please."

While John made his phone call ("Dude! I've got a great idea!"), she skimmed the prayer notebook for an exercise from Katherine that would be fruitful to explore together. It didn't take long to find one.

MEDITATION ON MARK 14:1-11
A Beautiful Thing

Quiet yourself in the presence of God. Then read the text aloud a couple of times and imagine you are with Jesus at Simon's house in Bethany. Use all of your senses to enter the story and participate in the scene.

> It was now two days before the Passover and the Feast of Unleavened Bread. And the chief priests and the scribes were seeking how to arrest him by stealth and kill him, for they said, "Not during the feast, lest there be an uproar from the people."
>
> And while he was at Bethany in the house of Simon the leper, as he was reclining at table, a woman came with an alabaster flask of ointment of pure nard, very costly, and she broke the flask and poured it over his head. There were some who said to themselves indignantly, "Why was the ointment wasted like that? For this ointment could have been sold for more than three hundred denarii and given to the poor." And they scolded her. But Jesus said, "Leave her alone. Why do you trouble her? She has done a beautiful thing to me. For you always have the poor with you, and whenever you want, you can do good for them. But you will not always have me. She has done what she could; she has anointed my body beforehand for burial. And truly, I say to you, wherever the gospel is proclaimed in the whole world, what she has done will be told in memory of her."
>
> Then Judas Iscariot, who was one of the twelve, went to the chief priests in order to betray him to them. And when they heard it, they were glad and promised to give him money. And he sought an opportunity to betray him.

For Personal Reflection (45-60 minutes)

1. Begin by picturing yourself as an onlooker in the story. What do you notice about the woman who anoints Jesus? What thoughts

and feelings arise within you as you watch her break the jar and anoint him?

2. How do you feel when you hear the disciples criticize her? What do you say about her? Why?

3. Think of a time when you judged someone else for the way they served or worshiped Jesus. What justification did you use for your judgment? What might God say to you about this?

4. Now imagine you are the woman anointing Jesus. What motivates you to pour out your perfume on him? Do you have any hesitation in breaking the jar? Why or why not?

5. How do you feel when you hear the disciples criticizing you and scolding you? How do you respond? Offer what you notice to God in prayer.

6. How do you feel when you hear Jesus defend you and the offering of your gift? How do you respond when he declares that you have done "a beautiful thing"? Offer what you notice to God in prayer.

7. What "beautiful thing" are you being invited to offer in sacrifice and love to Jesus? Do you have any hesitation in offering such a costly gift? Offer your longings, fears, and resistance to God in prayer.

For Group Reflection (45-60 minutes)

1. With whom did you most easily identify in the story—the woman or the critical observers? Why? Share what you noticed about your thoughts and feelings as you imagined yourself participating in the story.

2. What opportunities do you have for offering a costly sacrifice of love to Jesus? How can the group encourage and support you in this offering?

3. Offer a word of encouragement to the person on your left. What "beautiful things" have you seen him or her offer to Jesus? How has this offering inspired you? When you receive a gift of encouragement, take time to savor it before offering a word to the person beside you.

4. Close by silently meditating on the worth of Jesus. What is he worth to you? Pray for an increase in love, devotion, and courage for yourself and for your fellow travelers.

Mara

Each person dealt with sorrow in her own way, Mara reminded herself as she settled onto Charissa's couch, the prayer exercise on her lap. Hannah, evidently, preferred to deal with struggles by herself, by withdrawing from community. Mara, on the other hand, ran toward community, now that she had community to run toward. Or maybe Hannah preferred the community of a husband, now that she had one. What a lucky woman she was. Mara wouldn't know what that kind of community was like. "Should we call her and make sure she's okay?"

Charissa lowered herself into an armchair. "I think maybe we should just leave it for now. It sounds like they're leaving early in the morning for Chicago."

Where two or three are gathered . . .

Jesus was with them, even if it was only the two of them. But Mara didn't like the thought of the Sensible Shoes Club unraveling. If Hannah didn't value their time together, there was nothing they could do to force her to participate. But when should you let someone walk away, and when should you hunt them down? Mara offered a silent prayer for her friend, then looked at the text. "Want me to read first?" she asked. Charissa nodded and closed her eyes.

That woman sure was lucky to have something beautiful to offer Jesus. The jar looked like a treasure, like it was carved from marble. And when she broke it, the spicy aroma of the perfume filled the whole room and lingered. That woman was gutsy. Mara wasn't sure she would have had the chutzpah to pour the ointment out on Jesus' head during a dinner party. But maybe the rules for dinner parties were different back then.

The look in the woman's eyes caught Mara's attention as she imagined the scene unfolding, a look that declared the only person in the whole wide world who mattered at that moment was Jesus, and nothing—no one—was going to prevent her from pouring out her precious gift on him. Jesus had an intense look in his eyes too, this look of gratitude and love mixed with sorrow as he gazed at her. They did not break eye contact. Mara would have treasured a moment like that. What a lucky woman. "Blessed" was the better word. What a blessed woman to have a costly gift to offer. A blessed woman to think of offering it. A blessed woman to hear Jesus praise her for the gift and then say that everyone in the whole wide world would hear about it. Blessed. Like a star pupil in a class. Like a favorite child. Blessed.

Mara twirled her bangle bracelets, oblivious to the clicking sound until Charissa looked up from her writing. "Sorry," Mara mouthed. She crossed one leg over the other, wishing she could rest her bare feet on the coffee table. But Charissa had complained to her about the "punk kids" who put their feet up on desks and disrespected her with phones in the classroom, and Charissa's glass coffee table didn't invite smudges from feet. Her new rugs didn't invite shoes. She would be in for a shocker once they had a baby spitting up or a toddler spilling things. And if Bethany had those rocket poops like Kevin had . . .

Mara stared at the Christ candle, rolled her shoulders, and read the questions again. How did she feel when she heard the disciples criticizing the woman? Mad. That woman had every right to use her gift any way she wanted to. Who were they to tell her what to do with it? They had no right to judge her. What that woman did was between her and Jesus. They should just back off, leave her alone.

Jesus was mad too. Leave her alone, he said.

Yeah. You tell 'em, Jesus.

What a blessed woman to have Jesus defend her. Defend *and* praise. Wow.

If she put herself in the woman's place, Mara could imagine Jesus defending her against bullies. That's something Jesus would do—intervene and tell the bullies to knock it off. But praise? That's the part that kept her from imagining herself as the woman. For one thing, she didn't have a costly gift to offer Jesus, nothing that would cause him to praise her. Compared to that woman, Mara was the little kid drawing stick figures and coloring a purple sun or something to present to Jesus.

Jesus would take her drawing, of course, and he would smile and tell her it was pretty and hang it up on his fridge for a while to make her feel special. But she had nothing other people would regard as precious and valuable.

Mara scrunched her toes on the floor rug and then brushed the indentations away with the sole of her foot. What "beautiful thing" was she being invited to offer to Jesus? She had no clue. And thinking about all the beautiful things other people had to offer him only made her feel worse about herself.

She stared at her empty hands. How did she feel when she watched that woman pour out her gift upon Jesus? How did she feel when she heard Jesus defend and praise her?

Jealous. That was the honest word to describe how she felt. That was often the word to describe how she felt. Mara shook her head and sighed. How she wished that wasn't what she felt. But since it's the only thing she had, she poured it out and tried to imagine that the offering smelled like something other than stinking shame.

Charissa

It was possible, Charissa thought as she read through the prayer exercise again, that she was subconsciously drawn to texts that mentioned "Bethany." First, the raising of Lazarus story, now the anointing at Bethany. She rested her hand on her abdomen. Bethany was quiet after an active day. *Sleep, little girl. Sleep.* But if she slept now, would she be kicking all night?

Sleep. It was no alabaster jar filled with expensive perfume, but it was a costly sacrifice nonetheless, one that Charissa ought to accustom herself to making. She had read some new mothers' testimonies online, about how they had started using colorful words they had never in their lives uttered before, how they would never again take sleep for granted, how they wondered if they would ever sleep soundly again, what with worrying about whether their infants were breathing in their cribs or whether they could choke on a pacifier or whether they were getting enough nutrition or whether they would earn a merit scholarship to a prestigious college.

Charissa stared at the Christ candle and took a slow breath. Even after a few months of practice, it was far easier to analyze the story from a literary or psychological distance than to enter it with her imagination. What had caught her attention during her search for a text, however, was first, the timeliness of the story as they approached Good Friday and second, the opportunity to ponder a text that was similar to one that had impacted her months before, the story of the woman who, with scandalous devotion, crashed Simon the Pharisee's dinner party and wiped Jesus' feet with her hair. The same dynamic was at play in Mark's story: one woman's extravagant love for Jesus and others' harsh judgment of that love. With which characters, Charissa wondered, did she identify now? What progress had she made in her own journey toward expressing greater devotion and gratitude? Could she say she had become more loving, more passionate since embarking on the sacred journey at New Hope last fall? She wasn't sure.

She read the text silently, trying to envision the scene.

"Lavish" was the word that came to mind as she pictured the woman breaking open her jar to anoint Jesus. She saved nothing for herself. She didn't measure out the perfume by teaspoons, calculating the cost. Instead she poured out every last drop in love, devotion, and gratitude. While the chief priests and scribes sought the opportunity to arrest and kill Jesus, and while Judas sought the opportunity to betray him, this woman sought the opportunity to honor him, to anoint the Anointed One.

What opportunity did Charissa seek? She clicked her pen. The opportunity to follow him, yes. To be faithful, yes. But to give herself over in love with reckless abandon? Not most days, no. She was still cautious, still calculating, still measured.

If she was honest, she understood the criticism. Though she might have refrained from publicly denouncing the woman and her offering (hadn't she been striving the past few months to crucify her critical spirit?), she would have silently censured. It did seem a waste. Especially if the gift was worth what the disciples appraised it to be. Three hundred denarii could go a long way toward altruistic causes, toward kingdom work.

But Jesus received the gift and commended her for it.

Charissa stroked her abdomen. There were plenty of times over the past several months when she had reprimanded John for his impulse to "waste money." No, Bethany didn't need that high-end crib or state-of-the-art stroller. Charissa was constantly reining him in, reminding him of their budget, approaching their purchases from a cost-effectiveness perspective. She had tried to control his generosity and manage his prodigal tendencies.

But she also remembered the joy she had experienced the night she disregarded their budget and charged off to the store to buy groceries for Mara, not merely the necessities but also some treats for the boys. Or the time when she sent in the donation to Crossroads with the instructions to use the money to buy ingredients for Mara's famous snickerdoodle cookies so that the patrons would have something more than sandwiches or soup that day. Small examples, to be sure, but examples that reminded her that extravagance could have purpose when it was directed in love toward another.

It was the difference, perhaps, between sharing an expensive meal with a loved one to mark a special occasion and taking that same expensive meal and dumping it into the garbage without eating it. One was extravagance, the other waste. And what the woman in Bethany discerned correctly was that this was a moment when extravagant devotion superseded practicality. And so she poured out her precious treasure with abandon. In freedom. In love.

Charissa checked her watch. Twenty more minutes for silent reflection. Though she could spend the remaining time repenting of the ways she had judged others over the years, it might be more profitable to ponder her discomfort over imagining herself as the woman. *Learn to linger with what provokes you,* Nathan often said.

Okay, she would linger.

What had she ever offered that Jesus would deem "a beautiful thing"? What costly sacrifice had she ever given in love? Recently, she had given up her childhood church for John, but she hadn't really been thinking about Jesus when she agreed to attend Wayfarer. She had given up some of her time on Fridays to serve at Crossroads, but this practice benefited her as much as anyone. She liked the feeling of making a difference, liked helping Mara. Was she serving for Christ's sake? She wasn't sure. Was she serving for the sake of the poor? She wasn't sure. Was it possible that even her serving could be self-serving?

Weeds, weeds, and more weeds. Was it ever possible to offer anything that was pure and untainted by selfishness, or would her soul always be a mixture of wheat and weeds?

I have no beautiful thing to offer you, she wrote in her journal, then closed the book with a thud that caught Mara's attention and elicited a sympathetic sigh.

Though Mara was kind to name the ways Charissa had served her and helped Jeremy—"Those are beautiful things to me," Mara insisted—the encouragement did little to assuage the guilt over all the things that had not been beautiful in her life. Charissa had been trying to go the extra mile, to lay down her life in love for others. But it wasn't enough. She wasn't going far enough with sacrifice.

"You're way too hard on yourself," John said as they lay in bed later that night. "I don't think the goal of spiritual formation is beating yourself up over not being perfect, is it?"

No. It wasn't. *It's a journey, not an exam,* Nathan would say. Progress, not perfection. "You know who I kept thinking about tonight?" Charissa said. When John didn't guess, she answered, "Meg. She had this purity of heart that I don't think I'll ever have." Purity of heart wasn't something she could achieve by trying harder, either. That's what was so frustrating—her helplessness in making herself like Jesus.

John rolled toward her and propped himself on his elbow. "Yeah, but we never see other people's motives, do we? I mean, we can't know whether someone's heart is pure or not. If Meg had been here tonight, she probably would have been commiserating with you."

"I know. But she loved well. I can imagine Jesus greeting her with a big smile and saying, 'Well done.'" Charissa couldn't imagine Jesus doing the same for her. And if she focused on serving in order to receive Christ's commendation, then she was still living selfishly, wasn't she? She exhaled loudly.

"What?" John asked, his thumb to her cheek.

"I don't think I'm ever going to be free of my self-centeredness. Ever." John kissed her, and she turned off the light.

Becca

Another email from Hannah, the second this week. No, Becca hadn't confirmed her plans for the summer yet. No, she didn't know when she would be flying to Kingsbury. No, she didn't need Hannah to make any of the arrangements for her. If Hannah could just put enough money into her account to pay for the airfare, Becca would take care of it herself. She pressed Send and closed her inbox.

"She's as bad as my mom," Becca said to Simon, then immediately regretted it. "I mean, she's acting like a mom, and I don't need a mom right now." The words had tumbled out completely wrong. "What I mean is, I don't need someone else trying to be one." She was not going to cry. Simon was tired of her tears. He hadn't said that, not directly. But she could tell that her moods were becoming tedious. The last several nights he had been out late with work colleagues for drinks and hadn't once invited her to join them. She would need to get a better handle on grief management.

She sidled over toward his chair and squeezed in beside him, her leg draped over his. "How about takeaway curry tonight?"

He reached for a cigarette and lit up. "Quiz night."

"Another quiz—"

"I told you that already."

"Sorry. Forgot." She waved her hand in front of her face to shoo away a puff of smoke. She wished he would quit, especially now that her mom . . . "I can come cheer you on."

"Nigel wouldn't like that."

"Why not?"

He took another long drag on his cigarette. "Nigel's very intense, very competitive. He doesn't like spectators." Becca had never met Nigel. She hadn't met many of Simon's friends, in fact, and the few she had met didn't seem to like her. *They're jealous,* Simon said whenever she complained. *You should see their wives. Ghastly.*

"I won't cheer, then," she said. "I'll just sit and watch. I'll be so quiet you won't even know I'm there."

"Then why bother?"

"You don't want me there?"

"I said Nigel wouldn't want you there."

"Why should this Nigel get to say who's there and who's not there?"

"Rebecca, stop."

"I'm just saying, you should be able to take your girlfriend to quiz night without the others making an issue out of it."

Simon shifted as though he were rising from the chair. *No. Stay. Please.* She maneuvered onto his lap. She could make him stay. Nigel could find a different partner. She nuzzled Simon's ear. *Quiz night? What quiz night?* When his hands began to grope beneath her skirt, she thought she had won. But twenty minutes later, he was on his way to the pub without her.

She stared at the door after it closed behind him. Fine. He could go have his fun. But there was no point staying at the flat by herself. Maybe Harriet and Pippa were going clubbing. She texted both of them. *Dance night with killer band at Cargo*, Harriet replied. Good. Maybe she would take Pippa's advice for grief management and get totally wasted.

She opened Simon's closet and removed her favorite black leather mini-skirt and a low-cut blouse. A little flirting with strangers wouldn't hurt, either.

Carpe diem.

Hannah

Even after rehearsing the moment in her imagination during the three-hour drive south to Chicago, Hannah was unprepared for the emotions that overtook her when Heather opened the door to her bungalow and greeted her with outstretched arms and a bubbly, "Wow! You look great!"

Heather looked great too, her twentysomething face bright and fresh and without any visible evidence of ministry strain. The veteran indicators of the furrowed brow, the dark circles under the eyes, the slumped shoulders—those would come later. *Just wait,* Hannah thought, eyeing the perky potted pansies in unfamiliar matching swan urns on the porch. Heather had evidently made herself at home.

"And you must be Nathan!" Heather exclaimed before Hannah had a chance to introduce him as her husband. She had anticipated that moment on her doorstep, and now she'd even had that snatched away from her. Hannah summoned an appropriate smile. "C'mon in!" Heather said, stepping aside and sweeping her arm toward the living room.

She should have emailed Heather and asked for privacy, for the gift of returning home without being made to feel like a guest. Nathan was right: she didn't know how to ask for what she wanted, and now she wouldn't get a second chance to introduce her husband to her old life without someone else watching.

Once across the threshold Nathan stooped to remove his shoes. "Oh, that's okay, you can keep your shoes on," Heather said, and then added awkwardly, "unless Hannah, you want—"

"No, shoes are fine," Hannah mumbled, noting Heather's stylish flats before casting her eyes around the room.

"I hope you don't mind that I added some personal touches," Heather said. *Translation: I hammered holes into the walls to hang artwork everywhere.*

"You're a Monet fan, huh?" Hannah commented. The front room now contained several prints of gardens and bridges.

"Love him. The way he captures light—I could sit in front of his paintings for hours. You should take Nathan to the Art Institute while you're here."

This isn't a sightseeing trip, Hannah replied silently. Aloud she said, "Maybe another time. We've got our hands full, trying to get everything packed up."

Heather sat down in Hannah's prayer chair, the recliner where for years Hannah had engaged in her morning devotions beside the front window, and put her feet up. "I was going to help get your office ready by boxing up your books," she said, "but then I thought you might be sorting things out while you packed. Anything you don't want to keep, feel free to leave."

Nathan squeezed Hannah's shoulder as they sat down together on the couch.

"I should have asked you before about some of the furniture," Heather went on. "I'd be happy to buy some of your stuff if you don't want to move it."

Though Hannah knew she had no room for any of it in Kingsbury, her first impulse was to put it all in storage rather than leave it for Heather.

"What do you think, Shep?" Nathan asked when she took too long to reply.

"We'll talk about it."

They did—after Heather finally excused herself to lead a Bible study at the church. "Keep everything that's important to you," Nathan said as they assembled boxes. "We'll figure out how to consolidate everything once we get home."

Obviously, he wasn't entertaining her desire to move. Despite his declaration that they would "talk about it later," he hadn't initiated the subject on the drive down. After the first hour of relative silence in the car, Hannah assumed he preferred not to discuss it. In any case, she didn't intend to bring it up again. Once was too much.

She opened all the cupboards in her kitchen and stared at her old dishes and appliances. What sentimental attachments did she have to any of it? A few souvenir plates and mugs, that was all. She wrapped some pieces in newspaper and filled half a box. Heather could keep the rest or get rid of it. Hannah didn't care.

Did. Not.

"You okay, Shep?"

"I want my chair." She didn't wait for him to help her drag it toward the front door.

It was dark when Hannah and Nathan arrived at Westminster, the U-Haul only partially filled with boxes and a few pieces of furniture: her recliner, a roll-top desk, and an antique barrister bookcase that had been her father's. The rest Heather purchased with a check that had already been made out to Hannah and signed by Claudia Kirk, presumably her mother. Heather had scribbled in the total for her first month's rent plus the household items. She'd gotten a bargain, and she knew it.

Hannah unlocked her office door and breathed deeply. This had been the haven where she had spent the majority of her time over the past fifteen years, even sleeping on the couch many nights. She set down a stack of empty boxes and picked up a favorite blanket that was folded on one of the throw pillows. "I want this couch," she said. "And those lamps." The antique lamps with urn-shaped bases and scalloped shades had lit the dens in her childhood homes, and her mother had sent them to her when she got the job at Westminster. Nathan unplugged them from the wall and set them on the sofa.

"Are the bookcases yours?"

"No. Just the couch and the lamps. And all these books." Oh, how she had missed her books.

Nathan adjusted his glasses and leaned in for a closer look. "You've got good stuff here." He fingered some of the book bindings. "We'll find room, don't worry. I can take my books from home to school and give you that office space. You can even put your chair in there by the front window, have a place where you can close the door. We'll make it work."

Mm-hmm.

She opened her desk drawers. These, at least, Heather had left untouched.

Shocking.

"Are you going to sort books here or just pack them all up?" Nathan asked.

With her future in pastoral ministry still uncertain, she wasn't sure what she might need. "Just pack all of them." That was easier than deciding what to keep and what to leave behind. While Nathan cleared shelves, she cleared out her desk.

"Knock, knock," a voice called from the doorway.

Hannah looked up. "Steve!" She hadn't seen his car in the parking lot, and his office had been dark when they had arrived. So much for avoiding him while she packed up. She stepped around boxes to give him a one-armed hug.

"I figured that was your U-Haul out there," he said.

Before she lost another opportunity at an introduction, she motioned toward Nathan. "Steve, I'd like you to meet my husband, Nathan Allen."

Steve smiled warmly and extended his hand. "If I'd known you'd be here tonight, I would have invited you both for dinner."

"It's okay," she said. "We were working all day at the house and finally got it cleared out. Or everything I need to clear out, anyway."

"Well, thanks for being willing to work with Heather on that. She's very excited."

Feeling Nathan's gaze on her, Hannah pitched her voice correctly. "I'm glad she's worked out. It sounds like she's been a great fit for Westminster."

Steve nodded. "She had hard shoes to fill, but she's done a great job." He glanced again at Nathan. "Your wife was a great colleague. It's hard to let her go."

Nathan grasped her hand and held onto it. "Well, thanks for paying attention to the Spirit's nudges. If you hadn't given her the sabbatical, we wouldn't have reconnected."

"Glad to be part of God's plan." Steve paused and then said, "You sure you won't join me in leading worship tomorrow, Hannah?"

"I'm sure, thanks."

He was looking at her not with the shepherd's expression she had often seen as he ministered tenderly to the flock but with the senior executive's expression she had glimpsed at staff meetings when he was issuing correctives. "I'll be frank," he said. "There are some people in the congregation—not many but a vocal minority—who think I forced you to resign, that somehow your sabbatical was part of some grand scheme to push you out in favor of someone—"

Younger, she silently supplied when he hesitated.

"—new," he said, "or that you left because you're angry or because something happened between us."

"What? Of course not!"

"It just seems odd," Steve went on, "the way you resisted having a proper send-off here. If there's anything unresolved or unspoken between us, I'd like to talk it through."

Unresolved and unspoken. Yes, as a matter of fact, there was. And though Hannah resisted naming it—though her mind commanded her to disappear without naming any hurt or disappointment for fear of giving offense—her soul longed to speak the truth. If she didn't take this opportunity to voice her struggle face to face, she might not get another. "Nate, maybe you can give Steve and me a few minutes together, alone."

To Steve's credit he listened without interrupting, asking appropriate, clarifying questions. To Hannah's relief he did not become defensive when she said that even though she knew he had her spiritual health in mind when he insisted she take a sabbatical, the way it was sprung on her had felt controlling. He also understood that his reluctance to take her part-time proposal to the elders had left her feeling unappreciated. "I think I wanted you to tell me that you so valued my partnership in ministry that you'd go to bat for me," she said, "that you'd do anything you could to enable me to continue to serve here. Instead, you seemed eager to accept my resignation."

He visibly bristled for the first time. "Whoa. That's not what I remember from our conversation. What I remember is that I asked you about your sense of call. I asked you to consider whether you were feeling any sort of obligation to return to Westminster. I didn't say you couldn't return here in June. I never would have said that. I asked whether you were wholehearted about remaining here, or whether perhaps God was doing something new in your life. That's what I remember."

"No, you're right. I know that's what you said."

"There wasn't any hidden subtext to that, Hannah. I wasn't looking for ways to get rid of you. But if you've communicated something else to people in the congregation . . ."

"No! Of course not. I haven't communicated with anyone about it." If he was going to turn this around and accuse her of gossip or otherwise undermining the body, she wasn't sure she could keep from bursting into tears. She pulled a throw pillow to her lap and fiddled with the tassels.

Steve shifted in his chair, the faux leather squeaking. "Part of what I'm trying to do here is damage control. There's already been hurt and misunderstanding, and I'm sorry for that, for the part I've played in it. But if we don't do this ending well, it will cause even more hurt. And I don't want that. This congregation has deep affection for you, nothing but appreciation and affection."

Affection? It hadn't felt like affection, being cut off from communication about the life of the congregation for the past seven months. It hadn't felt like affection, being accused by some of exploiting the congregation's generosity by not returning to serve. And the one person who had maintained active communication during her sabbatical—Nancy—now refused even to meet with her for a cup of coffee. She could count on two hands the number of people from Westminster who had emailed her after she tendered her resignation, and there were even fewer who had bothered to send congratulations or well-wishes for her marriage. If this was what passed for affection, she didn't want to see apathy.

"We'd like to say a public thank-you in worship tomorrow," Steve said, his voice firm. "At both services."

For their sake, his sake, or hers? She made sure not to audibly sigh her frustration. Though she hated playing the appearance game, she supposed she shouldn't fault a senior pastor for attempting to unify the body and minimize collateral damage caused by the sudden resignation of a long-time staff member. For all she knew, he and the elders had had multiple conversations about how best to proceed. But the whole approach smacked of control.

"I'd also like for you to participate in worship," he said. "Call to worship, pastoral prayer, benediction—your choice. Let the congregation receive your blessing even as we pray God's blessing for you."

Hannah stared at her feet. "I'll sleep on it," she said. But that night she didn't sleep at all.

Becca

Becca turned over in a bed that was not hers, a bed that was not Simon's, and groaned. The sunlight streaming through a window pierced her. She shut her eyes and covered her face with her arms.

"'Morning," a voice said. *Too loud.* She lifted one arm to see who was sitting on the edge of the bed. "Drink this," Harriet said, handing her a mug.

Becca didn't have the strength to reach for it. She groaned again, the taste of vomit in her dry mouth causing her to gag.

"C'mon, Becks. Wakey-wakey!" Harriet nudged her until Becca propped herself up on her elbows, her head tilted back against a pillow that reeked like a parking garage stairwell. She took one sip of black coffee and spit it out on the floor.

Someone else in the room moaned. Becca squinted in that direction. "'Arrrry?" Pippa called from a tangle of blankets on the floor.

"Here, pet." Harriet kicked aside a pile of discarded clothes and offered Pippa the mug Becca had rejected. "I swear, you lot . . ." She plopped down on the edge of the bed again, causing Becca to bounce. *Stop. Bouncing.*

Pippa cursed.

"It's your own fault," Harriet said. "I told you you'd had enough. And you"—she poked Becca—"lucky for you I was there. You were a complete and utter madwoman, I tell you."

"With ridiculous dance moves," Pippa added, rising unsteadily. "Wish I could dance like that."

The way the two of them kept talking about Becca's dancing, she was pretty sure she hadn't been doing ballet on the floor. "I'd change your mobile number if I were you," Harriet said. "I heard you give it out to a dozen guys, and believe me, you don't want some of them calling."

Becca groaned again.

"Ooohh, but that one," Pippa said, "what was his name? Benjie? He was *fit.* Care to share?"

Becca did not remember a Benjie. "Did I—" She struggled to sit up in bed. "Did I, you know . . ." She rubbed her bare arms, knees pressed against her chest. She could not remember.

"You were getting friendly," Harriet said.

It was Becca's turn to curse. "How friendly?"

Pippa stooped to pull on her jeans, one hand on Harriet to steady herself. "Lighten up. A wee snog, that's all. Nothing serious."

"You told him all about Simon," Harried added. "Loudly. Should have heard yourself, going on about how you've found your one true love."

Becca breathed a sigh of relief and checked her phone. Simon would be worried, wondering where she was. She scrolled through dozens of missed calls and texts from names she did not recognize. But among all the calls and texts, one number was missing.

"Steady on," Harriet said when Becca tried to rise too quickly from the bed. "Where are you off to?"

Becca reached for her blouse—also covered with vomit—and winced. "Can I borrow some clothes?" She crumpled her skirt and blouse into a ball. "And use your shower?" She wanted—needed—to wash it all away.

─────◌⫯

A *stomach flu*, her mother had insisted to her grandmother the morning after Becca's first and, up until this morning, only hangover. Gran would have had a fit if she'd known Becca had come home from Lauren's eighteenth birthday party drunk. Becca was so sick that night, she didn't need a lecture. Her mother didn't give one. Instead, she held back Becca's hair and kept a cold cloth on her forehead while Becca vomited into the toilet bowl, vowing between retches that she would never do it again.

She stared at the ads inside the Tube as she traveled to Notting Hill Gate. With any luck, Simon would still be asleep when she arrived. He loved to have a long lie in on weekends. When she arrived at the flat, she made sure the gate and door did not slam behind her. But Simon was not there. "Simon?" she called, making a quick round of the place. No sign of him. She texted. No reply. She made herself a cup of black coffee and sat down on the couch to watch television. Four DIY shows later, Simon still had not contacted her. But Benjie, Luke, Kristofer, Ian, and Freddie had, each with proposals of varying degrees of vulgarity— enough to make her want to shower again.

Hannah

"Can I bring you something for breakfast?" Nathan straightened his tie and smoothed his mildly rumpled suitcoat. "Yogurt? Cereal? Bagel? Anything?"

The thought of food made Hannah feel sick to her stomach. "No, I'll be okay."

He sat down beside her on the bed. "What can I do for you?"

She wasn't sure. She just wanted the day to be over. She still hadn't decided what to do about Steve's request for her to participate in both services, and she was running out of time. "What should I do?"

"What do you want to do?"

"What I want to do is just hop into the U-Haul and drive home." She was certain, however, that there was a wide chasm between what she wanted to do and what she ought to do.

If we don't do this well, Steve's voice reminded her, *it will cause even more hurt.*

"I don't want to be there out of guilt," she said, "but that's about the best motivation I've got right now. Obligation and guilt." And fear. Fear of causing not only hurt, but damage. Much as she wanted to disappear with minimal interaction with the congregation, she knew Steve was right. She needed to leave well. And if this was her best opportunity to express gratitude for their fifteen years of life together, then she needed to get over herself and do what love required. "I'm not sure what I can offer from an authentic place right now. No way I can lead the congregation in prayer. I haven't even been praying myself. It would just be empty words." As for standing up front and receiving their gratitude or commendation or prayers or whatever Steve had in mind for the beginning of each service, she wasn't sure how she would manage that without disintegrating into a puddle.

"What else did he offer you?"

"Call to worship. I guess I could read the Scripture and just let it do what God intends it to do. At least my spiritual funk wouldn't get in the way."

He did not reply.

"He also offered me the benediction. But it would feel pretty weird to stand up there at the end of the service and pronounce a blessing without doing anything else." Nate was looking at her with his *I can see into your soul* look that was so unsettling. "What?" she asked.

"Nothing. I'm just listening."

"What would you do if you were me?"

"I'm not you, so—"

"No, I know." They'd had conversations like this before. "If you were in my shoes, what would you do?"

He took a slow breath. "Watching you, watching all of this, it brings back memories of leaving my own church years ago. With all the shame swirling around Laura's affair and my own anger and resentment about everything, I wanted to disappear out the side door. Like you. But a wise friend told me the same sort of thing Steve told you, that endings are crucial. Benedictions are important. Celebrating the good that's been shared in ministry is important, even when not everything can be resolved the way we want it to be."

"But with all the rumors circulating about my credibility, my integrity—I hate the thought of standing up there in front of people who think I tricked them or manipulated them or that I'm a hypocrite, a liar. I don't know what all they're saying about me." She shouldn't care so deeply. But she did. She didn't know how to keep company with Jesus as he surrendered his reputation. No matter how hard she tried, she couldn't get past her own ego, release what others thought of her, and crucify her pride. She couldn't.

As the minutes ticked by toward a decision she didn't know how to make, one phrase pursued her. *Keep company with Jesus.* If she had to stand in front of the congregation, where could she best keep company with the One who understood her wrestling and resistance, her sorrow and emptiness? Where could she serve without being the center of attention?

Suddenly, she knew. There was one place, one place she had always loved to stand. She picked up her phone and dialed Steve's number. "May I preside at the communion table with you?"

There was a moment's silence before he answered. "That's the perfect place to serve together."

—⁂—

To spare her the drain of pre-service narthex encounters, Steve offered Hannah and Nathan the small prayer chapel adjacent to the sanctuary. "You can stay here and then slip in during the gathering song, if that sounds okay."

Hannah nodded.

"I'm assuming you don't want to sit up front with me?"

No, she didn't want the vulnerable exposure of facing the congregation for the entire service. "I'll sit with Nate in the front row."

Steve scanned the printed bulletin. "All right. I'll summon you forward after the announcements to offer a word of thanks for your ministry and say a prayer for you. Then I'll invite you to join me at the table after the sermon."

"Sounds good."

Steve glanced at his watch. "Short prayer?" Hannah reached for Nate's hand on one side and Steve's on the other, then tried to stay focused as Steve asked that everything spoken, sung, and prayed would bring honor and glory and praise to the Most High. "And Lord, I thank you for bringing Hannah and Nathan here this morning. May she be encouraged and strengthened by our time together. Give her ears to hear the good words spoken over her life, not just by me but by you. In Jesus' name."

Hannah sniffled and murmured, "Amen."

"Amen," Nathan echoed, and kissed her wedding band. "You okay?" he asked after Steve left the room.

"I hope so." She smoothed her gray slacks with clammy palms. "Why do I feel like I'm going to a funeral?"

Nathan stroked her hair. "That sounds like a really important image to ponder," he said as they walked hand in hand to the front row.

six

Becca

At lunchtime on Sunday Simon finally texted to say he had spent the night at Nigel's flat after the quiz night went late and would meet Becca for dinner. "I've booked us an evening cruise," he wrote. She had been coveting one of those, and he knew it. *What a guy.* She would make sure she was appropriately "glammed up," to quote Pippa, as secret restitution for her *carpe diem* disaster. Humming, she rifled through her side of his closet for something suitable to wear. With her favorite blouse splashed with vomit, she didn't have many options. She texted Pippa: Need to get an evening gown asap.

Pippa replied: Know just the place.

"I wouldn't go long," Pippa said. "Go short. Tight." She thumbed through a rack of slinky cocktail dresses. "Here—this one. Look how fab this is." She held the sequined silver one up to Becca's shoulders. "You'll look great in this." It was the sort of dress her mother would have fainted over, and not in a good way. Becca took it to the dressing room and tried it on. "Hope Benjie isn't there," Pippa teased, peering over her shoulder into the mirror.

Becca blushed. "Please, Pip. Our secret, okay? Simon would kill me."

Pippa sealed her lips with her finger. "You don't have to worry about me."

But Pippa had not proven to be a reliable guardian of secrets in the past. Becca would need to make sure Simon didn't join them at the pub for drinks in the near future. She twirled to see herself from a different angle. "It *is* fabulous, isn't it?"

"You're fab in it," Pippa said, kissing her cheek. "You'll have everyone drooling over you. Just like last night."

"As long as Simon's drooling," Becca said with a last glance at her reflection, "I'll be happy."

———

"Champagne?" the server asked with a flirty, appraising stare. The dress didn't leave much to the imagination.

Becca crossed her arms against her chest. "Not for me, thanks." The thought of drinking alcohol again made her feel queasy.

"Something from the bar?" he asked.

"Ummm, do you have Appletiser?" With his double-take, she felt as if she had just ordered a juice box.

"Appletiser, it is." He gave a slight bow before disappearing with his tray.

"Did you just order an Appletiser?" Simon asked, sidling up to her. His free hand stroked the bare skin on her back while he held his drink to her lips. "Here, try this."

"No, thanks."

"Why not?"

"Not in the mood."

His hand circled lower on her body and squeezed. She jumped. "*Simon*," she whispered. "Stop." Maybe it was her imagination, but many eyes seemed to be fixed on her—and not with admiration. Most of the people onboard were wearing smart business attire. Maybe she and Pippa had overdone it.

Simon finished off his drink in one gulp. "Be right back." He wove his way to the bar and ordered another drink as the band began to play. How would she dance in these spiky heels? She'd only been wearing them a couple of hours, and already her feet were killing her. She would have blisters by the time the cruise finished.

"What's your dad drinking?"

"Sorry?" Becca spun around to face the server.

He handed her a glass. "Your dad—what's he drinking?"

"He's not my—"

He winked and slipped her a piece of paper with a phone number scrawled on it. As he left with a smirk, she caught a glimpse of her reflection in a window. *Becca,* her mother's voice pleaded. Setting her jaw, Becca turned away and tried not to hobble to the dance floor.

Hannah

Nervous and distracted, Hannah caught only snippets of what Steve spoke about her during the announcements: faithful servant, tireless commitment, grateful for her tenure. She hoped no one noticed her shaking hands when one of the elders gave her a bouquet of flowers and a card. After the congregation clapped politely, Steve prayed for her.

"Well done," Nathan whispered when, trembling, she took her seat beside him again.

During her quick scan from up front, she hadn't seen Nancy and Doug, who usually sat on the pulpit side at the first service, about four rows back. She cast a surreptitious glance over her shoulder. No sign of them. Tucking her hair behind her ears, she crossed her ankles and tried to listen prayerfully to the Scripture reading and the sermon. But if someone had asked her later what Steve preached about, she wouldn't have been able to say. She was thinking only of the moment when she would stand beside him at the table and offer the broken body and blood of Christ to the ones she had loved.

"On the night he was betrayed," Steve declared to the congregation, "Jesus took bread, blessed it, broke it, and gave it to his disciples, saying, 'Take. Eat. This is my body, broken for you. Do this in remembrance of me.'"

Sunday after Sunday Hannah had watched Steve break the bread. She had broken it herself at many services. But when Steve broke the loaf in half at the table, hands lifted high above his head so all could see, her eyes stung with tears. This is my body. Broken for you. Given for you in love. Take. Eat. Receive the brokenness and the fullness of my body. And remember me.

"In the same way after supper," Steve said, "Jesus took the cup, saying, 'This is the cup of the new covenant sealed in my blood. Take, drink, all of you. Do this in remembrance of me.'"

After the elders came forward to receive the elements for those seated along the side aisles, Steve gave Hannah part of a loaf and one of the chalices. Taking her position on the lectern side, Hannah served, bread in one hand, cup in the other. As many as she could, she called by name, and when she didn't know names, she called them "beloved." *Beloved, the body of Christ has been broken for you.* One by one, the worshipers tore off a piece of bread—some took large chunks, others only crumbs—and dipped it into the cup. *His blood has been poured out in love for you.*

Take. Eat. Drink. Remember.

Occasionally, someone would touch her hand while taking the bread or the cup and whisper a thank-you or a blessing, and Hannah would nod her gratitude. When Nathan came forward to receive, both of their eyes brimmed with tears. Her voice cracked as she said, "Beloved. Nathan. The body of Christ has been broken for you." He tore off a piece, his eyes riveted on her as she spoke the next words. "The cup of Christ has been poured out for you. In love." He dipped the morsel into the cup and placed it in his mouth, eyes closed as he chewed slowly. *Take. Remember.* With a touch of his hand to hers, he returned to his seat.

That's when she glimpsed Nancy and Doug rising from a row on the lectern side. They would be in her section! Her heart fluttered. *Oh, God. Mend. Heal. Restore. Please.* What a privilege to serve them, to share that holy moment with them. Hannah tried to stay focused on the people in front of her, but part of her was rehearsing the moment when she would be face to face with her wounded friend. *This is Christ's body, broken for you. Given in love for you. Take. Eat. Remember. Please.*

The congregation continued singing as the people streamed forward to receive. In the press of the crowd, she lost sight of Nancy and Doug, but they would be moving forward in her line, coming closer and closer. She offered a blessing to a little child in his father's arms, then took an opportunity to scan the faces again so she could mentally calculate how long it would be until—

She saw them.

There they stood, waiting to receive the sacrament from Steve, both of them avoiding eye contact with her. As she watched, they each tore off a piece of bread, dipped it into the cup, and returned to their seats on her side.

For a moment Hannah forgot there were others patiently waiting to receive. Trying to compose herself, she greeted the next in line. "Sarah," Hannah said—it was Sarah, wasn't it?—"this is the body of Christ broken for you." *Broken.* Her hand trembled as she offered the cup. *Poured out.* She quickly brushed aside a tear with the back of her wrist as the next in line moved forward. *Do this in remembrance of me.*

With many people wanting to greet her at the end of each worship service, Hannah didn't have a chance to tell Nathan about Nancy until they were loading a few wedding gifts into the U-Haul after the reception. "Maybe Steve's line was shorter," he said. "It would be awfully petty if they deliberately avoided you."

But it was hard to believe otherwise when Nancy did not make any effort to seek her out after worship or attend the reception. "Even if Steve's line was shorter," Hannah said, "it wouldn't have been by much. We finished serving at the same time." After she and Steve had finished serving the congregation, they had served one another. It was a moment she was grateful for.

She was also grateful for the kindness of many who had thanked her in specific ways for comfort she had provided or wisdom she had offered or the way she had encouraged them during times of trial. Her ministry, they affirmed, had made a significant difference, and this was something she needed to take to heart. As for whoever might be spreading rumors or believing conspiracy theories about her, they hadn't spoken them to her face. Not that she would have expected them to. Anyone could hide behind a smile and a hearty "Congratulations!"

"Anything else you want to do while you're here?" Nathan asked. The parking lot was nearly empty. She had survived the morning. Now she just wanted to click her heels and be back in Kingsbury.

"No." She had said her goodbyes. She had spoken her thank-you to those who gathered at the reception after the second service, some of whom didn't know Hannah but came for the cake. She had offered her well wishes to Heather, who would finish up her internship at the end of May and then officially be installed as an associate pastor.

"I'm proud of you, Shep." Nathan draped his arm around her shoulder. "You finished well. You wanted to keep company with Jesus, and you did."

In her own small way, she supposed she had kept company with Jesus in his sorrow, in his rejection. She had shared in the broken body of Christ. With a final glance at the steeple, she murmured, "Let's go home."

Mara

Promptly at six o'clock on Sunday night, the garage door opened and both boys entered with their duffel bags, Kevin grunting half a response to Mara's greeting and Brian brushing past her without speaking. "Nice to see you too!" she called to his back. From the window she watched Tom reverse out of the driveway. "Who's in the front seat with your dad?"

Kevin yanked open the refrigerator door and stood there, letting the cold air out. "Tiffany." He muttered something else Mara couldn't hear.

"Everything okay?"

He stayed hidden behind the fridge door. "Yep."

Mara turned down the Crock-Pot heat. "I've got that apple pork tenderloin you like," she said, removing the lid to stir the juice. "And mashed potatoes." She thought she heard him sniffle. "Kev?" He wiped his face against his shoulder before closing the door. "What's up?"

"Nothin.'"

"Everything okay with your dad?"

"Yep."

Since she couldn't think of any questions that required more than a one-word answer, she said, "Bailey missed you this weekend." As if on cue, the little dog trotted into the kitchen and flopped down in front of Kevin, who stooped to pet him. "And some of the boys at Crossroads were asking about you today, wanting to know when Mister Kevin is coming back to play basketball." Kevin kept stroking Bailey's stomach. "And oh! Almost forgot! Abby called and invited us all to come over for cake and ice cream on Thursday for her birthday."

"I've got practice."

"I know. After practice."

"I've got homework."

Since when had Kevin ever used homework as an excuse for missing a party? "We won't stay long. I thought maybe you'd like to see Madeleine. It's been a while and babies, they change really fast."

"I don't want to go, okay?" he said, then bolted up the stairs. Neither boy came when she called them for dinner half an hour later, and when she checked on them, both were sleeping—or pretending to be asleep—in blind-darkened rooms.

"I don't know what to do with them," Mara confided to Katherine at her spiritual direction appointment at New Hope later that week. Though she'd planned to be on a monthly rhythm, she hadn't met with Katherine since December. So much had happened since then, she had been talking Katherine's ear off for the past thirty minutes. Not that Katherine acted bored or annoyed. She always made Mara feel like she was being listened to without being judged. "Kevin's been the one to confide in me lately, but this time he's keeping quiet. Says there's nothing going on whenever I ask if he's okay. And then with everything going on with Jeremy . . . I just feel completely overwhelmed, you know? I try to pray, but it doesn't seem to do any good."

"In terms of what?" Katherine asked.

"In terms of making a difference in anything, changing anything. Tom's still a—" she caught herself before she said the word she wanted to say and substituted with "jerk. Brian's getting worse. I don't think I can take much more. Enough is enough." She exhaled slowly. "And I think I know what you're gonna ask me next. You're gonna ask if I have any sense of how God's with me in all this crap, right?"

Katherine smiled. "What a great question."

"Yeah, well, I don't. I mean, I know he is, but I just wish he'd do something to fix it, to make it go away. I know I shouldn't feel jealous, but it's hard to look at the blessings in other people's lives and not feel like I'm getting the leftovers. Which reminds me . . ."

As Katherine listened intently, Mara recounted her experience of praying with the story of the woman and the alabaster jar and how the only thing she had to offer Jesus was her envy, envy not just toward a woman who lived two thousand years ago but toward everyone whose life seemed to be easier than her own. She tried not to think about it, but

Charissa and Hannah weren't exempt from her jealousy either, much as she hated to admit it. "Pathetic, isn't it?"

"Not pathetic, Mara. Honest. A beautiful offering to Jesus."

Mara laughed, not joyfully but cynically. "Well, I've got plenty more where that came from. An endless stinking supply of envy." The Christ candle on Katherine's coffee table flickered and winked. "Charissa and I were talking about it, how discouraging it gets, seeing the same sins over and over and feeling like you'll never be free of them. It's like I've been jealous for so long, it's become part of me. I mean, it goes way, way back in my life, way back into my childhood with all the girls who lived on the right side of the tracks, you know? The girls who had everything going for them, handed to them. And then there's me, the rejected—"

No. Stop.

Not rejected.

Chosen. Loved. Favored.

That was the new script that replaced the old, the script she needed to keep rehearsing, keep living as her new reality, even and especially when circumstances screamed something contrary to that truth, even and especially when the old condemning voices clamored in her head.

"What are you thinking?" Katherine asked.

She sighed. "That I need Jesus to tell all the old voices in my head to shut up, like he told off the disciples. Maybe I need to practice listening to him say, 'Leave her alone!' whenever the voices get loud."

"Oh, I love that idea! What a good spiritual practice, to let Jesus do the quieting."

"Yeah, well, I just wish I had something other than my jealousy and failures and sin to offer him. I wish I had something precious and beautiful, like that woman had."

Katherine leaned forward slightly in her chair. "You do have something precious and beautiful, Mara. I hear it again and again in your story, how you're persevering in faith. In spite of everything you've got going on in your life—and it's a lot, believe me—you aren't giving up. You're pressing forward with hope. You're growing in confidence in God's love and care for you, even when it would be easy to doubt it. And you're finding ways to love others well. I say that's a beautiful thing. Those are all beautiful things."

Mara stared at her hands, her empty, open hands. She hadn't considered the possibility that she could be the gift, that her life was the broken and fragrant offering, that her faith in the midst of everything that was dysfunctional and ugly was beautiful. Precious. Costly.

Jesus.

Maybe she had something to offer him after all, something that pleased him, something—could it be?—something that perhaps Jesus would even praise. She shook her head with wonder and closed her eyes to listen and imagine.

—⟨˒⟩

When Mara left New Hope, she left with a brochure describing special Holy Week events: a "Journey to the Cross" prayer walk with Scripture and art, a Good Friday worship service, and a silence and solitude retreat on Holy Saturday. "Count me in on the retreat day," Charissa said on the phone later that afternoon. "I probably won't get much silence and solitude after the baby's born, so I might as well take the opportunity now."

"Great!" Mara said. "I've got to work on Good Friday, but I think I might try the art thing too. Katherine said it's eight different prayer stations with Bible verses and art about Jesus' death."

"Like paintings of the crucifixion?" Charissa asked. Mara could almost hear her wrinkle her nose.

"I don't know. She used the word, 'experiential,' whatever that means. I figure I'll try anything once."

"Well, I'll go with you if you decide to go. Just let me know which night." Charissa paused. "What about Hannah? Maybe we could all go together."

"I'll call and invite her," Mara said, but she wasn't optimistic, not after Hannah skipped their last meeting. There was no way to force her into community, no way to keep the Sensible Shoes Club from unraveling. Mara knew that. But if the group died . . .

She rubbed her forehead slowly. She wasn't sure she could handle one more loss right now.

Charissa

"You're sure saying yes to lots of stuff," John said. "What's up with that?" He peered over Charissa's shoulder at the skillet, where she was browning ground beef using the step-by-step instructions Mara had provided.

"Just trying to grow deeper in faith and be a good friend, go the extra mile." She poked at some pink meat with her spatula.

"Well, don't overdo it."

"I'm feeling fine. And I've got a good handle on my work right now." She'd had such a productive weekend of writing that for the first time all semester, she was ahead on both her personal papers and her lecture notes.

"Okay, Riss. I'm just saying, you have this tendency to try to be perfect and—"

"That's not why I'm doing it."

"Okay, no need to get defensive. I just want you to be careful, that's all."

She prodded the bits of beef more vigorously. The grease sizzled and spit.

"Need help with anything?" he asked, opening the fridge.

"That would be against the rules." She turned down the heat and leaned closer to the skillet to inspect whether all the pieces were evenly browned. Hard to tell. She flipped some of it over again. It looked gray. To be safe she gave the beef another minute and then drained the fat into a bowl, pursuing every stray morsel of meat until all was in its proper place.

John was standing at her shoulder. "What?" she asked.

"Nothing. Just watching."

"Well, stop, okay? You're making me nervous." Setting the skillet on a backburner, she turned her attention to the bell peppers, which she had chopped by herself—not as quickly and efficiently as Mara, but evenly and carefully, fastidiously removing all of the little white seeds from each slice, even after reading online that they weren't poisonous. She wasn't taking any chances.

"You can put some oil in the—"

"Eh-eh"—she thrust up her arm to cut him off—"shhh."

He opened a can of soda. She wished he wouldn't drink that stuff. Bethany would not be a soda drinker. "Isn't there some basketball game on?" she asked.

"Nope. Not until Sunday."

She motioned toward the front room. "Well, go watch news or something. I'll call you when it's ready."

"Yes, ma'am!" He saluted and left the kitchen humming "Hail to the Chief."

Charissa waited until she heard him turn on the TV before she poured some oil into a second skillet. Then she added broccoli and carrot slices to the yellow, red, and green peppers. Their dinner would be colorful even if it wasn't flavorful. John could add his own spices. Bethany didn't like them.

As she rotated the vegetables in the pan, she ruminated on his perfectionism comment. Quick to deny it as a motivation, she now considered the question again: Why did she want to go with Mara to New Hope?

She could give good answers. She desired to serve her friend well, to love well. She wanted to cooperate with the Spirit in crucifying her self-centeredness, and the discipline of service was a way to accomplish that. But was her interest in crucifying her self-centeredness also a self-centered pursuit? Why did she want to be free of selfishness? For her own sake or for the sake of others?

Ugh!

Ugh and gross.

The peril of self-examination, Charissa thought as she mixed the vegetables with the beef, was that it could easily deteriorate to self-analysis and self-preoccupation and a myriad of other self-focused remedies that kept her looking at her sin and failures instead of at the cross. *Jesus, help me,* she murmured, and turned down the stove.

When John offered to do the dishes, she didn't argue. She still had a couple of student essays to grade. With her feet propped up on an ottoman, she made her margin notes and corrections in red. They had already crossed the midpoint of the semester, and most of them still couldn't identify dangling modifiers, make subjects and verbs agree, or use apostrophes correctly. And if she read one more "should of" or "take for granite," she was going to scream. She had already given them a list of common errors that spell-check wouldn't catch. And these were just the micro-level edits. It was disheartening how many of the students still couldn't form a cogent argument with supporting details. What had she actually accomplished in the classroom? Not much, evidently.

John gave a "whoop" from the kitchen and came bounding into the family room holding his phone. "Dad scored tickets!"

"For . . ."

"The game in Detroit!"

She stared at him blankly.

"Final Four against Connecticut!"

As if to echo her father's exuberance, Bethany landed a kick that doubled Charissa over. John didn't notice; he was typing rapidly with his thumbs.

"Basketball, I assume?" she said, her hand on her abdomen.

"Michigan State, Sunday night in Detroit. Can't believe he managed to get them. I knew he was trying, but it was a long shot."

Charissa returned to her page. John sat down on the edge of the couch. She could feel his gaze upon her. "What?" she asked, not looking up.

"My parents are wondering about coming down here for the weekend, and then Dad and I can drive over to Detroit Sunday."

"They want to stay here?"

"No, no. They'll stay in a hotel. They were planning to come in April anyway, remember?"

Now that he mentioned it, yes. But an entire weekend? She was thinking their visit would be a day trip. "I've got a lot of work to do this weekend, John." She didn't relish the thought of entertaining Judi while John and his dad left for the day. "It's really not good timing right now."

"And when will it be good timing?"

She wrote "Good use of metaphor" in the margin and turned the page.

"Charissa?"

"Hmmm?"

"Can you put that down a sec? I'm trying to talk to you."

And I'm trying to grade, she silently replied. She set the essay on her lap and folded her hands primly.

"You said yourself that you've got a good handle on your work right now, that you've got extra time to give to Mara, to be at New Hope. Seems the same principle of 'going the extra mile' should apply to family, right?"

He had a point. She didn't like it.

"Do it for me, will you?" he said. "Please? They want to see the house." Subtext: the house for which they generously gave the down payment. "And they want to be able to buy some things for Bethany." Subtext: they're excited about their first grandchild and want to participate in preparing for her arrival.

She exhaled slowly. "Okay. Fine."

"No—if you're going to be that way about it, then forget it. I can just tell them you don't want them coming." He resumed typing.

He wouldn't, would he? "John, stop."

He looked up at her, thumbs still poised on his phone.

"I'm sorry, okay? You know I don't like things sprung on me. If they're going to stay in a hotel—"

"They've already said they will."

"Then, okay. But don't expect me to go on long shopping trips. I hate those." She had endured enough of them at Christmas. She wasn't doing it again.

"No, I know. It'll be fine."

"And you're going to have to rein in your mother if she starts offering all of her ideas about how to decorate the house or things to buy for Bethany or—"

"I know, okay? I know. I will."

"Okay." She picked up her pen.

He rose and kissed her on the forehead. "Thanks, Riss."

"Mmm-hmm." *If someone asks you to go one mile, go two,* Jesus said. Charissa was fairly certain he didn't mean you should walk those miles whining and complaining or acting like an imposed-upon martyr. She would need to do some serious praying before her in-laws arrived. And she'd probably be on her knees—figuratively speaking—all weekend long.

Becca

No amount of wheedling—and Becca had tried every possible angle for several days—persuaded Simon to change his mind. He was going to Paris for a writing weekend. Alone. "But why can't I come with you?"

His back was turned toward her as he stuffed clothes into a carry-on bag. "I told you, Rebecca. You're a distraction."

"I thought I was your muse." She flopped into his armchair.

"You are. But how will I get any words written if you're there with me?"

She was going to retort that he was the one who had invited her to spend an entire summer with him in Paris, and how was that going to work? Then she thought better of it. She didn't want him changing his mind about that. "I'll let you write. For hours and hours. I won't bother you at all. I'll go to museums, and you can do your Hemingway thing at the café. And at night . . ."

He zipped up his case.

"Simon?" Her fingers hovered at the top buttons of her blouse. "Simon, please." He couldn't just leave her like that. She couldn't bear the thought of an entire weekend at his flat without him, and she didn't want to be alone at hers. "Please, Simon. Take me with you. I'm—" *begging you,* she nearly said. But there was schoolgirl flirting, and then there was desperation. And she was skirting desperation. She needed to dial it back.

"I've got to catch my train." Giving her a quick peck on the cheek, he grabbed his bag and strode out the door. When the iron gate clanged shut behind him, she was still rooted in the spot where he had abandoned her.

"You didn't tell Simon about what's-his-face from the club, did you?" she asked Pippa on the phone later that afternoon.

"What? Of course not! When would I even see Simon or talk to him?"

"I don't know. Sorry." Becca lay back on Simon's bed, listening to the rumble of traffic from above. She had never noticed how loud his flat was, between the screeching hiss of buses and the pedestrians who streamed along the sidewalk carrying on loud conversations. Maybe she would go back to her flat to work. "He's just acting a bit . . ."

"A bit what?"

"Off. A bit off, that's all."

"Maybe he's stressed."

That was probably it. Simon didn't like his job, he wasn't making progress on his novel, and he needed some space to clear his head, to focus. If Pippa hadn't been in touch with him—and really, it had been paranoid to think she had—then there was no way Simon would have heard about the disaster at the club. And hadn't he acted fine on their dinner cruise? It was only the past couple of days that he hadn't seemed quite himself.

Becca rolled over on the bed, clutching Simon's pillow to her chest. If she believed in prayer, she would pray for him to have a productive writing weekend and then return to her rejuvenated in his passions. But she didn't believe in prayer. Her mother had believed in prayer, and a whole lot of good that had done her.

"You clubbing with us tonight?" Pippa asked.

"After last week? Not a chance."

"Oh, come on. Get your mind off Simon, off your mu—" Though Pippa broke off before she enunciated the final consonant, Becca felt heat rush to her face. "Off your books," Pippa said. "Off your classes. You've only got—what?—a month left in London? You've got to make the most of it, right?"

Right. And the list of things she wanted to experience in London in the short weeks remaining did not include another evening surrounded by drunk men trying to grope her. "I'm going to the National Gallery tonight." Becca said it as if she had decided on the plan hours ago instead of right at that moment. The museum was open late on Fridays, and though she had visited it several times already, the vastness of the collection meant she hadn't yet viewed some of the famous pieces she had studied in an art history course during her sophomore year.

With Simon away, it was the ideal opportunity to return. She had tried several times to persuade him to go with her, but he'd declared that if he never saw another lily pond or ballet dancer or bowl of fruit, it would be too soon. In Paris at Christmas he had humored her master-piece quest because it was her birthday, and she wanted to go to the Louvre. But while she followed the horde of tourists to the *Mona Lisa*, he had insisted on working on his manuscript in the café. He'd seen the painting, he said, and didn't understand what the fuss was about.

After working another hour on a paper, she left Simon's flat and rode the Tube toward Trafalgar Square, which, even on a chilly, damp April evening, was packed with people posing for pictures beside the foun-tains, clamoring upon the stone lions, and picnicking on the steps be-neath Nelson's Column. Demonstrators gathered there too, holding their signs about climate change and gay pride, while a tubby, bearded man with an American accent bellowed into a bullhorn, informing the masses that they were going to hell if they didn't repent from their sins and turn to Jesus Christ for mercy and forgiveness. "Believe the good news!" he shouted as he tried to shove pamphlets into the hands of those skirting by.

Becca hadn't anticipated being assaulted by a street evangelist, and she made sure she avoided eye contact when she brushed past him. "Be-lieve the good news!" he barked again. As far as she was concerned, there was nothing good about it. She hurried up the steps of the museum, her hands stuffed into her coat pockets. So much of her time with her mother at Christmas had been colored by her mother's attempts to share her faith, all of which seemed to be rooted in judgment and condem-nation of her relationship with Simon. Her mother had insisted oth-erwise, saying she only wanted to share her own growing sense of con-fidence in God's goodness and love, that she wanted Becca to experience God's love too.

Some love.

At least this museum didn't contain trigger points for grief. As far as Becca knew, her mother had not visited here during her weeks in London. Too bad, she thought as she steered clear of the tour groups filing toward the Impressionist wing. She would have loved Van Gogh's sunflowers.

—☙

Michelangelo, Titian, Rembrandt, Raphael. Becca methodically ticked the most famous artists off her list while recalling what she had learned about painting techniques and composition. *Chiaroscuro,* her professor would say as she pointed out the play of light and dark in Caravaggio's paintings. Becca lingered at *Supper at Emmaus,* Caravaggio's famous depiction of a beardless, resurrected Jesus sitting at a table with astonished disciples, and tried to appreciate the piece from a technical perspective: the shadowing on the garments, the light on Jesus' face. It was as if candlelight flickered from within the painting. But as for the depiction of Jesus, Becca preferred the mural of him at her old church, painted by some parent, probably. At least in that picture, Jesus had energy and spirit, like he was playing with the children. Here he looked mellow and detached, completely lacking vigor and passion. Resurrected? He looked like he had just been awakened from a nap.

She moved on through room after room of religious art. How many crucifixion scenes did they need? If Simon were with her, he'd be making snide remarks and looking at his watch. She glanced at her phone. Eight o'clock. She hoped he was working diligently on his own art right now. That's probably why he hadn't returned her phone calls or texts.

"Where's the Da Vinci drawing?" she asked a guard at the entry point to one of the rooms. She couldn't leave the museum without seeing *The Burlington House Cartoon,* a famous work they had studied in class.

He motioned over his shoulder. "Through that doorway there."

She nodded her thanks and entered a dimly lit room where several people perched on a bench admiring a large-scale charcoal drawing of the Virgin Mary seated on her mother Anne's lap while holding the Christ child. Leaning forward, Jesus stretched out his hand to bless the toddler John the Baptist, who stood on the ground beside them, looking up into his younger cousin's face. *Note the triangular form,* her professor's voice reminded her, *the unity of space, the play of light and dark. See how their glances keep the viewer's eye within the composition.* The drawing had stirred some controversy with a few of her fellow students—no doubt religious fundamentalist types—who had objected to Da Vinci portraying Mary with her mother when her mother had never been mentioned or named in the Bible. But it was a tender scene, and Becca had liked it.

Now that she was viewing it in person, what caught her attention was the tranquility of Mary's countenance as she smiled at her son. She was exquisite. Breathtakingly beautiful. Becca stared at her, transfixed. The Mona Lisa possessed nothing compared to this adoring young mother.

From behind her, a man cleared his throat. "Sorry," Becca said, stepping out of the way so that she wouldn't block the view. She sat down on the edge of the bench. The drawing, the posted caption reminded her, was preparation for a painting Da Vinci never made, and parts of the drawing were unfinished. The women's feet, for instance. And Anne's hand. Once the other visitors left the room, Becca moved closer. Mary's eyes were fixed on Jesus, but Anne's eyes were fixed on Mary, and she was pointing heavenward. Mary seemed oblivious to the gesture, all of her attention fixed on her child.

As Becca focused on the unfinished, pointing hand, she suddenly felt irritation swell within her, irritation she hadn't felt when they studied the piece in class a year ago. That hand spoiled the scene, and the fact that it was unfinished made it all the more jarring. Was the pointing to heaven really necessary? Did Mary need a reminder, a lecture in that moment? Wasn't it enough for them to enjoy sitting together?

Becca's eyes stung with unexpected tears, not merely tears of sorrow but complex tears of anger and regret. She was angry—angry that she would never have an opportunity to introduce her own children to her mother. She was angry—angry at her mother for giving in to the diagnosis, for not doing everything in her power to fight the cancer and live. She was angry—angry at fingers that pointed to a God who did not answer prayer. She was angry—angry at a God who had refused to listen to the anguished pleas she had sobbed into the darkness the night her mother told her the news. Angry.

That peaceful, happy girl sitting on her mother's lap and staring with adoration at her son—she had no idea the suffering her God had planned for her.

Poor duped girl.

Swiping her cheeks with the back of her hand, Becca pivoted away from the drawing and left the room.

seven

By Sunday morning of her in-laws' visit, Charissa was convinced of one thing: Ben Franklin's "Fish and visitors stink after three days" adage considerably overestimated the shelf life of the latter. "How about if you and your folks head to church, and I'll rest here," she suggested to John when he emerged from the bathroom wrapped in a towel. She hadn't yet taken full advantage of her pregnancy card during the past thirty-six hours of togetherness, and with twenty-four more to go, it was time to play it.

"But it's Palm Sunday! You don't want to be there on Palm Sunday?"

Palm Sunday had always been one of Charissa's favorite celebrations at First Church—the children processing with branches, the trumpet fanfares, the choral anthems—and she suspected Wayfarer would not duplicate any of those worship elements. "I'm feeling exhausted," she said. "I think I'd better rest here. What time will you and your dad head to the game?"

"He's antsy to get there. You know Dad, doesn't ever want to be late for anything. So I expect we'll hit the road right after lunch."

Oh. That would mean even more hours alone with John's mother. If she didn't go to church, she couldn't reasonably use an afternoon nap as an excuse for avoiding interaction. And since it was raining again, she couldn't ask Judi to be out in the garden identifying fledgling growth in the flower beds. She reformulated her plan. "Well, if that's the case, then maybe I should go this morning with all of you and then come back here and rest."

"It's up to you," John said. His tone of voice indicated he knew what was behind her change of heart.

It wasn't that she didn't appreciate her in-laws, she thought as she fidgeted in her sanctuary seat later that morning. (Why Pastor Neil was preaching about Jesus cleansing the temple and not the triumphal entry into Jerusalem, she had no idea.) Rick and Judi Sinclair were good people, kind and generous. But they had strong opinions about everything, and from the moment Judi had entered the house on Friday, it was clear she would have made different decisions about the kitchen and bathroom remodels. "I hope you didn't feel pressured to get things done quickly," she'd commented while inspecting the cabinets Jeremy had expertly updated. "Not that these aren't nice; it's just that I thought you'd be replacing them with new ones." She made a similar observation about the bathroom. "You can always decide to replace all the tile later if you want." The floors, at least, earned her approval. "Very nice," she said.

Rick agreed. "Does your guy want a job in Traverse City?"

Charissa gave him Jeremy's card. She wasn't sure how far afield Jeremy was casting his net for work, but he had confided in John a few days ago that he and Abby were feeling desperate.

She stretched her neck from side to side and scanned the sanctuary for them. Abby was sitting in the far back corner, but Jeremy was not beside her. In her pan around the room she also caught sight of Nathan and Jake, but Hannah was again absent.

"Did everything go okay in Chicago?" she asked Nathan after the service.

"We got everything packed up and moved, but Hannah was feeling pretty worn out this morning, so she's home resting."

Though his expression and tone of voice gave nothing away, Charissa wondered what "worn out" meant. "Tell her hi for me," she said. Then she introduced him to Rick and Judi, who, when they heard he was her PhD advisor, shared a cryptic look between them that John did not observe.

"Let it go," John said as they followed his parents' car to the restaurant. "You've got to let things go."

Like overhearing his mother quietly interrogate him about how they had chosen the name Bethany. ("Is it a family name or something?") Or biting her tongue when Judi commented that the family room was "very blue." Or turning the other cheek when Rick made some crack about going out to eat because he didn't want John to have to cook for them. "Charissa's learning to cook," John had said in her defense, "and she's doing a great job."

Let it go.

"I know they can be overbearing," he said, his eyes fixed on the road, "but they mean well."

She knew that. But it still didn't make being with them for extended periods of time any easier.

She and John had been engaged for a month when he invited her to go home with him to Traverse City. The Sinclair house, situated with stunning views of West Grand Traverse Bay, was easy to spot with its lighthouse mailbox and harvest flags. Judi, dressed in charcoal slacks and a chic cashmere sweater, had met them on the front porch and welcomed them into a home decorated with autumn accessories and brimming with collections of teapots, spoons, and seashells. Family photos adorned every horizontal surface, and the refrigerator was plastered with souvenir magnets holding old school pictures, missionary prayer postcards, and inspirational quotes. A minimalist in her decorating, Charissa had felt claustrophobic.

So when Judi mentioned at lunch that she would be happy to take her shopping to decorate the house while "the boys" were at the game, John nudged her under the table as if to say, *I've got this.* "I told Charissa she'd better rest this afternoon. She's been pushing hard lately, and I don't want her to overdo it."

Judi wiped her mouth with her napkin. "Well, exactly. I've been worried about that very thing. Those fainting spells—it sounds like maybe the stress has been too much, that you've taken on way too much this semester. You've got to be careful."

Charissa took a slow sip of water.

"She is careful," John said. "She's watching things." He reached in front of Charissa for the bottle of ketchup. "So what do you think our chances are tonight, Dad?"

Rick shrugged. "Well, I don't think anybody expected them to dominate Louisville like they did, and I'd say that UConn—"

Charissa concentrated on her bowl of soup. It was going to be a very, very long day.

———

As soon as John and his dad left for Detroit, Charissa made her move. "If you don't mind," she said to his mother, "I'm going to take John's advice and go lie down for a while."

"Of course! I'll make myself at home. Did you already have something in mind for dinner?"

Nothing she had already learned how to cook would meet with Judi's approval. "I've got makings for sandwiches, turkey, ham, cheese. I thought we could do that."

Judi hesitated, and her silence communicated volumes. "How about if I just quick nip to the store and pick up some things? John always loved my lasagna. I'll whip one up, and then he can have leftovers when he gets home."

Charissa was too weary to argue. "Sure." *Suit yourself*, she added silently. But she wasn't eating lasagna. She and Bethany were having a sandwich. Disguising her irritation with artificial sweetener, she said, "Can you find everything you need in the kitchen?"

Judi said she could. So, leaving her to root around in cupboards and drawers, Charissa went to her room and closed her door.

What's taking up sacred space? Pastor Neil had asked the congregation at the close of his sermon. *What's cluttering the temple, individually and corporately? What would Jesus desire to clear out in us and in his church?*

Jesus could start with her resentment. She was not in a "place of prayer" at the moment but a den of angry, passive-aggressive impulses. And the truth was, she didn't want to be cleansed; she wanted to be justified.

She looked at her watch. Even if she "slept" for two hours, that would still leave another two hours before the game started. Judi would want to watch the game, and Charissa could then excuse herself by claiming to have papers to grade or lectures to prepare. *Just try to hang out with her,* John had whispered when he left. *At least for a while. Watch a movie or something.*

Charissa wasn't interested in wasting a few hours on a movie. And she wasn't going to shop with her. Or cook. Or pretend to have a heart-to-heart chat. Or give her any opportunity to launch into a lecture about what she should do about her PhD or career after Bethany was born.

Her cell phone rang on the nightstand. "Hey, Mara," she said as soon as she picked up, "you don't have an emergency you need help with, do you?"

"What?"

Charissa moved toward the window, just in case her voice could be heard through a wall. "I need a good excuse to get away from my house."

"That bad, huh?"

"To quote John, she means well. But I'm about ready to lose it."

"What's she doing?"

The front door squeaked open and then closed. Judi was probably on her way to the store to buy all the things Charissa's kitchen lacked. "It's not even that she's saying or doing anything major to irritate me. But she has opinions about everything, and it drives me nuts." What was even more provoking was the fact that Charissa thought she had dealt with this exact issue weeks ago. After battling anger and resentment over what she deemed interference, she had reached a place of being grateful that she and John had options regarding Bethany's care, options that other new mothers like Abby did not have. "You know those whack-a-mole games at carnivals?" Charissa said. John loved playing those games. "That's what it feels like. Like I've gotten rid of something—pride or selfishness or bitterness or whatever—and then it pops up again."

"Yeah, I know what you mean. Like I'm never gonna be done with it. So frustrating."

Charissa lay down on the bed. "Sure you don't need me to immediately come to your rescue with something?"

"Want me to make something up? That's a miracle, isn't it? No stress to report." Mara paused. "Well, no new stress to report."

Bethany kicked. Charissa grimaced.

"Abby called a little while ago," Mara said. "She's getting baptized on Easter."

"What? Wow!" Charissa had waved to Abby from a distance after worship but hadn't had a chance to speak to her.

"Yeah, I guess she met last week with the pastor, and after talking with him a while, she knew it was something she was ready to do, something she wanted to do. So her parents are coming up Easter weekend to be there."

"Wow, Mara. That's fantastic news."

"Yep."

The flatness in Mara's voice did not jibe with the happy magnitude of such an occasion. "So . . . everything's okay?"

Mara gave a loud sigh. "I just wish Jeremy was getting baptized with her. Keep praying for him, okay? He sounds really depressed every time I talk to him. I'm worried. I know I need to stay out of it, let them work things out, but it's hard not to interfere and try to help."

Charissa wished she possessed quicker impulses to pray—like when she noticed Jeremy wasn't in worship, she could have offered a prayer for him and for Abby. That was a spiritual discipline she needed to start practicing: notice and then pray. But when she hung up the phone a few minutes later and closed her eyes, she immediately drifted off to sleep.

⸻ ☙ ⸻

Clutter. There was so much clutter. Old records, video cassettes, magazines, alarm clocks, limbless dolls, mounds of paper, lighthouses, family photos—every surface of the room was covered. Charissa could hardly breathe. She tried to kick aside some empty wicker baskets, but they were attached to the floor. She stooped to inspect. They weren't empty. They were filled with bits of moldy bread and rotting fruit infested with swarming maggots. Whose disgusting house was this?

Judi appeared in the corner of the room. "I'll help you clear this stuff out," she said. "You've got quite a mess in here."

"It's not my mess," Charissa argued. She was no hoarder.

Someone was knocking on the door, but there was no way to open it. There was too much trash on the floor. "Housekeeping!" a voice called.

"It's not my mess!" Charissa kicked at a stack of papers. "This isn't my house!"

But the knocking persisted.

"Ready for dinner?" Judi asked.

Eat? How could anyone eat in a place like this?

"Charissa?"

Charissa rubbed her eyes, disoriented. She was in her own tidy, uncluttered room, and Judi was standing beside the bed, backlit by the dim rays of a setting sun. Charissa blinked drowsily.

"The lasagna's ready, and I've got the table set."

Of course she did. Charissa was going to say, "I don't want lasagna, and I'd rather eat my sandwich in my room," but instead she said, "I'll be there in a couple of minutes."

She took her time getting up, far more time than necessary. When she entered the dining room fifteen minutes later, Judi was at the table, waiting for her. "I don't think it's cold," Judi said as she sliced into the steaming dish with a spatula Charissa did not recognize. She set a slice that was far too big in front of Charissa and said, "How about if I offer the blessing?" Charissa pursed her lips and nodded.

Hannah

Hannah reclined alone in her prayer chair, the one piece of furniture they had found room to integrate at the house. The rest of her possessions they had temporarily stowed in a storage unit. "We'll make it work," Nathan had assured her numerous times over the past week. "We'll figure this out. I just need to get through the end of the semester, and then I'll have more time to sort through things and get rid of stuff."

She strained to hear snippets of conversation from upstairs. Nate had spent the past hour on the phone in his office, but she couldn't tell from his cadence what kind of conversation it was.

"Hannah?"

She hadn't heard Jake enter the family room. "Hey, Jake, what's up?"

"I need a ride to Pete's house. I've been waiting for Dad to finish on the phone, but I'm already late, and we've got a project due tomorrow."

"I can take you, no problem." Hannah released the lever on the recliner and rose to get her coat and keys.

"I think he's on the phone with my mom."

Hannah stiffened, her arm suspended midair beside the key rack. "Is he? How do you know?"

"She texted me and said she's coming to Kingsbury for work or something. She wants to see me."

"When?"

"I don't know."

Hannah pocketed her keys. "No, I mean, when did she text you?"

"After church."

Nathan had neglected to mention this when he and Jake arrived home. In fact, they had now been in the house together for several hours, and he'd said nothing. When she returned after dropping Jake off, Nathan was sitting at the kitchen table.

"Were you on the phone with Laura?"

"Yeah."

"Why didn't you tell me she texted Jake?"

"I didn't want to burden you. You said you were worn out."

Chaucer sat down in front of her, paw in the air for her to shake. She ignored him. "You didn't think it was important to tell me she's going to be in town?"

He raked the fingers of both hands through his hair. "I wanted to work it out first with her. It wasn't a conspiracy theory to keep you in the dark."

Hannah sat down on the edge of a chair, still wearing her coat. "So when is she coming?"

"She's in town for a meeting the week after Easter." Chaucer rested his muzzle on Hannah's lap. She nudged him away. "Here, bud," Nathan said, snapping his fingers. "C'mere." He rubbed Chaucer's face with both hands. "Lie down." The dog flopped down on the floor, and Nathan stroked his fur with his bare foot, his "hineni" ankle tattoo visible beneath his trouser hem.

"You could have told me."

"Hannah—"

"You could have told me."

"I didn't want to burden—"

"I know. You didn't want to burden me because I'm"—she used her fingers for air quotes—"'worn out.'" She stood. "This doesn't help with that." She gripped her keys.

"Where are you going?"

"Meg's." It was the only place she could think of where she could be alone and undisturbed.

As the twilight sky deepened to the color of a bruise, Hannah sat in Meg's kitchen, listening to spring peepers chirp their melodies in the trees. *Disregarded.* That's the word that described how she felt. Disregarded.

Every new marriage had its growing pains. She knew that. She had counseled many newlyweds and understood the challenges of integrating separate lives, especially in blended families. But this seemed a particularly painful breach of the covenant she and Nate had made with one another. Shouldn't he have consulted his new wife before calling his ex?

Her phone buzzed with a message: Please come home so we can talk about this face to face.

Please come home.

Hannah cradled her head in her hands and cried.

Charissa

"It's actually not such an overwhelming color when you sit in here awhile," Judi said, her eyes scanning the unadorned aquamarine walls of the family room. "Rick's been saying he wants to paint the guest suite. What's this color called?"

"I don't know. John picked it." Charissa returned to the pretense of reading her composition textbook. She had set a stack of books on the coffee table in front of her, hoping the visual would communicate the sacrifice she was making in order to keep her mother-in-law company in front of the television.

"Ooh! I just saw them!" Judi waved at the screen. "The camera panned right over the section where they're sitting."

Unlikely, Charissa thought, but didn't correct her.

"I've got some artwork that would be beautiful in here," Judi went on, "to bring some life to the walls. I'd be happy to bring it down the next time we visit."

Which will be when? Charissa silently replied.

"There's a gallery in town—the owner and I went to college together—and she features local artists who paint fabulous views of Lake Michigan and the lighthouses."

Charissa flipped a page. "I promised my mom we'd shop together for décor when she comes up to stay." She'd had no such conversation with her mother, but Judi didn't need to know that.

"Oh? Are your parents coming soon?"

"My mother is, once the semester is over. Then my father will fly up with her after Bethany's born."

"I guess we need to think about coordinating grandparent visits," Judi said.

Right. Charissa didn't need both sets converging at the same time. As far as she was concerned, the maternal side had priority. But she and John hadn't negotiated those details yet. They hadn't even taken time to draw up the birth plan, which was supposed to be in place by now. Once she finished the semester, she could shift her focus toward preparing for Bethany's arrival.

"So will your mother come for the birth?"

Charissa flipped another page. "No, not until afterward. John and I are going to keep all the labor and delivery private."

"You don't want help while you're in the hospital? Those first few days can be really difficult."

"John's taking time off work." Charissa shifted position on the couch, her uterus tightening. She had been having quite a few Braxton Hicks contractions the past few days. Maybe she was dehydrated. She had read online that dehydration could increase their frequency. "Can I get you something to drink?" she asked, rising slowly to her feet once the contraction subsided.

"I'll get some coffee. Do you have decaf?"

"I don't think so." Charissa hadn't drunk coffee in months, and John usually drank the real stuff.

"Never mind, then. I should have bought some when I went to the store." She followed Charissa into the kitchen and poured herself a glass of water while Charissa removed the bottle of TUMS from the cabinet. Bethany did not like lasagna. She should have insisted on eating a ham sandwich. "Heartburn?" Judi asked. Charissa nodded. "I guess lasagna wasn't a good choice for dinner. You should have said something."

You should have accepted my offer of sandwiches, Charissa thought. She chewed two tablets slowly while Bethany kicked and somersaulted. *Sorry, baby girl.* The two of them would be up all night.

"Don't feel like you need to keep me company," Judi said when they returned to the family room. She motioned toward the stack of books. "I know you're busy."

Charissa felt a pang in her gut that wasn't a contraction or acid reflux. Judi's granting permission to disappear stung. She closed her textbook and placed it on the stack. "It's okay." Giving her attention to basketball was neither an admission of guilt nor an apology, but it was nevertheless a declaration of intent to be a more gracious host in the hours that remained. She put her feet up on the coffee table and asked, "What's the score?"

Mara

Mara picked at some chipped nail polish while she waited outside Dawn's office for her counseling appointment. Some mothers' prayers were answered, she told herself, and some mothers' prayers were not. Like Ellen. Ellen, Mara knew, had been praying for Abby to be awakened to faith, and now Abby had been. At some point over the past week, Abby had crossed a line into wholehearted belief, and she wanted to publicly declare her trust in Jesus Christ. She wanted to publicly repent of her sins, die to herself, and be raised into newness of life, washed clean.

"You'll be there, Mom, won't you?" Abby had asked on the phone Sunday afternoon.

Of course Mara would be there. She would give up Easter Sunday at her own church in order to witness Abby's entry into the body of Christ. She would sit beside Abby's parents as close to the front row as possible, and she would cry tears of joy. And tears of sorrow. Because her own fervent prayers for her son to awaken to faith and to be well and whole and happy had not been answered. The faith-filled part of her said, "Not yet." The discouraged part of her declared, "Not ever."

She reached for a magazine filled with glossy photos of attractive women with attractive families in attractive homes and then changed her mind. Why subject herself to more opportunities for envy and discontent?

Leaning back in her chair, she closed her eyes. It was hard not to question Abby's timing, hard not to resent her moving forward so quickly when perhaps she could wait and be baptized someday with her husband. Someday. Or no day. There was no guarantee Jeremy would ever turn fully to Christ. So why should Abby wait? In the midst of their financial stress and uncertainty about employment and Jeremy's relapse—several occasions he deeply regretted, Abby had reported to Mara—the Spirit had worked to draw her to Jesus. That was worth celebrating. Maybe the Spirit would work through Abby's awakening to draw Jeremy too.

"It's wonderful Abby is taking that step, isn't it?" Mara had said to Jeremy on the phone.

"Yeah. Great."

"But what about Maddie? I forgot to ask Abby what you're doing about her."

"What do you mean?"

"I mean, will she be dedicated or baptized or something along with Abby?" Mara wasn't sure what the infant practices were at Wayfarer Church.

"No."

Mara had decided to press. "Because . . ."

"Because according to the pastor, both parents need to be able to answer questions about faith, and I'm not going to stand in front of a whole crowd of people and be a hypocrite."

She admired him for his integrity, even as her heart broke that he was not able to believe. Though the Twelve Steps program had saved his life years ago when he was neck-deep in addictions, Jeremy's talk about "letting go" and "trusting a Higher Power" evidently lacked the specificity of trusting Jesus Christ as that Power.

Keep praying for him, Abby had said. Of course she would. But given her track record for answered prayers—praying for God to heal Meg, praying for her family life to improve, praying for the Sensible Shoes Club not to fall apart, and the list went on and on—Mara wasn't sure how much her prayers helped anyone. She kept going, though. What else could she do? She had to keep offering her faith as a beautiful thing to Jesus, broken and small as it was some days.

"Mara?" Dawn was smiling at her from the doorway.

Mara rose. "I've got lots to tell you," she said as she stepped into Dawn's office. "As usual."

Charissa

"You're sure you don't mind me going?" John asked as he put on his coat.

"Of course not," Charissa said. "Go." Somehow he had managed to snag a single ticket to the championship basketball game in Detroit.

"Thanks, Riss. I'll make it up to you."

"Just add it to your tab." He owed her big time for the weekend with his parents, he had insisted multiple times. She was just grateful they had survived the visit without any major damage.

He kissed her. "Hope you and Mara have a good time together, whatever the art thing is."

Charissa wasn't sure what to expect at New Hope either. In all of her years of attending church, she had never heard of this kind of Holy Week event. Maundy Thursday and Good Friday services, yes. But an experiential prayer journey to the cross? She couldn't picture it.

When she arrived at the retreat center an hour later, Mara was waiting for her in the lobby. "Thanks for coming," Mara said, embracing her.

"Sure." Charissa smoothed her hair and hung up her coat. "Is it just us, or is Hannah coming too?"

"No, she can't make it, said she had other things going on."

Charissa needed to remember to pray for her. From the expression on Mara's face, it seemed they both had drawn the same conclusion about her absence. "And how about you, Mara? Are you doing okay?"

Mara shrugged. "My counselor thinks I am, so that's encouraging. We keep moving forward, right?"

"Right. Or try to, anyway."

Progress not perfection, Charissa reminded herself as they walked down the hallway to the chapel where they had gathered for Hannah's wedding. How different it looked! No longer a place of joyful celebration, it was now a place of somber reflection and quiet reverence, the overhead lighting dim, with candles flickering and casting shadows around the room.

A middle-aged man met them at the entrance doors and handed each of them a small pamphlet. "The Scripture texts are posted at each prayer station," he said in a whisper, "along with art that illustrates the story and themes." He opened a brochure to show them. "In here are some prompts for how to pray. You can take this home with you."

Charissa read the front cover: *Welcome to Journey to the Cross. You are invited to accompany Jesus in his sorrow and suffering as he journeys to Golgotha. As you walk and pray, imagine you are watching the scenes unfold. Experience the details as you read and gaze upon the artwork. Though you may be tempted to skip past the sorrow of the cross to the joy of Easter morning, our capacity to receive the wonder of the resurrection is enlarged when we take time to ponder the sacrifice of Jesus Christ. May God lead you deeper into the reality of his love as you travel.*

She glanced over the man's shoulder. Inside the chapel about twenty people sat in front of different pieces of art to meditate and pray. "The journey starts in this corner here," he said, gesturing, "and then you move counterclockwise around the room. Take as much time as you like at each of the eight stations. There's no rush."

Murmuring their thanks, they entered the room, where mournful violin music played quietly over the speakers. As Charissa watched, Mara leaned against a wall and, as they had done weeks ago in this same space, removed her shoes.

While Mara took her time, Charissa only paused politely at the first two stations of Pilate questioning Jesus and releasing Barabbas in his place. Not much to capture her attention there. So she moved to the third station, where a long wooden beam several inches thick lay at the foot of a painting of Roman soldiers grabbing a man by his sleeve. Taking an empty seat, she read a single verse on the placard: "They compelled a passer-by, who was coming in from the country, to carry his cross; it was Simon of Cyrene, the father of Alexander and Rufus" (Mark 15:21).

Compelled. She didn't like that word. Here's a man minding his own business, and suddenly he's swept against his will into the drama of a stranger's execution. She opened the brochure to read the guide for prayer:

Imagine you are Simon of Cyrene, journeying toward Jerusalem to cele-brate the Passover. As you approach the city, you see a procession. A bloodied and bruised man is stumbling under the weight of a cross as Romans lead him toward the place of crucifixion. Crowds shout their accusations about his guilt. You pause to watch.

Suddenly, a rough hand grabs you by the shoulder. "You!" the soldier barks. "Carry his cross!"

What's going through your mind in this moment? Do you willingly take the cross, or do you try to resist? Why?

Now pick up the wooden beam on the platform. What does it mean for you to walk with Jesus in carrying the cross? What do you want to say to God in prayer?

Charissa watched a rail-thin teenage girl pick up the beam and stagger under the weight of it before setting it down for her mother to lift. The mother was crying. Charissa lowered her gaze. She had never given much thought to Simon of Cyrene's role in the crucifixion narrative, but since she had bristled upon reading the verse, it seemed like a potentially fruitful place to pause and pray.

She closed her eyes and tried to imagine herself as Simon, tried to imagine what it would feel like to be singled out and snatched from the crowd, coerced into carrying a bloodied crossbeam for a man who had obviously been convicted as a criminal, a man whose flesh hung in shreds on his back, whose eyes were nearly swollen shut, and whose brow was lacerated from thorns pressed into his skull. The crowd jeered at him, but he did not reply. He didn't look like he could make it much farther. She had heard about the particular agony and cruelty of cruci-fixion, and even if this man had committed a heinous crime, the pun-ishment was deplorable.

Much as she was moved by his pain, however, she didn't want to get involved. She tried to offer her excuses, but the Roman soldiers didn't listen. She didn't want to carry the cross. She didn't want other people to think she was the criminal. She didn't want to participate in the shame, didn't want to be guilty by association. Every part of her resisted being swept up into the narrative. Every part of her resisted being commanded to walk a mile or two against her will. Why couldn't she just mind her own business and get on with the purpose of her Passover journey? Let the drama play out according to God's plan. It had nothing to do with her.

She opened her eyes and glanced over her shoulder at the previous station, where Mara knelt on a cushion in front of a cross, looking up and weeping. Slowly, Charissa rose to her feet and returned to that station. Maybe she needed to see that it had everything to do with her. Maybe she needed to try again to enter the Barabbas part of the story.

While Charissa waited for chairs to empty, she read the single verse printed on the placard: "So he released Barabbas for them; and after flogging Jesus, he handed him over to be crucified" (Matthew 27:26). Pilate, looking to save his own skin, had done what was expedient: he gave in to the demands of the crowd. He handed Jesus over to be crucified. And Jesus did nothing to resist the handing over.

As soon as the station cleared, Charissa lowered herself to kneel where Mara had knelt, on a cushion before a life-sized cross. Nailed to the cross were single words painted on strips of wood: pride, vainglory, envy, sloth, anger, lust, greed, gluttony. At the intersection of the beams was a mirror angled forward so that someone kneeling on the cushion could glimpse her own face reflected there. Charissa scooted backward until her face was positioned in the dead center of the mirror.

There. That's what she had deserved for her sin. That's where she had belonged. On the cross like the other criminals. But Jesus—Jesus had taken her place, just like he had taken the place of Barabbas. Jesus, the guiltless one, had taken upon himself her sin, her guilt, her shame. He had willingly identified with Charissa, the sinner. All her pride, all her vainglory, all her selfishness and resentment and gluttonous desire for achievement and honor—all of this Jesus had borne for her, without resisting, without complaining, without making anyone understand that he himself was not the guilty one.

Tears wound down her cheeks as she looked up and saw with rinsed eyes the depths of her sin. But more than that—so much more than that—she saw the depths of his love.

The one who has been forgiven much, Jesus said to Simon the Pharisee, loves much. If Charissa—like the ill-repute woman who crashed a dinner party to anoint Jesus—if Charissa could see the depths of her sin and the love that had paid the price for all of it, could she be enlarged to love much in return? The gift, she realized as she stared at her reflection in the mirror, the gift was seeing the enormity of her debt. Self-righteous Pharisees could not perceive the enormity of their debts. But prostitutes who had routinely offered themselves to all the false gods that did not satisfy—honor, achievement, admiration, esteem—prostitutes could perceive the enormity of their debts and receive the enormity of forgiveness. And when Pharisees were converted to seeing themselves as prostitutes, what a gift. What a gift of mercy and grace.

So much grace.

Whispering her gratitude, Charissa returned to Simon of Cyrene's station and picked up the crossbeam. She wasn't ready to enthusiastically identify with Jesus in his shame—would she ever run to embrace that manner of suffering?—but she was willing to be made willing. And maybe that was a good enough place to begin. Again.

Mara

Some mothers' prayers were answered, and some mothers' prayers were not. Mara wiped her eyes and stared up at a painting of Mary and the other women gathered at the foot of the cross.

Oh, the anguish Mary must have felt watching her son suffer and die. Mara reached for another tissue from the box on the floor and blew her nose as discreetly as possible. The anguish. *You have no power to stop his suffering,* the prayer notes read, *and he is doing nothing to resist it.* How did she feel as she imagined the scene unfolding?

Helpless. Utterly crushed by sorrow. And comforted that she was not alone.

Mara made sure they were well out of earshot of any other visitors before asking Charissa what she thought of the experience. "It was powerful," Charissa said as she retrieved both of their coats from the rack in the lobby. "I'm glad I came."

Mara slid her arms into her sleeves. "Me too. I've never spent much time thinking about Good Friday. Just Easter." But somehow in the midst of watching the sorrow unfold, Mara had experienced deep and profound consolation. Jesus knew. He understood. And he kept her company in the midst of all the disappointment and despair.

The front door opened, and a gust of wind blew in some crinkled brown oak leaves from the sidewalk. Mara stooped to pick one up off the carpet. "Hey," a familiar voice said. "Am I too late to walk with you?"

"Hannah!" Mara pocketed the leaf and threw her arms around her friend.

"I'm so sorry," Hannah said when Mara released her from the embrace. "I wasn't going to come. But I couldn't ignore the voice telling me I had to be here." She looked like she hadn't slept in days, half-moons deep and dark beneath her weary eyes.

Charissa glanced at her watch. "I'm so sorry, Hannah. I wish I could 'onger, but I really should try to get some work done tonight."

"No, no, that's fine," Hannah said, returning her hug. "You go. I wasn't sure how long you two would be here."

Mara removed her coat. "I'll keep you company," she said. "Come with me."

Hannah

The last time Hannah had stepped through the New Hope chapel doors she was wearing a wedding gown. She paused at the threshold, remembering the faces turned toward her as she processed down the aisle, the nods and smiles and mouths whispering, "Beautiful," when she passed by each row, her father keeping in slow step with her, his eyes fixed ahead with tears dampening his cheeks, Mara and Charissa and Becca smiling at her from the front steps, each holding a bouquet of daffodils and a pair of sensible shoes. She saw her nieces toss their white rose petals and felt again her own bare feet treading upon the petals' softness as she moved closer and closer to Nathan, who, when her father gave her hand to him, pressed his lips to her fingers before turning with her to face the cross.

Dearly beloved . . .

"You okay?" Mara whispered. Hannah nodded. Weeks ago the room had overflowed with exuberant spring blooms and cascading white ribbons; now it was dark and somber, a place of mourning, not rejoicing. Like her own soul. "I'll sit here in the back and pray," Mara said, and patted her on the shoulder. "Take your time."

Thanking her, Hannah moved toward the first prayer station, where, on a cloth-draped table, a painting of Pilate washing his hands was positioned beside a towel and a basin of water similar to the one they had used for foot washing at Meg's. Hanging on the wall behind the painting of Pilate were robes, each one pinned to a painted fist and billowing above the heating vents. "Crucify him!" screamed the words scrawled in angry font above each fist. The whole scene pulsated with fervor and rage. *Crucify him!*

Hannah sat down in front of the table and read from Matthew 27 the story of Pilate questioning Jesus, offering to release Barabbas in his place, and then washing his hands of the whole ordeal when the crowd made their demands that Jesus be crucified. "Do you not hear how many accusations they make against you?" Pilate asked him. But Jesus gave no answer. "Not even to a single charge," Matthew wrote, "so that the governor was greatly amazed."

Hannah shifted in her seat. Maybe she should have ignored the persistent prompt to come to New Hope. The melancholy mood of the prayer journey would only amplify her grief, not alleviate it. And she had already pondered Jesus' silence before his accusers, back when she first became aware of rumors circulating at Westminster about her integrity. She had already prayed for the grace to die to her reputation, to keep Jesus company in his silence and his refusal to defend himself. It still hadn't done her much good. No matter how hard she tried, she still couldn't let it go, still couldn't move beyond the sting of Nancy avoiding her in worship, of refusing to offer forgiveness and be reconciled.

Unable to sit before the billowing, accusing robes any longer, she rose and walked toward the next station, where she chose not to linger or kneel before the mirrored cross. She didn't want to dwell on words like "envy" or "vainglory," didn't want to rehearse the ways she continued to feel wounded and slighted by Westminster's speedy replacing of her. She didn't want to think about how her resentment over Nathan being in touch with Laura had festered the past couple of days, causing her to lash out with retributive, taciturn reserve whenever he tried to communicate with her about other issues. *Please don't punish me with silence,* he'd entreated her multiple times. But she couldn't help herself. She was more afraid of the damage she might inflict on their marriage if she spoke her uncensored thoughts and feelings than if she kept those thoughts and feelings to herself.

After pausing only briefly in front of the reflection about Simon of Cyrene, Hannah approached the fourth prayer station. Near the place where she and Nathan had lit their unity candle and offered their promises to one another stood three dead trees secured in five-gallon buckets with duct tape and rocks. Draped through the bare branches of the trees was a long black cloth, at the top of which was painted the silhouette of a weeping woman. Blue beads and crystals representing tears hung from the branches, and at the base of one of the trees was a puddle fashioned from turquoise tulle.

Jesus Speaks to the Weeping Women, the sign read. Beside it was the Scripture text:

And there followed him a great multitude of the people and of women who were mourning and lamenting for him. But turning to them, Jesus said, "Daughters of Jerusalem, do not weep for me, but weep for yourselves and for your children. For behold, the days are coming when they will say, 'Blessed are the barren and the wombs that never bore and the breasts that never nursed!' Then they will begin to say to the mountains, 'Fall on us,' and to the hills, 'Cover us.' For if they do these things when the wood is green, what will happen when it is dry?" (Luke 23:27-31)

Hannah's visceral reaction to both the visual representation and the text was so overpowering, she sat down. *Blessed are the barren . . .* The phrase arrested her and would not let go. *Blessed are the barren.* She reached into her bag. Much as she had avoided the intimacy of journaling the past several weeks, she knew she couldn't fully process her response if she didn't write it down.

Tuesday, April 7
8:30 p.m.
I've studied this text before. I've preached this text. I know why Jesus is calling the barren women "blessed." When the devastation comes upon Jerusalem and the temple is destroyed, people will be distraught with grief. In that day of destruction and terror, it will be easier for the ones who don't have to watch their children suffer. Mothers will long for death to come quickly rather than watch their children starve or be tortured. "Blessed are the barren and the wombs that never bore and the breasts that never nursed." I can exegete the text and marvel at Jesus' compassion for suffering mothers and weeping women even as he's heading toward his own grueling death. His care and concern for the grieving in the midst of his own agony astonish me. His suffering never made him nearsighted. That's extraordinary.

But as has been true so many times these past few months, a single phrase grabs me, stirs me, confronts me, and demands that I pay attention to why I'm so agitated and upset by it. "Blessed are the barren and the wombs that never bore." I want to argue with Jesus and say, No. It's not a blessing to be barren. It's never a blessing to be barren. The women who long to be mothers, who would give anything to give birth to a child, you can't say they're blessed just because they won't have to endure their children's suffering. Being barren is its own particular heartache. Don't tell me, Jesus, that it's better this way. I don't want to hear it.

Over and over again I rehearse the same wounds, don't I? I'm like Rachel weeping for her children and refusing to be comforted. How long do I go on grieving the loss of my womb? Now that I have a husband, my barrenness devastates me in an even deeper sort of way, in a way I've tried not to think about and haven't wanted to talk about. And I don't know when I'll be free of it, Lord. I see Charissa's protruding belly, and I pray your blessing on her. Again. I imagine Laura's protruding belly, and I say, It's not fair, Lord. Again.

Loss after loss after loss. I think of my mother grieving all of those miscarriages years ago, and I understand in a new way her impulse to want the mountains to fall on her. Sometimes the pain is so great that you just want it to end. You don't think you can endure one more loss, one more trauma, one more devastation. I was about to write, I know my losses are nothing compared to some people's losses, but I'll stop right there with the measuring and comparing and say simply that I'm grieving. Still. So I string my tears to the branches of those desolate trees and watch them drip into the pool of gathered sorrow. I add my tears to the tears of the barren and the bereaved, to the ones who weep day and night wondering when relief will come.

"Blessed are those who mourn, for they shall be comforted."

When, Jesus?

I'm not ungrateful, Lord. I'm not. I know I need to keep rehearsing my thanks for all the blessings of abundance you have poured out to me these past seven months. Lavish blessings. I'm grateful, Lord. I am. But if I don't also offer you my lament, I know my sorrow will become toxic. I don't want to become toxic with bitterness and resentment.

And I feel bitter and resentful about so many things right now. I'm sorry, Lord. Forgive me. Cleanse me. Deliver me. Heal me. Please.

I know people could look at my life and say, Why are you so downcast? You've got a wonderful husband—and he is—and a lovely stepson—true—and a place to live with people who love you. All true. I think of women who would give anything for my life, give anything to be loved by a Christian husband the way Nathan loves me and is patient with me. I think of Mara, even, and everything she's going through and think, why I am so downcast? What's wrong with me?

But I can't fake joy, Lord. What I have right now to offer you is sorrow. Gratitude, too, but also sorrow. I miss my Meg. I miss my work. I miss my space. I grieve what was. I grieve what will never be. I grieve.

But I'm not the only one who grieves. I sit and stare at these dead trees watered by tears and find myself strangely comforted at the thought of being part of a community of the brokenhearted and the disappointed who keep watch for redemption. For resurrection. Blessed are those who mourn, for they shall be comforted.

Let that be true, Lord. Not just for me. For all of us.

Charissa

When Charissa finished revising a paper shortly after eleven o'clock that night, she turned on the television to check the Michigan State score. The clock on the national championship game in Detroit was ticking down, and it didn't look good for the Spartans. John would be crushed.

She hit the power button on the remote and flicked off the light. No way he would be home much before three o'clock in the morning. Good thing he hadn't lost his knack for pulling all-nighters. That would serve them well with a baby.

Her abdomen tightened in a contraction, and she winced, waiting for it to release. She needed to call and schedule their childbirth classes. Learning some breathing techniques might help her with the discomfort of these Braxton—

Oooof!

Charissa doubled over with a searing cramp. That was new. She tried to take a deep breath but couldn't get her diaphragm to fill. Maybe a warm bath would help relax her muscles. As soon as she could stand upright again, she filled the tub with warm water and lowered herself in, trying to extend herself comfortably. No use. The tub had not been designed for tall pregnant women. For once in her married life she wished she were at her in-laws' house. Their guest bathroom had a large whirlpool tub. Maybe she would let John have his new deck and hot tub too.

Oh!

Another cramp. She tried to swivel onto her side but couldn't manage the maneuver. She started to count off seconds. Ten. Twenty. Thirty. Sixty. Ninety. One hundred. She needed to get out of the bathtub and check online to make sure this type of thing was normal at twenty-six weeks. But the pain made her dizzy, and she wasn't sure she could lift herself out of the tub. *Drain the water.* She should drain the water in case she passed out. She pulled the plug and listened to the gulp and gurgle of the water circling down the drain.

Deep breath, she commanded herself, and don't pass out. Get to a phone. Get to a phone. *Please, God. Get me to a phone.*

Hannah

Though Nathan had teased her about it on more than one occasion, years of 2 a.m. phone calls had conditioned Hannah to keep her cell phone on her nightstand in case someone needed her in an emergency. Like Becca. Or Mara.

Or Charissa, who sounded frantic and frightened when she apologized for calling after midnight. She hadn't been able to reach Mara, she said, and John was still two hours away, and the online medical sites said she should go to the hospital to be checked out, just to be safe. "Because I think they might be real contractions," she spluttered, "and John says I have to go. He wants me to go. But I don't know if I can drive myself, the pain gets so bad."

As she had done on so many other occasions over the years, Hannah dressed in a hurry. This time, however, there was someone at the house to pray for her when she left. "Let me know if there's anything else I can do," Nathan said before kissing her goodbye.

There wasn't much else to do, except watch and wait and try to soothe Charissa with a non-anxious presence. Or at least the pretense of one. When a disheveled John skidded into the room at 3 a.m., Charissa was hooked up to an IV drip for fluids and a monitor to measure contractions. "You're okay, baby," John said. "You're okay." Hannah wasn't sure if "baby" referred to Charissa or to Bethany. To both, perhaps. "What's the latest, Riss?"

She shrugged, her eyes clenched tight, whether in an attempt to fight back tears or to endure another contraction, Hannah didn't know. John, who had evidently researched such things, began asking questions about dilation and effacement. When Charissa did not reply, Hannah repeated what the attending physician had said. "They're still trying to get labor to stop. So far the contractions are spread out at about fifteen minutes, and she's not dilated at all."

"That's good," John said. "Not being dilated is good."

Charissa, eyes still closed, murmured, "This can't be happening." She had murmured the same words all the way to the hospital in the darkness of Hannah's car. "This can't be happening."

John kissed her forehead and stroked her hand. "Don't worry, Riss. You'll be okay. Everything will be okay."

But whether this was a declaration of faith or a denial of terror, Hannah didn't know. "I'd be happy to pray with both of you."

John nodded. "Thanks, Hannah," he said, and bowed his head against Charissa's shoulder.

It hadn't been that long ago, Hannah thought as she pulled out of the hospital parking garage an hour later, that she and Meg had rushed Charissa to this same hospital after John was injured playing football. They kept her company in the Emergency Room, and only after Charissa was summoned to see John did Meg disclose that she had once staggered through those same doors to meet a chaplain who gave her the news that her beloved husband, Jim, was dead.

It hadn't been that long ago—though it felt like a lifetime—that Hannah had raced through those same doors with Becca after Meg collapsed at the airport. "She'll be okay, right?" Becca repeated again and again on the terrifying ride from the airport to the hospital. "She'll pull through, right?" Hannah couldn't remember what she had replied.

"I'll be praying for you," Hannah had promised John and Charissa when she said goodbye. But when John said again, "Everything will be okay," Hannah did not echo that reassurance. John hadn't seemed to notice.

Wednesday, April 8
9:30 a.m.
Maybe journaling two days in a row means I'll get back into a rhythm of processing my life with God in these pages. I've felt so desolate. So dry. Writing feels like taking a long drink from a neglected well. Why do I forget? Why do I avoid the practices that are good for my soul?

Especially when I'm feeling so much disequilibrium in every area of life. I'm sorry, Lord. Restore my soul. Please. I've been so out of sync with you, with others. I've been so consumed with my own grieving and losses that I haven't had energy to pour into anyone else. The midnight call jolted me awake, not just physically but spiritually. I am reminded—again—that our sorrow, our suffering is communal. Even when we feel so alone in it.

I keep thinking about John's insistence that "everything will be okay." I think what he meant every time he said it was, "Nothing bad will happen because we're trusting God." I remember being there years ago, believing that God would prevent every kind of suffering if I trusted him. "Daddy fix!" That was my image for God because that was my image of my dad. That was the image that had to die.

Maybe Meg's death is still too raw for me to approach any situation like Charissa's with hope and confidence in God's power. Maybe I expect things to go wrong because I'm still smarting from God not healing Meg, or at the very least, giving her more time. Giving us more time. Maybe I've seen too much over the years, presided at too many funerals for infants, sat at too many bedsides of dashed hopes.

I know you invite me to trust you as Redeemer, Lord. Not to expect you to be the God who fixes broken things or prevents the brokenness from happening but to trust you to be the One who redeems broken things, makes your presence known in the midst of all that is broken, and keeps us company as we grieve. You do make all things well. Like Julian of Norwich's prayer. All shall be well. And all shall be well. And all manner of thing shall be well. Someday. No matter what.

"All shall be well" means that even if I make my bed in Sheol, God is with me. It means that even if I dwell in the remotest part of the sea, even there God's right hand upholds me. It means that even when we walk through the valley of the shadow of death, we don't have to be afraid—not because nothing bad will happen to us in this life but because God is with us in anything and everything that happens to us in this life. Somehow, everything that happens to us in this life can form and shape and prepare us for life beyond this world as well.

In the meantime, Lord, please show your kindness to Charissa and John. Please show your love and care and power. Watch over little Bethany. Continue to knit her together in health and wholeness. Reveal your glory, Lord, in all these things. I don't presume to know what your glory will look like. But help us trust you. No matter what.

Being at New Hope last night helped reorient me to the cross. That's what I needed. I need to keep working with the Spirit to move against my desolation into consolation and hope. So I've decided to go with Nathan to the silence and solitude retreat on Holy Saturday. I know a day of retreat and meditation will be good for my soul, even as part of me continues to resist. Meet me in my resistance, Lord, and move me forward, deeper in my life with you.

Mara

When Mara discovered Charissa's frantic voicemail seven hours after she left the message, she kicked herself for having turned off her phone overnight. Leaving the boys to figure out breakfast and pack their lunches, Mara returned to her room, wrapped herself in her favorite afghan, and called for an update. John answered Charissa's phone. "They're saying 'high risk,'" he said, his voice quivering with emotion. "She's dilated to two centimeters, and the contractions are hitting every few minutes. They're trying to stop her labor, slow down the contractions, but . . ."

"Oh, John." All of Mara's babies had gone full term, even late. She knew nothing about preterm labor or premature babies. She had only seen pictures of little ones lying in incubators or cradled in the palm of a hand, hooked up to wires and tubes. She'd heard horror stories about complications and defects, with weeks and months spent in neonatal intensive care units and tens of thousands of dollars in medical bills. If the babies even made it that far. *Oh, God.*

"They're giving her steroids to help strengthen Bethany's lungs, but her cervix is thinning out. And there's nothing they can do to get everything to close up and thicken again. She's two centimeters and sixty percent effaced right now." He paused. "No. Seventy. Charissa just said seventy."

Jesus, help. "What can I do, John?"

"Nothing. If everything goes well, they'll keep her here for a couple of days, then send her home."

"Are you still in the ER?"

"No, they've got her in the labor ward now." His voice broke, and Mara waited in the awkward silence for him to pull himself together and say something else. He did not.

"Is she up to having a visitor? I'd be happy to come by and sit with you guys. If you want company."

John repeated the offer to Charissa, then said, "We're okay for now, thanks. But if you know of any prayer chains . . ."

"I'm on it." She had activated them for Meg. She'd activate them again. As many as she knew in Kingsbury and beyond. "And if you think of anything else I can do . . ."

"I'll call you."

"Give her a hug from me. And one for you too."

"Thanks, Mara. I will."

Mara leaned back in her rocking chair and stared out the window at brown thatched yards beginning to green. Across the street in Alexis Harding's perennial garden, golden daffodils—the frilly kind with long noses—collectively bowed their heads in rows. They looked like they were praying. A whole community joined in prayer. That's what Charissa and John needed. To be wrapped in a community of prayer. Mara would begin by calling the prayer coordinator at church, and then she would let the people at Crossroads know. Ever since Charissa's fainting episode in the kitchen, some of the guests had become concerned about her. They would want to know she was in labor. They would want to be with her in prayer. They would want to pray for the baby. For baby Bethany.

"Hold on there, little girl," Mara murmured. "Hold on."

Becca

Why Hannah thought it necessary to let her know Charissa was in the hospital in premature labor, Becca did not understand. "Please keep her in your thoughts," Hannah had written in her email. It was the sort of thing her mother might have done, asking her to pray for someone she hardly knew. The larger purpose of the email, however, was to pin Becca down on the dates she would be "flying home."

What home could she return to? All that awaited her was the shell of a musty old house crammed with stuff that would remind her of everything she had lost. Maybe she should just tell Hannah to get rid of all of it. Or sell it. Becca didn't much care. All the things she thought she would want to do after her mother died—like returning to Kingsbury so she could sort through her mother's life, organize pictures, and visit her grave before going to Paris for the summer—now held no appeal for her. At all. She needed to move on with her life, not get stuck fixating on the past. Living in the past wasn't good for her. Move forward. Move on. That's the sort of advice she had heard her grandmother give her mother many times.

"I think I'm going to tell Hannah I'm not coming," she said to Simon, who was typing away on his novel. Ever since returning from Paris, he had spent every waking moment glued to his computer. "Simon?"

He did not look up from his screen. "Hmm?"

"I said, I think I won't go back to Kingsbury when the semester ends. I think I'll just come straight to Paris with you."

He raised his eyebrows and glanced up at her. "That's not what we planned."

"I know, but there's no reason for me to go. Hannah can take care of everything." That was no doubt why her mother had put Hannah in charge: Hannah could be counted on to take care of all the details Becca did not want to be bothered with. She tried to squeeze in beside him. He shut the computer screen. "What?" Becca said. "What's the matter?"

"Nothing." He reached into his pocket for another cigarette.

"You don't act like it's 'nothing.'"

"I'm right in the middle of a scene, Rebecca. I really don't have time to discuss your travel plans right now."

Fine. They would talk about it later. In the meantime she would reply to Hannah and let her know she had changed her mind about flying to Kingsbury at the end of the month. She skimmed Hannah's email one more time. *I'm keeping you in prayer,* Hannah wrote. *I hope you're doing okay.*

Becca was fairly sure Hannah's definition of "doing okay" would be different from her own. But if "doing okay" meant making decisions to suit herself rather than other people, then she was doing just fine.

Charissa

Viable, the doctor said. At twenty-six weeks the "fetus" was "viable." While John visibly bristled at the clinical comment, Charissa was more focused on the best-case-scenario details of what would be required of her in order to give Bethany the greatest chance of making it to full term. "Bed rest," the doctor said. "That's the best remedy. As little movement as possible." There was no way to reverse what the contractions had already accomplished. They could only try to stop the labor from going further. That was the best case scenario. Worst case? She wasn't even going to think about it.

"You can do it, Riss," John said once the doctor left the room. "I'll help."

Be bedridden for three months? Three and a half, if you calculated full-term pregnancies at forty weeks. She was going to have to do nothing but stare out a window or up at a ceiling for three and a half months?

"You can read. Or watch movies. Or do research for your garden."

"There won't be a garden," Charissa said. "I won't be able to plant anything." It seemed an odd thing to feel upset about, given their circumstances at the moment, but her eyes brimmed with tears. And what about her classes? Her teaching? Her students? She still had three weeks left of classes to teach. And they had done nothing to prepare for a baby. The room wasn't ready. The clothes weren't bought. They hadn't even put together a registry or had a baby shower yet.

She stared at columns of marked drawers filled with syringes, needles, and masks.

"Charissa?" John said. She turned her head toward him. "It'll be okay. Everything will be okay."

She wished he would stop saying that. Everything was not okay. So many things were not okay. She winced as another contraction seized her.

Not okay.

eight

Hannah

The Maundy Thursday service at Westminster had always been one of Hannah's favorite services of the year: the Scripture passages focusing on Jesus' last hours, the acapella singing of "When I Survey the Wondrous Cross," the gradual extinguishing of candles and dimming of lights until the entire sanctuary was plunged into darkness, into silence.

As she sat beside Nathan at Wayfarer's evening service, her thoughts wandered to a little church in rural Ohio where she had served as an intern her second year of seminary. They had finished the Maundy Thursday service by ringing the steeple bell thirty-three times, once for each year of Jesus' life. But before each bell tolled, the long attached rope lashed and cracked with a violent snap. By the end of the tolling, Hannah was in tears. She wasn't the only one. It was as though they had traveled across two millennia to hear the ruthless strike of a whip against the bruised and beaten flesh of the man from Galilee.

Nathan reached for her hand as a soloist began to sing: *O sacred Head, now wounded, with grief and shame weighed down, now scornfully surrounded with thorns, thine only crown: how pale thou art with anguish, with sore abuse and scorn! How does that visage languish which once was bright as morn!*

Hannah fingered the nail she had picked up from a basket outside the sanctuary. At the end of the service, they would be invited to come forward and drop the nails at the foot of the cross. But first they would be invited to come forward for foot washing in remembrance of Jesus' command to love one another. She would not go forward. She could not bring herself to offer her feet to a stranger when Meg was the one who had washed them right before she died. That was the memory she wanted to cherish, the memory of being loved and served in such a poignant way. She was not ready for a new memory to be layered upon the old.

The lights dimmed further at the second stanza, with more voices blending in melancholy harmony: *What thou, my Lord, has suffered was all for sinners' gain; mine, mine was the transgression, but thine the deadly pain. Lo, here I fall, my Savior! 'Tis I deserve thy place; look on me with thy favor, vouchsafe to me thy grace.* The lyrics brought to mind the mirrored cross at New Hope and the cushion where Hannah had chosen not to kneel. Perhaps the prayer stations would still be set up on Saturday for the silence and solitude retreat. Perhaps she would take time to kneel and meditate on Christ taking her place.

What language shall I borrow to thank thee, dearest friend, for this thy dying sorrow, thy pity without end? O make me thine forever; and should I fainting be, Lord, let me never, never outlive my love for thee.

Amen, Hannah whispered. Amen.

———୧୨

Thursday, April 9

10 p.m.

I was worried that I would sit at Wayfarer tonight and lament the ways the Maundy Thursday service wasn't like Westminster's. Instead, I was able to enter into the beauty of what was offered, even as it was different from what I loved for fifteen years. Tonight's service was another opportunity to be reoriented toward wonder and awe at the suffering of Jesus. "What wondrous love is this?" we sang together. What wondrous love, indeed. And when we sang the final verse, I wept. Because as we sang, I was reminded that beyond the veil, beloved voices also testify to the truth: "And when from death I'm free, I'll sing on, I'll sing on, and when from death I'm free, I'll sing on; and when from death I'm free, I'll sing and joyful be, and through eternity I'll sing on, I'll sing on; and through eternity I'll sing on."

I've spent so much time the past couple of months thinking about death—not just physical death but all of the ways I've been invited to die—that maybe I've lost sight of life and resurrection. I know that grieving all of the losses in their full power has the capacity to enlarge me, not diminish me. And I do want to be enlarged, Lord. I want to experience the depth of suffering and sorrow so I can also experience the joy of resurrection and life. You are the Resurrection and the Life. Keep reminding me. None of my losses end in death but in life.

Something significant is shifting in my spirit. I perceive it, a move from desolation toward hope as I fix my eyes on the cross and meditate on your victory and love. Hineni, Lord. Here I am.

Charissa

It wasn't the way Charissa had expected to spend Good Friday, still hooked up to an IV and a monitor. She had expected to serve alongside Mara at Crossroads. She had expected to attend an afternoon worship service at the university chapel. She had expected to fix another dinner as part of her bet with John. And as long as she was counting off expectations . . .

She had expected to finish her semester strong. She had expected to use May and June to prepare for the baby. She had expected her pregnancy to be straightforward. She had expected to carry their baby to full term. She had expected.

She stared at her hand, where bruises from unsuccessful IV prods had darkened. She ought to be grateful, grateful that they had managed to stabilize her, grateful that she had not yet given birth, grateful that she could go home and sleep in her own bed. But she was too disappointed to be grateful.

"Mom said she was on bed rest with Karli for a few weeks," John had unhelpfully offered that morning.

Well, "a few weeks" was not ten or twelve or fourteen. And John's younger sister had not been born premature. So if Judi thought she understood what Charissa was going through, then she was wrong. No one could understand unless they were experiencing all the losses she was experiencing right now.

John entered the room with a sandwich from the cafeteria. At least he hadn't gone for fast food again. "You want a bite?"

Charissa shook her head. She would be getting a tasty tray of dry, stringy chicken and one of those mixed fruit snack cups any minute. Yum.

"Hannah called while I was downstairs, wanted to know if she can help with anything once we get home. I told her we'd let her know."

Charissa did not reply.

"And I told Mom again that we really can't handle company right now, even though she's desperate to help." Charissa had told her parents the same thing. Having them in town would stress her out even more. If John could keep up with the shopping and cooking and Mara could help with cleaning and the occasional meal, as she had offered, then they could keep both sets of parents at bay by reassuring them that they had everything covered. "And it's not like you'll have to spend every moment lying in bed. You'll be able to sit in a chair and read or write or do online shopping or—"

Charissa covered her eyes and exhaled loudly. It wasn't his body, wasn't his time, wasn't his life, wasn't his responsibility. He couldn't possibly understand what she was feeling. No matter how hard he tried.

Mara

Mara was stirring a pot of tomato soup on the stove at Crossroads when Hannah entered the kitchen. "What are you doing here?" Mara exclaimed. She was so surprised to see her that she nearly dropped the ladle.

"Well, I know Charissa has been helping out, and I didn't want you to be down a volunteer."

Mara removed her gloves so she could hug her friend. What a gift to have Hannah back! "Thank you," she said. "Thank you so much for coming."

Hannah reached into the box of plastic gloves on the counter.

"Hairnet too." Mara pointed toward another box. As Hannah tucked her hair behind her ears and covered it with the mesh, Mara noticed there was some light in her eyes again. "You look good. Rested or something. Like a shadow got lifted." Amazing, the change since she had last seen Hannah at New Hope. Maybe her prayers had made a difference for someone after all.

"You're right," Hannah said. "I can feel it." She clasped her gloved hands together and stared at the stove. "So point me in the right direction. What can I do to help?"

"Can you chop some carrots and celery for the salad?"

"Sure," Hannah said, and reached for a knife.

"I've put her on every prayer list I can think of," Mara said as they set the food out half an hour later. "I told John I'd help with cleaning and cooking, but I guess it wouldn't hurt to get them on the church's list for meals, if they do that sort of thing." Mara wanted to do everything she could to help, but she was strapped for cash. It would be hard to supply more than a meal or two each week. Not that John had asked for help. Until their bet, he reminded her, he had always done all of their cooking.

Hannah placed some tongs beside the salad bowl and straightened a pile of napkins. "Nate says Wayfarer has a meal coordinator. He'll call and let them know it's going to be a long haul."

If they're lucky, Mara thought. The longer, the better.

"Where's Miss Charissa?" Billy, one of their regulars, asked as he ambled into the dining room. "She ain't sick again, is she?"

He obviously hadn't heard the news through the grapevine yet. "Miss Charissa is in the hospital. Her little baby tried to come early."

Billy whistled and rubbed his crewcut back and forth. "Poor little baby. It don't know it's not done cookin' yet." He fumbled around in his coat pockets and pulled out a crumpled receipt. "You take somethin' to her for me?"

"Sure," Mara said.

"You got a pencil?"

Hannah reached into her purse and pulled out a pen.

"Thanks." He sat down at one of the round tables and scribbled something on the scrap, folded it in half, and gave it to Mara. "Tell her Billy's praying for her, okay?"

"You bet."

He tilted his head back and sniffed the air. "Tomato soup today?"

"Yep."

He looked at Hannah and said, "Miss Mara makes the best soup."

"Yes, she does."

"You one of her friends too?"

"I'm Hannah." She reached out her hand to shake his. "Nice to meet you, Billy."

He thrust his nose into the air again. "You got those cookies today too, Miss Mara?"

"Not today, I'm afraid. Sorry."

He looked disappointed. "Ohh. Those are good. I like those cookies."

"Mara's famous snickerdoodles?" Hannah asked.

"Yeah. Knew it was some funny name."

Mara made a mental note to buy the ingredients. "I'll make them just for you next week, Billy."

"All for me?"

Mara laughed. "Not all for you, but I'll make them because of you. In honor of you."

"In honor of me?"

"Sure. Why not?"

"You hear that, Joe?" he said, bumping another regular patron with his elbow. "Miss Mara's making cookies in honor of me."

"What kind? Chocolate chip?"

"You like chocolate chip cookies, Joe?" Mara asked as she filled his bowl with soup.

"Yes, ma'am. My mom used to make us kids chocolate chip cookies. I used to lick the batter right off the spoon."

"I used to let my sons do that too," Mara said.

"My mom always left the chips on the beaters for me," Joe said. "I liked that. Haven't had chocolate chip cookies in a long time."

"Well, I'll make snickerdoodles in honor of Billy next week and chocolate chip in honor of you the week after that. How's that?"

Joe lit up with a toothless grin. "If I get here early, can I lick the batter?"

"I'll save a little bit for you, okay?"

"Okay. Deal."

Like wildfire word spread through the line that Mara was making cookies in honor of people. "Tell you what," she said, after half a dozen guests made special requests for their favorite kinds, "I'll talk with Miss Jada and see about having a whole bunch of cookies some week, okay? Lots of different kinds to choose from." She'd made her dozens of assorted Christmas cookies for Tom's office for years. Why not do something similar for Crossroads?

"Like an all-you-can-eat buffet restaurant!" Ronni said. "The kind where you can keep going back to the dessert bar for as much as you want."

What a great idea! She could bake more than cookies as a treat for them.

"I wish we could do something like that, Mara," Miss Jada said when they were cleaning up the kitchen after lunch, "but there's no extra money in the budget."

"What if we get donors?"

"Donors for cookies? I don't know how many people would give money for that."

"Just for the ingredients. Like we got that time before." Mara didn't mention that she'd discovered Charissa had been the anonymous donor. "I'll figure out how much it would cost to make what I want to make. And then we'll have a big celebration."

"A celebration of what?"

"No special occasion. Just a celebration of them. To make them feel special." If Billy and Joe and Ronni and the others could have one place where they knew that they were important, that they were seen, that they were known, that they were loved, then it was a start.

Miss Jada sighed. "I love your spirit. If you can figure out how to make it happen, I'll leave that up to you."

"I'll help," Hannah said after Miss Jada left to take a phone call. "I think it's a wonderful idea."

"It's a start." Mara eyed her reflection in the microwave. Beloved. Favored. And chosen to bear Christ. What a beautiful thing. "At least it's a start."

—☙

Half an hour before Tom was scheduled to pick the boys up for the weekend, Mara found Kevin sprawled on his bed. "You packed?" Mara asked, picking up an empty bag of Doritos off the carpet. Bailey followed her with his nose to the ground, scouting for nacho cheese fragments. "Kevin?" On top of a chair piled high with rumpled clothes—dirty or clean? who could tell?—was his empty duffel bag. She nudged his foot. "Hey. You gotta get going. Your dad'll be here soon."

Kevin rolled over to face the wall.

"Kev . . ." Bailey vaulted onto the bed and licked his hand.

Kevin didn't acknowledge either one of them.

"I said your dad—"

"I know, okay?"

"Okay. You know he doesn't like to wait." If the boys weren't ready on time, Mara would be the one blamed for it, and she wasn't up to a confrontation with him. She nudged Kevin's foot again. "C'mon, Kev." Tom wasn't the only one on a schedule. She had promised Abby she would babysit so that Abby and Jeremy could have a night out together before her parents arrived on Saturday. They needed time together, just the two of them.

Kevin, his face concealed in the crook of his elbow, said with a muffled voice, "Why do I have to go?"

It was the first time Kevin had ever voiced any objection to spending a weekend with his father. "Because it's your dad's weekend. And I know he looks forward to being with you." For all of Tom's faults—and they were legion—he had always been devoted to spending time with his two sons.

"Yeah. Right." The scoffing noise Kevin made when he said these words startled Mara. Though she knew he had been upset about something when Tom dropped him off two weeks ago, Kevin had never confided any details. She figured maybe they'd had an argument. Kevin, with all his teenage bravado, could be moody and sensitive, and Tom didn't tolerate it. *Stop being such a sissy,* Tom had barked at Kevin many times over the years. *What are you, a momma's boy?* He'd never accused Brian of that. Brian had never been and would never be a "momma's boy."

Mara sat down on the edge of the bed. What were the chances of her resolving this before Tom showed up in the driveway? "You wanna talk about what's going on with your dad?"

"I just don't want to go."

"But you have to."

"Just tell him I'm sick. Tell him I'll cough all over Tiffany and her kids and get them all sick."

Ahhh. So it *was* about the girlfriend. She reached out and placed her hand on his dry forehead. "You do feel a little bit clammy. I'm thinking you're running a fever. And is your throat sore?"

He swallowed hard and said, "Yeah."

"Well, then. I think you'd better stay home this weekend and get better so you don't miss any school next week."

When he rolled over again to face the wall, she thought she heard him mumble, "Thanks."

It wasn't a tactic that would work long term. But when Mara texted to say Kevin was sick and was concerned about getting a pregnant woman and her kids sick, Tom replied with a single word: Okay.

She felt like running a victory lap. With a single text she had managed to communicate that she knew all about the pregnant girlfriend, and she had done so in an ostensibly reasonable and court-appropriate manner. As soon as Brian was out the door, she returned to Kevin's room, where he was sitting at his computer watching some comedian on YouTube. "All set," she said. "Your dad seemed fine with it." She didn't tell him that his father never even bothered to ask for details or that he didn't seem upset about the change of plans. "How's your throat?"

"Better." He clicked the pause button on the video.

"Glad to hear it." She sat down on the edge of his bed. "We don't have to talk about it now, but we'll need to talk, okay? I'll need to know what's going on with your dad so that I can help you." Try to help, anyway. There was only so much she could do to negotiate around the court settlement.

Kevin nodded without looking at her. If he knew she would be his advocate, then that was also a victory. "I was just going to make myself a frozen pizza before I go babysit Maddie. Want some?"

"Yeah, okay," he said, and pressed play.

Charissa

The first thing Charissa noticed Friday night after John helped her up the front stairs and into the house was that the rug on top of the hardwood floor in the family room had been carefully vacuumed into the precise sawtooth pattern she prized. "Thought you would notice that," he said when she thanked him. "You want to lie on the couch for a while or head back to bed?"

She wasn't tired and couldn't bear being horizontal again. "I'll sit here."

John pulled the ottoman toward her. "Then put your feet up." She obeyed. "Hannah said there's a recliner at Meg's house that they can bring over."

Charissa did not want Meg's cancer chair. "This will be fine."

"But a recliner would be so much better for you. You've got to make sure you're—"

"Resting. I know. But I can't have you treating me like an invalid. I won't survive that." If he hovered around her for the next however many weeks, she would go crazy. Helping was one thing; monitoring her every move was another. She couldn't live under that kind of intense scrutiny, not from John, not from his mother, not from any other well-meaning, concerned friends. She had heard the doctor's instructions. She knew what was at stake. She knew that every hour, every day, every week that Bethany could remain in the safety of the womb meant a better chance for her health and survival outside of it. She knew that. And if someone called into question her level of activity, it would be like calling into question her level of commitment to her child. She wouldn't tolerate that. Not from anyone.

"What can I bring you?" he asked. "Something to drink? Something to read?"

"My laptop."

"You're not going to work on—"

"The doctor said I couldn't do physically taxing things. He didn't say anything about not doing work for school."

"But you can't go back to—"

"I know that, okay? I'm not going back to my classes. I'm not going back to teaching. But I'm still going to write the lectures and grade the papers and finish my own assignments for the semester. I'm supplying the substitute with everything they'll need to teach the class well." As far as Charissa knew from her email and phone interaction with Dr. Gardiner, the substitute had not yet been decided on. But she had been reassured that there was no reason why she couldn't continue to work from home. She would finish the semester, and she would finish it well.

John retrieved her computer and brought her a tall glass of water. "Thanks," she said.

"Yeah."

While he sat down on the couch to check his phone, Charissa opened her inbox to find dozens of new messages, most of which were inquiries about her health from peers, faculty, and students. Why couldn't her body be her own business? She had no desire to supply details or answer probing questions. And though many of the messages contained well-intentioned expressions of care, she knew that some people were simply being nosy. She clicked her mouse on one from an unfamiliar address with the subject, *Coordinating meals.*

> Hi Charissa,
>
> My name is Stacy Jones, and I'm the food ministry coordinator at Wayfarer Church. We've received word that you are in need of meals for the next few months, and I'll be taking care of setting up the schedule. Please let me know if there are foods you cannot eat or do not like so we

Charissa slammed her laptop shut. "Did you call Wayfarer?"

John looked up from his phone. "Call Wayfarer?"

"Yeah. Did you call the church and put us on some list for getting food?"

"No."

"Well, somebody did."

"I asked Mara to help by getting us on prayer chains but—"

"Why would you do that?"

"Do what?"

"Ask her to recruit people I don't even know to be praying?"

"You were there in the room when I asked her to."

"I didn't hear you say that, John. And I wouldn't have asked for it." Why in the world would she want strangers knowing her business?

"It's for prayer," he said. "It's what people do. They ask for prayer."

"Not from absolute strangers, they don't." It was bad enough that the grapevine at Kingsbury University had made her private affairs public knowledge. And now to have people at Wayfarer—people she did not know—spreading word about her being on bed rest and recruiting strangers to come to the house to deliver meals? No. Not okay.

"I think you're overreacting, Riss. It's not like people are sitting around constantly talking about you. It's just prayer. And food. That's all."

There were people who loved posting every intimate detail of their lives on Facebook, people whose newsfeeds vomited information. She wasn't one of them. And this felt like a deep violation of trust. Just as she was about to continue her rant, the doorbell rang. *Great. Now what?*

John jumped to his feet and opened the door. "Hey, Mara!"

Speak of the devil, Charissa thought, and then immediately felt guilty for assigning such a label to her. But the timing was interesting.

"I can't stay," Mara said. "I'm on my way to babysit Maddie, but I just thought I'd come by and drop these off." She entered the room carrying a bouquet of tulips. "How're you doing?"

Charissa shrugged.

"Here," John said, reaching for the flowers, "I'll put these in water. Come sit down."

Mara sat on the edge of the couch. "I can't stay long. Just wanted to drop by and see you, let you know I'm praying for you. Lots of folks are praying for you."

"So I hear." Though Charissa heard the terseness in her own voice, Mara didn't seem to notice.

Reaching into her pocket, Mara pulled out a crumpled little slip of paper. "Here's a note for you."

Charissa read it, heat rising to her face. *Dear Miss Karisa, So sorry to here about your little baby. Get better soon. Love, Billy*

"Crossroads Billy?" Charissa said.

"Yeah. He was worried about you, wanted you to know he's praying for you."

"You told Billy?"

Mara nodded. "He was first in line today, hoping there would be snickerdoodle cookies, so I told him I'd make them special for him next week to honor—"

"How many others?"

"What?"

"How many others at Crossroads know about this?" Charissa made a sweeping motion with her hand toward her abdomen, her lap, her whole body.

Mara looked confused. "About what? About you having to be on bed rest?"

John entered the room and placed the vase of tulips on the end table beside Charissa. Then he signaled with his hand for her to calm down.

No. The fury within her billowed. "Did you tell everyone at Crossroads?"

Mara fiddled with her bracelets. "I uh . . ."

"They all know, don't they?" Charissa gripped her knees and leaned forward. "Do you have any idea how it makes me feel to think that the whole homeless population of Kingsbury now knows about—"

"Charissa," John murmured.

"—me being alone here during the day and—"

"Charissa," he said a little louder.

"Here I am, not knowing who could track down an address and—"

"Charissa, stop." He stared at her, his mouth half open.

Mara looked as if she'd been slapped. "I'm sorry." Her eyes welled with tears. "I'm so sorry. I didn't mean to cause any harm."

"It's fine, Mara," he said. "Everything's fine. But I think maybe—"

"Yeah. I'll go." She rose slowly to her feet and cast Charissa a mournful, apologetic glance. "I'm so sorry. Please forgive me. Me and my big fat mouth."

Without replying, Charissa turned her face away.

Hannah

"I'll call Charissa and apologize to her," Nathan said when Hannah finished recounting what Mara had told her in tears on the phone. "I'm the
one who called Wayfarer to ask about the meals."

Hannah shut the dishwasher and selected the light wash cycle. "Because I asked you to, Nate." She sighed and leaned back against the
kitchen counter. "I feel awful. I should have specifically asked Charissa
what kind of help she wanted instead of following Mara's lead. But Mara
was just trying to be helpful. She wasn't trying to violate any personal
boundaries; she was just trying to show love for a friend. She's devas-
tated by it."

Hannah had offered to go over and keep her company while she
babysat at Jeremy's apartment, but Mara had refused. She did not want
to be comforted; she wanted to punish herself. She hadn't said that directly, but it wasn't hard to read between the lines. "I guess it's a really
painful reminder to all of us," Hannah said, "not to assume what love
looks like." She kicked herself again for emailing Becca the news. She
never should have violated Charissa's privacy like that. Not even with
one person.

Though Hannah had not said this to Mara, she had listened to the
story with some measure of sympathy for Charissa. She wouldn't want
her private business broadcast widely without her permission either,
even for the purpose of prayer. Like Charissa, she preferred to dispense
personal information on a need-to-know basis, under careful control.
But unlike Charissa, Hannah told herself, she would not have lashed out
at Mara as if she had deliberately betrayed her. She would have hidden
behind a smile and told her that everything was fine, that she wasn't
upset at all. Just like she had done with other friends over the years. Hide.
Conceal. Deny. And then try to get over it.

Maybe, she thought as she wiped down the kitchen counter, maybe
Charissa and Mara had a better chance of authentic reconciliation because they each knew something was badly broken.

"Shep?"

"Yeah?"

"Come sit for a minute, will you? I'll finish cleaning up later."

Something in Nathan's tone unsettled her. She wrung out the dishcloth and draped it over the faucet before sitting down at the table across from him. He reached for her hand. "Laura called."

She stiffened. "When?"

"When you were on the phone with Mara."

"And?"

"And she came into town early. She wants to meet with me tomorrow."

"Tomorrow? What time?"

"Around lunch."

"But we're supposed to be at New Hope together for the retreat day."

"I know. I'm sorry. I tried to put her off to next week, but she wants to see Jake on Easter. And I'm not going to let her see him until I've met with her face to face. So it's got to be tomorrow."

"I'll go with you." She could skip the silence and solitude day. She had plenty of days with silence and solitude.

He shook his head. "Not a good idea. Not for our first meeting."

"But we talked about this, how we need to be a team, to stand together against her!"

Nathan stroked her wedding ring. "I know. And we will. But tomorrow it just needs to be the two of us, trying to work things out for Jake."

He was right, of course. She knew he was right. "Does Jake know?"

"Not yet. I'll tell him when I pick him up at Pete's. In fact, I'll probably take him out for ice cream, if that's okay with you."

"Yes. Of course." She didn't need to be a third wheel in that conversation either.

He leaned forward. "Thank you."

"For what?"

"For wanting to come with me and for understanding why you can't. Thank you."

She nodded, cupped his chin, and kissed him.

—☙

Good Friday
9 p.m.
I've spent the last hour reviewing journal entries from the past few months while I wait for Nate and Jake to come home, particularly my entries about Laura. Here we are again, yielding to her demands. I've already written so many words about my envy, my resentment, my begrudging God's generosity to her, my struggle to pray God's blessing upon her and her husband and their unborn child because it still doesn't seem fair that she, who abandoned her marriage and her son, gets to waltz back into Jake's life even as she prepares to welcome another child into the world.

And I hear the whisper of the Spirit, again, reminding me that what I want for myself is grace. Abundance. And I'm invited to desire that for others as well. Not fairness. But grace. The "unfairness of grace."

I read again my pondering about what it would mean to wash Laura's feet and how that question led us to give up our Holy Land trip—a trip we would have been leaving for in three weeks—because she threw a fit about not being consulted. I read my words about what love looks like, about what dying to self looks like, about what turning the other cheek and offering the cloak and walking the extra mile looks like.

It occurs to me that what each of those things has in common is the going beyond what's demanded. Take more. Here's more. You want to slap one cheek? Slap the other one, too. You want my tunic? Take my cloak, too. You demand one mile from me? I'll walk the extra one.

It's all about freedom, isn't it? The first mile is demanded. The extra mile is freely given. Only the extra mile can be given as a gift of love, from a posture of freedom. And so that's the mile where Jesus' life shines brightly. That's the mile that can stun the world with its beauty and grace.

That's where I want to walk, Lord. In freedom. In the power of your Spirit. In love. But it's so hard to keep company with you in all the deaths to self. It's so hard to embrace your call to love, to sacrifice, to trust, to persevere in hope that death is never the end with you. To believe that in all of these dyings there are also risings.

Tonight you invite me to keep company with the disappointed and the hopeful, to remember the ones who kept watch with you as you died, who were crushed and perplexed and heartbroken. And uncomprehending.

Watch and pray, you say. Help me watch and pray.

Mara

The good thing about trying to soothe a crying baby for two hours, Mara thought, was that the little one's frantic sobs could distract you from indulging your own. When Madeleine finally wore herself out, Mara laid her down in her crib and watched her sleeping baby twitches. Poor little lamb.

The front door opened, and Abby poked her head into the room. "Everything okay?" she whispered.

"Yes, fine. She just conked out."

"Cried the whole time?" Jeremy asked from the doorway.

"Not the whole time." Mara bent over to kiss Maddie's forehead, then stepped aside so Jeremy and Abby could also kiss her goodnight.

"Thanks for taking care of her," Abby said, closing the door with a gentle thud behind them.

"Any time. You know that. Any time." Mara retrieved her coat from the couch. "When do your parents get in tomorrow?"

"Late afternoon. If you'd like to join us for dinner, you're welcome."

What a kind offer. "Thanks so much. But I'll let you have that time together. Kevin's home this weekend, and I'll be gone most of the day tomorrow for a retreat so . . ." Not that Kevin would want to spend an evening with her, but she wanted to be home. Just in case there was an opportunity for conversation.

"Kevin is welcome to come too," Abby said. "Just let us know. You think he'll want to come to lunch with us after the baptism?"

Mara hadn't even thought that far ahead. What were the chances she could persuade Kevin to come to church with her on Easter? She couldn't remember the last time one of the boys had come to worship. "I don't know. I'll ask him."

Jeremy was staring at the floor, shuffling one foot back and forth across the carpet. Much as she longed to probe and ask him how he was doing, she kept her mouth shut. Her big fat mouth that had gotten her into trouble again. If Jeremy knew she had told Charissa and John and

Hannah about his struggles and Abby's worries and their financial stress and his previous battles with addictions, what would he say to her? Would he explode like Charissa? Would he feel betrayed? She had only wanted other people praying for him because she loved him so dearly. She had only wanted other people praying for Charissa and John because she loved them dearly too. She hadn't meant to hurt anyone.

"You okay, Mom?" Abby asked. When Jeremy looked up, the sorrow and despair in those hazel eyes of his shattered her heart again.

"Yeah, I'm fine. Thanks for letting me spend time with Maddie." There was so much more she wanted to say, but if she didn't get to her car soon, Jeremy and Abby would have front row seats on an emotional geyser erupting, and it wouldn't be pretty. After kissing both of them goodbye, Mara hustled to the apartment parking lot, where, behind the protection of her tinted windows, she let it all go.

Kevin was watching a movie in the family room when Mara entered through the garage. "Hey," she called.

"Hey," he called back, his eyes fixed on the television.

Bailey trotted into the kitchen to greet her and flopped onto his side. He would need a walk. Without taking off her coat, she grabbed the leash off the hook. "I'll be right back. Gotta take Bailey out."

"Already did."

"You already took him out?"

"Yeah. He had to go, so I took him for a walk."

Mara stared at the back of his head.

"And yeah, he pooped. So I cleaned it up."

She looked at Bailey, who was now wagging his tail in anticipation of another outing. She gave him a treat instead. "Thanks, Kev."

"Yep."

She hung her coat up in the closet. "What are you watching?"

"*Bourne Identity.*"

"Want some popcorn or something?"

"Yeah, okay."

She grabbed a bag from the pantry, tossed it into the microwave, and hit the timer. As the bag inflated and the kernels popped, she practiced her mirror reflection discipline again: I am the one Jesus loves. He has chosen me and will never reject me.

No matter what, she added. She wiped her eyes with the back of her wrist. *No matter what.*

"Here you go," she said, making sure she didn't block the television screen when she handed him the bowl.

"Thanks." She was just about to retreat to the kitchen when he said, "Have you seen this movie?"

No. She hadn't. "Is it good?"

He shrugged. "I like it." Tires screeched and sirens blared in a chase scene. "You might like it." Without saying another word, he slid over a couple of inches on the couch, eyes glued to the screen. Sitting down next to him, Mara dipped her hand into their communal bowl and ate.

Part Three

Rolling Away Stones

When the Sabbath was over, Mary Magdalene, Mary the mother of James, and Salome bought spices so that they might go to anoint Jesus' body. Very early on the first day of the week, just after sunrise, they were on their way to the tomb and they asked each other, "Who will roll the stone away from the entrance of the tomb?"

But when they looked up, they saw that the stone, which was very large, had been rolled away.

MARK 16:1-4

nine

Becca

Since Simon insisted on spending the entire weekend working on his manuscript at the flat, Becca decided to spend the entire weekend ticking off more boxes of must-see London treasures, including one of Degas's famous paintings of ballerinas, a poster of which had hung in Becca's room since high school. Miss Kennedy, her longtime ballet instructor, had given her the gift after she danced the part of Giselle. "Like a gossamer thread floating across the stage," Miss Kennedy had raved. "Pure poetry, Rebecca."

Remember? Becca nearly said aloud as she stood in front of the painting at the Courtauld Gallery. But there was no one to remember the triumph with her. Mom, Gran, Miss Kennedy, they were all gone. Like the dancers who had moved out of view from the painting, they had shared a brief moment on life's stage, and then they were gone. As she leaned in to examine the brush strokes, lines from a Shakespeare monologue she had memorized years ago came to mind. "All the world's a stage, and all the men and women merely players. They have their exits and their entrances."

C'est la vie, Simon's voice commented in her head. You live. You die. The end.

Her mother would not agree. Her mother would say, You live. You die. You live again. That's what her mother *did* say. On the day they laid daffodils on her father's grave, as she wept in her mother's arms, Becca had heard her whisper, "It's not the end. It doesn't have to be the end. If you could only believe . . ."

If she had only known at that moment that her mother would be gone the very next day, she never would have spent the rest of that Saturday with Simon. She would have spent that last day looking at more pictures, asking more questions, begging for more stories. She never would have accepted her mother's invitation for Simon to join them for dinner. She wouldn't have made that their last meal together. She would have insisted on changing her flight. If she had changed her flight—if she had told Simon to head back to London without her—then her mother wouldn't have collapsed at the airport. The emotional stress had been too much. The goodbye had been too hard.

Becca bit her lip as she stared at *Two Dancers on a Stage*.

You enter. You exit.

C'est la vie.

—೮

"Simon?" she called when she returned to his flat. No answer. She flipped on the light. No sign of him. On his leather chair was his computer, still open.

She checked her phone. No messages. Odd. He had insisted he wasn't leaving the flat until he'd written five thousand words, and he'd said it would take him at least eight hours to hit that mark. She had only been gone for about four.

She set her bag of souvenir postcards on the counter and picked up his laptop. She had been dying to read his manuscript. And why shouldn't she? If she was his muse, then she ought to be able to read what she had inspired. And besides. What he didn't know wouldn't hurt him. She clicked the space bar, the screen flickering to life.

But the screen was not open to the manuscript. The screen was open to Simon's instant messaging app. What filled the window were not words but a picture, a picture of a woman, scantily clad. Not a random model from a website. That would have been disturbing enough. No. This was a photo of a friend. And beneath her photo were the words, "Harriet just left. Come on over, professor."

Pippa.

Her body shaking, Becca scrolled upward through their thread, with its multiple provocative photos and text after text arranging hookups, dating back several weeks. Beginning, in fact, the week Becca had buried her mother. On the day she was wearing her mother's gown and standing in her place as Hannah's maid of honor, Simon and Pippa had been together. One smiling photo taunted her more than any other: the two of them in front of the Eiffel Tower.

Becca closed the screen, backed away from the chair, and staggered to the bathroom, where she knelt on the cold linoleum, her head suspended above the toilet, and heaved.

She wouldn't mention Paris, she thought as she rinsed out her mouth. If she mentioned it, Simon and Pippa would know she had invaded their privacy. She wasn't even sure how she could confess to seeing the first photo, except to say that his computer was open to it. Maybe she had arrived right after he left, and the screensaver hadn't yet concealed it.

Becca splashed water onto her face and wiped herself dry with her sleeve.

There was a Manet painting at the Courtauld Gallery—a painting they had studied in her art history class—of a forlorn barmaid staring forward, both her back and her view reflected in a mirror behind her. "Stand in front of it," a docent had said to a small group of visitors, "and see if perhaps you're in the place of the man whose reflection you see in that corner there. He's likely asking for more than a drink." Becca had watched the tourists take turns looking squarely at the woman. "See the bowl of oranges on the counter in front of her?" the guide continued. "Manet routinely associated oranges with prostitution in his paintings. The girl is not only a barmaid but a commodity. Something to be purchased. Used."

She yanked her clothes off the hangers and thrust them into two grocery bags. With any luck she would be gone before Simon returned from their rendezvous, and he could wonder why half the closet was empty. Or not.

Love? No, he had never claimed to love her. Becca had never asked for such a declaration. Not with words. She thought his body had declared it, thought his passion had spoken it. But the texts and pictures were evidence that he had communicated nothing to her that he hadn't also communicated to Pippa. And likely to others.

Oranges. She ought to buy some oranges and put them in a bowl.

Hadn't she felt shamed by the appraising stares and the overt propositions on the dinner cruise? Hadn't she seen her own reflection in the boat window and heard her mother's voice pleading? Hadn't she?

She hadn't been purchased, no. She had given herself freely, completely, without reserve, with naïve trust.

She set his key on his dresser, picked up her bags, and shut the door behind her.

Poor, stupid, duped girl.

———⌒⌒———

Somewhere between Notting Hill Gate and Holburn station—Becca wasn't sure exactly where—she stared at her forlorn reflection in the Tube carriage window and felt anger overtake her shock and sorrow. Why should she be made to feel guilty over snooping through Simon's account? She knew where Simon and Pippa were. Right this very moment. She could end this definitively, not by cowering away in anguish but by confronting.

Once she dropped off her bags at her flat, she marched down the hallway and pounded her fist on Harriet and Pippa's door. Silence. She pounded again. Silence followed by a thud and shuffling feet. "Just a mo!" Pippa's voice called. She was probably scrambling to get dressed. As soon as she unlatched the door, Becca pushed past her. "Becks!" The look of astonishment on Pippa's face morphed into casual surprise as she straightened her sweatshirt. "I thought you were at the museum today."

Becca hadn't told her that information. "Finished early." She scanned the room. Under the bed? In the closet? The bathroom door was closed. She laid her hand on the doorknob, watching the color drain from Pippa's face.

"Becks—"

"I left something here." Becca opened the door. Simon was stooped beside the bathtub, wrapped in a towel. "Ahhh," she said. "Found it."

Without waiting for explanations or excuses, she turned on her heels and left the two of them to commiserate in their shock, determined not to cry until she was out of the building and wandering the London streets alone.

You enter. You exit.

C'est la vie.

Charissa

If Charissa was forced to be on bed rest, then she might as well take advantage of it and stay in bed all day Saturday and pretend she didn't notice the disenchanted look on John's face whenever their eyes met. "She didn't mean any harm," John had said after the incident with Mara. "She was just trying to help, trying to show love."

Okay, fine. But still.

Rain pelted the windowpane, blurring the view outside. Good. The greening of the earth only taunted her. Though Judi had offered through John to plant her garden this year, there was no way she would accept. It could lie fallow. Or bloom with what had already been planted. She didn't care.

"Can I bring you anything?" John asked, poking his head just far enough into the bedroom to be heard.

"No, thank you."

The door clicked shut again.

Nathan had called to apologize: He had stepped out of turn by contacting the church without checking directly with her, and he was sorry. He had violated her privacy, and he had been wrong to do so. *Please forgive me.* She told him she did. If Mara had called to reiterate her regret, Charissa might have listened and offered her forgiveness. She might even have confessed that she had overreacted and was sorry. But for some reason she couldn't bring herself to make the overture toward mending the friendship. Why?

She stared up at the ceiling.

Maybe she wanted to stew in her irritation. Maybe she wanted to wallow in self-pity. Or maybe—she shut her eyes tight at the dawning revelation—maybe she wanted a target for her resentment other than God.

She glanced at the clock. Soon they would be gathering at New Hope for the silence and solitude retreat, a retreat she had planned to attend. Oh, the irony. She would now have days, weeks, months to enter into the wilderness where all her familiar props were stripped away and where she could potentially experience the furnace of transformation. Or—and this was a tempting alternative—she would have days, weeks, months to whine, wallow, and brood over all that was not going according to plan.

Choose, a voice from deep within commanded. Choose well.

Silence and Solitude Retreat
Waiting for Morning

You are invited on this Holy Saturday to inhabit the threshold space between death and resurrection, to grieve the sorrows, disappointments, and losses while simultaneously rehearsing confidence in God's steadfast love, power, and faithfulness.

Today we practice waiting. Today we remember the women who waited to anoint Jesus' body, who expected to find death and who instead encountered the risen Christ. Today we offer our fragility, our confusion, and the ashes of our dreams to Jesus so that we may also discover and embrace new life in him. We wait and watch in hope.

Today we practice silence, not simply as a fast from speech but as an engagement of deep listening to God and to our own souls. We also practice solitude, not simply as a way to be alone but as a way to be fully present to God. In silence and solitude we let go of the things that keep us busy and distracted so that we can enter into a vulnerable place where God can both comfort and confront us.

As you keep silence, you may wish to meditate on one or more of the following Scripture texts:

Lamentations 3:17-26

Psalm 130

Matthew 27:57-61

Mark 16:1-4

2 Corinthians 4:7-11

May you know the presence of the crucified and risen One as you keep watch today.

Hannah

Hannah had hoped when she arrived at the retreat Saturday morning that the prayer stations would still be assembled in the chapel. Instead, everything had been stripped bare. Even the cross on the center platform, which had been draped in white for their wedding and black during Holy Week, was unadorned.

After distributing handouts with Scripture verses for meditation, Katherine stood beneath the cross to give a word of welcome and brief overview of the day. "The silence may feel awkward and unsettling," she said, "especially when practiced in community. But perhaps you'll discover a different kind of fellowship with others today, wordless communion and solidarity with those who are longing to hear God's still, small voice."

Mara, who had already warned Hannah that she felt like a geyser ready to erupt at the slightest provocation, spent the first half hour beside a window with a box of Kleenex and her Bible on her lap. Hannah, meanwhile, spent the first half hour trying to quiet the distractions and clamor in her soul. But pushing down the loud and racing thoughts about Nathan and Laura and Jake and Mara and Charissa and Becca and Westminster and all the rest was like trying to keep a beach ball under water. Though she had hoped to begin the day in wordless, unperturbed communion with God, she was going to need to use her words. She opened her journal and wrote her prayer.

Saturday, April 11
10:00 a.m.
Lord, I release all that clamors within me, all the racing thoughts, the worries, the cares and concerns, the wondering about Nathan's time with Laura, the bitterness that still grumbles within me. I don't have the power to silence the noise, Lord. So, please. With the same authority you used to silence the raging sea and the storm, silence the turmoil

within me and bring me to a place where I can be still and know that you are God.

Peace, be still! you commanded. Lord, I want to obey.

———

There, Hannah thought, as she closed her journal and leaned her head back. Something right in that moment had shifted in her spirit, from striving to rest, from clamor to quiet. Jesus had just spoken with authority, and her soul had responded. *Peace, be still.*

She breathed deeply once. And again. And again.

Peace, be still.

She was. Quite remarkably, she was. With gratitude, she offered her hushed response: *Speak, Lord. I'm listening.*

Mara

Mara wished she had a wider radius of solitude surrounding her. Between her sniffling and her growling stomach, the others near the chapel windows were probably not experiencing the gift of silence. Too bad it was raining. The courtyard would be a more private place for her to disintegrate. Or erupt.

She glanced again at the verses from Lamentations. *My soul is bereft of peace.* Yep. Katherine had told them they would likely notice the noise of their thoughts and feelings once they tried to be quiet, and it was true. Maybe she would try the palms down, palms up prayer that Katherine led for their opening exercise: Palms down, cast all your cares on him. Palms up, receive God's care for you. They had done that exercise in the sacred journey group, and she had completely forgotten about it. She was always forgetting everything she learned.

She turned her palms over again on her lap. *Lord, I release my worries about Jeremy. My regrets about Charissa. My guilt and shame and—what does Dawn call it?* She thought a moment. Self-loathing. That was it. *I release my self-loathing. And my despair. And my fears about Jeremy and Abby and Maddie moving away. And my broken relationship with Brian. Jesus, I release it all to you.*

She turned her palms up to receive God's gifts: peace, presence, hope, faith, forgiveness, mercy, grace, and the steadfast love and faithfulness God promised was new every morning. *By faith, Lord, I receive. I receive. Help me receive.*

The problem was, she so quickly returned to thoughts about her cares and concerns. Like Lamentations said: her soul continually thought of her affliction and was bowed down within her. She frequently rehearsed her trials and disappointments and needed to frequently rehearse God's faithfulness and provision. It needed to be more than standing in front of a mirror and declaring her belovedness. She needed to continually call to mind God's care and concern for her and for those she loved. *But this I call to mind, and therefore I have hope. The steadfast love of the Lord never ceases; his mercies never come to an end.* If she could keep calling that to mind, then maybe she would be able to wait quietly for the Lord to act instead of fretting her prayers all the time. *The Lord is my portion, says my soul, therefore I will hope in him.*

Portion.

That was an interesting word. She used to ask Nana for an extra portion of chicken and dumplings because that was one of her all-time favorites, and Nana would always dish out a large, generous portion. But there were many nights at home when the portions weren't large, when Mother hadn't gotten her paycheck yet and they had to scrimp by. Mother would take a very tiny portion of Spam and baked beans for herself and say she wasn't very hungry and that Mara should eat her portion. Mara believed her and ate. Double portion.

Her stomach rumbled again, and she cleared her throat to cover the noise.

What did it mean to say that God was her portion? God was a pretty huge portion, wasn't he? Not just a scraping-to-get-by sort of portion but something that filled, that satisfied, that was enough. God was enough. More than enough. *The Lord is my portion, says my soul, therefore I will hope in him.* Mara leaned her head against the window and closed her eyes, the gentle patter of the rain soothing her soul.

Hannah

1:30 p.m.

I don't think I've ever experienced silence in community quite like this before. It's one thing when you're scattered into solitary places for prayer, but when you're sitting together at round tables for lunch, not talking to anyone, it can feel pretty uncomfortable. All you hear is the sound of spoons clinking against the soup bowls or the sound of water being poured into glasses. Or throats clearing. Or you sneeze, and someone mumbles, "God bless you," and then quickly covers her mouth because she wasn't supposed to say anything, and you share this smile between you that communicates you're with one another in both the discomfort and the invitation of it all. It was actually a gift after a while, not having to come up with things to say. I felt myself relax into it and became more aware of the rhythm of my breathing, my chewing, my slow thoughts about God.

I had to fight the temptation as we finished lunch to duck into a secluded corner to check my phone for messages from Nate about his meeting with Laura. I release that clamoring anxiety, Lord, and ask that you help me return to waiting. With peace. With hope. With quiet confidence in you. "I wait for the LORD, my soul waits, and in his word I hope." That's the text I was praying with this morning: keeping watch for the dawn in dark places. I want to be like the watchmen scanning the horizon for the first signs of morning. I want to wait in the darkness, confident that God's light will shine. Not just for me. For all who wait and keep watch.

Now my attention is drawn to the text of the women going to the tomb. It's their question to one another that shimmers for me and invites me to linger with it: "Who will roll away the stone for us?"

They're on a mission. They're going to finish the act of love they had not been able to perform for Jesus after he died. They're going to anoint his body and say goodbye. But there are obstacles to the mission. They know a stone has been rolled into place—they had watched Joseph of Arimathea roll it into place against the tomb.

But it's interesting that they didn't take men with them that morning to help. Maybe they asked and couldn't find anyone to go with them. Maybe they didn't think about it until they were already on their way there—they had been so single-minded about getting the spices and anointing the body that they hadn't considered the logistics of it.

And so, in the early light of the morning, they're saying to one another, "Who will roll away the stone for us?"

That's what I need, Lord. What we need together. We need you to roll away all the impediments that keep us from seeing resurrection. We return to places of death, expecting to find death, expecting to tenderly embalm the losses. We come prepared to do so. We've got our spices and oils, and we're ready to weep. We think that what we need help with is rolling away the stone so we can grieve. But we need the stones rolled away so that we can rejoice. So that we can see again that death never has the last word.

Speak, Lord. I'm listening.

—☙

At five o'clock Katherine broke the silence by offering a prayer to commit them into God's safekeeping. "And as you carry in your mortal bodies the death of Jesus, may you also carry within you the life of the One who was crucified, who was buried, and who rose again."

Amen.

On their way to the parking lot, Hannah reached into her bag. "A little something for you." She handed Mara a piece of paper torn from her journal. "A poem. Well, not really a poem. Just some lines that came to mind today as I prayed for you. For all of us. I was thinking about death and darkness and light and resurrection and your image of the geyser erupting, and this poured out."

As Hannah listened, Mara read the short lines aloud: "'Keep watch for geysers of grace, faithful but unpredictable eruptions that refuse to be controlled or tamed. Wait. Watch. Hope. Pray. Delight in being startled and awed by the explosive force of dancing water no depth of darkness can contain.' Ooh, that's good." Mara folded the paper and put it into her purse. "It feels explosive, all right. And it would be great to think that it's grace erupting, not sorrow. Or despair. Thank you. Thanks for the reminder." She wrapped Hannah in a bear hug. "And thanks for coming today. I wasn't sure I was going to make it the whole time, but I'm glad I stayed. It was good."

"For me too," Hannah said. "It took me a while to settle in to the quiet, but once I got there, it was a meaningful time with God." Nathan had told her he usually went away for silent retreats a couple of weekends a year. Maybe she would join him, and they could share the silence and solitude together.

Mara was checking her phone, a frown tugging at her lips.

"Everything okay?" Hannah asked.

"Looks like Charissa tried to call. Hope it wasn't to chew me out some more." She pressed the phone to her ear. "Nope, didn't leave a message. Should I call her?"

Hannah wasn't sure. "Maybe send a text to say you see she tried to call, and does she want to talk?"

Mara shoved her phone back into her purse and sighed. "I don't think I can take another round of anger right now. And I've already tried to apologize. Unless you think I should—"

"No. I don't have any advice about it. Just prayers for mending."

"Yeah." Mara jingled her keys. "See you tomorrow?"

"Tomorrow?"

"For worship. Abby's getting baptized and—"

"Right! Sorry. Yes, I'll see you there." Easter. It was hard to believe it was Easter. After a goodbye hug Hannah headed to her car and checked her messages to find one uninformative text from Nathan: Can you meet me for dinner at Timber Creek at 5:30?

She replied: Be there soon.

When she arrived at the restaurant, Nathan rose to meet her at a corner booth. "Everything okay?" she asked.

He helped her out of her coat, then waited for her to sit down. "Yeah, okay. Do you want something other than water to drink?"

She shook her head.

He slid along the bench across from her.

"So? How'd it go with Laura?" In the few seconds it took for Nathan to answer, Hannah tried not to leap to any conclusions.

"Better than I expected. It took a while to get there, but in the end we managed to agree about what's best for Jake right now."

That was surprising. Astonishing, actually. Even when it was the very thing they had prayed for.

"I know," he said, replying to her raised eyebrows. "I was shocked. She even said she was willing to take it slow with him, not to try to force her way back into his life. But she wants to start building bridges with him, and I need to encourage that. So we'll start tomorrow. She's going to meet him for ice cream tomorrow afternoon."

Again, surprise. No demand for Easter lunch? Easter dinner? Going out for ice cream seemed about as innocuous a first visit as possible. "I'm stunned," Hannah said. "Given the way she's interacted with you the past couple of months, making her demands, coming off as controlling and threatening . . ."

"Yeah. I know."

So why didn't he seem elated? "Did something else happen?"

Nathan removed his cutlery from his napkin and slowly set each piece down on the table. "God held up a mirror to my life, and it was pretty humbling."

Being with Laura again after so many years, Nathan said, had stirred up old memories that he had stuffed away. Being with her—now as a newlywed again—had brought back memories of their early days together as a married couple and how he had expected Laura to fit into his life, his ministry, his schedule. Being with her reminded him of how she had become a casualty of his ego, how his need to be busy in ministry and his drive to be respected and honored and adored and needed by his congregation had impacted her. "Sitting across from her today, Shep, I saw how angry she still was, how much she still resented me. She didn't admit any of that, she didn't have to. It seeped out of her as she was ranting and demanding her rights as Jake's mother."

Hannah communicated to the approaching server that they needed more time, then turned her attention back to Nate, who was fiddling with his straw wrapper, smoothing it and then folding it methodically into triangles.

"I was about ready to shut her down," he said, his gaze still fixed on his hands. "I was ready to spit back my own venom and lash out at her for abandoning her son—our son. But then suddenly I realized that I never once apologized to her for the way my sin had wounded her. Not once. So I did. I asked her to forgive me." His voice broke. "I interrupted her, right in the middle of her accusing me of all sorts of things, and I asked for her forgiveness. She was so stunned, she couldn't speak. She just looked at me. And then she started to cry. It's like it all broke loose, right there in the booth. God broke the pattern of blame and resentment. Not only did she forgive me, but she asked me to forgive her." He removed his glasses and wiped his eyes. "It was amazing, an amazing work of God. And we moved forward from there, able to talk about what's best for Jake."

Hannah swallowed hard and rearranged her napkin on her lap. "That's . . ."

The word "incredible" caught in her throat and lodged there, scraping. She tried again. "I'm . . ."

The words "amazed," "so happy," and "so excited about what God did" bumped into "incredible" and stayed put too. She cleared her throat. "Wow," she said, and shook her head slowly.

"I know." Nathan put on his glasses, pushed aside the straw wrapper, and picked up his menu. "So much more than I'd hoped for. Why am I always surprised by the Spirit's work?"

Hannah stared at the flickering candle on the table. Yes. Amazing, the Spirit's work. Amazing, how Nate had seen with fresh clarity all the ways he had disregarded Laura in their marriage, expecting her to fit into his routine, his life, his schedule. How lucky Laura was to be the recipient of such insight and confession, the fortunate recipient of the Spirit's work.

Wow.

She straightened her silverware, then took a long sip of water. Amazing, too, how Nate seemed not to recognize that fifteen years later, he was repeating the same pattern of disregarding his wife, of expecting her to fit into his house, his life, his routine.

Wow.

Nathan glanced up from his menu and motioned to hers, still closed on the table. "Do you already know what you want?" he asked.

Oh, yes. She did. But she wasn't sure she was ready to say it out loud. "Give me a minute."

"Take your time."

She opened her menu and made a pretense of studying entrees. Amazing, how, with all of his keen powers of observation and insight, he could be so oblivious to his current wife's state of agitation. He had obviously not considered the possibility that she could be anything other than overjoyed by the Spirit's work of enabling him and Laura to move forward together, amicably cooperating for the sake of their son.

Wow.

The words blurred on the page. What did she want?

She took a deep breath. "Nate?"

He glanced up from his menu.

She set hers down. "I'm feeling really upset and angry right now."

If a restaurant booth could become holy ground, then theirs did, not because the conversation was straightforward or easy but because after speaking candid, difficult words about feeling disregarded, Hannah knew she had been heard.

"You're right," Nathan said after she laid it all out before him. "You're absolutely right. Even after you were brave to say what you wanted and what you needed, I went right on thinking you could blend in to my world if I just cleared enough space for you." He reached across the table for her hand. "I'm so sorry, Hannah. Will you forgive me?"

Since speaking too quick an answer might belittle his request, she paused. No denying. No minimizing. No disregarding his need for her forgiveness with a dismissive, *Oh, it's okay. No big deal.* Offering forgiveness was a way of admitting her hurt, a way of moving forward together in authentic and intimate vulnerability. "Yes, Nathan," she said, "I forgive you."

Mara

"A whole day of keeping quiet," Mara said to Kevin as she stirred a pot of spaghetti on the stove. "Can you believe your mother managed to do that?"

From his barstool at the kitchen counter, Kevin smiled slightly but did not reply.

"Well, I didn't think I could do it, either. Gotta say, it was pretty weird sitting with a whole bunch of people at lunch and not saying anything to each other. Not sure I would do it again, but it was a good experience for a day." She emptied a can of tomato sauce into a pan and set the burner to medium heat. "Hear anything from your dad today?"

"Nope." Kevin did not seem upset about this. But it was odd that Tom never even bothered to text him to see if he was feeling better. Maybe Tom knew he had been faking it. Maybe Tom knew and didn't care.

Mara decided to pry. What did she have to lose? "You wanna talk about the real reasons why you didn't want to spend the weekend with him?"

He shrugged.

"If something happened, maybe there's something I can do to help." Or maybe there was something her attorney could do to help.

"I just didn't feel like hanging out with him, that's all."

"You sure?"

"Yeah."

She'd try one last time and then leave it alone. "When you got back two weeks ago, you seemed upset. That's why I asked."

He looked down at his phone and typed something. "He was being a jerk."

"To you?"

"Just a jerk."

"Did he say or do something to hurt you?" If he had, she would take care of it. Immediately.

"Nah . . . nothing like that."

"Like what, then?" She gave the spaghetti another stir and then set down the spoon to give him her full attention. When he did not reply, she said, "You can trust me, okay? I've gotta know the truth about what's going on so I can help you."

He scratched at a pimple on his chin. "He promised to take Brian and me to Hawaii this summer. That's why he bought me the surfboard at Christmas." Mara had already suspected that. She figured Tom had planned some expensive holiday for the boys, a way of continuing to win their affection. "But now he's taking Tiffany, and he said we couldn't go."

"Tiffany and her kids?"

"Nope, not the kids. Just him and Tiffany."

How romantic.

"They're getting married there."

Of course they were. Tom had done plenty of other things that had taken her by surprise. This was not one of them. "When?"

"Sometime in July."

Uh-huh. He was giving the divorce what? A few weeks to be final? "When's her baby due, do you know?"

He shook his head. "But she's like, huge."

Nothing ventured, nothing gained. "Has your dad said whether"— *Go for broke,* she told herself—"whether he's the father or . . ."

"Tiffany says he is, so yeah. I guess."

Uh-huh. She ought to be furious that Kevin knew that detail. Paternity test "gotcha" moments from Jerry Springer episodes came to mind. Given her own past with Tom, Mara knew she wasn't someone who could throw stones; Kevin had been her "gotcha" pregnancy. But at least Tom was the only one who could have been his father.

"I'm sorry, Kev." No wonder he hadn't wanted to spend the weekend with his dad. He'd been betrayed. Replaced. "Wish I could do something to make it up to you."

He didn't answer, but he also didn't vacate the barstool. When the tomato sauce began to spit in the pan, she turned down the heat and stirred. "What about Brian? What does he think of all this?"

"He doesn't care. Dad says he's taking all of us to Disney World instead. That's all Brian cares about."

Brian wanted to go to Disney World? That was surprising. "Your dad's taking all of you? As in all Tiffany's kids too?"

"Yeah. And I told him I don't want to go."

"What'd he say to that?"

"He got mad, said I have to, that it's part of the rules or whatever."

Mara wasn't sure about that. "I'll check, okay? I don't know if he can make you or not. But, Kevin?" He looked up at her. "I'll be your advocate, all right? If there's anything I can do, I'll do it. I promise. And I'm sorry. I'm really sorry."

She thought she heard him mumble, "Thanks."

After dinner Mara pored over her temporary custodial order documents. There was no way to know for sure until she spoke with her attorney, but it looked like they could appeal with a judge if they needed to. If Kevin felt that strongly about not going out of state with a new stepmother and her kids, then maybe a judge would grant his request. Tom was entitled to his vacation time, that much she understood, but he also was required to give her written notice when he intended to take the boys out of state. She would remind him of this by email so she had it for the record.

"What does it say?" Kevin asked when he entered a few minutes later with Bailey trotting beside him. He hung up the leash on the hook and gave the dog a treat from the jar on the counter.

"I'll call my lawyer on Monday to double-check." She wasn't going to get his hopes up about a judge listening to him. She might be reading it wrong. "But maybe the first thing for me to do is tell your dad you don't want to go. Are you okay with me doing that?"

"Yeah."

"If I do that, he'll know you talked with me about it. You're okay with that?"

"Yep."

She wouldn't have the conversation with Tom face to face—that didn't feel safe—but she would email him after he dropped Brian off tomorrow night. That way she would have a record of his response if she ever needed it. And if he said no way, then she could let him know she was pursuing it with her attorney.

Kevin sat down on the edge of a chair, still wearing his coat. "You're okay with it?"

"With what? Emailing your dad?"

He nodded.

"Yep," she said. "I'm okay with that."

"He'll get mad."

Mara patted his hand. "It's all right. We've got to work these things out." She would ask some friends to pray. Maybe that would be her excuse for calling Charissa. On second thought, asking for prayer might stir up Charissa's resentment about the prayer chains.

"Can you drive me over to Michael's house?" Kevin asked. "He's invited a bunch of us over for laser tag."

"Sure." She had one more question to ask, a question that had been swirling around in her mind all day. "Say . . . Abby's getting baptized at church tomorrow, and since you're home this weekend, I wondered if you'd like to go. For Easter. And then we're all going out for brunch afterward."

He leaned over to rub Bailey's back. "Yeah. Okay."

Really? She did not voice her astonishment or squeal her delight. She simply said, "Okay, cool," and tried to remain so.

Becca

What was meant to be a short walk to catch her breath and collect herself after confronting Simon and Pippa ended up stretching into hours. Mile after mile Becca walked. She walked across bridges and along the river and through parks and down medieval alleyways. She walked past museums and churches and government buildings and squares filled with monuments. And then, since she felt desperate for some kind of link to her mother, she walked to the hotel near Russell Square.

No one was standing at the welcome desk, and the dining room was dark. Becca hesitated at the threshold, staring at the table where the two of them had shared pots of tea, the table where she'd first seen the ultrasound picture and her father's card, the table where she had announced she wanted to spend her twenty-first birthday not with her mother but with Simon in Paris. Not knowing what else to do, she sat down and tried to imagine her mother sitting with her, comforting her. Because one thing her mother had never said—one thing her mother would never say—was, "I told you so."

"Hello? Someone there?" The overhead lights switched on, and Becca squinted, the glare harsh after an hour spent in the dark. "Oh, hey," Claire said, her expression softening in recognition. "I was just getting ready to lock up and thought I heard something."

Becca wiped her eyes. She hadn't expected to see her again, and now Claire might assume she had come to the hotel specifically to track her down. "I'm sorry," Becca said, "I was out for a walk and got tired." She picked up her wad of tissues.

Claire sat down across from her, her coat draped over her arm. "I could ask if you're okay, but I can tell you're not. Is there something I can do to help?" When Becca did not reply, Claire said, "How about if I fix us both a cup of tea?"

They sat together in front of the unlit fireplace with their mugs, Claire listening and Becca speaking far more than she had intended. The compassion of a slight acquaintance in the wake of the betrayal by both a lover and a friend was a gift Becca hadn't known she needed when she entered the hotel lobby. "My mom knew Simon was no good, and she tried to make me see it, but I wouldn't. I didn't. I defended him. I defended us, said he was the best thing that had ever happened to me and that I wasn't giving him up just because she didn't approve."

Claire handed her another tissue.

"And now what do I do? I can't go back to my flat—not with Pippa there on the same floor. And how am I going to finish the semester?" In the course of just a few weeks her entire world had imploded. She had lost everything. And there was no restoring any of it. She wished she could just go to sleep and not wake up. Or wake up and realize it had all been a bad dream. There was nothing left. She was completely alone in the world.

"How about this?" Claire said. "How about if tonight you come stay at my flat? It's not much, but I've got a sofa you can sleep on."

It was a kind, generous offer, and Becca couldn't think of any better options. "Are you sure? I don't want to impose."

"No worries at all. C'mon." Claire put on her coat. "It's just a short walk from here."

ten

Hannah

Early on Easter morning, while it was still dark, Hannah drove to the cemetery with two bouquets of daffodils. When she arrived, the gates were open and dawn was breaking on the horizon, the purpling sky a painted canvas for intricate silhouettes of awakening trees. Meg's marker was easy to spot on the greening hillside, her tombstone not yet weathered and softened by time, her epitaph chiseled with definitive strokes: *Beloved*. That's the one word Meg had requested, along with part of a single verse, from Luke 24:5. "Why do you look for the living among the dead?"

A reminder, Meg had said to Hannah after she submitted her memorial service notes to her pastor. *A reminder for anyone who might come to visit.* Like a daughter, Hannah thought as she laid one bouquet on Meg's grave and the other on Jim's. Or a grieving friend.

A reminder.

While mourning doves cooed to one another in the trees, Hannah rested her hand on the cold granite and whispered her prayer.

Becca

She couldn't avoid the inevitable forever. While Claire got dressed for church on Sunday morning, Becca formulated her strategy. She would confront Pippa first and then compare her story to any rubbish Simon might attempt to feed her when she confronted him. Unless, of course, the two of them had already conspired to make their stories match. Maybe there would be no discovering the truth.

"I'll be praying for you," Claire said when she hugged her goodbye on the sidewalk half an hour later. Becca thanked her, not for the prayers but for the place to stay. She hadn't slept well, but at least she had slept some.

As she walked past the British Museum, she texted Pippa: We need to talk.

To Becca's surprise, Pippa replied: Okay.

Just after eleven the two of them met at the garden café at Russell Square, Pippa avoiding eye contact by staring into her coffee mug while Becca interrogated her. As the photos indicated, their liaison had begun after Simon returned from Chicago. They had run into each other one night at the Cat and Mouse Pub. He was lonely, Pippa said, and he didn't know how to handle everything. When Becca asked what "everything" meant, Pippa said, "You know, you freaking out over your mum dying and everything."

If they had been alone in a room, Becca might have shrieked her astonishment and anger. But surrounded by other patrons, she commanded herself to keep it together. "Whose idea was it?"

Pippa did not reply.

"Whose idea?" she demanded, her voice becoming more shrill.

"His." It was only going to be a one-off deal, Pippa insisted. She had only planned to offer him a bit of comfort, a bit of fun to take his mind off of everything. But then . . .

Becca waited while Pippa stirred her coffee with a spoon. "I know about Paris." Pippa's head shot up, her expression horror-struck. "Whose idea was it, yours or Simon's?" Pippa looked like she was trying to determine the safest answer to give. Becca snatched the spoon from her hand. "I said, whose idea?"

"His. It was his. He said he needed to do some research for his novel, and he didn't want to be there alone, so . . ."

"So he asked you to go with him?"

"Ummm . . . I can't remember if he asked directly or if it was just implied, but I said yes. I mean, it was Paris, right? And you were still in the States."

"For my mother's funeral, Pippa! For my mother's funeral! And for her best friend's wedding." Becca flung Pippa's spoon down on the table and grabbed her purse from the floor.

"Becca, wait! Stop! It wasn't serious at all."

And that was supposed to make things better? Easier? "That's your excuse? That's your apology?"

"Becks, I'm sorry."

Becca threw up her hand. "Save it. Just save it."

Cockamamie. That's the word her grandmother would have used for Simon's side of the story. Becca stared out her window blankly, replaying their brief phone conversation. Pippa had flung herself at him, he claimed. She had gotten him drunk and then taken advantage of him.

"And Paris? Did she get you drunk and shove you onto the Eurostar?" He hadn't replied.

"My mother knew I was too good for you," she'd said before hanging up on him. "She was right."

Her mother had been right about everything. If only she could tell her that she was sorry. If only she could tell her that she regretted not listening. If only she could hear her mother's voice say, "I know, honey. I know." But the only voice Becca heard was her own, chiding her for being such a stupid, gullible girl.

Mara

"Christ is risen!" the pastor called from the front of the sanctuary.

"He is risen indeed!" the congregation responded.

The pastor stepped toward the baptismal pool. "As the church has done since its earliest days, we celebrate baptism on Resurrection Sunday, rejoicing in God's promises and the work of the Holy Spirit to draw people to Jesus Christ. Baptism is the sign and seal of God's promises to his covenant people. By God's grace, he forgives our sins, adopts us into the body of Christ, renews and cleanses us with his Spirit, and raises us up to eternal life. All of these trustworthy promises are made visible in the water of baptism."

He swept his hand through the water and then let it slowly drip from his cupped palm into the pool. "Our Lord Jesus Christ declared, 'All authority in heaven and on earth has been given to me. Go therefore and make disciples of all nations, baptizing them in the name of the Father and of the Son and of the Holy Spirit, and teaching them to obey everything that I have commanded you. And remember, I am with you always, to the end of the age.' We celebrate and give God thanks for these new disciples who today publicly declare their faith in Jesus Christ, even as we remember the waters of our own baptism and give God thanks for the ways he has marked us as his own, by his grace."

It had been years since Mara had taken time to remember the waters of her own baptism, which took place not on an Easter Sunday but on her twenty-fourth birthday. On that day she stood before a congregation with four-year-old Jeremy, who watched wide-eyed with his thumb in his mouth while his mother, robed in white, knelt in a trough as the water was poured out upon her, running down her hair, her face, her shoulders, a steady stream until she was soaked right through. And when the preacher helped her out of the trough, someone handed her a towel and, with a kiss planted on each wet cheek, said, "Welcome to God's family, Mara."

Jeremy probably wouldn't remember any of that. She hadn't done a good job remembering herself. Maybe she should buy a pitcher and a bowl as a reminder. She could buy one for Abby too.

"Beloved of God," the pastor said, "you stand before us today to receive the sacrament of baptism . . ." Abby, dressed as the others were in white, looked as if she were getting ready to say her wedding vows again. With the same earnestness in her voice as on the day she offered her promises to Jeremy, Abby spoke her yes to Jesus Christ. And when she rose up from the water, spluttering but beaming, her face was shining. It wasn't just the sanctuary lighting. Abby looked radiant. "She's beautiful," Mara whispered to Jeremy, who nodded and repositioned Madeleine on his lap. Mara squeezed her little foot. As Abby dried off with a towel and followed the other newly baptized to change out of their wet clothes, Ellen whispered something to her husband.

What a special moment for them, to hear their daughter affirm her faith and offer her promise to live for Christ. "And we pray for Jeremy, our son," Ellen had said when she greeted Mara with a warm embrace outside the sanctuary that morning. *Our son.* Maybe God would hear their prayers. All of their prayers.

"Congratulations," Mara said with a hushed voice when Abby returned to their row during the final song. Abby smiled her thanks and scooped Madeleine into her arms before taking her place between Jeremy and her mother. As Abby laid her wet head against his shoulder, Jeremy draped his arm around her and sang the words on the screen with his baritone voice. Mara was surprised he knew the tune. "Crown Him with many crowns, the Lamb upon His throne. Hark! How the heav'nly anthem drowns all music but its own! Awake, my soul and sing of Him who died for thee, and hail Him as thy matchless King through all eternity." Oh, for the day when those words were Jeremy's heartfelt testimony. *Please, God. Awaken his soul.*

Kevin, who stood on Mara's right, pulled out his phone. She nudged him, and he pocketed it. He had at least feigned attention during most of the service and had seemed genuinely interested when the children went forward to hear the story about Mary Magdalene mistaking the risen Jesus for the gardener. *For all my boys, Lord. Please. Awaken them. Help them recognize you.* She wondered how Brian and Tom were spending Easter morning. Not at church, that was for sure. Sleeping in, probably. Maybe meeting Tiffany and her kids for a big brunch buffet. Brian loved brunch buffets. She hoped Tom took him somewhere that had Belgian waffles. Brian loved piling toppings on Belgian waffles. So did Kevin. Kevin would get to enjoy an Easter waffle and omelet and anything else he wanted because Abby's parents were treating all of them to a fancy brunch at their hotel, the sort of brunch Mara wished she could afford on special occasions. Maybe someday.

"Crown Him the Lord of life! Who triumphed o'er the grave, who rose victorious in the strife for those He came to save. His glories now we sing, who died, and rose on high, who died eternal life to bring and lives that death may die." Ooh. That was a good line. Amen to that. She glanced over her shoulder to the section where she'd seen Hannah sitting with Nathan and Jake. She wondered if Hannah was thinking about Meg when they sang that line. Probably. John was sitting over in that section too. Mara wondered if he'd seen her sitting with her family. Probably. They were pretty conspicuous visitors in the second row, the most racially diverse row in the whole place. Maybe her church was one of the few in Kingsbury that had so many races and ethnicities worshiping together. After worshiping there for so many years, Mara had stopped noticing. She wouldn't take it for granted anymore.

After the music finished, they remained standing as the pastor, wearing dry clothes again, ascended the steps in the front of the sanctuary and raised his arms in a blessing. "Christ is risen!" he exclaimed.

And the congregation shouted in reply, "He is risen indeed!"

When Mara and John happened to make eye contact after the benediction, Mara knew she couldn't leave the sanctuary without wishing him a happy Easter. And once she hugged him and wished him a happy Easter, she couldn't leave the conversation without asking about his wife. She switched Madeleine's empty carrier to her other hand and said, "How's she doing?"

He shrugged. "Okay. Or as okay as she can be, I guess. You know Charissa. Staying down like this is about as hard as . . . well, it's hard for her."

From the expression on his face it was clear it was going to be hard for him too. She was going to say, *Tell her hi from me, tell her I'm praying for her*, but since she wasn't sure what kind of reaction such a message would provoke, she fiddled with the smiley sun mirror dangling from the carrier handle.

"I'm really sorry, Mara, about what happened the other night. She was tired, upset, stressed. This isn't anything like what we were expecting, what we were hoping for."

"No, I know."

He laid his hand on her shoulder. "She knows she overreacted, and she's sorry about it. I think she tried to call you."

"Yeah. She didn't leave a message."

"Right. I don't know if she'll try to call you again. I think she feels pretty embarrassed about the whole thing, so maybe if you could call, check in with her sometime . . ."

"Yeah, I'll call her." That was good news, that Charissa wasn't still mad at her. "Tell her happy Easter from me, and I'll check in with her later. I'm going out with my family"—she gestured toward the front of the sanctuary where Ellen was taking photos of Jeremy, Abby, and Madeleine—"so maybe tomorrow or something?"

"Yeah. Sounds good. Thank you." John gave her another hug and said, "Christ is risen!"

Mara replied, "He is risen indeed."

"Where's Kevin?" Mara asked when she joined the others near the Easter lilies.

Jeremy motioned over his shoulder toward the baptismal pool, where Kevin stood, his hand in the water. "Just wanted to see if it's warm," he said when he saw his mother looking at him. He quickly dried off his hand on his jeans.

"Well, come on over here for a picture. Let's get a few with everyone together, okay?"

"Here, let me help," Hannah said from behind her.

"Oh, thanks, Hannah!"

"No problem." While Hannah set down her bag, Mara took her place on the steps between Jeremy and Kevin. "Everybody scooch in together," Hannah said, "Kevin, closer there by your mom, that's it. Look here, everyone." With Kevin's shoulder pressed against her and her hand resting on Madeleine's little arm, Mara looked at the camera and smiled.

Charissa

"Mara's not mad at you," John said when he entered the house with a bag of Subway sandwiches. It wasn't the Easter brunch Charissa had envisioned a week ago, but she was choosing not to complain. Gratitude was the spiritual discipline she could not afford to neglect.

"She's way more forgiving than I am." Charissa slowly shifted to an upright position on the couch and unwrapped her ham and cheese sub. She was going bland. Nothing to agitate Bethany. "So should I call her again?"

"She's out for lunch with her family. Abby's parents are in town for the baptism."

Charissa had completely forgotten about that momentous occasion. What an awful friend she was. To Mara and to Abby. "How was it?"

"Beautiful. I can't even remember the last time I saw adults get baptized. So powerful." He probably didn't mean it as a slight against First Church, but even so, she bristled.

"Infant baptism is beautiful too," she said.

"Yeah, I know. But when you get to witness a new believer going down into the water and coming up again, there's nothing like it."

She wasn't going to argue with him. Charissa had been baptized as an infant; John had been baptized as a teenager. They'd had that conversation during their premarital counseling with the Reverend Hildenberg and had agreed that their children would be baptized. John might not remember. But she wasn't going to argue. Not now. She was going to stay calm and practice letting go. Over and over and over. She had to. "You want to say grace?"

"Yeah, sure." He reached for her hand and prayed.

There was a tree outside their bedroom window, visible whenever Charissa lay down to rest, that was in need of some serious exfoliating. Her online research identified it as a river birch, prized by some for the beauty of its peeling bark. But every time she looked at it, she felt agitated, overwhelmed by a desire to march out there and rub it smooth. That was precisely what she could not do, not just because of the mandatory bed rest but because, according to the experts, stripping the bark would harm the tree. "I swear that tree is taunting me," she said when John entered the room to deliver a cup of lemon tea after lunch.

"Want me to close the blinds?"

"No. I'll still be thinking about it."

"It's just doing what it's supposed to do."

"Well, it's driving me nuts." She was surprised she hadn't noticed it when they first moved in. Maybe it hadn't been shedding then. She took a sip of tea. "Okay, maybe close the blinds." He reached for the string. "Not all of them, though. I want some sunlight." He maneuvered one side closed. But then they weren't even. "Maybe just angle the slats up a bit—yes, like that. Thanks."

He sat down on the edge of the bed. "Anything else you need?"

She had a stack of books, her computer, her tea. "No, I'm good. Thanks."

"Okay." He kissed her forehead. "I'm heading over to Tim's for a little while. They put in their new deck and—"

"Yes, I know. It's awesome."

"It is. But ours will be more awesome."

She shooed him away. "Go on. Go covet your deck."

"*Our* deck." He motioned toward the window. "If you want, we could just take that tree out, make the deck bigger."

"I'm not going to kill a perfectly good tree." Even if it drove her crazy.

"Well, then. What is it you always say about being provoked?"

"Linger with what provokes—"

"Yeah," he said, "that. Do that."

It was, Charissa realized as she finished her tea, the exact same impulse she'd identified several months ago with her urge to kick at car tires to dislodge muddy snow. She wanted smooth and pristine, not ragged and shedding. Not slow. Not passive. Would the tree eventually shed its bark? She didn't know. And even if it did, wouldn't the bark grow right back and resume its same ugly process of shedding? It was that whack-a-mole image all over again. Even if she shed some of her deeply ingrained patterns of pride, she was never going to be completely free of it. So why couldn't she be at rest in that? Why couldn't she rest in grace and yield to the slow process of becoming more like Christ?

Because she was a perfectionist, that's why, and she didn't have much hope for ever being otherwise.

If only she could be as tranquil and yielded as that shedding tree, at rest in the process of gradually letting go. If only.

She opened her computer. She had papers to write and lecture notes to prepare for her substitute. Still no final word on who that would be, but she would make sure that whoever it was had excellent content to offer the students. If she was going to be physically immobile, at least she didn't have to be intellectually so. She would make it across the semester's finish line, even if she had to do so lying down.

Mara

The hotel brunch was as lavish a spread as Mara had ever seen, with elaborate ice sculptures of rabbits and eggs and flowers adorning some of the buffet tables. "Look at the design on that egg," she said to Abby as they made their way through the line. It looked as if it had been etched on glass. Mara held out her plate for some seasoned skillet potatoes to go along with her vegetable omelet.

"All that work for such a short amount of time," Abby said. "Wonder how long it takes them to do that." She pointed out the sculpture to her mother and said something in Chinese. Ellen nodded.

"Please tell your mom how much we appreciate them treating us to all of this. It's a feast."

Again, Abby spoke quietly in rapid syllables. Ellen turned toward Mara and said, "Celebration. Thank you, Jesus."

"Amen!" Mara replied. "Thank you, Jesus." She wished she could privately communicate her desire for Ellen to pray fervently for Jeremy. She didn't want to ask Abby to translate. No need to cast a shadow of anxious thoughts over her daughter-in-law's special day. "Kevin, look at that dessert table." Beneath an ice sculpture of a woven Easter basket was a variety of layer cakes, cheesecakes, brownies, assorted cookies, and fresh fruit. "I wish I could do something like that for Crossroads."

"You could bake like that," he said.

"Yeah, but it would cost a lot of money to buy all the ingredients. I'll be stretching it just to make all the cookies I want to make."

Ellen and Abby exchanged something in Chinese, a back and forth conversation that ended with Abby saying to Mara, "My mom asked what Crossroads is, so I told her how you work there, that you cook meals for them. She says she wants to help you cook a special meal for the people there. A feast."

"No ice," Ellen said with a grin. "Food. Much food."

"Oh," Mara said, "that's very kind of you, but we don't have much of a budget for a feast. Just at Thanksgiving and Christmas." That's when the donations from the community poured in. The rest of the year was lean.

Abby said, "Sorry! I mean, my mom doesn't want to help you cook. She wants to pay for the food. Give a donation for a feast."

Mara stared at Ellen, unable to speak.

"My parents support a shelter in Ohio," Abby said. "She says she's happy to support one here too."

Mara used her free hand to tap her heart. "Thank you, Jesus!"

And Ellen added, "Amen!"

———✿———

Mara had just cleared off her plate and was contemplating a trip to the dessert table when Kevin ducked his head behind her and said, "Dad's here."

"What?"

"Dad's here." He gestured toward the end of the line. Mara followed his pointing finger. Tom, strutting like someone who used to be attractive and still considered himself to be so, had just entered the dining room with Brian, a frizzy-haired pregnant woman she assumed was Tiffany, and several small, bickering children. He took a plate off the top of the stack, his back still turned toward their table.

Mara spun around in her seat, trying to figure out if there was somewhere she could hide. But Jeremy had already gone back for seconds, and it would only be a matter of time before Tom or Brian caught sight of him. Of all the rotten—

"They see us," Kevin said. "Brian just looked over here."

Without thinking, Mara turned around. Right at that same moment, Tom also turned. Their eyes met, and his face reddened. She felt the color drain from her cheeks. Of all the places to end up for Easter brunch! And now what should they do? Brian wouldn't acknowledge her; he had already turned his back. Tiffany, her attention focused upon a little boy who was grabbing for a plate, was oblivious to any drama. And by the look on Tom's face, he wasn't eager to divulge anything. Brian nudged him forward in line, and Tom held out his plate to the woman serving scrambled eggs.

They could ignore and avoid each other. That was the appealing option. Or . . .

Maybe . . .

Mara rolled her shoulders and stood. "Want me to bring you a piece of cake or something, Kev?"

He leaned forward on his knees and pretended he was enthralled with the sleeping baby in her carrier on the floor. "No, thanks."

Breathing a prayer for help and courage, Mara timed her arrival at the dessert table to match Tom's. "The chocolate cake looks good," she said. Tom did not reply. "Hi, Brian." Brian reached for a piece of raspberry cheesecake. "No Easter hug for your mom, huh?" Tiffany, her heavily made-up eyes wide with curiosity and perhaps a bit of fear, looked first at Brian, then at Mara. No way she was even half Tom's age. "You must be Tiffany. I'm Mara. And who are these cute little guys?"

Tiffany, full plates in each hand, rested her elbow on the blond head of the oldest, took a moment, and then said with a squeak, "This is Caleb, that's Drew, and the little one's Mikey."

Three spirited little boys plus one pouty thirteen-year-old, a fifteen-year-old who wanted nothing to do with her, and a baby on the way? Mara looked at Tom's soon-to-be-wife and was overwhelmed not by anger and resentment but by pity. "You've got your hands full there," Mara said, noting the enormous diamond ring on her finger. "Can I help you carry something to the table?"

Tom looked like he wanted to strangle her with a single bare hand. Tiffany passed Mara a plate and said, "Okay. Thanks."

"Brian, help your"—Mara struck her forehead—"oh! I was going to say 'brothers,' but not yet, right? Never mind, you can still help these little guys. It looks like maybe they'd like to have some dessert too." She bent toward the littlest one, a hand on her hip. "You tell Brian what you want, okay? He'll get it for you." Brian, scowling, ignored her and turned away from the kids—two of whom were now hitting each other—to get a second plate for himself.

As Mara accompanied the waddling girlfriend and three whining children to a table at the opposite end of the restaurant, she could feel two sets of hate-filled eyes boring into the back of her head.

"Everything okay, Mom?" Jeremy said, hastening to her side. He must have only just figured out what was happening. And oh, the look of confusion on Tiffany's face! Priceless.

"Yes, hon, everything's great. Just meeting Tom's new family. This is Tiffany"—Jeremy's eyes widened as he glanced at Tiffany's enormous belly—"and these are her sons, Caleb, Drew, and Mikey. Tiffany, this is my oldest son, Jeremy. And of course, you know Kevin." She motioned over her shoulder, but Kevin was still concealing himself by attending to Maddie.

Mara glanced toward the dessert table where Tom and Brian were still deliberating. Or avoiding. This was her open door, and she was going to plow through it head down like a running back into an end zone, just like she'd seen Kevin do countless times on the football field. Evade the tackles and go, go, go! "Kevin was telling me about Hawaii, Tiffany. That sounds wonderful! And Disney World, wow! You guys excited about that?"

The little boys stared at her, and the middle one, his finger shoved up his nose, nodded.

Mara leaned toward Tiffany and said with a confidential tone, "Not sure Kevin's too keen on that, though. A little old, maybe. And it would be a shame for him to spoil the fun for your little guys. You know how moody teenagers can be."

Tiffany looked like she was taking this information to heart. Even if she didn't have prior experience with adolescent boys, she had probably spent enough time around Brian and Kevin to know how difficult they could be.

"Just a thought," Mara said. "You and Tom should talk it over, make sure you're on the same page." She held her hand up in front of Caleb and said, "Hey, bud, gimme five!" He slapped her palm hard. She pretended to be hurt, and he laughed. Then the other two clamored for the same. When she finished getting her hand slapped and feigning injury, Mara said, "Well, I'll let you all enjoy your meal together. Great to meet you, Tiffany."

Tiffany seemed too stunned to reply. But after Mara strolled away, she watched from her peripheral vision as Tiffany whispered at length in Tom's ear.

"You sure you're okay?" Jeremy asked once they were out of earshot.

Mara felt like her knees were going to buckle. She wove her arm through her son's to steady herself. "Yeah, fine." But there was no way she and Kevin were going to be at the house that night when Tom dropped off Brian. "I was so busy getting dessert for the others, I forgot to get something for myself." She let go of Jeremy and returned to the buffet. She was going to enjoy every bite of a piece of that chocolate layer cake. To celebrate Easter. And victory.

Hannah

"Are you coming with us, Hannah?" Jake asked as he put on his shoes.

No, not for the first time he saw his mother. "I think it should just be you and your dad today. I'll meet your mom another time, okay?"

"Okay."

"But thanks for inviting me."

"Yeah." He stood a few feet in front of her, posture erect, arms stiff at his side.

"Okay if I give you a hug?" she asked. He nodded. "I'm proud of you. I know this is a big deal."

"Thanks."

"Ready, bud?" Nathan asked as he entered the kitchen.

"I guess."

He patted Jake's shoulder. "Okay, we're outta here." He kissed Hannah on the cheek. "Be back soon."

She nodded and said, "Jake, how about if the three of us pray together before you go?"

Jake stared at the floor. "Yeah, okay," he said, offering one hand to his father and the other one to her.

—☙

According to Nathan, who returned home with the first report forty-five minutes later, Laura was already inside when they drove up. As he described the scene, Hannah pictured it: a mother scanning for a son she hadn't seen in years, looking in the opposite direction and not noticing that Nate and Jake were in the car watching her.

"Jake said he thought she looked nervous, and he was right. All the bravado she'd had in our phone conversations, all that was gone. She was just sitting there in the booth, fidgeting with her hands. Waiting. Watching." And for the first time ever, Nathan said, he put himself in her shoes and thought about how hard it would be to reenter a child's life, how much she had missed with him, and how that guilt must feel soul-crushing at times.

Hannah hadn't considered that either, all the gifts Laura had lost. Forfeited.

Nathan took her hand in his. "I always told myself that she abandoned Jake and didn't look back. That was the narrative that justified my resentment when she reappeared. But I never thought about her regret. And when she saw him—when she saw me walk in with him—the tears welled up in her eyes, and she raced toward him and then skidded to a stop because Jake put out his hand to greet her with a handshake, not a hug. And I saw the pain on her face, Shep, this awful agony on her face that she tried to recover from. But it was there. And even if we hadn't had that breakthrough yesterday, today would have shattered my heart. I've been saying for months that we've got this long road ahead of us, not even thinking about what it will be like for her to try to form a relationship with him."

Hannah took a deep, steadying breath. This moment was not about her, she reminded herself. It was good that Nathan was feeling compassion for Laura, good that he saw the reality of her struggles, good that he had shifted from wanting to punish to wanting to encourage. It was good.

And so hard. She didn't want to shut down Nathan's story, didn't want to say anything that would keep him from confiding his thoughts and feelings to her in the future. But oh, how hard she fought to stay deeply attentive to him while her own wounded places were tapped again.

He brushed a wisp of hair from her forehead. "Are you okay?"

She wanted to be. She wanted to rejoice and give thanks that Nathan and Laura could move forward as Jake's parents, work together for his flourishing, discuss his struggles, and find a new equilibrium as exes who didn't resent and hate one another. She wanted to be okay.

"I will be," she said, and leaned her head against his chest.

Easter Sunday
5:30 p.m.
Another opportunity to practice honesty with Nate. I didn't want to make it about me, but there was no concealing my grief, and he said he

was grateful I didn't try to hide or work it through on my own.

I told him it felt easier to me when the two of us were allies united against a common enemy. I knew how to support him in his anger because I was angry, too. And it was easier when I was the one encouraging him a few months ago to find ways to wash Laura's feet. Now that he's kneeling, I'm struggling. I hate that I'm struggling, but I am.

I should be happy they've forgiven one another. I should be grateful for God's work of healing and transformation. Instead, I feel threatened and insecure. I'm sorry, Lord, but that's where I am. Meet me here.

Nate apologized for disregarding me again, for not thinking about how this could wound me, for only thinking about the removal of his anger and the deepening of his compassion as an answer to prayer. I asked for his forgiveness for my insecurity, because that says as much about my view of him as it says about Laura. I need to trust his love and commitment to me. I do trust it. I want to trust it even more.

We pledged honest communication as we move forward, that neither one of us will conceal what's stirring in us in the deepest places. I know God can use this to shape me, to shape us. If wounds are getting tapped and are painful because of the tapping, then there remains something to be healed. Help me trust your slow healing work, Lord, and the promise and beauty of resurrection.

Becca

Becca had one visitor Sunday afternoon, Harriet, who wanted her to know that she had not been a co-conspirator in the affair. "I was as stunned as you," she said from the doorway, and then looked as if she wished she could take that statement back. "I mean, I had no idea anything was going on. I promise."

It didn't matter. In two weeks Becca would leave it all behind her, return to Kingsbury for the summer, and hope that for the rest of her life she would associate London with something other than betrayal and regret. She was determined to do everything she could to enjoy the city before she said goodbye, and that meant not hanging around her flat or wondering if Pippa was hanging around Simon's. When her phone buzzed with a text, she excused herself from any further conversation with Harriet. "How are you?" Claire wrote.

"Ok."

"Meet for tea?"

She might as well. Claire sent the address of a café near Trafalgar Square. "One hour?"

Becca wrote back, "See you there."

—☙

If Becca had known that Café in the Crypt was located at St. Martin in the Fields, she might have said no. She hoped Claire wasn't attempting to manipulate her into going to some worship service. That wasn't going to fly. Maybe she'd suggest the café at the National Gallery instead. It was just across the street.

"Hey!" Claire greeted her at the steps of the white steepled church. "I'm so glad you could come. Have you been here before?"

"To the church? No."

"They host a lot of classical concerts here, so I wondered if maybe—"

"No."

"Well, the café is lovely. Probably a bit chilly to sit outside, but the crypt is open."

Becca followed her into the back of the church and down a staircase to a room with brick vaulted ceilings and plenty of atmosphere. She was surprised she hadn't heard of it before. "They do jazz concerts here sometimes," Claire said. "Good food too."

As they made their way toward the cafeteria-style line, Becca glanced down at the floor. Tombstones? Real ones? Was this some kind of bad joke?

"You okay?" Claire asked, correctly interpreting her body language.

"When you said crypt, I wasn't thinking literal crypt."

Claire covered her mouth with both hands. "Becca! I'm so sorry. I wasn't even thinking!" She looked mortified. "Want to go outside instead? Or somewhere else? The museum? They've got a café there. Come on."

"No, it's okay. I'm okay." Becca had been in Westminster Abbey plenty of times, and it had never bothered her. But that was before—

"You sure? Because we can go somewhere else."

"No. This is cool. I'm fine."

"My treat, then, to make it up to you."

The food smelled good, and she hadn't eaten since breakfast. "Yeah, all right," she said, and she picked up a tray.

"Sorry I freaked out," Becca said as she finished off her bowl of soup. "It's just, graveyards . . ."

"No, I know. I get it. You don't have to apologize."

"It's been hitting me hard today, how I'll be going back to Kingsbury now for the summer and how I'll have to sort through all my mother's things, and I know it will hit me all over again that she's gone. Especially having to be in that house all by myself. I don't know how I'm going to manage it."

"Have you got other family to help?"

"No. No one. My mom had one older sister, my Aunt Rachel, but she's not around at all, hasn't even returned my phone calls lately, so I'm on my own." Almost immediately the words floated through her mind: *I'm a little lamb who's lost in the wood.* She bit her lip. And now there was no one to watch over her. Not Simon. Not Rachel. No one.

"What about your mum's friend, the one you mentioned that got married. Helen?"

"Hannah." She needed to email Hannah and let her know her plans had changed. Hannah had offered to help, plenty of times. In every email: *Whatever you need.* Maybe she would take her up on the offer. What other options did she have? "It's just that I had already told her I wouldn't be coming back at all, and I really don't want to have to tell her everything that happened with Simon. She's a pastor, and I don't want her pastoring me, you know? I mean, no offense—I know you go to church and everything, but I'm just not interested in hearing about God right now."

"You've been through a lot," Claire said. "I think I'd be disappointed too."

Disappointed? Is that what she was? Becca swallowed a bite of her apple crumble and said, "I think you'd have to believe in God to be disappointed by him."

—☙

They left the café as people were entering the sanctuary for an evening service. "Since it's Easter," Claire said, "I think I'll stay."

Easter. Becca had completely forgotten about Easter. Her mother had always loved Easter. That's probably why she had picked those Easter verses for her funeral and for her tombstone. *You live. You die. You live again.* That's what her mother believed. That's what Hannah believed. That's what Claire believed.

"Want to come with me, Becca?"

Had Claire not been listening? Had she not heard her specifically say she wasn't interested in church or in God? "Not my thing," Becca said. "Definitely not my thing. But you go enjoy it. And thanks for dinner."

Call it disappointment, call it anger, call it stubbornness: if Jesus himself were to stand in front of her and speak her name, Becca still wasn't sure she would believe.

Charissa

"You awake, Riss?"

Charissa rubbed her eyes and yawned. What time was it?

John sat down on the edge of the bed. "You've got a couple of visitors."

She glanced at the clock on the wall. Almost six. Had she really been asleep all afternoon?

"Mara and Kevin are here."

Mara. She rolled over quickly to get up.

"Whoa!" he said, thrusting out his arm. "Bed rest, remember? Take it easy."

Right.

Right.

"I told her I'd check on you, see if you're up for her coming back here to see you for a minute."

Charissa caught a glimpse of herself in the mirror and grimaced. How she wished she could take a quick shower and wash her hair.

"You want me to ask them to come back another time?"

"No, no, it's fine. Tell her to come. Please."

Moments later Mara entered the room carrying a wicker basket tied with pink ribbons. "Easter delivery," she said.

Grace, grace, and more grace. Charissa pushed down the lump in her throat and reached for Mara's hand. She didn't deserve a friend like this.

"Mara, forgive me. Please. I'm so sorry. There's no excuse for the way I acted toward you."

"Well, there is, actually. I should have asked you before blabbing my big mouth to everyone."

"No. John asked you to help spread the word for prayer, and you did. I need to get over myself. Truly." In so many ways, that's what she needed. Grace to get over herself. "Will you forgive me?"

"Of course," Mara said. "Forgive me too?"

"Yes."

Mara handed her the basket and kissed her on the cheek. "Just a few goodies to keep your spirits up."

"Snickerdoodles?"

"Mara's famous snickerdoodles, fresh out of the oven. And some cashews for protein. And cheese, the British kind you like."

How Mara remembered that, Charissa had no idea. "Thank you," she said, peering into the basket. "Can you stay and visit?"

"Just long enough for Tom to drop Brian off at the house. Don't want to be there when he arrives."

Charissa replied with her eyebrows.

"Yeah, I've got lots to tell you," Mara said.

Out in the family room John asked Kevin which video games he liked to play, and Kevin replied with a list. "Some of my favorites!" John said. "I've got all those."

Charissa reached into the basket for a cookie. "So," she said, offering the plate to Mara, "tell me everything."

Weekends would be easier, Charissa thought as she watched John pack up his briefcase early Monday morning. At least on weekends she wouldn't be mentally rehearsing all the classes she was missing. "You sure you have everything you need?" he asked.

She lay back on the couch and eyed her computer, the stack of books, a selection of snacks, and a pitcher of water on the coffee table. "I'm sure."

"A mug. I'll get you a mug."

She was going to say that she would get it herself but then remembered she shouldn't. This bed rest restriction was going to require far more discipline than anything else in her life up until now, and she would have to fight the temptation to cheat when John wasn't monitoring her. Keeping Bethany in mind would help with that, she hoped.

He filled a mug with water and brought it to her. "Thanks," she said.

"Call if you need anything, okay?"

"Okay."

"Promise?"

"I promise. Go. You'll be late."

He kissed her on the forehead, then stooped to kiss her abdomen. "Be good, Bethany. Stay put. Both of you."

If only it were that easy, she thought as she watched him back the car out of the driveway. She reached for her computer and skimmed through her email, aware of her continued agitation about the sheer number of people who had heard the news and were "keeping her in prayer." *Let us know what we can do to help,* a few of them said. Maybe if they really wanted to help, they could offer something specific she could accept or reject.

Judi had also written again. Though Charissa had heard John tell his mother multiple times on the phone that there was nothing they needed right now, she was evidently finding that difficult to believe. *I can be there in just a few hours. I hate feeling helpless.*

Right. Join the club.

At least her own mother was accepting the boundaries without arguing. She was busy with work but would happily rearrange her schedule if Charissa needed her, she had said. Charissa had assured her she was fine.

She was just about to close the inbox when a new email appeared from Dr. Gardiner. "Substitute," the subject line read. Charissa clicked on it, expecting to see the name of some graduate student sliding in to take her place. Instead she read, "Nathan Allen is willing to take your class. He can start tomorrow."

She exhaled slowly. That was good news. With all of his other commitments, she had never considered the possibility that he could sub for her. As painful as it was to relinquish her teaching, at least her students would be in the best possible hands. She spent the rest of the morning editing her lecture notes, emailed the document to Nathan with a word of thanks, and then polished a Milton paper until it shone. One day down, she thought as she heard John's car pull into the driveway, another seventy or eighty—God, help me—to go.

eleven

Hannah

The text from Nathan on Tuesday morning asked if Hannah could meet him on campus for lunch. He had an idea he wanted to run by her, he said, and he wanted to talk with her about it face to face. Once she finished running errands and paying bills, she headed to the university.

All along the campus walkways, gray trees were erupting in color, some bursting into pink, white, coral, or burgundy blossoms, others garbed in tentative, astonished green, as if not yet convinced of their resurrection. Swollen tulips in raised beds awaited the command to open, while white and yellow daffodils swayed in a rippling breeze. Overnight, it seemed, the earth had undergone a profound change. Even the browns of the dirt had been transformed from the sleeping brown of death to a reddening brown, a hopeful and livening brown, expectant and waiting and full of possibility.

He is risen indeed!

Nathan met her inside the campus center. "Everything okay?" Hannah asked.

"Yeah, fine."

"I thought maybe something happened with Laura or Jake."

"No, it's not that. Though she did email a little while ago to say how much she appreciated the time with him, and she looks forward to more. So we've got that to negotiate." He stared up at the sandwich board. "Give someone an inch, and they'll take a mile."

Or two, Hannah added silently.

"She says she wants to see Jake as much as possible before the baby's born. She seems to forget we agreed to take things slow, that it's important for Jake to set the pace. And Jake wants to take things slow. I think that was hard for her to hear, like maybe she expected him to love his time with her so much that he'd be clamoring for more."

Hannah fought back the temptation to be delighted about this. She should long for reconciliation between a mother and her son. She should. But she didn't. Not yet.

"Want to eat outside?" Nathan asked after they ordered. "There are some benches down by the pond."

"Perfect."

On the lawns surrounding the campus center, some students, exulting in a cloudless, sixty-degree day, tossed footballs and Frisbees in short-sleeved shirts while others lay on the grass reading. Hannah and Nathan found an empty bench beside a weeping willow, its branches sweeping the water. "So, don't keep me in suspense," Hannah said after they thanked God for their food. "What's going on?"

He opened his bag of chips. "Got a call from Neil this morning. The seminary intern, Joel, is down with chicken pox, of all things."

"Oh, no!"

"Yeah. Poor guy. He was scheduled to preach this Sunday, and Neil desperately needs a Sunday off—he's exhausted after Lent and Easter— so he was calling to see if I'd be willing to cover for him."

"That's great!" It had been years since Hannah had heard Nate preach. What a gift to be able to listen to him again.

"Well, I told him I didn't think I could do it."

"Why not?"

"Because I know someone else who would be a wonderful supply preacher, and I think she should take the opportunity." Hannah stared at him. "So what do you say? Your sabbatical's not technically over yet, but . . ."

Preach? At Wayfarer? "Did you mention me to Neil?"

"Yes."

"And?"

"He's going to call and invite you. He thought it was a great idea."

She set her sandwich down on her lap. When she said goodbye to Westminster, she'd had no expectation she could be in a pulpit again any time soon.

"Hope you don't mind me telling you first," he said, "but I thought maybe you'd want a bit of time to think about it, pray about it before he calls."

"Yes, thank you! I mean, I'm shocked. An opportunity like this wasn't anywhere on my radar."

"Well, I think it needs to be. You're a pastor, Shep. And I don't pretend to know what ministry will look like for you in the future, but you can't be anyone other than who God has created and called you to be. I say it's time to start looking at possibilities."

⸻ ☙

Tuesday, April 14
1:15 p.m.
I've been sitting here by the campus pond reading Easter season texts, trying to figure out what to preach. I've got sermons I could recycle, but I think the discipline of writing something new would be good for me. I'm a different person today than I was nine months ago, and my preaching—even my preparation for preaching—ought to reflect that.

It means so much to have Nathan's wholehearted affirmation of my call, to have him encourage me to explore opportunities, even if that means serving someday with a different congregation. He said we should throw the doors wide open and see what God does. There's something both liberating and terrifying in that. I don't trust myself to return to full-time pastoral work. That's the truth. I don't trust that all of my compulsions toward busyness and productivity and my addictions to usefulness and affirmation are well and truly dead. But I trust you, Lord. I trust your work in my life. I know your work isn't fragile. If you say I'm ready to return to preaching—even if only for this Sunday—then I say, Hineni.

As I think about the process of discernment, it occurs to me that I'm way overdue for spiritual direction. I think I've done okay with naming the losses and processing the upheaval of the past few months, hard as it's been. But I need some help naming what's rising to new life and identifying what God might be calling me to do. I've always been a sunset sort of person, better able to reflect on the past than hope for the future. I think God's calling me to be a sunrise person as well, to practice that posture of keeping watch for the dawn, like I was praying about on Holy Saturday. To be anticipatory with hope. I've practiced watching sunsets as a spiritual discipline in the past, stirred by the imagery of dwindling light. Maybe I need to practice watching in the darkness for the sunrise, waiting for that light to break forth. You call me to keep watch, to wait, to hope. More than watchmen for the morning. More than watchmen for the morning. Thank you for the glimmering light on the horizon. I see it, and I give you thanks.

Charissa

When the doorbell rang just before five o'clock, Charissa tried to see who it was without shifting too much on the sofa, but the view to the porch was blocked. Since she wasn't expecting anyone, she didn't want to invite whomever it was to simply come in. The screen door creaked on its hinges, and the visitor knocked. "Charissa?"

Nathan. "Come in!"

He entered carrying two paper bags. "Sorry! Should have called first."

"No, that's okay." She overcame the temptation to sit up and greet him properly.

"How're you doing?"

She smoothed her hair and straightened her maternity shirt. "Still here, so that's good." If she could keep her attention riveted upon Bethany's health instead of ruminating on everything she couldn't do, then the days might pass more fruitfully.

"I've got some food for you and John, one chicken casserole that's hot and another one you can freeze for later. Okay if I put them in the kitchen?"

"Sure. Thank you."

"Hannah sends her love, says she'll drop by tomorrow afternoon to see if you need any laundry or cleaning done."

Charissa smiled. "She knows me well."

"I know she's happy to help. Just make a list of what you want done, and she'll do it." She heard him rustle the bags in the kitchen. "I'll put the oven on low heat for this until John gets home and put the other one in the freezer. There's a salad here too."

"Great. Thank you so much. He should be home soon." Thankfully, John had a boss who was sympathetic and made sure he was on his way out the door by five. Not everyone was so fortunate.

"Can I bring you anything?" Nathan called from the kitchen doorway. "Something to eat? Drink?"

She hated being waited on hand and foot. So humbling. "Just some water, thanks." John had filled a couple of pitchers before he left for work, both now empty. She'd tried to consolidate trips to the kitchen and bathroom, but she still wasn't in the habit of thinking strategically. She wouldn't tell John how many times she had actually gotten up from the couch that day.

When Nathan returned to the family room, she invited him to sit down. "So how did my students do?" She had been waiting for a report all afternoon.

"Pretty well, I think. They were all very concerned about you, wanted to know how you're doing. I didn't give many details, just that I would be finishing out the semester for you."

"Thanks."

"I used your lecture notes, and that went well. Good material, clearly presented."

Truth was, Nathan could teach freshman composition in his sleep. The fact that he was willing to use her content was also a gift of grace. "I'm almost done with the lecture for next week," she said. "I'll email you the notes by tomorrow morning."

"No rush."

"And if they've got any questions about the essays due next week, they can email me."

"I'll remind them."

"I'm planning to do all the consultations for their final papers by telephone." No way she could meet with any of them face to face. "I'll send out a schedule with available time slots starting later this week."

"Sounds like you've got everything covered."

At least he didn't argue with her and tell her she shouldn't be trying to write lectures or grade papers or finish up her own coursework for the semester. Maybe he could talk with John and reassure him that being physically inactive did not mean giving up her work. *It's the stress level, Charissa,* John insisted. Well, she would be far more stressed if she were doing absolutely nothing but lying around all day.

Hands clasped together, Nathan tapped his chin, a gesture which usually indicated he was deep in thought. "You're in a Milton seminar this term, aren't you?"

She held up crossed fingers. "He and I are like this. Why?" Maybe she would do one more round of revisions on that paper due next week. It wouldn't hurt.

"I was thinking about one of his sonnets today," Nathan said, "'When I consider how my light is spent . . .'"

Charissa knew that one well. Over the years she had written several papers on it, committing it to memory. *When I consider how my light is spent, Ere half my days in this dark world and wide, and that one talent which is death to hide, lodg'd with me useless though my soul more bent to serve . . .*

She stopped her silent recitation. He had just used Milton to bust her, and she'd walked right into it. *God doth not need either man's work or his own gifts,* the sonnet went on. *Who best bear his mild yoke, they serve him best.*

She smiled wryly. "So you're in league with John, huh? Conspiring to shut me down completely? Make me give up my work?"

"No, I would never presume to do that. I just offer it as something to ponder as you rest."

She ran the final lines of the sonnet through her mind: *Thousands at his bidding speed and post o're land and ocean without rest. They also serve who only stand and wait.* Yes, well, she didn't like waiting. And the only thing worse than standing around and waiting was lying down and waiting. "You know what?" she said. "You really should make T-shirts."

He eyed her quizzically.

"T-shirts that say, 'Linger with what provokes you.'"

He laughed. "Not sure many people would buy it, it's so provoking."

"Exactly." She turned the whole poem over in her mind. Milton, upon losing his sight, was worried that God would judge him for burying his one talent. He was worried that God would be harsh with him, that God would "exact day labor, light denied." Would God ask him to do a task and then deny him the means of doing it? Is that the kind of God he served? The voice of Patience—the very voice Charissa struggled to obey—supplied the answer as Milton listened: No. God was not that sort of God.

And what about her? What drove her to want to disregard her limitations and press through with her commitments as best she could? Love for her work and her students or love of something else? It was the likelihood of "something else" that agitated her, the thought that her desire to finish the semester valiantly, commendably, was not about responding to God's bidding but to her own ego's drive.

The front door opened and John entered. "Hey, Nathan! Wondered whose car that was outside." He leaned over the couch to kiss Charissa on the forehead.

"Nathan brought us dinner."

"Dude! You're a star. Thanks."

Charissa wondered when Nathan had last been called "dude." If ever.

"Can you stay and eat with us?" John asked as he hung up his keys.

"No, thanks, not tonight. Jake and Hannah are waiting for me."

"Another time, then. When all of you can come."

Charissa echoed the invitation. "I'm not going anywhere. At least, not any time soon, I hope. So do come some night. We'd enjoy the company."

"I'll talk with Hannah about that, see what might work. Maybe next week? She's preaching on Sunday, did I mention that?"

"No," Charissa said. "Where?"

"At Wayfarer."

"And I'm going to miss it!"

"Well, I hope this will be the first of many more. She's a gifted preacher, I know that." He smiled conspiratorially. "Don't tell her, but I've listened to some of her archived messages online from Westminster. Good stuff."

"Wish I could be there. They record them, don't they?"

"I know they do," John said. "I've listened to a couple of Neil's sermons online."

"Good. At least I'll be able to do that." She could also pray for Hannah as she prepared to preach. She would add that request to her list.

"I'm going to change my clothes," John said after Nathan left, "and then we'll eat. Sure was nice of him to bring food."

Yes. It was. The casserole smelled delicious and would go down easy. It was the food for thought he'd offered that would take a bit more time to digest.

Mara

She would give herself several weeks to plan the feast at Crossroads. With Ellen's generous commitment to fund the meal—not just dessert, she had insisted, but a lunch buffet with flowers on every table—Mara was going to approach it as if she'd been hired to cater a special event. "I've been thinking about it," she said to Miss Jada when she arrived for work Wednesday morning, "and I don't think we should advertise. I'd like it to be a surprise for the regulars, make them feel really special when they arrive." If they did it on a Friday, they could count on about fifty guests. That was manageable, especially for the first time.

"I sure didn't think you'd get donations lined up so fast. But this is good, Mara. This is real good." She looked at her calendar. "So end of May, you think?"

"Yeah. That Friday there." Mara pointed to the last one of the month. Hannah had already promised to help. Jeremy too, if he wasn't working. *But I hope you'll be working,* Mara had said. And he'd said, *Yeah, you and me both.* Being together in worship and at the brunch on Easter had given her an extended time to observe him, and apart from being quiet at church, he'd seemed okay. She had confirmed this with Abby later. At Abby's insistence he was back at his AA meetings, and his sponsor was regularly checking in with him. Jeremy had told Abby he was committed to staying sober for her sake and for Madeleine's. For his own sake too, Mara hoped.

"So you need any help from me," Miss Jada said, "or you just gonna run with this?"

"I think I'm good. It's a challenge, but it's something I used to dream about doing—cooking big meals for lots of people—so this'll give me a chance to try it, see how it goes."

"Well, they'll be grateful for anything, you know that."

She did know. Mara had once been one of them. She never wanted to forget that.

"How's Miss Charissa doing?" Billy asked when he arrived for lunch a few hours later.

"She's doing okay," Mara said. "Thanks for praying for her. And that reminds me"—she reached into her apron pocket and pulled out a small envelope—"she asked me to give this to you."

Billy grinned broadly as he read the note. "Well, that's real nice. Real nice of her." He shoved it into the inside lining of his coat and patted it. "Do I smell cookies?"

"Yes, you do. Snickerdoodles in honor of Billy Hamilton today."

He turned around to the crowd in line behind him, held up his hand for attention, and called, "Hear that? Billy's being honored today. Miss Mara's famous cookies for everyone!"

And the crowd cheered.

Charissa

"All right, put me to work," Hannah said after she removed her shoes and draped her sweater over the back of Charissa's couch.

"I wish I didn't need this," Charissa said. "But thank you."

"My pleasure. I remember what it was like after I had my hysterectomy. I hated asking for help. Much easier for me to give care than receive it."

Charissa wasn't sure she could say the same. Both the giving and the receiving, it seemed, required practice.

"So where do you want me to start?" Hannah asked.

Gesturing toward the cleaning supplies on the coffee table, Charissa gave some brief instructions. Hannah reached for a duster and began with the fireplace mantel.

"Did your husband tell you he busted me with Milton last night?"

Hannah laughed. "No. What did he do?"

Charissa gingerly repositioned herself on the sofa. "He reminded me of a poem I know well—really well—and then he didn't have to say anything else. I got the message." As Hannah cleaned, Charissa described Milton's sonnet and her pondering.

"I'm surprised he didn't give that one to me last fall," Hannah said, "with all my struggling to embrace my sabbatical."

Charissa hadn't even made that connection between their stories. Hannah, as much as anyone, would appreciate how difficult it was to be stripped of productivity and forced to rest.

"It feels like death, doesn't it?" Hannah said.

It did. But Charissa felt guilty for saying so because there were so many people who had it so much harder than she did. What she didn't want to disintegrate into was a self-pitying whiner. Day after day she had to choose gratitude. "I'm trying to keep a good perspective about it, but it's hard. It's hard to imagine lying here in the house for another two and a half months." Then again, it was even worse to imagine *not* lying there and what might happen if she went into labor this prematurely. "I was thinking again last night about all my compulsions, my drive to succeed, to achieve, to be perfect—all the things I've seen the past few months. None of this is new. It's just a new context for the same old struggles to surface. But this time it feels like much more is at stake." She stroked her abdomen.

"When you say 'at stake,' do you mean your PhD program? Or pregnancy? Or . . ."

"Not the program, no. I'm the one who's driving myself to finish the semester, no one else." In fact, she had received several kind emails from faculty members—Dr. Gardiner included—to remind her that her first priority was her health and that she shouldn't feel obligated to complete her coursework on time. There would be grace. "What I meant was Bethany. And I guess the formation of my own soul, come to think of it."

Those stakes were always high, weren't they? She could resist the deep work of God or she could yield to it. And maybe what she had been doing was resisting it.

"There's a question that came to me months ago," Charissa said, "back when I had my students writing papers about only having forty days to live. I was pondering that memento mori exercise in the prayer notebook and got to thinking about why I've always wanted to teach. Then I pushed it all aside; I didn't want to think about it because I wasn't sure what true answer would emerge. Am I teaching because I love it? Because I want to invest my life in students and their intellectual growth? Or am I teaching because I've always loved honor and recognition?"

Teach me to number my days, the psalmist said, *so I may gain a heart of wisdom.* Charissa was numbering her days in a different sort of way now, but she wasn't sure she was growing in wisdom as a result of it.

"Those are penetrating questions," Hannah said. She set the duster down on the mantel. "What are you seeing?"

"That I'm a mixed bag of motives." Charissa sighed. "I think I chose the academic path not because I love scholarship but because I was addicted to achieving, and I wanted the initials after my name." Had she ever said that out loud before? She wasn't sure. It sounded so prideful and shallow and ugly. Hannah, however, was looking at her with compassion, not disgust.

She plowed forward. "I think I gravitated toward teaching because I crave authority. I love respect. That's why a couple of students have really pushed my buttons this semester." She supposed she ought to be grateful to Justin Caldwell and his posse for revealing in new ways her addictions and idolatry. If they were pushing buttons, then there were buttons to be pushed.

"As far as whether or not I love teaching, I don't know. There are parts of it I enjoy—watching students light up with understanding or insights, or getting to see progress in their abilities to develop thoughtful arguments and write effectively. That's gratifying." She paused. "But I don't know, Hannah. When Meg was dying, I saw so clearly that what I wanted was to make a difference in this world, not for my own name and recognition but for the sake of others. I know teaching can be that. And maybe I can be that sort of teacher someday. But the truth is"—she looked up at the ceiling as the confession formed fully—"the truth is, I'm not writing lectures and grading papers and pushing to complete the semester for the students' sake. I'm doing it for my own. Because I've never been one to quit anything. And I don't want to be the one on the receiving end of grace. Not for this."

Hannah sat down on the hearth, cross-legged. "I understand what you mean."

In the two hours Hannah spent at the house, she didn't get much cleaning done. "But this was better," Charissa said. "This is what I needed." More than mopping or vacuuming or scrubbing, what she needed was someone listening to her life with compassion and asking probing questions that prompted reflection. What she needed was someone who understood the wrestling, someone who could remind her that God could use anything to shape and form her into Christlikeness, even unexpected pregnancies and missed presentations and punk students and relational conflicts and bed rest. What she needed was someone who could invite her to see God at work in the midst of everything. "Thanks, Hannah. This has been a gift to me."

"To me too. And I promise, I'll come back and clean for you later in the week."

"Or come back and visit. The cleaning can wait." If John had overheard that, he would have turned cartwheels.

Hannah rose to her feet and stretched. "I was thinking earlier that I really want to get back in a regular rhythm of meeting with the Sensible Shoes Club. Would you be up for that?"

Charissa smiled. "'Up' probably isn't the operative word for me at the moment, but let's get a date on the calendar. I'd love to keep walking together. In a metaphorical sort of way."

Hannah

"Good time with Charissa today?" Nathan asked as they cleared the dinner table together.

"Yes." One of the best conversations Hannah had ever had with her, in fact. "I didn't accomplish anything I planned to, but I think God had other plans."

"Evidently." He pulled his phone from his pocket. "I got an email from her just before I left campus. She's going to write one more lecture and then turn things over completely to me."

Wow. One thing about Charissa, when she made a decision, she moved ahead quickly. "Are you okay with that?" Hannah asked.

"Yes, fine. I'm more intrigued by her process of letting it go." He adjusted his glasses as he peered at the screen. "Here's what she wrote. She said I could share it with you. 'Hannah reminded me today that the spiritual life is about yielding to God's invitations. As we talked, it became clear to me that my invitation right now is to rest, to lay everything down. Thanks for being willing to finish out the semester for me, with all that involves. I'm going to say yes to this latest opportunity to be enlarged and stretched in grace. I trust that what God wants to do in me while I rest is more urgent and important than driving myself to complete my responsibilities as teacher and student. So I'm letting go.' And she goes on to say that she thinks you'd make a really excellent spiritual director and that you should consider training for that."

Hannah chuckled. "She mentioned that part to me as I was leaving. She thinks both of us should go through training. Did she tell you that?"

He nodded. "It's something I've thought about for years, but it's never been the right time." He tucked his phone away. "But maybe that's part of our journey together. I'd love to grow in that process of prayer and discernment with you."

They had laid down their pilgrimage to the Holy Land. Maybe this was the pilgrimage they would make together instead.

Jake appeared in the doorway, trumpet case in hand, wearing a striped bowtie and a suit. "Looking good, bud!" Nathan exclaimed.

"Thanks. You're coming, right, Hannah?"

"Wouldn't miss it." She hadn't been inside a middle school gymnasium in years. She gave Chaucer a couple of treats and rinsed off her hands in the sink.

"I played saxophone in my high school band," Nathan said as they walked out to the car together. "Did you know that, Shep?"

She did not. She gazed up at a sky seeded with stars. There were so many things she didn't yet know, so many things she looked forward to discovering.

"What about you?" Jake asked Hannah. "Did you play anything?"

"Clarinet," she said. "And very poorly. I remember this one concert; I was probably a little older than you . . ."

Mara

Mara was mashing potatoes when she heard commotion upstairs, bodies thudding against the floor and voices crackling with anger. Shouting and wrestling matches had been commonplace between the boys when they were younger. *Boys will be boys*, Tom always said, but Mara was usually the one trying to dodge blows while yanking them apart from one another. She turned off the mixer and eavesdropped through the ceiling, trying to determine if it was serious enough for her to intervene.

"It's your fault!" Brian yelled. "You ruin everything!"

If Kevin replied, he did so in too low a voice for her to hear. When something crashed against the floor—a lamp, maybe?—she charged up the stairs. "What's going on up here?"

Brian, who in the past couple of months had shot up several inches, had managed to pin his shorter, stockier brother to the floor and now had his fist poised above Kevin's face.

"Hey, break it up!"

Kevin spit into Brian's face and when Brian recoiled in disgust, Kevin flipped him onto his back.

"Kevin, stop! That's enough!" Mara shoved his knee with her foot. "I said, break it up!"

Kevin released him, and Brian scrambled to his feet, his nostrils flaring, his face scarlet with rage. Mara touched his shoulder, and he shoved her hand away. "Deep breath, Brian. C'mon." Kevin stormed out of the room. "Kevin, wait! Get back here. C'mon. Both of you. Sit down."

Brian paced, muttering. Kevin reappeared in the doorway. "Brian started it!"

"Because you ruined everything!" Brian charged him again, and Kevin swerved.

"Hey! Stop it, both of you. I mean it." She held out both arms like a referee and signaled with her chin for Kevin to sit. He rolled his eyes and flopped onto his bed. When Brian looked like he was going to bolt, she blocked the exit. "C'mon, Brian. Let's talk this through." She motioned toward a chair covered with clothes. Brian flung the pile onto the floor.

"Hey!" Kevin yelled, ready to start all over.

"Kevin, leave it. He needs a place to sit. And you can put your clothes away when we're done." When both boys were sitting with their arms crossed defiantly against their chests, she breathed a sigh of relief. She couldn't remember the last time Brian had cooperated with her. *Thank you, Lord.* "Okay, Brian, fill me in."

"Why does Brian get—"

Mara cut Kevin off with her hand. She had money in the bank with Kevin. Now was her chance to try to make a small investment with Brian. "What did your brother ruin?"

Brian answered without looking at her. "Everything."

Kevin pivoted away from her toward the wall. Mara sat down on the edge of his bed. "How about being a little more specific?"

"Disney World!"

Mara felt her face flush. "How did he ruin that?"

Brian kicked one of Kevin's shoes across the carpet. "Dad says that because Kevin doesn't want to go, I don't get to go, either."

She hadn't anticipated this move from Tom.

"It's not my fault Tiffany doesn't want you there," Kevin muttered.

Oh.

Mara, feeling sick to her stomach, decided to play dumb. "Tiffany doesn't want you to go?"

Brian shrugged and slouched deeper into the chair.

"What did your dad tell you?"

"I told you. That I don't get to go because Kevin doesn't want to."

"Why would I want to go to some stupid kid place with her?"

"It's not stupid!" Brian, for a fleeting moment, resembled a younger version of himself, a child who—she should have remembered—had loved their trip to Disney World when he was little and for years had begged for another.

She hadn't intended to ruin anything for him. She had just been trying to help Kevin.

Brian sent a second shoe careening across the floor. "You're just mad because you don't get to go to Hawaii!"

"I don't want to go to Hawaii, Hawaii's stupid."

"Okay," Mara said, placing a hand on Kevin's knee, "enough with the 'stupid.' It sounds like there's been a big misunderstanding here, that's all. I'll talk with your dad and work it out." Her voice sounded much more confident than she felt. "Let's take a time out here, give each other some space, and I'll see what I can do."

To fix what I broke, she added silently. She had been so eager to have her "gotcha" moment with Tom, so eager to be Kevin's hero, she hadn't thought about other consequences.

Brian wiped his cheek, a quick, slight gesture he would be mortified to know his mother saw.

In that instant her heart broke.

Much as Brian reminded her of Tom, she often forgot that he was not Tom. He was a thirteen-year-old boy whose parents were getting divorced and whose father's attention was now divided. He was a thirteen-year-old boy who had always hero-worshiped his father, and now his father had let him down. And if she didn't find ways to extend herself in love for him—love that he did not reciprocate—then she was no better than his father.

On her way back down to the kitchen, the boys in their respective rooms, Mara replayed the scene at Easter brunch. She shouldn't have been snide with Brian in front of Tiffany, shouldn't have done the whole "Help your brothers" thing. Tiffany had obviously taken Mara's "You know how teenagers can be" advice to heart, combined it with what she had already observed about Brian, and decided she wasn't going to let him ruin her kids' trip.

She texted Tom: What's going on with Brian and Disney World?

He did not reply.

Hannah

Friday, April 17

6 a.m.

After praying about a couple of possibilities for sermon texts the past few days, I woke up this morning knowing what I'm called to preach: Jesus' revelation of his wounds. I've been studying John 20:19-29 for the past hour, making lots of notes and seeing the truth with fresh eyes. When the resurrected Jesus wanted to reveal who he was to his frightened, bewildered, wondering disciples, he showed them where he was pierced. In his resurrected body, the marks of his suffering were still visible. And they testified to the depths of his love, to the reminder of his humiliation and death. The Wounded One is now the Resurrected One.

But the Resurrected One is still the Wounded One.

In a Botox world where perfection is pursued and idolized, wounds and scars are ugly and shameful. Our culture says, Numb the pain. Erase it. Or at least, cover it up. Conceal it. Don't show it to anyone. That was the message I heard for many years.

But the testimony of Easter is that suffering isn't erased from Jesus' resurrected body. His wounds have been made glorious. They point to what he has done and how the Father has been glorified in the suffering, death, and resurrection of the Son. The wounds tell the story of our salvation and God's victory over the forces of evil, of death. Life wins.

If we're honest—if I'm honest—it's easy to equate resurrection with perfection. Don't I often think of resurrection as the removal of everything that has brought hurt and suffering and death in this life? Don't I often envision a day when pain will be erased? When the evidence of suffering will be removed? Glorified, resurrected bodies shouldn't still show signs of torture, torment, and death, right?

Jesus shows another way, that resurrection means that even our wounds are made glorious because of the power of God. And our wounds can also testify and tell a story: this is where I suffered. This is where I hurt. This is where Jesus healed and offered comfort. This is where God redeemed my pain and suffering. Our wounds and our scars can tell stories that make Jesus' love and power visible to others. If we have courage to open our hands and show them.

Words of an Easter hymn we sang on Sunday came to me as I prayed this morning: Crown him the Lord of love; behold his hands and side, those wounds, yet visible above, in beauty glorified. All hail, Redeemer, hail! For thou has died for me. Thy praise and glory shall not fail throughout eternity.

Jesus, may your wounds take in all of our hurts. May we glimpse in them the reminder that our story of salvation is a story written not merely with pen and ink but with blood and tears. A story of love and hope. For all of us.

Speak, Lord. I'm listening.

—⟨⟩

"Have you got a scar story?" Hannah asked Nathan as the three of them ate breakfast later that morning. She brushed some crumbs off her flannel pajamas.

"Physical, you mean?"

"Yeah." She wasn't going to ask him to divulge emotional or mental or spiritual wounds in front of Jake.

He rolled up the left sleeve of his robe and pointed to a mark on his forearm. "Dog bite. I was seven, and it was the neighbor's dog. But it was my fault. I was tormenting him." He looked at Jake. "Your dad was a troublemaker. Just ask your Aunt Liz sometime."

Jake smiled from behind his orange juice. "She's already told me stories."

"Yeah, I bet she has. You've got plenty of ammo if you ever need it, don't you?"

"Yep."

Nathan reached for another slice of toast. "Jake's got a scar story, don't you, Jake?"

Jake lifted his bangs and pointed to a faint jagged edge Hannah had never noticed before. "Fell off my bike when I was—what, Dad? Like, seven?"

"Eight, maybe."

"Yeah, eight. And then you wanted to put this cream on it or something. I don't remember exactly. You tell it."

"I wanted to put scar removal cream on your forehead but you said you didn't want me to because—"

"Because I said, 'If you take away my scar . . .'"

"'You take away my story,'" they said in unison.

Hannah laughed and said, "Oooh. That'll preach. Can I use that, Jake?"

"Yeah, sure."

Nathan slathered his toast with strawberry jam. "Watch out, bud. You've got a preacher living in the house now. Gotta be careful or you'll end up in a sermon."

Jake eyed Hannah like he wasn't sure if his dad was teasing or not. "I'll never use you as a sermon illustration," she said, "unless I ask your permission first. Deal?"

"Deal."

"Same deal for husbands?" Nathan asked.

Hannah licked a bit of milk from her cereal spoon and then wagged it at him. "If you behave."

"I'll try." He crossed his heart. "I know another scar story. A good one."

"I'm listening."

"A friend of mine's a surgeon in town, and he was on call one day when the ambulance brought in a young guy in his twenties, motorcycle crash, didn't think he'd live. But Ken did the emergency surgery, and the kid pulled through. A few months later, Ken's out near the hospital loading dock when a nurse comes out and says there's someone who wants to see him. So he goes back in, and there's a guy standing there he doesn't recognize, and he has that awkward moment of knowing he should know who the guy is but doesn't."

"I know that feeling," she said. "I hate that feeling."

"Yeah. Exactly. So the guy says to Ken, 'You don't know who I am, do you?' And Ken says, 'No. Sorry.' So the guy lifts up his shirt, shows him his chest, and then Ken says, 'Oh, hey, Sam, how're you doing?' Recognized the scar pattern immediately."

"It was the motorcycle guy?" Jake asked.

"Yeah."

Hannah shook her head slowly. "Ooh . . ."

"That'll preach," she and Nathan said in unison.

Mara

Tom couldn't ignore her forever. She would give him the weekend, and if he still didn't reply to her multiple texts inquiring about the Orlando trip, she would send an email on Monday morning and copy in her attorney. "You coming to church?" she asked Kevin. He was awake uncharacteristically early for a Sunday.

He poured some cereal into a bowl and said, "Nah."

No surprise, but it was worth asking. "Well, Hannah's preaching this morning, so I'm going back to Wayfarer. And then I'll call you afterward and see what you want me to bring home for lunch. I haven't had a chance to get to a store." Babysitting Madeleine all day Saturday so that Jeremy and Abby could get away for the day had been far more fun than her usual shopping outings. Especially since Maddie had happily demonstrated her new trick of rolling over. *She's gonna be like you, Jeremy,* Mara said when they got home. *That's how you got around; you could roll in any direction.* Not that he'd had far to roll in that one-room apartment his father had rented for them in secret.

She poured herself a second cup of coffee. "You haven't heard anything from your dad, have you?"

"Nope."

"Nothing at all?"

"Nope."

"What about Brian, has he said anything about—"

"Nope."

"No, he hasn't heard anything, or no, he hasn't said anything?"

"He's not talkin' to me."

"Not since the Disney World thing?"

"Yep."

Brian hadn't been talking to her, either. She had tried multiple times. Daily she reminded him that she was serious about going to bat for him with his dad but that she just hadn't heard anything back yet. *But don't worry,* she'd say. *We'll get it sorted.* Brian never replied.

Kevin picked some marshmallows out of his bowl of Lucky Charms and popped them into his mouth. "I don't know what he's so mad about. Dad would just be going on all the baby rides with Tiffany and her kids. It's not like he'd be paying any attention to what Brian wanted to do."

Mara understood what Brian was mad about. He'd been replaced. She'd be mad too if she cared a whit about Tom. Which she didn't. "Well, just try to understand how he's feeling, okay? You're happy because you don't have to go. He's sad because he wanted to." Kevin was staring at his bowl. "Kevin?"

"Yeah, okay."

"Okay. Thanks."

Before she returned to her room to finish getting dressed for church, Mara quietly opened Brian's door. When he was sleeping he looked like the little boy she'd had to frequently protect from Kevin's teasing. She wished she could plant a kiss on his forehead, but if he woke, he would freak out. She pressed her fingers to her lips and then held her hand a few inches from his face. He didn't stir.

Ever since meeting Hannah, Mara had assumed she was a good pastor. She'd experienced Hannah's pastoral gifts firsthand. But she had never thought much about what kind of preacher she might be. As soon as Hannah began to speak, Mara knew. She was a deep kind of preacher. A compassionate one. Hannah had a pastoral presence in the pulpit—not charismatic like her own Pastor Jeff, whose preaching cadence was like music pulsating with energy and rhythm, but like a shepherd speaking gently to sheep who were wounded, frightened, and bewildered.

The resurrected One is the wounded One. Mara chewed on this as she listened. What did the wounds of Jesus reveal to her? Love. So much love. And understanding. The wounds revealed a suffering-with-us God who did not withhold himself from any of the trauma and pain. Not physically. Not emotionally. Not psychologically. Not spiritually. *Thank you, Jesus.*

What did the wounds of Jesus reveal? Not just suffering and compassion but victory. Victory! Victory over sin and evil and death. Victory accomplished not through fighting against evil and death—and here was a deep mystery—but by submitting to it. Mara wasn't sure she would ever understand the paradox of victory accomplished through suffering, of power revealed in weakness. Mystery. But oh, what a glorious mystery!

Jeremy was on the edge of his seat, listening. Mara could tell. Abby was too. In fact, apart from some sniffling Mara heard from behind her, you could hear a pin drop.

What about her own scars? How did they reveal Jesus?

She didn't have any physical scars that told a story. Her wounds were the invisible kind, the psychological and emotional ones she had tried for years to conceal, but which, by the grace of God, had been brought into the light of loving community and touched by a wounded, risen Savior. She did have scar stories. And maybe they could point others to Jesus.

From the corner of her eye she could see Nathan and Jake in the front row, and oh! the adoration and respect on Nathan's face as he listened to his wife was something to behold. Mara wondered what her life might have been like if she'd had a husband who loved her like that.

But she wasn't going to be jealous of her friend. She would rejoice for her. Thank God with her. Because Mara knew one thing for certain: you didn't preach about hurt and pain and wounds and healing and comfort like that if you hadn't experienced suffering yourself and been comforted by the wounded Healer.

Hannah

Nine months, Hannah thought as Nathan lit their unity candle Sunday night. It had been almost nine months since Steve entered her office and announced that she was being given a sabbatical, almost nine months since she first arrived in West Michigan, bewildered, disoriented, grieving, and yes, resentful. Nine months. The imagery wasn't lost on her. Maybe the barren, wombless one had been pregnant after all.

Never in her tenure at Westminster had Hannah preached a sermon that evoked such a deep and passionate response from listeners. *Anointed,* Neil said when he shook her hand and thanked her. She'd had the privilege of bearing the Word, and the Word had taken on life, a life far beyond the words printed on her page. In the mystery of God's grace, the Word had been enfleshed through her. Hannah didn't yet know what it would mean, but something new, something beautiful was being born.

Part Four

All Things New

_"Forget the former things; do not dwell on
the past. See, I am doing a new thing! Now it springs up;
do you not perceive it? I am making a way in the
wilderness and streams in the wasteland."_

Isaiah 43:18-19

twelve

Having read Monday's missive from Tom twice, Mara read the last part of the email again. If Brian was upset about not going to Orlando, Tom said, then it was Mara's fault. She was the one who suggested to Tiffany that the boys not go.

One boy, Mara thought. She had suggested that one boy not go. And when she suggested it, she'd only had one of her boys in mind. That's where she had failed. She had only regarded Kevin's desires and needs.

Tom was right. Brian losing out on Disney World *was* her fault. And if Tom ever told him—and Tom would, she knew he would—Brian would never forgive her.

She lowered her head onto her desk. Now what? She could try to spin it, tell Brian that his soon-to-be stepmother was the one who had decided she only wanted her kids to go and that his father had sided with her and against him. Brian's moodiness—that was putting it mildly—was no secret. That approach might work.

On the way to the orthodontist later that afternoon, when she had a few private moments with Brian captive in the car, she decided to implement her strategy. "I finally got an email back from your dad about Florida. It sounds like Tiffany thinks you"—she caught herself before she said "would ruin her kids' trip"—"like Tiffany and your dad are worried it won't work to have you there with her kids. Any idea why they would think that?"

"Nope."

"Has something happened between you and the boys?"

"Nope." He sounded just like Kevin. What she needed was an open-ended question, something that might invite a multi-word answer.

C'mon. Think.

"So why would they . . ."

He flicked his seatbelt and pounded the car door with his fist. "I don't know, okay? I don't know why they would think that."

"Okay. I just wondered if maybe something had happened to make Tiffany—"

"Tiffany's stupid. And her kids are stupid too. I don't want to go with them anyway."

But the crack in his voice betrayed him. "Okay, then I won't push it with your dad. But maybe you and Kevin can go somewhere else with him—just him—this summer. Want me to talk with him about that?"

"I don't care. Whatever."

"Well, I'll see what I can do."

She had dodged a bullet. *Thank God.* She had possibly even set herself up to be a hero, whether Brian acknowledged those heroics or not. She ought to feel relieved. Elated. But she did not.

If she didn't find some way to be truthful with Brian about her role in everything, it would come back to bite her. Tom would make sure it did.

"Brian, I want to apologize to you." Had she ever said those words to him before? She couldn't remember. She felt sick with apprehension speaking them now. "I played a part in your dad's decision." He did not move his head but looked at her from the corner of his eye. "I talked with Tiffany at the hotel that day about Kevin not going to Florida—I'd promised Kevin I would try to help get him out of going—but I think she misunderstood what I said. I didn't say anything about you. But she obviously took it that way, and I'm sorry for that. I never meant for your dad to take the trip away from you. I know it meant a lot to you, and I'm really sorry. If there's something I can do to fix it, I'll do it." He was silent. "If you want me to try."

She drove more slowly than necessary through the parking lot and up to the front door, where she turned to face him. The vein on his left temple was pulsating. "I can try, Brian, if you want me to."

He flung open the car door.

"Brian?"

Over his shoulder he said, "Yeah, okay. Whatever."

When he slammed the door behind him, she drove to a secluded parking space, lowered her head on the steering wheel, and deep-breathed her way into prayer.

"I know it doesn't sound like much," she said to Charissa when she dropped off an egg casserole and blueberry muffins just before five, "but it's huge that he didn't lash out." Mara had been marveling over that for the past two hours.

"Exactly," Charissa said from the couch. She adjusted the waistband of the sweats Mara had seen her wearing the day before. "I think you were brave to tell him the truth. You took away Tom's power over you when you did."

"Right. At least now if Tom tells Brian it's my fault, Brian heard it from me first." If nothing else, it was progress in her relationship with him, even if it seemed like a baby step forward. Maybe Brian would someday come to view her as an advocate rather than an adversary. That would be a miracle. "It's Disney World he wants," Mara said, "so he must've figured his best way to get it is to have me help him."

You're gonna have to show Tiffany and your dad that you can be good with the boys, she'd told Brian when he finished his appointment, *that you're willing to play with them, have fun with them. Maybe the little boys will even beg for you to come.* That was obviously a strategy that hadn't occurred to him, and he'd seemed intrigued by it. Not grateful—no, that would be overstating it. But open. And that was progress. Maybe she and Brian would one day be united as allies against a common adversary, like she and Kevin had been. What a miracle that would be.

She stretched her bare feet and wriggled her toes. She could do with some color on her nails. Maybe she would bring over some bottles from her massive collection and paint Charissa's toenails too. It might be nice for her to stare at something fun and sparkly if she had to lie on the couch all day. "I think I'd go nuts if I were you," she said.

Charissa fiddled with her ponytail. "It makes you see how many ordinary things you take for granted every day. Like showering. Or washing my hair."

"So how about if I wash it for you?"

"My hair? No."

"C'mon. You can sit in a chair, and I'll wash it at the sink."

"You've already done enough, bringing over more food."

"Anybody can bring food. How many people have offered to wash your hair?"

Charissa laughed. "One."

"Okay, then."

"I'm sure John would help me again if I asked nicely."

"Well, John's not here, and I am." She rose to her feet. "Didn't I ever tell you I dreamed of being a hair stylist when I was a little girl? Well, that and a chef."

"You're already a chef. A good one. Just ask anyone at Crossroads."

Mara had never thought about it that way, that her job at Crossroads was in some sense a fulfillment of a childhood dream. "Thanks for that." She was no fancy chef at an elegant restaurant, but she cooked simple meals for grateful guests, and that was its own reward. As she headed down the hall for towels and shampoo, she caught a glimpse of her reflection in a mirror. Beloved. Chosen. Blessed. And favored to bear Christ. That was the gift. She had been chosen in love to bear Christ with love. Mara found the stack of plush white towels in the cupboard and grabbed one to roll beneath Charissa's neck and another to dry her hair. "You got any chairs with wheels?" she called.

"Back in the bedroom at the desk."

When she found it, Mara rolled it out into the living room. "Your chariot awaits," she said, and Charissa laughed again.

It was the water, the sensation of water running through her fingers that brought to mind another occasion of washing, not of hair but of feet. As Mara gently massaged Charissa's scalp, she remembered Meg pouring water into a basin. She heard again her soft, high voice explaining why she had chosen the prayer exercise about Jesus washing the disciples' feet. She wanted to take the opportunity to remember Jesus together while they had the chance, Meg said. She didn't know how much longer she would have, she said, and she wanted to take the time to express her love and gratitude to her friends. As it turned out, she only had another day. Life just wasn't fair. Why was it that people like Meg died and people like Tom got to go right on their merry way? It didn't make sense.

Mara shielded Charissa's forehead with her hand as she rinsed out the shampoo with the sink sprayer. "Hannah said Becca's coming home next week."

"I heard. Becca emailed me. She's going to need her car back."

"Oh. I didn't even think about that."

"Well, it's not like I'm going anywhere any time soon. I hope."

"I hope not too," Mara said. "Something must've happened with Simon, don't you think, to make her change her mind about Paris?"

"She didn't say that, but it's not hard to read between the lines."

"Poor girl. Hope she's the one who broke his heart and not the other way around." Mara paused. "What do you think she's gonna do? I can't imagine she'll want to stay in that big house all by herself."

"I don't know. It's not like she has family she can go to."

"Her aunt's still not—"

"No. Not in the picture at all, as far as I can tell."

The front door creaked open, and Mara leaned sideways, sprayer still in hand. "Hey, John!"

"Hey! What's this?"

"Full service salon," Charissa replied. He set down his briefcase.

Mara finished rinsing and turned off the tap. "Just helping out."

"Not 'just helping out,'" Charissa said. "This is way beyond 'just helping out.'" She leaned her head back far enough to make eye contact. "If I'd had a sister, I don't think she would have loved me any better than you."

Mara wrung out some water from Charissa's hair, reached for the towel, and said, "That's what sisters are for."

Becca

Becca spent more time at the library during her last two weeks in London than she had all school year. It was one surefire way to avoid running into Pippa. Early in the mornings she would leave her flat, grab a coffee and a pastry, and head to campus. Then, when she finished her classes and assignments, she would spend the afternoons at museums. That was one surefire way to avoid running into Simon.

As her departure date approached, she inventoried the places she wanted to see one last time and methodically checked them off her list: the Globe Theatre, Kensington Gardens for a picnic, shopping on Oxford Street. And because Claire had been kind to her—and to her mother—Becca had invited her to see a West End production of *Stomp*. It was one of the few shows she knew would not make her cry. "I'll ride with you to the airport on Wednesday if you'd like some company," Claire said when they left the theater. "I've got the morning off."

"Then don't spend it going to the airport. I'll be fine."

"Sure? I don't mind. I don't fancy the thought of you being all alone."

But "all alone" was Becca's life now. She might as well get used to it. "I'll be fine," she said, and tried to believe it.

Becca was emptying her closet into suitcases Tuesday afternoon when there was a knock on the door. "Becks?"

Pippa. Becca snatched two more blouses off hangers.

"Can I please come in?"

Becca tossed the blouses onto the growing pile of clothes on the bed. She would never fit all the stuff she had accumulated into two bags.

"Please?" It sounded like her face was pressed right up against the door. "I need to see you."

Becca pitched a pair of shoes toward a suitcase, a heel thudding on the wood floor.

"Please. I know you're leaving tomorrow, and I wanted to say goodbye."

"Send a text," Becca called out. "Or better yet, a picture from Paris."

"Please. I'm not leaving until you open the door."

Rather than risk her making a scene in the hallway, Becca opened the door just wide enough for eye contact, nothing more.

"Can I come in?"

"No. Whatever you want to say, you can say it from there."

Pippa waited until someone passed by in the hallway and then said with a low voice, "I just wanted to say again that I'm sorry and that I'm gutted over everything."

"Gutted? Why? You got what you wanted."

"Can I please come in?"

With a frustrated sigh Becca flung open the door, then returned to packing. Pippa closed the door behind her. "Simon and I are done."

Becca rolled up a pair of tights and stuffed them between some sweaters.

"Becca?"

"I'm sorry you won't get to go to Paris."

"That's it?"

Becca shrugged. What else did she want her to say? That she was happy? Surprised? Sad for her? She was none of those things.

"I just felt too guilty, you know, every time Simon and I . . ."

Amazing, how that guilt hadn't prevented her from sleeping with him in the first place.

"Anyway, I wanted to tell you in case, you know, with it being your last night and everything that you might want to . . ."

Becca spun around. "Want to what?"

"I don't know . . . say goodbye to Simon?"

"You're kidding, right?"

Pippa was not.

Becca shook her head, speechless. Was that all sex ever was to Pippa? A bit of fun? A distraction? Was that all Pippa thought it had been to her?

She removed from her closet the sequined cocktail dress Pippa had helped her pick out for the dinner cruise. "Tell you what," Becca said, tossing it to her, "you keep this, okay? A goodbye gift. You'll get way more use out of it than I will."

If Pippa caught the barb, she didn't respond to it. Instead, she fingered the sequins. "Text or email or something?" Pippa said after a few moments of awkward silence. But it was clear from the expression on her face that they both knew Becca wouldn't.

There was one place in London her mother had loved more than any other, a place Becca had told herself she would not go. But she was so worked up after Pippa left that she needed something that might soothe, and music might soothe, especially music offered by a choir her mother declared sang like angels. On her last night in London Becca wanted to be somewhere her mother had been. So she rode the Tube to St. Paul's and walked to the cathedral, carillon bells boisterously ringing the top of the hour from a nearby church tower. She paused to listen beneath the branches of a large evergreen and glanced up at the massive dome, a masterpiece of architecture and engineering. There would be music at the evensong service but no sermon. What she didn't want was a sermon. What she needed was peace. What she hoped for was a sense of presence, a connection with her mom.

Just as she was ascending the front steps, her phone buzzed with a text. *Simon.* After a moment's hesitation, she read the words on the screen: Terrible mistake. Need to see you. Want you to come with me to Paris. Please say you'll come. Waiting for you.

Weak in the knees, Becca lowered herself onto a step out of the way of foot traffic and read the words again. And again. And again. She leaned her head against a pillar and closed her eyes. She could cancel her flight. She could. It wasn't too late to cancel. She could go to Simon's flat and scold him and then forgive him and spend the summer in the most romantic city in the world, far away from the sorrow of Kingsbury and a lonely, empty house.

She could.

She typed the words, "On my way," then paused, her finger hovering over Send.

Could she?

Could she really?

She stared at the screen. One little word would make all the difference. "Home," she typed. *On my way home. We're done.*

And she pressed Send.

Hannah

The last time Hannah was waiting for Becca to appear at the end of the concourse, she was waiting with anguished impatience and worry, Meg having been whisked away by paramedics after collapsing—there, right about there—on the terminal carpet. When Becca emerged this time, her dark eyes were not wide with terror but diminished with weariness or sorrow. Unsure whether she would welcome an embrace, Hannah rested her hand on Becca's shoulder and said, "Welcome home." At this, Becca collapsed, sobbing, into Hannah's arms.

—◌

"How's she doing?" Nathan asked when Hannah returned to the house.

"Okay. She insisted she wanted to be by herself, so I didn't push anything." She leaned forward to rub Chaucer's muzzle between her hands. "Some of her high school friends are home from college, so that helps. She doesn't have to be alone if she doesn't want to be. And she's already lined up a barista job at a coffee shop where she's worked the past few summers. She starts this weekend."

It's not Paris, Becca had said with a rueful sigh, *but at least it's something.* Something familiar in the midst of everything that had shifted with cataclysmic force.

"Did she say anything about Simon, about what happened?"

"Nothing." Curious as she was, Hannah had avoided asking any probing or manipulative questions. If Becca wanted to confide in her, then she'd do so when she was ready. "I invited her over for dinner tomorrow, but I don't think she'll come."

"At least she knows you're here. That's no small thing."

Hannah didn't argue with him. But how she wished she could do something more for Meg's girl.

"This came for you today," he said, offering her an envelope immediately identifiable by the uneven handwriting. Hannah pried it open along the seam. With all the other things that had required her attention lately, she had forgotten about the note she'd sent. How kind of Loretta Anderson to respond.

Dear Hannah,

I've had my share of heartaches over the years, but few compare to my sorrow over your news about our Meg. She was the daughter I never had, and I loved her with all my heart. Thank you for letting me know. It's been many years since I've seen Becca, but please know that I will be in fervent prayer for her as she grieves and tries to find her way. I know how much her mother adored her and how much Becca must be suffering right now.

I'm grateful for the gift Meg was and continues to be to so many. May God comfort all of us who were privileged to call her friend.

Peace to you,
Loretta Anderson

"You okay?" Nathan asked as she tucked the note back into the envelope.
"I will be," she said, and reached for his hand.

Thursday, April 30
10 a.m.
I'm sitting in the labyrinth courtyard at New Hope on the bench where Meg and I first sat together last September in a bower of late summer roses. The whole world is greening. I don't remember ever noticing so many shades of green before. Maybe we notice resurrection more keenly when we're emerging from the valley of the shadow.

I just met with Katherine for spiritual direction for the first time since the wedding. Before I went I looked back in my journal to see what we talked about the last time we were together in February. I had told her about my struggle with endings, and she had recommended keeping company with Jesus as he said goodbye to loved ones. "Do not cling." That was the word I needed to embrace in the midst of everything that was changing so rapidly. "Do not cling." An Easter word to Mary Magdalene and to me.

We talked about that today, all the ways I've been invited to let go
with open hands and to receive with open hands. We talked about Easter
as a season, not merely as a day, and what it means to share in the power
of his resurrection even while we share in the fellowship of his sufferings.
Dying and rising. This is our daily rhythm. Day after day after day. We
die. We rise. And sometimes we discover, by God's grace, that the
darkness we thought was the shadow of death is instead the shadow of
the Almighty, covering us with his wings.

Katherine asked me what it was like to preach again. I told her that
the words might have sounded similar to words I've preached before,
but they flowed from a different, deeper place. "Integrated," she commented. That's a good word. I preached from a place of having come to
glimpse God's love for me in the depths of my being, and so I was able
to offer that hope to others. By confronting some of my own wound-
edness the past nine months and exposing those wounds to others, I
know the fellowship of his sufferings and the power of his resurrection
in deeper ways. I know his wounds take in my hurts. And my scars can
reveal his glory.

I told her, too, about some of the responses to my message. A few
people thanked me for not giving an "Everything's great because Jesus
is victorious over the grave!" sort of sermon. They thanked me for the
reminder that we hold the sorrow and the joy in the same overflowing
cup and trust that Jesus reveals himself in each. Christ IS victorious. And
we still groan in our sufferings. This, too, is Easter. I told Katherine about
a young woman who came up to talk with me after worship. She wanted
to show me the scars on her arms from where she had cut herself as a
teenager in self-loathing, in depression. She was so numb in her soul, she
said, she needed to feel physical pain. Now she counsels teenage girls
who struggle with the same impulses. That's the kind of stewardship of
sufferings we're called to. That's the kind of stewardship I want to embrace in ever-deepening ways.

When I expressed that longing, Katherine asked what was stirring in
me about desires for ministry. "Do you want to return to pastoring?" she
asked. I do, if God has that for me. But what amazed me as I sat there

with her is that I don't feel anxious about it. I don't feel the need to grab for something as a source of identity and significance anymore. And that's a paradigm shift I couldn't have imagined when I arrived in Kingsbury. "Just give God nine months," Steve said last August. I had no idea what God would form in me during that time. I still don't have a full picture. I know I'll need to find some type of employment to help with our monthly expenses. It's been a gift to have the time off from work, but it's time to return. I'm not assuming I'll be able to receive a paycheck from a church, but I know I'm called to ministry. Maybe that means the next step is tentmaking. Or hospital or retirement home chaplaincy. God knows what we need to live on, and I want to approach this prayerfully with Nate.

Here's one thing I do know: I want to be alongside others as they explore what it means to notice and name the presence of God in the midst of all the ordinary circumstances of a day. I want to be alongside others to encourage them to know the height and depth and length and breadth of the love of God, to rest in the love of God. To celebrate and savor it with joy. I stare at the labyrinth, at the flower shape in the middle, and I'm reminded that what I want is not to wear myself out delivering flowers to Jesus or to others but to keep Jesus company as he gives the flowers away. Lavish, abundant, beautiful signs of his love. That's what I long to do.

Katherine says that sounds like a call toward the ministry of spiritual direction, and she may be right. Charissa may be right. That may be a next step forward while I explore employment opportunities as well. Watch and pray. Those are ongoing words for me. Watch and pray.

The Holy Land group leaves on the pilgrimage next week. Katherine asked where I would like her to pray for me. I was so touched by that. I had hoped to pray there myself, to walk in the footsteps of Jesus with Nate. With Jake. I asked if she would pray twice: once in Cana for our marriage and once near the Garden of Gethsemane for me, that I would continue to have the courage to say, Your will be done.

Becca

Becca was so exhausted when she arrived from London that she went straight upstairs to her room without thinking about anything else. It was only the next afternoon when she awoke that she discovered Hannah had stocked the refrigerator and cupboards with food, and there were pink and white ruffled tulips in a vase on the kitchen table.

She poured herself a bowl of Cheerios and sat down in the music room on the antique sofa where she and her mother had often watched movies together, the collage of smiling photos confronting her.

She couldn't do this. Not by herself. She had thought she might have a sense of her mother's presence with her in the house. But all she felt was her dreadful absence.

She couldn't do it. Her mother wouldn't blame her for that. Her mother hadn't been able to return to her own house after the car accident. She'd told Becca that story, how she went home from the hospital, packed up her life in a couple of suitcases, and staggered back to her childhood home because she couldn't bear the grief of living alone, surrounded by memories.

Maybe that's what she ought to do. Leave the house. Sell it. Close the door and never return.

If only she had asked her mother for advice about what to do after she was gone. But Becca had avoided all those sorts of conversations. She had lived in denial—or was it foolish hope?—convinced that her mother would live, regardless of what the doctors had predicted.

"I'll help you," Hannah had said many times. "Whatever you need, you can lean on me."

Becca glanced outside at a yard that would need to be tended to, at chipping paint on eaves and a sagging porch with railings missing. What was she supposed to do with a decrepit old house? She couldn't be burdened with it. Her mother wouldn't want her burdened with it. Her mother had always encouraged her wings, even when those wings took her places her mother didn't approve of.

Her hand shifted from her lap to the butterfly tattoo on her shoulder. Her wings. Odd, how she hadn't made the connection before. Leaning forward, she pulled from the collage the photo of her mother with a butterfly resting on her shoulder. Becca glanced at her tattoo. It was inked in almost the same place as the blue one that had landed on her mother. Maybe it was some kind of sign. A sign of what, she didn't know. But a connection. A thread weaving them together somehow.

Maybe Hannah could help her clear out the house. It was a tomb. A crypt. And Becca needed to fly. To be free. Maybe the butterfly was the sign.

"Take it slow," Hannah said on the phone later that afternoon when Becca called to thank her for the food and flowers. "I know it's hard. But you don't want to make any rash decisions you might regret later."

Becca emptied the coffee pot into the sink. "But I can't take care of everything. I know I can't. My mom couldn't, either. She said so after my grandmother died. She didn't know how much longer she would keep the house."

"I know. She told me."

"So what did she expect me to do with it? Did she tell you anything about what she was hoping for?"

"All she said was that she wanted you to finish your senior year. She was really adamant about that. She didn't want her"—Hannah paused as if reconsidering her words—"she didn't want you to put your life on hold in any way."

Becca stared out the window at the chickadees gathered at the feeder. "So that's my answer, right? Sell the house, go back to school for one more year, and then figure out what's next."

Hannah paused and then said, "How about if you join us for dinner tonight, and we can talk about it in person?"

It wasn't a bad plan. Becca didn't relish the idea of eating alone at the house, and she wasn't prepared to sort through any of her mother's belongings. Not yet.

"It's pizza night here, an Allen Family tradition."

"Yeah, okay," Becca said, and went upstairs to shower.

Hannah

Nathan and Becca had plenty to talk about at dinner, with her being a literature major and him being a literature professor, with her spending a year abroad in London and him spending a year abroad in Oxford. Their lively conversation ranged from metaphysical poets to favorite Beatles albums. Jake entered that debate enthusiastically, arguing good-naturedly with her about the merits of "Abbey Road" versus "Revolver." Hannah, who knew nothing about either one of them, listened attentively and waited for natural segues into discussion about Becca's departure from London, her process of grieving, or her thoughts about moving forward. It wasn't until Jake excused himself to do homework and Nathan made coffee that Becca shifted gears.

"What if I spend the summer getting everything sorted out and then put the house up for sale?"

"I think it might be wise to move a little more slowly," Hannah said, "give yourself a year to process everything."

"Yeah, but it's a huge responsibility, and I'll be away at school, and it shouldn't just sit there empty." Becca reached for another cookie. "My mom didn't like the place. She said it felt lonely and sad when she was there by herself. And it does. It's awful. Like a tomb."

Hannah had thought of it as a funeral parlor, but tomb was an apt description too.

"Mom didn't know what to do with it, either. She didn't feel like she could get rid of all my grandmother's stuff after she died, so she just stayed trapped, stuck."

Hannah was going to defend Meg. She was going to say that she wasn't stuck but praying about what her next steps were when she was struck down with cancer. But she decided to keep this to herself.

"And ever since my mom told me what happened to my grandfather, well—the house just seems especially creepy now. I don't even know if I can stand it all summer. I might stay with a friend at her flat. She's got a futon."

"Might not be a bad idea," Nathan said. "Surround yourself with people who love you, who can support you through all of this."

"Yeah." She set her jaw. "But I've made up my mind. I want to sell it."

Hannah managed to avoid sighing. "It's yours to do with as you want, Becca." Meg had left the house and everything in it to her daughter. All Hannah could offer was advice. But as Meg had told Hannah on multiple occasions, Becca was strong-willed. There would be no arguing with her. If she had decided she was going to sell it, then she had decided. Period.

"So what do I need to do?" Becca asked.

"Decide what you want to keep," Hannah said, "and start getting rid of the rest."

"You'll help?"

"Yes." And if there were things of Meg's that Becca was quick to discard, Hannah might secretly save them in boxes in case Becca ever regretted her decision.

Becca sat back in her chair and breathed out a slow sigh. "Okay. I can do this. We can do this. Thank you." She finished off her coffee and looked at her phone. "I'm going out with some friends tonight. Better get going. Thanks for dinner."

"Any time," Nathan said, rising. "You're welcome here any time."

"Thanks." She gave him a hug and turned toward Hannah. "Can we plan time for sorting through things once I know my work schedule?"

"Absolutely."

Hannah and Nathan stood at the window watching as Becca pulled her mother's car out of the driveway a few minutes later. "I've got a crazy, crazy idea," he said.

Hannah raised her eyebrows.

He kissed her. "How about another cup of coffee?"

Nathan was right. It was a crazy idea. A crazy, ridiculous, and quite possibly divinely inspired idea. She planted her elbows on the table and stared at him. "You heard Becca. It's like a tomb."

"I know."

"You've been in the house, Nate, you know what it's like."

"Yes. And I seem to remember suggesting once before that you could move into it and bring some life to it."

He was right. Last December he had suggested she stop commuting back and forth from Nancy's cottage at the lake and stay instead at Meg's house while she was in London. When Meg returned home she commented that she had never seen the house so beautifully decorated for Christmas.

"What about Jake?" she asked. "He won't want to move."

"Don't be so sure. He'd have way more space in a place like that. And it's not like we'd be moving far. What is it? A couple of miles?"

Hannah fiddled with her small diamond ring, the gem catching the light. What if?

"We can talk to him about it," he said, "see what he thinks. And we don't have to decide anything fast. We'll need to make sure Becca really wants to sell it, give her all summer to think about it, longer if she needs to. But in the meantime, we can pray about whether there's new life for an old house, whether God would call us to move there together."

A funeral parlor transformed, a tomb thrumming with life, not death. Hannah pondered the images long after Nathan fell asleep that night. What if?

Meg would beam with delight to think that not one but two houses that had been places of sorrow and loss could be transformed into places of joy and new life. She would be thrilled, thrilled to know that her daughter would always have a room to return to if she wanted, thrilled to know that Hannah and her fledgling family would make it their own together.

And oh, the possibilities for ministry in a large house like that, for hospitality, for providing a resting place for the weary in need of deep renewal. What if?

As she drifted off to sleep, her head resting against Nathan's shoulder, one verse rang in Hannah's spirit again and again: *Behold, I am making all things new!* She could almost hear Meg's voice echo, Amen.

thirteen

"Musical houses!" Mara exclaimed after Hannah finished sharing with the Sensible Shoes Club what she and Nathan were prayerfully considering. She glanced over at Charissa, who was lying on her couch in a pair of striped linen pajamas. "Crazy to think that both of you could end up living in Meg's old houses." That hadn't come out quite right. "I mean . . . that you would move into places where Meg lived." She hated using past tense for her friend. She would always hate it.

"I know," Hannah said. "You're right. It is crazy. But please don't say anything to Becca about it if you see her. There's still a lot for us to think through. I know from conversations with Meg that the house is in pretty rough shape, that it needs lots of repairs and significant updating. So it would be a huge project."

"Well, I know a great handyman who could do some of that work," Charissa said, smiling at Mara.

Now, wouldn't that be something? "I bet Jeremy would love it," Mara said. "He loves old houses, always has."

"Well, if this is where God is leading, Nate and I are going to need someone like that. I don't have a clue about remodeling. No idea what would be involved. But something about this feels right. We'll wait and see where it all goes." Hannah removed her Bible and journal from her bag. "I'm glad it worked out for us to be together tonight. There's a lot to think about. Pray about."

Charissa nodded and said, "Let's pray for Becca right now."

They did. They lit the Christ candle and prayed for God to comfort her, reach her, rescue her, and reveal his love for her. They prayed for the seeds Meg and others had planted in Becca's life to sprout, grow, and flourish. They prayed for all the places of death and despair to be transformed into life and hope. They prayed fervently for Meg's child as if she were their own. And when they finished praying for Becca, they continued in prayer with the Bible story and exercise Mara had selected for them to ponder together.

MEDITATION ON JOHN 21:9-22
Embracing the Call

Quiet yourself in the presence of God. Then read the text aloud a couple of times and imagine you are on the beach with the disciples and Jesus. What do you see, hear, smell, taste? Pay attention to the thoughts and emotions that are stirred within you as you listen.

When they had gone ashore, they saw a charcoal fire there, with fish on it, and bread. Jesus said to them, "Bring some of the fish that you have just caught." So Simon Peter went aboard and hauled the net ashore, full of large fish, a hundred fifty-three of them; and though there were so many, the net was not torn.

Jesus said to them, "Come and have breakfast." Now none of the disciples dared to ask him, "Who are you?" because they knew it was the Lord. Jesus came and took the bread and gave it to them, and did the same with the fish. This was now the third time that Jesus appeared to the disciples after he was raised from the dead.

When they had finished breakfast, Jesus said to Simon Peter, "Simon son of John, do you love me more than these?" He said to him, "Yes, Lord; you know that I love you." Jesus said to him, "Feed my lambs." A second time he said to him, "Simon son of John, do you love me?" He said to him, "Yes, Lord; you know that I love you." Jesus said to him, "Tend my sheep." He said to him the third time, "Simon son of John, do you love me?" Peter felt hurt because he said to him the third time, "Do you love me?" And he said to him, "Lord, you know everything; you know that I love you." Jesus said to him, "Feed my sheep. Very truly, I tell you, when you were younger, you used to fasten your own belt and to go wherever you wished. But when you grow old, you will stretch out your hands, and someone else will fasten a belt around you and take you where you do not wish to go." (He said this to indicate the kind of death by which he would glorify God.) After this he said to him, "Follow me."

Peter turned and saw the disciple whom Jesus loved following them; he was the one who had reclined next to Jesus at the supper and had said, "Lord, who is it that is going to betray you?" When Peter saw him, he said to Jesus, "Lord, what about him?" Jesus said to him, "If it is my will that he remain until I come, what is that to you? Follow me!"

For Personal Reflection (45-60 minutes)

1. Imagine you are one of the disciples having breakfast with Jesus. What would you dare to ask Jesus? What have you come to believe about him?

2. Imagine you are Peter. How do you feel when Jesus keeps asking you if you love him? How do you feel about what Jesus asks you to do to demonstrate your love?

3. To what places and experiences have you been taken where you have not wished to go? How has God been glorified in these kinds of deaths?

4. In what ways are you tempted to compare your path of following Jesus to someone else's?

5. What is your response when Jesus says, "Follow me"?

For Group Reflection (45-60 minutes)

1. In what ways is Jesus calling you to demonstrate love for him by loving others?

2. In what ways are you being asked to die to yourself as you walk with Jesus?

3. What does it mean for you to keep your eyes focused on Jesus without comparing your journey to someone else's?

4. How can the group pray for you as you embrace his call to follow him?

Mara had always loved Peter, a fellow open-mouth-and-insert-foot-er. Peter gave her hope because when he failed—and he failed miserably—he got up again. She liked that about him.

Peter's frustration was something Mara also understood. Jesus had asked her the same questions over and over again too. Sometimes she felt frustrated, not that Jesus asked the same questions but that Jesus *needed* to ask the same questions.

Mara, do you love me?

Yes, Lord. Of course she did. Not as much as she wanted to, not as much as some other things in her life sometimes, not as much as some other people loved him, maybe, but yes.

Mara, do you love me?

Yes, Lord, but . . .

Mara, do you love me?

Yes, Lord. She loved him. As much as she was able to, she loved him. And she wanted to love others well too. Even if she didn't like where that path led. Because when Jesus talked about loving others, he wasn't just talking about the ones who loved her back. That was the hard part about love, about "going the extra mile," like Charissa had been talking about the past couple of months. Because you didn't get called to walk the extra mile with people who made it easy to walk it. That was the hard part.

She stared at her shoes. In the past few weeks her bitterness against Tom had found different forms of expression: her desire to win, to punish, to play "gotcha" games with him. She had told herself it would be a miracle if both Brian and Kevin became fellow allies in a battle against a common adversary. But was that really the miracle she wanted? That her boys would turn against their dad and develop and nurse their own bitterness and resentment to equal hers? Is that what she wanted?

There was an awfully wide gap between her honest answer to that question and what she knew was the "right answer."

Help, Jesus.

She rubbed at her chin, her fingertips finding a couple of wiry whiskers. The real miracle, she knew, would be to have her heart changed toward Tom. The real miracle would be for her to long for Tom to turn to Jesus and be rescued. The real miracle would be for her to pray for that. She snorted and then covered her mouth. What a miracle that would be.

Charissa

Charissa smoothed her pajamas and tried to find a comfortable position for writing in her notebook. Thirty weeks. She had made it to almost thirty weeks. But oh! the days were tedious. She stared at the handout. To what places and experiences had she been taken where she had not wished to go?

That was the easy part to answer. It was the second part of the question that was harder: How has God been glorified in these kinds of deaths?

She had no idea.

What she'd glimpsed of the glory of God had been revealed through others laying down their lives to love and serve her well, not through her own yielding and dying to self. Much as she affirmed the principle of cruciformity as a way of life, in practice she continued to resist. *I understand that,* Hannah had said one day when Charissa voiced her resentment over her enforced rest and her guilt over feeling resentful. Love for Bethany ought to translate into a willingness to embrace the cost, right? Instead, she caught herself griping. Constantly. And when she considered all the blessings she had been given, she felt even more guilty for complaining.

Follow me, Jesus said. And like Peter, she was looking over her shoulder to see how other people were doing it and objecting if their way looked easier. Especially now. But it was none of her business what discipleship for others looked like, none of her business whether others were called to die in painful ways or whether they lived fruitful, comfortable lives of ease. None of her business.

What is that to you? Jesus asked, exposing her heart.

Nothing, Lord, she responded. But in reality, it was something.

How hard was it to lie at home and rest? John tried to understand and be patient, but she could tell he wasn't entirely sympathetic. "Think of all the books you can read or the movies you can watch," he'd said multiple times. Though she had tried to devote more time to Scripture meditation and prayer, as the end of the semester approached, her thoughts drifted to chronic rehearsing of what she had laid down, some of it forced, some of it chosen, all of it hard. She wished it weren't so hard. She wished the cruciform way were something she embraced more readily, more enthusiastically. Her sorrow, she realized, was not that Jesus asked multiple times for an affirmation of love; her sorrow was that she kept failing to demonstrate it. After all the ways he had loved her, all the evidence of grace in her life, could she not pick up her cross and follow without chafing every step of the way?

"Pray for me," she said to Mara and Hannah when they shifted toward the group discussion time. She didn't want to die.

But die she did, daily. Most days blurred together without anything remarkable to note. Daily Charissa chronicled gratitude because that was the one spiritual discipline that helped her press forward: thanks for a good night's rest, for white blossoms on a Bradford pear tree in the front yard, for a thoughtful card or meal offered in kindness, for visits from friends, for the opportunity to devour literature for pleasure rather than productivity, and for one more day of Bethany being safe. At John's urging, she joined him in reading about their baby's development day to day, week by week, giving thanks for tiny fingernails growing in secret and elbows that poked her ribs, even as she tried to give thanks for heartburn and every other kind of discomfort that reminded her that she was still pregnant and that she was grateful to be so. Thanks to Mara's help and the convenience of online shopping, she also supervised the decorating of the nursery, including John's assembling the crib, which took three times as long as the instructions claimed.

She was browsing a baby clothing website one morning when her inbox dinged with an email from the Academic Affairs office. *Evaluations.* If she had remembered that she would be receiving student evaluations, she would have daily monitored her inbox for them. Charissa clicked on the attached document, the first part of which was a summary report assessing "teaching effectiveness" in such categories as "establishing rapport," "stimulating student interest," and "classroom experience." The second part contained student comments.

She skimmed the numerical grades first. *On a scale from one to five, five being high, rate your instructor in the following areas.* The more she read, the more agitated she became. Though it would have been naïve to think she would receive perfect fives all the way across, to consistently receive mostly threes made her heart sink, especially when her averages were compared to the "overall averages" of other faculty members. It wasn't just Justin and his back row posse that had graded her harshly. In categories like "explained course material clearly and concisely," she had received mostly ones and twos.

She skimmed the comments page. "Lectures too much" was one of the kinder remarks. A few students wrote that though they were sorry Ms. Sinclair had gotten sick, they had benefited from having a "real professor" finish the course.

Charissa closed her inbox, overcome by heartburn not caused by pregnancy.

—⟨⟩

"These aren't as bad as you made them out to be," John said when he got home that night. He stared at her computer screen. "Look here: 'Ms. Sinclair assigned writing themes that helped me think about life in new ways.'"

"That would be from Ben. Or from Sidney." Both of them had responded thoughtfully to the memento mori exercise she had given months ago. "Those are probably the only two who even gave me any fours."

"That's not possible. You got mostly fours in the 'demonstrated importance of subject matter' category. Look."

She leaned forward and shut the screen. She was tired of looking at it. "I'm obviously not cut out to be a teacher."

"Don't say that. It was your first semester, with lots of extenuating circumstances."

"I'm not going to make excuses for myself. It is what it is." She covered her eyes. "Maybe I should just withdraw from the whole program."

He pried her hands from her face. "You're kidding, right? All your life all you've ever wanted to do is teach."

"For my own selfish reasons. And this just shows how foolish it all has been."

"I don't buy it. And I bet if you talked with other faculty members—I bet if you asked Nathan, he'd tell you he's gotten plenty of lousy evaluations over the years." He picked up her phone and handed it to her. "Call him and ask."

"I'm not going to call and—"

"Call him, Charissa. He's your advisor. Call him."

She exhaled loudly and stared at the phone. She could tell by the look on John's face that he wasn't going to let it go. "Fine," she said, and dialed Nathan's number.

Regardless of what the students had indicated on their forms, Nathan said, he had worked with them for three weeks, and he had seen the fruit of her labor among them. Not only did they write reasonably well for freshmen, but they were thinking critically and asking good questions. "So don't be discouraged by this," he said. "Believe me, I've read plenty worse about myself over the years." Teaching, he said, was a daily exercise of failure, an ongoing practice in humility. And it might be exactly the right profession for her but not for the reasons that had initially drawn her to it. "You're gifted, Charissa, and you know me well enough to know I tell the truth. Don't give up over this, hard as it is."

Okay, she promised him. She wouldn't make any rash decisions. She would continue to move forward at whatever pace was necessary with an infant and explore her vocational call in spite of this setback. She would trust that somehow God was at work to shape her in the midst of it, hard as it was. Hard as everything was.

When Charissa hung up the phone, she lay back on the couch, palms resting open on her abdomen, and tried to practice letting go. Day after difficult day, she practiced letting go.

Becca

Sleeping on a childhood friend's futon was an adequate arrangement when that friend was single. But two weeks after Becca moved into Lauren's one-bedroom apartment with a duffel bag, Lauren started dating a guy from her office. "Sorry to kick you out," she said to Becca as they ate their ramen noodles one night, "but Dan and I . . ."

"No, I get it. Of course. You've already done way more than you needed to." Maybe she could afford a small studio apartment for the summer. Or find another friend eager to share rent for a few months. Quite a few of her high school friends still lived in Kingsbury. She ought to be able to work out something, anything to get her away from the house. Each hour spent there made her more resolute: she wanted it cleared out and ready to sell by the end of summer.

So she started purging one room at a time. When she wasn't working extra hours at the café, she was on her knees at the house, dividing everything into three categories: pitch, save, give away. Her aunt, at least, made it easy for her. Rachel had already taken everything she wanted, she told Becca on the phone one night, and she wanted nothing to do with anything else. "Unless you find something worth a fortune," she'd quipped, "and then we'll talk."

But apart from photos and mementos from her childhood, there weren't many things Becca desired, either. Her plan was simple: box up the treasures she wanted to keep and then host an estate sale before she went back to college. Let the vultures descend and do the work of stripping the carcass down to nothing. Whatever didn't sell could be donated to Goodwill. "You're sure about all of this?" Hannah had asked multiple times.

She was sure. By the end of May the only bedroom she hadn't yet sorted was her mother's. Many nights she entered the room with the intention of packing it up, but all she could do was bury her face in her mother's clothes in search of her familiar scent, or weep over blonde strands of hair still caught on the bristles of a hairbrush, or cry herself to sleep on a mascara-stained pillowcase she couldn't bear to wash.

As the fragrance of lilacs drifted in through the open window one evening, Becca sat cross-legged on her mother's bed, studying a sketchbook she had left on her desk. Gnarled and twisted trees filled many of the pages. Flowers too. "Amaryllis, flowers in winter," the caption read beneath a particularly detailed rendering. The last sketch was the one she had drawn of Becca a few days before she died. Becca traced her finger over the nose ring in the picture. Her mother hadn't approved of the nose ring, but she'd included it. Beneath the drawing were the words, "My beautiful girl." Becca closed the book before tears splattered and ruined the page.

It wasn't just the drawings that made her sad. It was the blank pages at the end of the book, too many blank pages. She set the sketchbook in a box along with other things she knew her mother had treasured: a box of love letters, a small wooden cross, and a framed sketch of Jesus holding a little lamb, all of which were on her nightstand when she died. Draped on the nightstand too was a burgundy shawl. A prayer shawl, her mother had told her, knit by someone from Mara's church.

Well, it hadn't worked.

Her mother had worn it every day of their visit together. She had wrapped herself in it when they watched movies and when they sorted photos into albums and when they drank milkshakes in front of the fireplace.

It hadn't worked.

Becca fingered the yarn and pressed her face against it, searching for a scent. Nothing.

She folded it and set it in the box, her gaze lingering on the picture of Jesus nuzzling the little lamb, a picture her mother said gave her comfort because she saw herself as a little lost lamb that Jesus had found and rescued. Becca stared at the lamb, an expression of contentment and rest upon its face. Oh, to be safe and securely held like that. To be loved and cared for, a little lamb with someone to watch over her.

Her mother had trusted Jesus to watch over her, to protect and love and care for her, and look what faith had done for her. Nothing.

That picture provoked her. Much as her mother had loved it, she couldn't bear to keep it. Maybe Hannah would like it. The prayer shawl and the cross too. Those were things Hannah would probably appreciate receiving as gifts. Becca set them aside in a separate box, scrawled "For Hannah" across the lid in permanent black marker, and left the room.

Mara

Comfort food, Mara decided. After weeks of fussing over fancy menus and elegant dishes, she decided that the real gift to the Crossroads patrons would be to make them feel like they were enjoying a home-cooked meal. So she casually worked into conversation questions about favorite childhood foods, and then she composed her list: macaroni and cheese (the real gooey kind, Billy said), meat loaf and mashed potatoes (several of them echoed agreement with Constance when she gave that answer), and chicken and dumplings. When Mara said that her grandmother had made chicken and dumplings for her when she was little, Ronni got a little teary and said, "Me too."

"Can I skip school and go with you?" Kevin asked the night before the big day.

Mara eyed him from across the dinner table. "Because you want to serve or skip school?"

He half-smiled and shrugged.

"You willing to work?"

He nodded and took a second helping of pork tenderloin.

"Work hard?"

"Yeah."

"Okay. You can come. I'll write you a note."

Brian, who had actually joined them at the table to eat, scoffed at this. "How come he gets to and I don't?"

Mara was going to answer, *Because he's served there before and knows everyone*, but instead she said, "You want to serve at the shelter?"

Brian stirred his mashed potatoes and green beans together on his plate. "Yeah, okay."

"It'll be lots of work. You don't get to go and just sit."

"Okay."

"You'll need to welcome the guests, treat them nicely and—"

"I said, yeah. Okay."

Okay. Mara took a spoonful of applesauce. "I'll write you a note."

She thought she heard him mumble, "Thanks."

—ᏻ

"Pray for us," Mara said to Charissa on the phone that night. "I can't believe this is actually happening." Never in her wildest dreams had she imagined both boys would want to come with her to Crossroads. "I'm not naive; I know they just want a day off school, but still."

"It's still incredible they want to go," Charissa said. "I'll definitely keep praying. Wish there was more I could do."

"That's plenty. All the good that's happening right now, I know it's only because people are praying. So thank you." She switched her phone to the other ear. "And what about you? How are you?"

"Still here." Charissa sighed. "And that's a gift. I know it's a gift. Almost thirty-four weeks now."

Mara whistled. "You're getting there. Just hold on, little Bethany. Almost there." Kevin entered the kitchen and stood waiting, hands behind his back. "Hang on, Charissa." She pressed the phone to her shoulder. "What do you need, Kev?"

He held out a piece of paper. "I thought maybe they might like it if they had menus and stuff, like they could order at the table and Brian and I could be, like, the waiters or something."

She stared first at him, then at the sheet of paper. *Crossroads House Restaurant,* it read at the top in fancy script. Below was a list of all the food she had mentioned she would be cooking.

"You're a genius! Can you print out fifty of these?"

"Yep," he said, and left the room.

Mara waited until she heard him reach the top of the stairs and then said to Charissa, "Wait till you hear this."

Hannah

Had she ever seen Mara looking so happy, so at ease? While Hannah watched her friend bustling around the Crossroads kitchen, managing the chaos with joy, she marveled over the beauty of someone flourishing in what God had called her to do. Not only that, but Brian and Kevin were both taking instructions without arguing. At least, not verbally. Brian rolled his eyes every once in a while but for the most part was cooperative, not only with his mother but with the other volunteers. "A miracle," Mara whispered to Hannah as she slid large casserole dishes into the oven. "Keep praying."

When the doors opened just before noon and the patrons entered a room with cloth-covered tables, flickering votive candles, and fresh flowers, Hannah and other volunteers were poised and ready to greet them. "What's all this?" Billy exclaimed, arms extended wide. "A party?"

"A big party," Hannah said.

"What kind of party? Birthday party?"

"No, not a birthday party. Miss Mara just wanted to throw a special party for all of you."

"A 'just because' party?"

"Yes. Just because." As Kevin, Brian, and others showed guests to their seats, Hannah returned to the kitchen. "I think you estimated about right. I counted fifty-two."

"Good. We'll have extras. 'Cause I prepped for sixty just in case."

"Put me to work," a voice called from the doorway.

Mara spun around. "Jeremy!"

"Or, I should say, put me to work on my lunch break. Can't stay long, Mom. Sorry."

"I'm thrilled you can't stay long! Another job?"

"Boss says we got a couple of big contracts, so it looks like we'll have some jobs to keep us busy for a few months, thank God."

The way he said those last words, Hannah thought, it didn't sound like a throwaway line. Mara motioned toward the dining room. "Well, your brothers are here." Jeremy raised his eyebrows. "I know, both of them, and they're gonna be out there taking orders at the tables and then delivering food."

"I'll help them out." Jeremy kissed his mother on the cheek. "And I promised Abby I'd take pictures so her mom can see." His eyes brimmed with emotion. "It looks amazing out there, Mom. I'm so proud of you."

"Well, you haven't tasted anything yet"—the timer beeped and Mara grabbed her oven mitts—"but thank you, honey. Thanks for coming."

Hannah was dishing generous portions of macaroni and cheese onto plates when her cell phone buzzed with a text. She decided to wait to check it. "Is that you or me?" Mara asked.

"Me," Hannah said. She handed two plates to Kevin.

"Oops! Mine too," Mara said. She set down her spatula and reached into her pocket, her brow furrowing when she read the screen. "It's John."

Hannah whipped her phone out of her jeans. *Strong contractions. Heading to hospital right now. Pls pray.*

"Two more meatloaf," Brian called out, entering the kitchen, "and an extra large chicken and dumplings." He looked at Hannah. "Please."

Mara was typing on her phone. Hannah loaded up two plates and told him to come back for the third. "I'll take that one," Jeremy said, reaching out his hand for the third order.

Mara shoved her phone back in her pocket and wiped her brow. "Guess we don't make a prayer announcement here, right?"

"Right," Hannah said. Charissa wouldn't want that.

"So, deep breath," Mara said. "And help, Lord Jesus."

Charissa

Charissa had hoped to make it farther. She had hoped to make it another month. But what more could she have done? She'd been doing nothing—*nothing!*—for seven weeks. "You did everything you were supposed to do," John kept repeating on the drive to the hospital, and the nurses echoed that after she was admitted to the labor ward. *Threshold,* they said. She had made it to a significant threshold as far as the baby's health risks were concerned.

She ought to be grateful she had added almost fifty days to Bethany's life inside the womb. And she was grateful. She just didn't like being told she ought to be grateful—not by John, not by nurses, not by the voices inside her own head. She also didn't like the thought of their baby having to stay in the neonatal intensive care unit for a few weeks of monitoring after birth. The logical part of her brain reminded her that it could be worse. Others had it worse. She had seen pictures online. She had read their stories. Their horror stories had motivated her to fight temptation and do as close to nothing as possible as she ticked off the slow days of waiting.

She stared up from her hospital bed at the fluorescent lights. As soon as the nurse finished putting in the IV line, she was going to get up off that bed and walk around. Or kneel. Or rock. Or scream into a pillow. The contractions could be her excuse to shout or cry loud and long about everything that had not gone according to plan.

John rubbed the blanket. "You warm enough? Too hot?"

"No, I'm okay." Well, not okay. She winced and tried to hold still as she breathed her way through another contraction.

"All set," the nurse said, pressing the tape gently around the needle. "The anesthesiologist will come by soon to talk with you."

"I don't want an epidural," Charissa said.

"You might change your mind about that, hon," John said, and the nurse nodded her agreement.

"Stay open-minded," she said, "and play it by ear."

"I said, no epidural." She didn't have control over much, but she was going to have control over that. She would have a natural childbirth. The way Bethany had been eagerly trying to get things rolling the past few weeks, there wouldn't be long to wait.

Mara

Mara glanced at the clock above the microwave. Seven. John had called more than seven hours ago. She decided to text again. *Nothing yet,* John replied. She called Hannah. "Still no baby. I don't want to keep bugging them, but I can't help feeling a little worried about everything." None of her babies had required the emergency care little Bethany would need. But at least Charissa had a husband like John alongside. That was a gift. Tom had been more of a hindrance than a help in the delivery rooms, demanding and obnoxious to nurses, who weren't amused by his crude jokes or sexism.

"Keep me in the loop if you hear anything," Hannah said.

Mara knocked on the window to get Kevin's attention outside. She mouthed, *Dinner,* and then said, "Okay, I will. And thanks again for helping today."

"My pleasure. It was wonderful, Mara, a wonderful success."

Yes, it was. The whole thing had come off without any hitches, which was, Miss Jada had said, truly remarkable. *You did real good,* she said afterward.

Mara couldn't have been more pleased. Not only had the guests raved about the food, but Kevin's idea of serving them restaurant-style had given Miss Jada some ideas about how to regularly make their patrons feel valued and cared for, ideas she was confident the board would approve. "I think it'll be the first of many," Mara said. "Who knows? Maybe with some fundraising we can do something like that once a month."

"Well, count Nate and me in. He's already said he wants to help out next time. Jake too."

Maybe even Brian. When Mara asked him in the car on the way home if he'd had a good time, he'd shrugged and said, "Better than school." Not exactly a ringing endorsement, but she'd take it.

After Kevin entered through the garage a few minutes later, Mara and Hannah said their goodbyes. "Call your brother for dinner, will you, Kev?" She tucked her phone in her pocket. Better keep it close in case John called.

"He's riding his bike."

She sighed. She had told Brian they would be eating at seven because Tom was picking them up for the weekend at eight. "Okay, we'll eat without him." She removed some of the leftover meatloaf and macaroni and cheese from the oven. "So what'd you think of today?"

"Yeah, okay."

"Just okay?"

"Good. It was good."

"Your idea was amazing, Kev. Did you see how happy everyone was?"

He spooned a large helping of mac and cheese onto his plate. "Yeah. Billy said he hadn't eaten in such a good restaurant since he was a little kid. He was in the Marines, did you know that?"

"Yeah. Did he talk to you about it?" She poured two glasses of milk and followed him to the table.

"Yeah, he was telling me stories about these secret tunnels that the Viet Cong used to hide out from the Americans and . . ."

Mara didn't have to ask any questions to keep him talking. Twenty minutes later when Brian came in, Kevin was in the middle of telling a dramatic story about Billy stalking an enemy sniper in the jungle. Brian loaded some mashed potatoes and meatloaf onto a plate and shoved it in the microwave.

"Did he get him?" Brian asked.

"Yeah. And the Viet Cong put this bounty on him because he kept killing off their men."

Brian looked impressed by this. "How many confirmed kills?"

Mara made sure she didn't sigh out loud. The boys played way too many Call of Duty games. "Dunno," Kevin said. "Lots, probably. I'll ask him next time."

"Or you can ask him, Brian," Mara said. Might as well seize any open door for conversation.

The microwave beeped, and Brian brought his plate to the table. He didn't reply, but he also didn't roll his eyes.

"Billy's got lots of cool stories," Kevin said.

Brian took a bite of mashed potatoes. "Not as cool as Leon."

"Yeah, definitely as cool as Leon."

"Leon's a boxer, like a heavyweight champion or something."

Kevin scoffed. "He's not a heavyweight, no way."

Mara let them argue. If they were determined to fight about who was the coolest patron at Crossroads, she wasn't going to interrupt. She rose from the table, put some snickerdoodles on a plate for them, and sat down again to listen.

Charissa

"You're holding steady at four centimeters," the nurse said after checking Charissa's dilation progress.

Nine hours of intense contractions, and now Bethany was going to take her time? Not okay. If she thought she could do jumping jacks without fainting, she would. Charissa fiddled with the laces on her hospital gown and tried not to cry.

"You're doing great," John said, and stroked her forehead. She swiped his hand away.

Hannah

"What was it like for you when Jake was born?" Hannah asked Nathan as they got ready for bed. When he didn't reply right away, she said, "I'm interested in all the details. Anything you remember."

"Really?"

"Really. The unabridged version." She sat down on what had once been his side of the bed and watched his reflection in the bathroom mirror while he squeezed out toothpaste. These moments of observing him in the mundane details of his daily routine—brushing his teeth, combing his hair, shaving—these were the sort of unguarded, familiar moments that reminded her of the gift it was to share life together.

He caught her gaze in the mirror and smiled. "I remember I was a nervous wreck," he said, "drove like a maniac to the hospital when we thought it was time. False alarm, and they sent us home." He brushed vigorously, then spit into the sink. "Next day, same thing. Race to the hospital, and they say nothing's happening and send us home. Third day, race to the hospital, and they say, yes, she's at three centimeters."

He finished brushing, spit one last time into the sink, and wiped off his mouth with the back of his hand. "I think it was three centimeters. Anyway, she suddenly started dilating fast, went from three to ten in half an hour or something crazy like that"—he rinsed his hands under the faucet—"and tells me she needs to push. I run to get a nurse, grab the first one I find and yell, 'She's pushing!' So the nurse grabs a wheelchair and races down the hallway because we've got to get her into the birthing room. We get her there, and I'm helping her up onto the bed when her water breaks all over me. And the next thing we know, Jake's crowning—right there—and the midwife, who's literally just entered the room, puts on rubber gloves and basically catches him." He dried off his hands. "Nurse, looks at me—she's as shocked as I am—and says, 'Can I get you a towel?'" He laughed. "True story."

Hannah scooted up against her pillow as he slid into bed. "Incredible," she said.

"Yeah."

"And then what?"

He rolled over to face her, propped on his elbow. He was silent a moment and then said, "It's like people say, you don't have words. You try, but you can't describe the feeling of wonder and awe and relief you have in that moment."

She could see him mentally debating whether or not to say anything more. She reached for his hand. "It's okay," she said. "I want to hear everything. Promise." She wanted to participate somehow in his moment of becoming a father, wanted to enter into the birth narrative of the young man she was growing to love as her son.

"I was overcome," Nathan said, "utterly overcome by love. And overwhelmed with gratitude for the gift she'd given to us. To me." His eyes brimmed with emotion. "Maybe I shouldn't have said that."

No. She was glad he did. His speaking the truth was what she wanted, what she needed. "If you hadn't loved her in that moment, Nate, what kind of man would you be?"

He tucked a strand of her hair behind her ear and murmured, "Thank you." The depth of love and devotion in his eyes—adoration, even— spoke more profoundly than any other words.

It was good, Hannah thought as she rolled over and turned off the light, it was very good that Jake was spending the night at a friend's house. Though she would never share the intimacy of childbirth with her husband, there were other intimate moments of communion they could share. And enjoy.

Charissa

Forget natural childbirth, she wanted drugs. Every flavor of drugs. "I want an epidural," Charissa said. John looked up from the chair where he was typing on his phone.

"Are you sure? You said—"

"I know what I said! I changed my mind." She glared at his phone. "And whoever you're bringing into the delivery room with us with your texting or Facebook or whatever, stop."

John stowed away his phone.

Charissa watched the monitor as another contraction seized her. A big one. "Epidural," she hissed as she breathed her way through it. "Now."

Becca

Nighttime was the worst part of the day, that moment when Becca, weary after a ten-hour shift on her feet, would stumble through the front door and hear only the jingling of her keys and the echoing of her footsteps on the hardwood.

She tossed her name tag onto the kitchen counter and made herself a cup of chamomile tea. She might as well pack up some more boxes. She hadn't yet done any work in the music room or in the parlor, and since the music room was still filled with too many reminders of her mother's life and death, she decided to purge the parlor.

All the furniture would go into the estate sale, and if there were fans of Victorian and early-twentieth-century decor who descended on the house, they would score plenty of treasures. The few things in the room that had been her mother's she would keep: some framed photos, the snow globe from Harrods, and a china tea service they had used on special occasions. Becca had always loved the weekends when her grandmother was out of town. That's when her mother was willing to break the strict house rules about toys staying in bedrooms, and they would have tea parties with Becca's dolls in the parlor. Becca had found pictures in a box: she with her cockeyed pigtails, surrounded by dolls and beaming impishly from the settee. She wished her mother were in the pictures. But there had been no one else to take photos.

She picked up a magazine from the coffee table, its pages open to sample bridal bouquets, and tried to think of something other than Paris or Simon. He hadn't contacted her after she'd refused his offer her last night in London. Some nights when she lay in bed by herself, her thoughts drifted toward him, and once she typed a text to say hi, and she nearly sent it—she was so close to sending it—but then she remembered the betrayal and how he had never loved her but loved using her, and her anger kept her from opening that door.

She put the magazine into Hannah's box, covering the face of Jesus and the little lamb.

Maybe she would change her number so she could stop wondering if she would ever hear from him again. Cut the cord, shut that life down, change her email address too. Claire was the only one who had written to her since she'd been back in Kingsbury—kind notes to say she was "thinking of her," which probably meant she was praying. Whatever. As weary as she felt, Becca would take whatever help the universe was willing to throw her way, which most days didn't seem like much.

She was on her way out of the room when she spied a small book lodged between the seat cushion and armrest of a chair in the corner. Her mother's journal. She had seen her writing in it the last week they were together, but then she had forgotten about it.

Flipping through the pages, her eyes landed on an entry dated the fourth of August, the day she dropped Becca off at the airport. *Take care of my daughter, Lord. Please. Watch over her and*

Becca closed the book, curled up in the chair, and cried.

Charissa

The epidural did what it was designed to do: it removed the pain. But it also took away Charissa's sense of control. Now the only touchstone, the only connection she had to her own body and to her baby was provided by wires, a monitor, and the report of medical personnel who regularly checked her progress. "There's a big one," a nurse commented as she watched the monitor. Charissa felt only moderate tightness. When her water broke moments later, she felt nothing at all.

"How about a fresh gown?" John said. "And maybe some new sheets?"

Charissa bit her lip and nodded.

—ᘓ

Just before dawn the monitor, which had been of marginal interest to the staff during the night, suddenly became the focus of a flurry of attention. "What's going on?" Charissa asked, the panic rising in her voice as one nurse hurried out of the room.

"What's happening?" John echoed, leaping up from the chair where he had grabbed snatches of sleep the past few hours.

"OB's on his way right now," another nurse said, patting Charissa's shoulder.

"What's happening?"

"The baby's showing some signs of distress," the nurse said, her voice irritatingly calm.

Moments later a doctor swept into the room and introduced himself. He looked way too young to be in charge. A baby doc. For babies. *Oh, God, help.* "What's happening?" John asked again.

"Heart rate's dropping," he said. "Baby's not happy at the moment."

God, help. Please help.

The nurse fiddled with the monitor and turned up the volume slightly so that the heartbeat was now audible as well as visible.

"I'm going to check and see how far dilated you are," the doctor said, "and then we'll see what we need to do." While John held her hand, the doctor donned gloves and did his exam. Charissa, feeling nothing, watched his face, which revealed nothing. "Okay," he finally said, "you're good to go. But your baby's getting tired, and we need to move fast"—*God, help!*—"so I need you to focus and push with everything you've got, okay?"

Push? How could she push when she couldn't feel anything?

"You can do it," John said, his voice taut. "I know you can."

God, please. She bore down and imagined herself pushing as hard and long as she could.

"Keep going, that's it," the doctor said. "Good job! You made good progress there. Take some deep breaths for me, rest a bit."

"You're doing great, Riss." John squeezed her hand and kissed her forehead.

"Where's the heartbeat?" she asked, trying to prop herself on her elbows.

The nurse moved the ultrasound probe lower on Charissa's abdomen.

"Where's the heartbeat?" John echoed.

Oh, God!

The nurse, still maneuvering the transducer in one hand, turned up the volume again. Still nothing. The doctor, leaning sideways around the nurse to check the screen, motioned for her to position the transducer lower. "It's harder to pick it up when the baby enters the birth canal," he said.

"But she's okay?" John asked. "Everything's still okay?"

"We're going to get her out with the next push," he said, his hand on Charissa's abdomen. "There's another contraction building now, so take a deep breath and push as hard as you can for me again."

He hadn't answered the question. Why hadn't he answered the question?

John gripped her hand even more tightly as, once again, Charissa commanded herself to do what she could not feel. Chin tucked to her chest, she closed her eyes and with a loud cry, pushed until she thought she would turn herself inside out.

"Keep going, Riss, keep going . . . Please . . ."

"Okay, gentle now, Charissa," the doctor said. "She's almost here. Just little pushes, you're almost there. That's it. You've got it. We're there."

Suddenly, there was a flurry of movement between the nurses and the doctor, lots of movement but no noise. Silence. No cry. Why was there no cry? The doctor lifted up a tiny, dusky gray—*Was that a baby? Oh, God, no!* She stared at a terror-stricken John for some indicator of what was happening. *God!* And then, after the interminable, deafening, screaming silence there was a whimper, a tiny mew, the most fragile, resilient, reverberating witness to life and hope Charissa had ever heard. "Call neo," the doctor commanded. John covered his face in his hands and sobbed.

There were moments in the life of a new mother that Charissa did not realize were important to her until she was robbed of them, like the father cutting the umbilical cord or smiling parents cradling a seconds-old newborn and marveling over tiny hands and feet before posing for photos. When Bethany was whisked away for oxygen without any chance to hold her, Charissa tried to tell herself that the Hallmark moments weren't important, that what was important was that their daughter would be receiving the emergency care she needed over the next few minutes, hours, days, weeks, even. "Go," Charissa said to John when the nurses invited him to accompany Bethany in her transport incubator to the neonatal intensive care unit. "Go with her. Please. I'm okay. I'll be okay." But after John left the room, Charissa lay back on the pillow and let the tears flow.

fourteen

Becca

Becca arrived at the coffee shop bleary-eyed on Saturday morning after staying up late to read her mother's journal. The intimacy of her hand-written thoughts, fears, longings—and yes, prayers—brought her mother to life again. Some of the words soothed, others pierced and wounded. Such was the price of hearing her mother speak, the bitter-sweet price of hearing her voice, raw, honest, uncensored, and full of love and hope and regret.

"The usual?" she asked one of their regular customers when she came up to the counter.

"Yes, please."

"Small decaf cappuccino for Ann," Becca called over her shoulder.

"You okay?" Ann asked as she swiped her card.

"Yeah, just tired."

But by noon Becca wasn't sure how she would make it through the rest of her shift. "Go home," her manager said. "It's okay. We can cover you."

"You sure? I don't want to leave you stranded."

"We're fine. Go home and get some rest. You look awful."

Becca didn't disagree or argue. But she didn't want to spend all day ruminating over her mother's words in an empty house. She texted Lauren. No reply. Maybe she could take a power nap and then tackle some errands. Or she could go for a run. She hadn't gone for a good run in a couple of months. That might do her a world of good. She drove to the house, changed her clothes, and laced up her favorite pair of shoes.

As her feet pounded the pavement mile after mile, her mother's words pursued her: *Rescue her, Lord.* So many of her mother's longings were summed up in that prayer. She had viewed Simon as a dangerous predator, and she had pleaded with God to do something to rescue Becca out of his hands. *I want my daughter back,* she wrote in one particularly distressing entry.

Well, Becca thought as she rounded the corner near her old elementary school, *I want my mom back.* The cruel irony was that her mother's wish had been granted only when it was too late for both of them to enjoy it. As for Becca's wish, there would be no granting of it. Ever. She pressed her fingers to her neck, checked her pulse, and quickened her pace for another couple of miles until, exhausted, she came to rest beneath a towering oak tree in a park and stared up at the sky.

That's where, as a little girl, she had thought heaven was. Some days she would lie on her back in their yard, squint her eyes at the clouds, and imagine she could see angels. Some days she would ask angels to deliver messages to her dad, like how she wished he could take her to the daddy-daughter dance at school, or how she had passed a spelling test she was worried about, or how she had gotten the part of a bunny rabbit in the Nutcracker ballet, and she would get to pull the tail of the evil Mouse King. One day she closed her eyes very hard and bypassed angelic messengers altogether. *Daddy, if you can see me,* she whispered to the sky, *please tell me.* But no answer came. What answer had she hoped for? A breeze through the tree above her head would have sufficed. But the day was still—not even birdsong—and it was the last time she had talked to the sky.

Tears ran hot down her cheeks as she lay down in the shade and closed her eyes. *Mom, if you can hear me . . .*

Charissa

The first time Charissa had the opportunity to gaze at her daughter for more than a few seconds was when she was wheeled on her gurney to the NICU before being moved to the postpartum recovery ward. Bethany, now a few hours old, lay in an incubator (a "koala," the hospital staff called it), wires and cords taped to her tiny pink body, a breathing apparatus attached to her nose, a feeding tube in her mouth, an IV hooked to her perfect little hand. *Oh, God.* John kissed Charissa on the forehead. "Hey, Mommy," he said, his hand resting on Bethany's shoulder, "meet our beautiful girl."

She looked nothing like the chubby cherubic babies in the movies. But oh! She was beautiful. Beautiful in her fragility. Charissa managed to squeeze out a broken whisper. "Can I hold her?"

Nodding, a nurse offered her a bottle of hand sanitizer. Then she gently lifted Bethany out of the koala, adjusted a blanket, and carefully placed her on Charissa's chest.

Oh, God.

Nothing could have prepared her for that first moment of touching her daughter. With a single finger Charissa stroked her cheek, then watched mesmerized as her little body rose and fell in steady breaths. "She's doing really well," the nurse said. "I know it can look pretty scary with all these wires and cords, but everything's looking good. Her vital signs are very good. And she's already had a good wet diaper."

Charissa moved her finger to stroke Bethany's hand. "How long?" she asked. "How long does she have to stay?"

"If everything goes well, about three weeks. We've got some markers we watch for—eating, breathing, swallowing on her own. We want to make sure she's gaining weight, that she's able to maintain her own body temperature. Right now the koala is taking care of that, making sure she's not too hot or too cold."

John stroked Charissa's hair. "I told them, you watch. Little Bethany will be an overachiever, just like her mommy."

Charissa kissed the pink cap on Bethany's head and looked at her fingers, each with a perfect tiny pearl of a fingernail.

"The key is to take it a day at a time," the nurse said, "and to make sure you're getting your rest too. She's in good hands here, I promise. We'll take good care of her."

Charissa's throat constricted, and she murmured, "Thank you." She rubbed Bethany's back, caressed her little thighs, her knees, her feet, her toes. Her impossible, perfect toes.

"Let's get you off to your room so you can rest," another nurse said, "and then you can come back later when you feel up to it."

"Not before some pictures," John said. "Lots of people are waiting for pictures."

Charissa hardly wanted to take her eyes off her daughter long enough to look at a camera. But she smiled for a few photos with John before returning her attention to Bethany. "We'll let you come back later," the nurse said. "Promise."

Reluctantly, Charissa shifted Bethany in her arms and prepared to hand her over. But just before the nurse took her, Bethany opened her eyes and locked onto Charissa's face with a long, probing stare, a glimmer of eternity in her gaze. And when her little eyelids closed like shades and opened again, Charissa silently marveled at all that could change with the blink of an eye.

John fingered Bethany's pink wristband. "She doesn't have a middle name yet. What shall we call her?"

Charissa looked at their daughter and immediately knew. "It's Grace," she said.

All grace.

Mara

"Four pounds, thirteen ounces, eighteen inches long," Mara reported on the phone to Hannah, "and John says Mom and baby are both doing well, thank God." Thank God, thank God, thank God.

"Oh, that's good news," Hannah said. "Thanks for letting me know."

Mara closed the kitchen window as the über-mower next door fired up his John Deere for the second time that week. "He says they'll keep Charissa for a couple of days. She's really sore, guess she tore pretty bad"—that was probably not information Charissa wanted widely shared, come to think of it—"and then Bethany will be there for a couple of weeks, they think."

"Did John say anything about meals? Anything we can do to help?"

"I got the impression they plan to be at the hospital as much as possible. He said we could drop by late tomorrow, as long as everything's going okay. He'll let us know."

"How about if I order flowers from the two of us?"

"That would be great," Mara said. "Thanks."

"Good. I'll take care of that tonight. And I should go. Nate's grilling burgers, and he just called out the three-minute warning."

"Enjoy! And once John says yay or nay on tomorrow, I'll let you know."

After Mara hung up the phone, she stared out at the back deck where for years Tom had cooked burgers on the grill. Maybe she'd teach herself how to use it. She could host backyard barbeques for friends and family. Maybe Jeremy could make her a picnic table. She had always wanted a picnic table.

She checked her watch. One more hour before Jeremy and his family came over for bratwurst, potato salad, and apple pie. Tom was probably grilling hot dogs for the boys. They always camped at Lake Michigan the last weekend in May, and Kevin had enthusiastically packed his surfboard, hoping the weather would cooperate. Maybe Tom would give them undivided attention without Tiffany and her kids hanging around. That would be good for them. Good for all of them.

She whistled for Bailey, who came running. "C'mon, little dog." She reached for his leash while he whirled in happy circles at her feet. "Walkies."

Up and down, up and down. Madeleine never tired of being bounced up and down on Mara's knee.

"Eat your pie," Jeremy said, reaching for Maddie. "She'll keep you going all night long if you let her." He blew a raspberry against her tummy, and she laughed.

Mara picked up her spoon.

"I never said thank you, Mom."

"For what?"

"For offering to turn your basement into an apartment for us."

"Oh, well, I shouldn't have."

"No, it was really kind of you, and I was wrong to be insulted about it. It was my pride, and I'm sorry." He passed Madeleine to Abby, who continued the raspberry game.

"Well, it was just an idea," Mara said. "And not a very good one."

"No, actually, a really good one. Abby and I were talking about it, and if we get desperate come fall—if the work slows down and we need a place to land for a couple of months . . ."

"It's not a great space for a family, Jeremy. You wouldn't have enough privacy."

"But if we get desperate."

Mara reached across the table for his hand. "Then you'll have a place you can stay."

"Thank you." He leaned forward and kissed her cheek. "Abby and I have been talking about something else too."

Much as Mara loved babies, she hoped they weren't going to say they were trying for another right now, not with Jeremy's work so unpredictable. She shifted her weight in her chair.

"We've been talking about having Madeleine dedicated at Wayfarer."

Mara stared at him. "But don't you have to get up in front of the church and answer questions about faith or something?"

"Yes."

"And you're ready to do that?"

"No. Not yet. But I signed up for a Bible study with the pastor." Jeremy took hold of Abby's hand. "I figure that's a good place to start. I believe in God, but I want something more. I need something more. Like what Abby has, what you have."

Mara's eyes welled with tears. Too much. Too full.

"So you'll be there whenever we make our promises?" he asked. "When I'm ready to make them?"

"Honey," she said, her hand pressed against her heart, "nothing in this world could keep me away."

Charissa

Almost forty-five minutes of pumping her breasts, and all she had managed to extract was a syringe-full. "You're doing fine," the nurse said. "Don't worry, in a couple of days your milk will come in, and you'll be a pro at this." Charissa didn't feel like a pro at anything. She covered herself with her gown. For now, any milk she was able to pump would be given to Bethany through her feeding tube. And then once Bethany was able to breathe without the CPAP, Charissa would be able to give her a bottle.

She wanted to breastfeed. She had said she didn't want to—she had insisted for months that she would have nothing to do with it—but now that she couldn't, she wanted more than anything to cradle Bethany to her breast and nurse her. She wanted intimacy without tubes and wires and monitors. *You'll get that,* John had said several times. *But for now . . .*

She knew. She didn't need to be told that her time would come. And she didn't need to be given updates on the other babies in the NICU bay, all of whom, according to John, were far worse off than Bethany. In the few hours Charissa had been recovering in her own private room, he had been getting to know the other families on the neonatal ward. She didn't want to hear their stories. What she wanted was a private room where she could be alone with her daughter. As soon as the nurse left, Charissa voiced this desire again.

"I told you, hon," he said, "it's all luck of the draw, and there aren't any private rooms open."

"But we're on a list, right? A waiting list or something?"

"I'll check. But I tell you, I think she's better off where she is. The nurses are there all the time. If she's in her own room, the nurses aren't there to watch her."

"I'll be there to watch her. You can be there."

"Not twenty-four seven." He rubbed her shoulder gently. "Give this a chance, okay? It's what we've got right now, and it's good. The nurses are great, you'll see."

"I want to go see her."

"Eat something first."

"I'm not hungry."

"C'mon, you've got to keep your strength up too."

"I'm fine. I just want to go see her. I'm missing everything."

"Charissa . . ."

"Tell the nurse I want to go see her. Now. Or you wheel me down there."

"I don't think I'm allowed to."

"Then get a nurse." She wasn't going to have an argument about it. They had told her she could see Bethany as soon as she had rested. Well, she had rested. She had rested all afternoon, and she wanted to be with her daughter. Now.

Hannah

When the doorbell rang late Saturday afternoon, Hannah was putting away food. "Got it!" she called to Nathan, who was scrubbing the grill. Chaucer accompanied her to the door and didn't bark when she opened it. "Becca!"

"Hey." Becca held out her hand for Chaucer to sniff, then stroked his head. Tucked under her other arm was a small book Hannah immediately recognized.

"Come on in," Hannah said, stepping back into the foyer. "We just finished eating. Are you hungry?"

Becca shrugged.

"I'll fix a plate for you. Burger okay?"

"Yeah, thanks."

Nathan came in to rinse his hands. "Hey, Becca! You just missed my grillmeister feast."

"We've got plenty of leftovers," Hannah said, motioning to the meat, cheese, and buns still on the counter. "How about if we sit outside? Too nice a day to be in."

"Yeah, I went for a long run. It felt good."

"Want some lemonade?" Nathan asked.

"Sure. Thanks."

While he poured her a drink, Hannah wrapped a paper towel around a hamburger patty and heated it in the microwave. "I'll let you help yourself to anything you like, ketchup, mustard, lettuce"—she popped the lid off the pickle jar—"and there's fruit salad on the top shelf of the fridge."

"Okay, thanks." Becca set her book down on the counter and opened the refrigerator. With her back turned toward Becca, Hannah caught Nathan's eye, gestured to the book with her elbow, and mouthed, *Meg's journal.* He nodded.

"I promised Jake a Frisbee match at the park," he said, "so I'll leave you two to connect together." He called upstairs to Jake and put on an old

Cubs cap Hannah remembered him wearing in seminary. "Okay if Chaucer stays with you, Shep?"

"Yeah, fine. Have fun." Hannah waited for Becca to finish serving herself before spooning out some fruit into a second bowl. Might as well keep her company with food. "Go easy on your dad," she said to Jake when he came downstairs in his running shorts and Star Wars T-shirt.

"No chance," he said, waving to Becca.

"See you, Jake." Becca tucked the journal under her arm before following Hannah outside with a bowl in one hand, a plate in the other.

Wherever she is, Lord, Hannah prayed silently, *whatever she needs, help me be alongside. Please.*

There was one particular entry in her mother's journal, Becca said after she finished eating, an entry that she couldn't get out of her head, and she wondered if her mother had talked to Hannah about it. She passed Hannah the open book and pointed. "This one. A letter to my dad."

Seeing Meg's handwriting caused Hannah's eyes to sting. *My dearest Jim.* She didn't read past the first line. "Your mom told me she wrote one. She was being really brave about feeling the pain of your dad's death again and grieving and letting go. But she never showed it to me."

"Go ahead and read it."

Hannah cleared her throat and smoothed the tear-stained page, whether from Meg or from Becca's tears, it was impossible to tell.

My dearest Jim,

I'm writing this letter for myself. If you were here, I know you'd understand. You always told me I needed to be kind to myself. You tried to help me understand that loving myself wasn't a selfish thing, but a way of opening up to God's love for me. You always knew God's love in a way I couldn't comprehend, and you used every day of our life together as an opportunity to show me what it meant to be loved and treasured.

Thank you, Jim. I understand now.

I'm letting go of you in a new way tonight. Or maybe I never truly let go before. Maybe I just buried you so deep within me that over the years I forgot you were there. But tonight I'm saying I love you, and I miss you.

By admitting how much I still love you, I'm also saying how much it hurt when you died. I died that day, too. Except I had to go on living. I just didn't know how. I wish I could have done it differently. I wish I hadn't been so afraid. But you'd be so proud of your beautiful daughter. She's not afraid. She has your love of life and love for other people. I'm praying she'll come to know your love for God, too. Or rather, that she'd come to know how much the Lord loves her. You would have shown her that, Jim. You would have lived in such a way that Becca would have never doubted how much her Heavenly Father loves her. I'm praying I'll be able to point her to God's heart. Lord, help me.

I remember you told me once that you were praying I would come to know how much the Lord loved me. You said you hoped someday I'd realize your love for me was just a shadow of God's love for me. I'd forgotten about that until recently. I can't believe I forgot that. But in the years after you died, I forgot so many things. I lost my way.

I'm found now, my love. I'm found. I just wanted to say thank you for this, your last gift.

And I love you. Always.

Hannah wiped her eyes and handed Becca the journal, still open to the page.

"I ended up at a park today," Becca said, "and I was looking up at the sky, trying to connect with my mom, you know? Sometimes I hear her voice in my head, things she used to say, but today I felt like I needed something more from her, some message that she's okay, that she's still with me somehow, watching over me or something, that she knows I'm"—her voice cracked and she pressed her palms against her eyes— "I'm sorry for everything." Her shoulders heaved, and she leaned forward.

Hannah scooted her chair closer, wondering if she should wrap an arm around her or wait. She decided to wait.

Becca took a deep, steadying breath. "Do you think she knows that? That I'm sorry?"

"She told me how sorry you were, Becca, and I know she forgave you."

"But the whole thing with Simon . . . I mean, what if that's what killed her? Putting on that dinner for us and then taking me to the airport, it's like it was all too much for her. Like the grief was too much for her."

Hannah placed her hand on Becca's shoulder. "Your mom hosted that dinner because she loved you. She wanted you to know that she loved and accepted you. She wanted a way to show you love, to serve you. And Simon too." Meg had made up her mind she was going to kneel and wash their feet that night, and she had done it. She had done it beautifully.

"He was awful to her," Becca said. "I was awful to her."

Hannah wasn't going to argue that point.

"My mom was right about him. She was right about everything. I turned into this different person when I was with him, and I didn't even see it." Becca wiped her nose against her wrist. "I'd give anything—anything to have that time back with her. But it's too late. It's all too late." She motioned to the journal. "And I read a letter like that, about how she felt lost and alone, how she felt like she died after my dad died, and I understand what that feels like. Because that's what I feel like. Like I've died too."

Hannah stared at the page. If only Becca could see what it meant to be found, if only she could take to heart her mother's prayer, if only she could say yes to the love of God seeking her, finding her, bringing her to life, giving her a home. *If only . . .*

"I wish I could tell my mom that I love her and miss her. I wish I could believe that I'll see her again, like she believed she'd see Dad again. I wish I could." Becca shook her head slowly. "But how can I believe in a God who lets dads die before they get to hold their baby daughters? How can I believe in a God who lets moms get cancer and die before their daughters grow up? How could my mom believe in a God like that? How could she talk about his love for her in the midst of all that?"

Hannah waited to see if she was asking a rhetorical question or whether she was waiting—hoping—for an answer.

Becca looked up into Hannah's eyes. "How do you believe in a God like that?" There was nothing accusing or angry in her tone. This was a girl who was broken, confused, and searching for something more than glib answers.

"Faith can be hard sometimes," Hannah said. "Making sense of suffering is hard. But you're right. Your mom grew to have this beautiful confidence in God's goodness and his love, even in all the heartache. Especially in the heartache. Jesus' suffering gave her hope. And she was confident that death wasn't the end. Isn't the end."

Becca stared off into the yard, a faraway look in her eyes. "Mom was wrong about one thing," she said. "I *am* afraid. I feel really afraid." She took a long slow breath and closed her eyes. Hannah did not speak, just in case Meg's girl was offering her own silent prayer.

—☙

Saturday, May 30
8:30 p.m.
There are people who would say I missed an opportunity to bring Becca straight to Jesus today. But I had such a strong sense of the Lord saying, Wait. Go slow. I need to trust that God is gently tending to seeds that have been planted, and I don't need to rush the process.

But oh! how I long for Meg's prayers—our prayers—to be answered. If Becca can come to see herself as that little lamb being found, nuzzled, and cradled with wounded hands, what a gift that would be! She told me she put Meg's picture of the shepherd and the lamb in a box for me along with Meg's prayer shawl and holding cross. But when I told her I already had a copy of it and that maybe it would give her some comfort to look at it, she didn't argue. I told her it's Jesus' wounded hand that catches my attention these days, that he knows the anguish and sorrow we feel, and he holds us in it. Keeps us company in it. She almost looked like she understood that.

Lord, bring her to yourself. Draw her with your love. Help her see what kind of God you are, a God who is with us. A God who did not withhold yourself from sorrow and suffering but endured it for our sake. In love. Lord, let her see your love. She's longing so deeply for her mom, for a sense of connection with her mom. Help her see what her mother saw, that the veil between this life and the next is very thin. Bring Becca from death to life, Lord. Bring her home.

Charissa

Early Sunday morning when the room phone rang, Charissa had just finished eating her breakfast, and John was on his way to the hospital. "Bethany's doing so well," the nurse on the phone said, "that we've taken her off the CPAP."

Charissa stiffened. Why hadn't they called her so she could be there to watch? She had wanted to be there the moment the mask was removed so she could see Bethany's full face. She had missed it. She had missed another milestone.

"She's doing really well without it," the nurse went on.

This was good news, wonderful news. *C'mon,* Charissa commanded herself. *Be grateful, not resentful.*

"So well that we're going to try to give her a bottle. Would you like to come down and watch?"

What a stupid question. "Yes, of course! Yes." She pushed her tray away and eyed the wheelchair in the corner.

"We'll need to do it within twenty minutes."

"Okay. I'm coming. Thank you." She hung up the phone and dialed John's number. "Where are you?"

"McDonald's drive-thru. Want something?"

"They're feeding her, John. They took the CPAP off."

"That's great!"

"No, I mean, they're going to give her a bottle, her first bottle, and I'm still in my room."

"So we'll go down together when I get there. Hold on a sec." He spoke an order into the microphone and then said, "You want a smoothie or something?"

"No!"

"That'll do it," he said to a cashier and then to Charissa, "I'll be there soon."

"How soon?"

"Fifteen, twenty minutes?"

Not good enough. "I need to get down there now. I'm not going to miss this."

"Just ask them to wait until I get there. I'm on my way. I don't want to miss it either."

"They said twenty minutes. I have to be there within twenty minutes."

"Okay, get a nurse to wheel you down, and I'll meet you there."

Charissa pressed her call button. Someone would be there soon, the voice said. But precious minutes passed. She pressed it again. The nurse tech was with another mother, the voice said. Someone would be there soon. But precious minutes ticked by. When the clock on the wall shouted the twenty minute mark, Charissa buried her face in her hands, too angry to cry.

"I thought you were on your way," John said when he arrived in Charissa's room.

"You got there in time?"

He looked sheepish. "They were just getting ready to give her the bottle, so I wasn't going to leave her. But look. See? I got some pictures, some video. Here. Watch."

Charissa overcame the temptation to turn her head away and instead watched her little one latch onto the nipple. She pressed her hand to her breast, a surge of heat rushing through her. "She did it."

"Of course she did it. I told you, she's a high achiever." John kissed the top of Charissa's head. "I'm sorry, Riss. I'm sorry I wasn't here to get you there in time."

It wasn't his fault. None of it was anyone's fault. "Thanks for taking video," she said. "I wouldn't have thought of that." She had missed the moment, but he had captured it for her. She could be resentful, or she could be grateful. She wanted to choose gratitude. *Help, Lord.*

"How about if I wheel you down there to see her?"

Charissa reached for his hand, and he helped her into the chair. She would spend as much time as possible on the ward with Bethany and John. She would spend every possible minute savoring Bethany's second day. She would be there to feed her the second bottle, and regret would not rob her of joy. As John wheeled her down the hallway to the elevator, she opened her hands in her lap and let go.

Mara

Mara was packing up a gift bag to take to the hospital Sunday afternoon when the garage door opened. "What are you guys doing home so soon?" she asked Kevin as he traipsed through the kitchen. They were supposed to be at the lake with Tom through the evening.

"Tiffany's having her baby."

"Today?"

Kevin shrugged. "I guess."

Brian flung his duffel bag onto a kitchen chair and stooped down to pet Bailey. "She was, like, in her bathing suit making this sand castle with Mikey—"

"When she started shouting for Dad and—"

"Hey!" Brian said.

"Let him tell it, Kevin." Brian telling her a story was an occasion to be celebrated.

"When she started shouting for Dad," Brian said, with a pointed glance in his brother's direction, "and she was all, 'The baby's coming, the baby's coming!'" Brian mimicked her with arms waving in the air. Mara tried not to laugh. It wasn't funny. "So Dad told us all to get in Tiffany's van, and he drove like crazy to the hospital. And then we had to watch her kids in the waiting room until her mom got there."

"And they were totally hyper," Kevin added.

"Yeah. Totally. But I told Dad I would watch them if he let me go to Disney World"—Mara pressed her lips together so she wouldn't beam at Brian's skillful maneuver—"and he said, yeah, okay, whatever."

She rubbed her chin slowly. "Well, that's good. That'll be good. I'm glad he gave you his word on that." She hoped Tom would keep it. "Which hospital?"

Kevin said, "Saint something."

"St. Luke's?"

"Yeah, St. Luke's."

So Tiffany and Tom were at St. Luke's the same time Charissa and John were there. Small world. She fought the temptation to calculate

Tiffany's months backwards in order to date Tom's infidelity. "So who brought you home? Dad?"

"Yeah."

"You should've called me. I would have come to get you." It was an odd feeling, hoping that Tom would make it back to the hospital in time for the birth, very odd for her first thought to be, *I would have helped,* instead of, *I hope he pays.*

In fact, she would take that first thought one step further. She stared at her reflection in the microwave and prayed for them. For Tiffany. For Tom. For the baby. And oh! what freedom she felt in that moment. What surprising, delicious freedom. Maybe when she was at the hospital visiting Charissa, she would stop in the gift shop and have something delivered to Tiffany's room. Not a "gotcha gift" but a sincere offering. A blessing. A letting go.

On second thought, maybe the gift was not inserting herself into their moment. She could send the baby a present another time. "Do they know if it's a boy or girl?"

Kevin said, "Boy."

Four boys. No, wait. *Six* boys. Oh, boy. "And what about you guys? Did you get to go surfing? Get some time with your dad, or was Tiffany . . ."

"No, we got time," Kevin said. "The surf was awesome, like four foot—"

"Five," Brian said.

"Yeah, maybe five-foot waves, and Brian caught this one . . ."

As the two of them recounted each sweet wave they'd either wiped out on or successfully caught and surfed, Mara offered God thanks for every good and perfect gift.

Entering the NICU was a far more complicated affair than visiting Jeremy and Abby after Madeleine was born. "Kinda like Fort Knox," Mara whispered to Hannah after they signed in and received their security badges. Mara removed her rings, bangles, and watch, then scrubbed her arms up to her elbows before being admitted onto the ward. "Did you do a lot of NICU visits in Chicago?"

"Some. Especially with the families that were there a long time."

"That must've been hard."

"Yes. Very hard."

Mara didn't press for details. Even if the babies lived, she imagined some of the marriages might not survive the long-term stress and trauma.

John met them on the other side of the security door. "So glad you're here!" He greeted both of them with a hug. "Good timing too. Bethany's awake."

"How's she doing?" Hannah asked.

"Really well. So much better than what we thought. She may even be able to go home in two weeks instead of three."

"Thank you, Jesus!" Mara said.

"Amen!" John pointed down the hall. "This way," he said, "follow me."

The same glow of serenity that had surrounded Abby as she cradled Madeleine radiated from Charissa, even in her visible weariness. "Hey," she said, looking up with a smile as Mara and Hannah entered the bay. "Come meet Bethany."

Oh, what a tiny little pink body! Maddie was huge by comparison. And with so many stickers and cords and tubes and a red light pulsating from some kind of monitor on her foot, Mara would have been overwhelmed with anxiety. But oh! Bethany's eyes were bright and locked onto her mother's face. "Look how she's watching you!" Mara exclaimed.

"I know. She doesn't blink very often, but the nurses say that's normal."

Mara studied Bethany's face, trying to figure out who she resembled more. Dark hair like Charissa and maybe like John around the mouth, though with a feeding tube it was hard to tell. "She's so bright," Mara said, "look how alert she is! It's like she's taking everything in."

Bethany thrust out her little fists and yawned. "Did you see that?" John said. "Big, big yawn for a little girl. You tired, baby girl?" Charissa leaned forward to kiss Bethany's nose as her eyes closed partway.

"She's not giving in, is she?" Hannah said. "She doesn't want to miss anything."

Mara remembered what it was like, holding each of her boys in those early days. Every breath, every cry, every yawn, every blink, every kick of their little feet, every bit of it was spellbinding. "So what's the schedule? And what can we do to help?"

"Not much at the moment," John said. "My folks are coming down just for the day tomorrow." Mara watched for a change of expression on Charissa's face but didn't see one. "I've got to go back to work in a week, much as I hate to. They think they'll send Charissa home on Tuesday."

"But I'm going to be here as much as possible," Charissa said. "I'm not going to leave her."

Mara understood. "I'll keep you company, if you want company."

"That would be good. Thanks, Mara."

"Me too," Hannah said, "whatever you guys need. Meals, cleaning, company, let me know."

"Prayer would be good," Charissa said. "Not just for us." She glanced around the room and lowered her voice. "Some of the babies are really struggling. I try not to feel guilty but . . ."

"It's hard not to," John said, "especially when your baby's thriving and you want the others to thrive too."

"Yeah," Mara said. "I get it." She watched a nurse hurry over to a monitor that was beeping fast, the young father's face clouded with worry as he held his wife's hand. Being in a place like this for an extended period of time would take its toll. Or enlarge you with compassion and gratitude.

Hannah

"So how are they doing?" Nathan asked, scooting over on the couch to make room for Hannah.

Hannah had logged many hours alongside anxious mothers who hardly took their eyes off the monitors, who refused to leave the bay to rest or eat, and who were insulted when nurses gently suggested they needed to take care of themselves so that they could better care for their babies. But Charissa, who had often spoken about her struggle with control, seemed to be taking the experience in stride. "They're all doing really well. Bethany's hitting every marker for progress, and Charissa's listening to advice about getting rest." She laid her head against Nathan's shoulder. "She said to tell you that this whole spiritual formation journey she's been on has made a big difference to how she's approaching everything now. She said she's seeing lots of opportunities to let go, so she's trying to practice."

Nathan laughed. "Amazing she's thinking about that while she's under that kind of stress. Good for her."

Yes. It was very good. *Grace upon grace,* Charissa had said, smiling. *Evidence of the Spirit's work.*

"And how was it for you, Shep, being there?"

Hannah thought a moment. "Good. Hard. Mostly good, though. Guess we've all come a long way." What a journey it had been. All the endings, all the beginnings, the life, the death, the new life. "I had this moment of insight as I watched Charissa holding Bethany, how she was *beholding* her with complete delight. It was like glimpsing God, his heart for us, his love for us."

Nathan nodded slowly. "Even before we know our own names," he said quietly. "Beloved. Treasured."

"And securely held," Hannah added, grasping her husband's hand.

fifteen

Welcome home! the banner on the front porch read. It had not been there when she and John left for the hospital early that morning. "Mara, I bet," Charissa said as she carefully unstrapped Bethany from her car seat. The pink balloons were the giveaway.

"Wait, wait!" John said. "Let me get video."

Charissa didn't sigh, roll her eyes, or argue. Though she refused to be the mother who would document every waking and sleeping moment, this was one to add to John's video collection of first things: first bottle, first time being held by grandparents, first bath, first time being dressed. "Okay," he said, "look this way. Hey, Bethany! Look here, baby girl." John snapped his fingers to try to get her attention.

Careful to cradle her head, Charissa lifted a very alert Bethany to her shoulder and turned so that he could film her face. Two and a half weeks old, and already it seemed she had been part of their lives for years. Charissa adjusted Bethany's pink pants and followed John, who was walking backwards, up the front steps and across the threshold.

Home.

They were home.

Charissa hadn't expected to cry. She waved for John to stop recording. Some moments were too precious, too intimate for other eyes to see.

Mara

So that was it. On the twentieth of June, one week after celebrating her fifty-first birthday with family and friends, Mara Garrison returned to being Mara Payne. She stared again at the final divorce decree. She hadn't predicted the odd cocktail of emotion. She had thought she would feel a euphoric rush of joy and relief. Instead, she was surprised to feel sorrow. Not sorrow over losing Tom—no, not that—but sorrow over broken things, over broken people, over broken relationships. That kind of brokenness was worth lamenting.

"Everything okay?" Jeremy asked as he came down the stairs, paintbrush in hand. He was almost finished painting her bedroom Caribbean blue.

"Yeah. Just not what I expected to feel, now that it's actually over."

He rinsed the paintbrush off in the sink.

"I thought it would be, 'Good riddance,' you know? Move on with life, be free."

"You *are* free, Mom."

"Yeah. I know. It's just an odd feeling."

All her life she had wanted to be free of Payne, to be free of all the grief that name had brought her. Now she was embracing it again, and by doing so she was declaring that God could redeem all the broken, painful parts of her journey. God had already done so much to heal her and transform her and give her hope. Now she was stepping again into unfamiliar territory. A new adventure with Jesus.

Jeremy was eyeing her with compassion. "I love you, Mom, and I'm with you. We're with you."

"I know you are," she said, embracing him. "Thank you."

Beloved. Chosen. Favored. Blessed.

And not, thank God, alone.

Hannah

Amazing, how much Becca had accomplished in clearing out the house. With most of the furniture and accessories now sold off in a very successful estate sale, the house felt less like a funeral parlor and more like an empty tomb. "I'm proud of you," Hannah said as she helped Becca box up the few things that remained. "Your mom would be proud of you; I know she would."

"Thanks. Now I just need to get it ready to sell. And I don't even know where to start."

"I'll help you with all of that," Hannah said. In fact, maybe this was as good a time as any to mention her ongoing conversations with Nathan about possible next steps. "How about if I make us both a cup of tea?"

If Becca could have signed paperwork on the house tomorrow, she would have. *How soon?* was her only question. How soon would they be willing to buy it? Hannah explained that there were probate issues to be explored, and she was happy to do that if Becca wanted to move forward. "Yes! As soon as possible. Please."

"We also need to make sure you get a good solid price for it," Hannah said. Fair market value and higher, she and Nate had agreed. Once they knew what repairs would be required and what they would be looking at for costs to renovate it, they could determine a generous offer. "And there's something else Nate and I feel really strongly about."

"What's that?"

"That you always feel welcome here. That you know you have a place to come and stay, whenever you need it."

Becca stared at her lap. "Okay. Thank you." She took a deep breath. "I think I know how Mom felt after Dad died, how she just wanted to be rid of their house, how she couldn't bear the thought of being in it again. So once I'm done with this place, I don't know whether . . ."

Hannah waited for her to finish her thought. But when the silence billowed, she said, "No pressure. Just an invitation."

Becca nodded. "The cottage was where my mom was happy, where life was good for her." She ran her finger around the rim of her mug. "I've been thinking about it, and maybe I'm ready to take Charissa up on her offer and go over and see it sometime."

That seemed to be a significant step. Hannah tried to keep her expression neutral. "The roses are in bloom."

Becca eyed her inquisitively.

"There are these beautiful pink climbing roses your dad planted."

"On the arbor?"

"Yes."

"He built that for her," Becca said. "She told me about it. But she didn't tell me it was still there."

"He built it for their first wedding anniversary, I think," Hannah said.

"I'd like to see it."

"Well, Mara and I are going over there to visit this weekend. I'm sure Charissa would be happy to have you join us." When Becca hesitated, Hannah added, "Just for a picnic. Not a prayer group."

"Oh," Becca said. "Okay. Yeah. Maybe. I'll call her."

"That's great news," Nathan said when Hannah called half an hour later to tell him about Becca's reaction to their idea.

"And you're sure Jake is okay with it?" she asked. He had seemed okay when they first mentioned it, but maybe he had privately communicated something else.

"He's more than okay. I even heard him telling a friend about it the other day, and he was excited. Like Becca, he's wondering how soon it might be able to happen."

"Then I'll call the attorney tomorrow, see what we're looking at for timing." As she backed her car out of the driveway, she looked up at the Victorian house that might one day be home.

"And how about New Hope?" Nathan said. "Did you get us registered for the program?"

"I'm heading there now. I told Katherine I'd be dropping off a check for both of us, and she's thrilled. She said she's been gently encouraging you for years to train as a spiritual director."

"That's true. She has. Maybe I was just waiting to train with my wife."

Next steps, Hannah thought as she wound her way there. These were all good, grace-filled next steps, ways to embrace God's call and offer a wholehearted *hineni*. Together.

Becca

Charissa greeted Becca at the door Saturday afternoon with a warm embrace. "So glad you're here! C'mon in." Glancing around the room, Becca stooped to take off her shoes. "Oh, leave them on. The floor's a mess anyway. And we're going to eat outside. Mara and Hannah are already out there."

She peered over Charissa's shoulder into a ballet-slipper–pink room decorated for a baby girl. "Is she sleeping?"

"No, Mara's got her." Charissa smiled. "And I'm afraid she won't hand her over very easily."

"Oh, that's okay. I was just wondering if that room there . . ."

Charissa followed her gaze. "Right! Yes. Your mom said that was—"

"Going to be my room?"

Charissa nodded. "If you want to spend some time looking around, that's fine with me. Just excuse the mess. It's been a bit chaotic the past couple of weeks, trying to get used to everything."

Becca wished she had said yes to visiting the house while her mother was alive. She had thought it would be morbid, walking through the rooms and hearing stories about her parents' life in that space. Now she wished she could hear the stories. She imagined her mom as a young bride being carried across the threshold, imagined her parents sitting together in front of the fireplace, imagined them gardening outside.

"There used to be a porch swing on the patio," Charissa said, motioning toward the front door. "The hooks are still there. Your mom said she and your dad loved sitting out there. And in the garden too. It's a beautiful garden. My mother-in-law says someone took a lot of care planning it. Someday I may actually get out there and do some weeding."

"I wouldn't mind helping," Becca said. She wasn't much of a gardener, but she could probably figure things out.

"Really?"

"Yeah. I don't head back to school until August, and I've pretty much cleared out the house now, so I've got lots of time on my hands."

Besides. Working in the garden her parents had once worked in might be therapeutic.

"Ahhhh, here she comes," Charissa cooed as Mara carried Bethany into the room, followed closely by Hannah.

"She just fell asleep," Mara whispered, handing her to her mom. Becca had never seen such a tiny baby. "Isn't she gorgeous?" Mara said to Becca after greeting her.

"She's beautiful." Like a fragile little doll. She returned Hannah's hug.

"So glad you're here," Hannah said.

"Thanks."

They all stood in silence, each staring at the sleeping baby. She looked so peaceful. So content. Becca wished she had some photos of herself as an infant cradled in her mother's arms, but in all of her sorting, she hadn't found any. There was no baby book with details, no record of her milestones or her mother's musings, probably because she was in too much grief to think about taking pictures or writing anything down.

All Becca had was a single story, a story her mother had told her a few days before she died, a story about a chaplain coming to the hospital room to pray after she was born, some story of coincidence her mother had marveled over, but Becca hadn't paid enough attention to the details, and now it was too late to hear them. One more opportunity lost.

Unless.

Maybe.

She cleared her throat, breaking the silence. "I was wondering," she said, looking around the circle, "did my mom ever tell you guys a story about when I was born? Something about a chaplain?"

Mara and Charissa shook their heads. "No," Mara said. "Sorry."

But Hannah said, "Yes."

While Charissa gently rocked Bethany in her arms, Hannah recounted the story of how Katherine, the woman who had led the retreat where they all met, had been the chaplain on duty when Becca was born on Christmas Eve.

"You're kidding," Mara said.

"No. And they only made the connection during one of Meg's spiritual direction sessions. Meg remembered a female chaplain coming into the room to pray with her, and it turns out it was Katherine." Hannah looked at Becca, her eyes brimming with emotion. "Katherine held you and prayed a blessing over you. And it meant so much to your mom to remember it all and make that connection because she had felt so alone when you were born. So frightened. Suddenly she realized she hadn't been alone, that God—"

When Hannah cut herself off mid-thought, Becca sensed she was debating how much more to say. Not wanting to miss any details her mother might have shared, she gestured permission for her to continue. "That God . . ." Becca repeated.

"That God was watching over her and taking care of her. That God was with both of you, loving you."

Becca's eyes burned.

Like a little lamb lost in the wood, she thought. Lost and found. Found by someone who would watch over her. Someone, her mother would say, with wounded hands.

"That's incredible," Charissa said. "Such a small world."

A coincidence without meaning, Simon would have insisted. But what did she believe? "Can I see the roses?" Becca asked.

So this was the trysting place her mother had spoken about, the place her parents were sitting when the pair of mourning doves landed on the arbor and nuzzled their necks like lovers. A holy moment, her mother said, and they hadn't dared breathe for fear of frightening the birds away. A holy moment, her mother said, because their wedding verses were about doves calling in springtime and a lover summoning the beloved. A holy moment.

Becca sat down and traced with her finger the words carved on the bench: For the woman I love.

Was it sentimental to imagine her parents being reunited? Sentimental to imagine them seeing her and loving her, even here, even now?

Was it only sentiment and a desperate longing for connection that prompted and stirred her thoughts about their faith and their God?

Words from her mother's letter echoed in her mind. *I'm praying I'll be able to point her to God's heart, that she'll come to know how much the Lord loves her.*

Why couldn't she grant the answer to her mother's prayer? Say yes and cross the line of faith? Becca's heart said, *You can give her that gift. Even here, even now.* But her head replied, *How can I trust God's love when this world isn't safe?*

If only the universe, heaven, her parents, God, Jesus—someone!—if only someone would give her a sign, send a dove, a butterfly— something!—to help her believe. Something. But the only sound she heard in the garden was a gust of laughter wafting from the small deck behind the house, boisterous laughter that welcomed others to join in.

Becca picked up a fallen rose petal and stared at the sky. *If you can see me . . . If you're listening . . .* But there was no coo of a mourning dove, no rustle of the wind.

Nothing.

She glanced over her shoulder as she heard someone approach.

"You okay?" Hannah asked.

"Yeah. Just thinking."

"I don't want to interrupt."

"No, it's okay." Becca scooted sideways to make room.

It was silly to want a sign, she thought as Hannah sat down, silly to plead for a mourning dove to appear, silly to expect an answer like that. Maybe holy moments weren't for her. She rubbed the petal between her fingers. "I've been sitting here remembering a story my mom told me about mourning doves and why they were special to her."

Hannah nodded. "Her wedding verses."

Yes. Wedding and funeral verses. They were also the verses Hannah had been reading aloud in the hospital room when she died, which meant—she hadn't thought about this before—they might have been the last words her mother heard. *Arise, my love, my beautiful one, and come.*

Becca scanned the sky again. Still no sign.

Nothing.

She sighed and stared at her feet. What was the old saying? A journey of a thousand miles begins with a single step? She slipped off one sandal, then the other, and scrunched her toes against the soft grass. "I don't really like sensible shoes," she said.

Hannah laughed. "Then wear heels. Or go barefoot. Your journey doesn't need to look like your mom's."

True. She wasn't being called to walk in her mother's footsteps. She couldn't do that even if she wanted to.

She breathed deeply, listening. No rustling of a breeze. No cooing of a dove.

Nothing but a single word summoning.

Arise.

Acknowledgments

The LORD bless you and keep you;
the LORD make his face to shine upon you and be gracious to you;
the LORD lift up his countenance upon you and give you peace.

NUMBERS 6:24-26

With love and gratitude . . .

For Jack, my dearest companion. I thank God for the gift of life together and for all the ways you have revealed his love to me. I love you. Thank you for sharing the journey with me.

For David, our beloved son. I thank God for the gift of who you are, and I look forward to reading your scripts and books someday. I love you, and I'm so proud of you.

For Mom and Dad. Thank you for the gift of life and love and for always encouraging me in my dreams. I love you and thank God for you.

For Beth, the best sister in the world. You've brought me so much joy over a lifetime. Thanks for being my first audience as I write the stories. I love you and thank God for you.

For beloved longtime friends who have been witnesses to me in word and in deed, sacrificially modeling the love of Christ. You know who you are, and you have helped make me who I am. I love you and thank God for you.

For the ones who gently led me toward Jesus long ago, with wisdom and grace. Special thanks to Kathleen, John, Sarge, Colleen, Paige, and Katherine. I am eternally grateful.

For Mary V. Peterson, who walks with me. Thank you for all the ways you hold my story with tenderness and compassion. You are such a trustworthy companion.

For my faithful midwife team: Sharon Ruff, Debra Rienstra, Rebecca DeYoung, Amy Boucher Pye, Martie Bradley, Marilyn Hontz, Lisa Samra, Carolyn Watts, Elizabeth Musser, and Amy Nemecek. Thank you for your keen insights, prayer, and encouragement as I labored to cross the finish line.

For Jennifer Oosterhouse, whose artistic and prayerful vision for Redeemer's annual Holy Week journey forever imprinted me. Thank you for giving so generously of yourself so that we all could be brought closer to Jesus in the beauty of his suffering and sacrifice.

For Shalini Bennett, who led the team of artists in Scripture meditation and prayer. Thank you for being so devoted to the ministry. Your wisdom lives on in these characters.

For the family of Redeemer Covenant Church. Our life together shaped me in such rich and profound ways. I thank God for the years he gave us to partner with one another in ministry.

For the original Sensible Shoes Club. I thank God for our season of walking together. Thank you for sharing the journey of formation with me.

For Julie and Mark VanderMeulen, who gave me a beautiful writing retreat space. Thank you for lavishing me with kindness and hospitality. You were an answer to prayer.

For Mindy Van Singel, who happened to answer the phone the day I called the hospital for research. Thank you for so generously giving your time to answer all of my NICU questions, both that day and afterward.

For all who assisted with research, particularly Sharla Ulstad and Anna Rapa. Your expertise is a gift to me.

For all who shared anecdotes that became part of the characters' experiences, particularly Jeremy, Denise, Catherine, and Jim. Thank you for the gift of your stories.

For the wonderful team at IVP, and especially for my talented editor, Cindy Bunch. How grateful I am that you said yes! Thanks for bringing all of your gifts and wisdom to my books. It's a joy and honor to work with you. Thanks, too, to Lori Neff, my creative marketer; Cindy Kiple, my intuitive cover designer; Allison Rieck, my gracious copyeditor; and Jeff Crosby, who is the best kind of leader and friend. I thank God for all of you.

For readers who have loved these characters wholeheartedly and who have encouraged me along the way. I'm so grateful for you. May the One who loves you continue to draw you deep into his heart.

And for you, Lord. All and always for you and in you and through you. You are my everything. Thank you. I love you. *Hineni.*

Amen! Praise and glory and wisdom and thanks
and honor and power and strength be to
our God for ever and ever. Amen!
Revelation 7:12

Also Available

An Extra Mile Study Guide

Blessed are those whose strength is in you,
whose hearts are set on pilgrimage.
As they pass through the Valley of Baka,
they make it a place of springs;
the autumn rains also cover it with pools.
They go from strength to strength,
till each appears before God in Zion.

PSALM 84:5-7

For those who would like to go deeper into the themes of this book, we have created *An Extra Mile Study Guide*. There you will find eight weeks of material for individuals and groups to explore the spiritual formation themes in this book. The guide is ideal for the seasons of Lent and Easter but can be used anytime. Week four includes an expanded experience with the Journey to the Cross.

May the Lord guide you deeper into his love as you walk the pilgrim way.

Journey to the Cross

For years during Holy Week our congregation hosted a Journey to the Cross very similar to what I've described at New Hope: eight prayer stations with art and Scripture telling the story of Jesus' road to Golgotha. Our journey was an adaptation of a historical prayer practice of the Catholic Church, Stations of the Cross. Annually we invited people from our community to walk in the footsteps of Jesus on a spiritual pilgrimage of meditation on his suffering and death in order to prepare for the glory of his resurrection. Members from our congregation prayed for months with the Scripture texts and then created art that invited reflection. The first four stations described at New Hope (the angry fists and billowing robes, the cross with the mirror, the crossbeam to lift, and the tears draped and pooled among the dead trees) are based on the art our members created for us. I am indebted to the prayerful, creative people who made our Holy Week experience such a meaningful one. Perhaps you'll find ways to offer a similar journey in your own churches.

Listed below are eight texts you can use for personal and group meditation. Each text is well-suited for either imaginative prayer (placing yourself within the story) or lectio divina (reading slowly and listening attentively for a word or phrase that captures your attention and invites you to ponder and pray). If your group is so inclined, you might also create artwork that accompanies each text so that you can experience a multisensory engagement with God's Word.

Matthew 27:1-2, 11-25	John 19:23-24
Luke 23:23-25	John 19:25-27
Mark 15:21	Mark 15:33-39
Luke 23:27-31	John 19:28-37

The Sensible Shoes Series

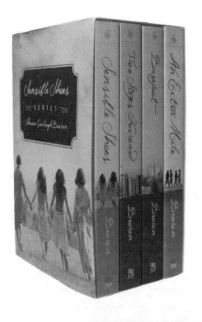

Sensible Shoes

Two Steps Forward

Barefoot

An Extra Mile

STUDY GUIDES

For more information about the Sensible Shoes series,
visit ivpress.com/sensibleshoesseries.
To learn more from Sharon Garlough Brown or to sign up for her newsletter,
go to ivpress.com/sharon-news.

formatio
TRADITION. EXPERIENCE.
TRANSFORMATION.

Formatio books from InterVarsity Press follow the rich tradition of the church in the journey of spiritual formation. These books are not merely about being informed, but about being transformed by Christ and conformed to his image. Formatio stands in InterVarsity Press's evangelical publishing tradition by integrating God's Word with spiritual practice and by prompting readers to move from inward change to outward witness. InterVarsity Press uses the chambered nautilus for Formatio, a symbol of spiritual formation because of its continual spiral journey outward as it moves from its center. We believe that each of us is made with a deep desire to be in God's presence. Formatio books help us to fulfill our deepest desires and to become our true selves in light of God's grace.